minis.

UNRATED QUEER FICTION: AUTHOR'S CUT

raymond g. neal

This *Author's Cut* edition contains revised and expanded material. Portions of this work previously appeared in the first edition published in 2025 under the title *minis*.

Brought to you by:

blendahead press, LLC

1702 W. Allen Street #1510
Allentown, PA 18104
blendaheadpress@gmail.com

This collection contains fiction, flash fiction, and autofiction. The Reflections chapters draw directly from the author's lived experience; the Short Story and Flash Fiction chapters are works of imagination. Names and identifying details have been changed or omitted throughout. This is a work of literature, not a record.

To all the girls I've loved before:

*Glenn, Christopher, Eric, Brad, Elio, Monkey, Jason
and the girl I love right now, Jude.*

And to Travis, my oldest, dearest, oldest queer friend.

Thank you for making my journey so rich and delicious.

You all are really something.

Table of Contents

FLAVOR KEY:

■ Short Story

✳ Flash Fiction

◯ Reflections

⌗ Verse

CAUTION: DO NOT READ WHILE DRIVING.

Flavor Guide

■ Short Stories

The Castle Down the Block
Just Like Ricky Did
In the After Hours
Cracked Xmas
Bandages (an awakening)
Spin
Cool (Former) Sk8er Guncle
The Roosterfish
Mad About You

* Flash Fiction

Bathroom
Rings
Henrietta
We
Surprise
Jared
Blue
Boxes
Quarantine

◯ Reflections

My Showgirl, My Self
Plugs 1: Dean
Agent Orange
Heavy Metal Lover
Jesus H. Christopher
Earthquake Weather
Plugs 2: Victor
Hit It Early, Hit It Hard
BRAD!
Married Alive
Enter the Monkey
Plugs 3: Jason
Feature, Not Bug

⊞ Verse

Red Headed Blanket
Super Cupid/Thru the
Ringer/Until I Forget
Write Down the Dream/One
More Time
Study You
Gutter/Man This Coat's Big
I Really Do Like You/
Bubblehead
Gameplay Instructions
tl;dr/fu

01. The Castle Down the Block

■

Once upon a time, a large group of women decided they'd had enough of playing house with their husbands and children; that the roles they'd assumed as wives and mothers had been foisted upon them by a patriarchal society that wanted to stifle their independence and hold them back from realizing their full potential. They rebelled against the roles they'd assumed. Some cut their hair short. Some burned their bras. Many became...earnest. They called themselves "feminists" or "women's rights advocates."

One such women's rights advocate, Diana, found herself in a predicament. She had a husband named Dean, along with two young children: five-year-old Ray and two-year-old Heather. Diana longed to reclaim her true identity, but her two young children threatened to hold her back.

After days and weeks of serious thought, Diana came up with a plan: she would find another mother, a mother who wasn't interested in joining the feminist work force, one who had no interest in self-actualizing, one who was happy staying home to bake bread and change diapers. Diana would leave Ray and Heather with this other mother while she herself jumped into the feminist fray. The mother Diana found lived right down the block and had two children of her own. This other mother's name was Kathy.

Kathy was no feminist, but she certainly was the queen of her castle. She was somewhat short as queens go, but she made up in intensity for what she lacked in size. Her smile was tight like a fist. Her black hair was styled in a deceptively perky swing cut, which she would flip back over her shoulders frequently, as if she were a model in a shampoo commercial. Kathy's daughters, Missy and Tiffany, were smaller, unfinished versions of their mother: predatory, misshapen, deceptive in nature.

Kathy may have been the queen of her castle, but it was her husband Rick who ruled it with an iron fist. Rick was a cop, an imposing male figure, and young Ray was in awe of him. Here was a specimen of adult male that Ray had never come across in his short life: large, intimidating, totally unreadable and capable of immense wrath. Ray steered clear of Rick as much as possible, which wasn't difficult since the man was hardly ever there. Ray admired Rick secretly, and from afar.

On their first day in captivity, Ray and Heather were given a brief tour of the castle by Kathy and her daughters. It was made quite clear from the outset that Ray and Heather were not family, nor were they guests in the castle; rather, they were "other" children who did not enjoy or deserve full house privileges. Included in the castle tour was the room shared by Missy and Tiffany, which was filled with an overwhelming array of little girl treasures: stuffed white poodles, lace curtains, rampant floral prints and rows of dolls that had vacant eyes and freeze-dried lips.

Flanked by her grinning daughters, Kathy explained quite firmly that the bedroom and its contents were OFF LIMITS to Ray and Heather. In fact, all rooms in the castle, and all contents of said rooms (including toys) were OFF LIMITS, except for the den (a large rectangle with white walls, high windows and a single door), which they were thrown into immediately. Picking at discarded Tinkertoys and Pick-Up Sticks, Ray and Heather stared at each other as the reality of their predicament sank in. They were at Kathy's mercy, and with the full consent of their mother.

One day Kathy beat up Ray in the bathroom. He had arrived home from school and been instructed to change into his play clothes. "But don't take your shoes off!" Kathy snarled before slamming shut the bathroom door. Then she barked, "I just cleaned and waxed the floor in there!"

Ray sat on the toilet for a moment, wondering just how he was supposed to change into his play clothes without taking off his shoes. He leaned over and looked at the bathroom floor. The linoleum did, in fact, look shiny and clean. Ray came to the realization that there was no way to avoid what was about to happen. It was inevitable, in fact. It was going to happen regardless of what he said or did. He may as well just make the most of it.

Ray slowly unlaced his shoes and removed them from his feet. Then he quietly sprinkled the copious amount of sand they contained from the school playground, all over Kathy's freshly cleaned and waxed linoleum floor. He did this intentionally and relished the act of defying Kathy. Of purposefully stepping into her trap. Ray savored the opportunity to make her mad, on purpose.

By this time, Ray hated Kathy. He hated her for being an adult who chose to be cruel to children. He hated her for putting him into this ridiculous situation. Most of all, he hated her for not being his mother. And though Ray's hatred was directed at Kathy, he also harbored similar feelings for Diana, feelings that he avoided thinking about or paying attention to.

Diana was the reason he and Heather were stuck in this castle every day, being subjected to Kathy's mistreatment of them. Diana would rather go to work than protect Ray and Heather. She'd rather be at work than spend time with and take care of them, so she dropped them off at Kathy's every day to fend for themselves.

Kathy, who had been poised outside the bathroom door, waiting to make her banshee-like re-entrance, stormed back into the bathroom. "I told you not to take your shoes off!" she shrieked. Whap! Whap! Whap! She was hitting Ray upside both sides of his head, again and again. She had hold of his arm with one hand and was wailing on him with the other. Whap! Whap! Whap! Kathy grunted as she continued hitting him but didn't speak.

Neither did Ray. In fact, he didn't make a sound. He did not once cry out in pain or surprise. He just let her do it. He went limp and eased into her blows as best he could. Ray figured, this'll end soon enough, and it did. She dragged him out of the bathroom, down the hallway, through the kitchen and out the back door. She plopped him down on a lopsided chair, went back into the house and slammed the back door shut.

Ray sat there while his head spun in twisted circles, his face tingling, his ears ringing and his vision rocking from side to side. Ray felt a sense of accomplishment as he sat there and regained his senses. He hadn't given her the satisfaction of tears or an apology or of pleading with her to stop. Ray was satisfied with how he'd handled himself, very satisfied indeed.

On another day, Missy and Tiffany were eating Kool-Aid from the packets and not letting Ray have any. As their sugar buzzes intensified, so did their taunts. "Mmmmmmm! This is so gooood," they teased, "but you can't have any!"

Girlish cackles followed, sounding like the squawks of newly hatched buzzard chicks. Having tried the tack of asking nicely, and being fed up with groveling, Ray snapped, "Fine! I don't want any of your damn Kool-Aid anyway!"

Missy's eyes widened in naked shock, as if Ray had just pulled his pants down and dumped a big brown one right there on the patio. Then she ran toward the house, with a confused Tiffany in tow, yelling, "I'm telling my daddy on you! You're in trouble! My daddy's gonna get you!"

The back door slammed shut and they were gone. Ray was left alone in the sunlight to think about what he had done. Missy sounded very sure of herself, and it made Ray nervous.

Rick was inside (a rare occasion) and he was sleeping. Ray was overcome with dread. His big moment of defiance was about to be wiped out by that huge man, who would stumble out the back door in a blind rage and rip Ray to pieces while Kathy, Missy and Tiffany watched and cheered him on.

After a nearly unendurable period of silence, a loud bellow emanated from inside the house, which caused Ray to freeze in terror. Certainly, Rick was about to come crashing through the back wall of the house, pounce on Ray and kill him! But after the loud bellow came nothing but silence. Ray stood still, waiting for something to happen, but nothing did. No one came out the back door. No one made a sound.

Ray finally deduced that it was Missy and Tiffany who'd been the objects of Rick's rage. Rick had yelled at them! Ray ran across a few feet of lawn, picked up a torn open and discarded Kool-Aid packet, and licked the insides of it, dancing a jig and humming to himself.

He felt vindicated by Rick's rage and great satisfaction in picturing Missy's and Tiffany's terrified faces as they cowered under their dad's menacing presence. Ray was thankful to Rick for being able to see how mean-spirited and petty his little hellions could be.

There was just one time Ray and Rick were alone together. They were in Rick's sports car as Rick drove back to the castle. The day was dank and gray, and Rick was pointing to some clouds in the distance. He told Ray that, if you looked closely, you could see the rain coming down out of them. It looked like straight black lines coming out of the sky. Could Ray see them? Ray couldn't, but he said that he could because he didn't want to disappoint Rick.

That afternoon, Ray observed a relaxed tenderness that Rick held in check when Kathy and his daughters were around. Ray imagined the two of them going off somewhere and living together as father and son. He had a sense that Rick would appreciate and love him in a way that his own father never had, because Rick only had his two bratty daughters to go home to, and they were no fun. What Rick really wanted was a son.

Ray and Heather's last day at the castle started out like any other. Late in the afternoon, however, Kathy and her daughters ridiculed Heather for pooping in her diapers.

Now, Heather was only two, and Ray felt that teasing her for pooping in her diapers was in extremely poor taste, and not something he could just let go. He rubbed Heather's shoulder and consoled her, telling her not to listen to them, they were just being mean, and Mom would be there to pick them up very soon.

That night, he told Diana what had happened. One revelation led to another, and before long Diana was marching down the block so she and Kathy could have a talk.

"And how does this tale end?" you've asked me. You tell me you can't remember. Well, Heather, what can I say except…it doesn't. Not really. We get older, we're shuttled to other castles in the neighborhood, most of them more pleasant than Kathy's, a few of them not.

I'd like to tell you that Diana came to her senses after that first time; that she realized her mistake, made us the centers of her universe, and that we all lived happily ever after.

But you wouldn't believe me.

Would you.

02. Bathroom

*

Bathrooms are quite large when you're eight, even when they are small.

I shut myself in the bathroom.

The way I remember it, all the surfaces are white except for the chrome faucets on the sink, the sliding shower door's frame and towel rack, the handle I push down on to flush the toilet, and the edges of the mirrored medicine cabinet.

The rest is all white: the tub, the walls, the ceiling, the light fixture, the tile on the floor, which isn't tile but linoleum and has flecks of grey so barely noticeable that I don't consider them worth remembering.

My towel is white. I remove it from my waist, which it was wrapped around, and drop it to the floor. I'm fully erect and it's sticking out in front of me like an arrow pointing the way to the happiest place on Earth.

The large flat mirror on the wall over the sink only goes down as far as the white countertop, which comes up to the top of my rib cage, just below my nipples, which I do not see, and my mind does not process, and that I won't become aware of in any significant way for another twenty years or so.

I cannot see it in the mirror because the sink is too high. Climbing onto the countertop seems more troublesome and dangerous than it's worth, and also much harder to explain should my dad surprise me by opening the bathroom door while I'm up there.

I look back down at it from on high. I find it fascinating. It's still stiff, still pointing the way toward a better place. I touch it, grip it, tug on it, let go. It's beginning to hurt. I know there's something I could do, there must be something I can do, to make it do what it's supposed to do. But I don't know what that is.

And I'm frustrated. Whatever it can do must be good. There must be something to it. And somehow, I know that whatever it does is something good. I'm beginning to have my doubts, though, because it really does ache. Not in a painful way that makes me want to cry, but in a way that makes me need to make it go away.

I am standing naked in the bathroom and it's sticking straight out. I imagine people looking at me, admiring me. I place my hands on my hips and thrust my hips forward a bit, point it toward the corner between the toilet and the bathtub. Pivot and point it at the corner between the mirror and the medicine cabinet. I'm proud, I'm naked, and it's hard, but this isn't enough. The view from on high is already boring. And it still hurts.

My dad raps his knuckles on the bathroom door and asks if I'm all right in there. Yeah! I say, too quickly.

I pull the shower door open and turn the water on. I pull the knob on top of the faucet, so the water sputters to a halt, gets choked back, then spits itself out of the showerhead.

I turn around, pick up the towel and hang it on the rack. Steam billows out of the shower. I look at the medicine cabinet, and it hits me.

I put the toilet seat down with a bang and a piece of one of the white plastic stoppers chips off and flies into the bathtub.

I scramble up onto the toilet lid and look at my reflection in the medicine cabinet mirror.

And there it is from a different angle. Sort of. It's a ghost. It's fading. And now it's gone.

The steam has fogged the medicine cabinet mirror.

03. Rings

*

When I remember Cynthia Nelson now, the word that comes into my mind and slaps itself across her forehead is "FRAIL." I see the word in large, black, uncaring letters that stand out against her pale white skin like scars.

I knew Cynthia when we were both in the third grade, and back then the reason I liked her so much was because she was as much a boy as I was a girl. We both inhabited a sort of gray gender area that most of the other kids had the luck, or the presence of mind, to steer clear of.

I was quite a kid, third grade me. The girls liked me because I could giggle with them and not menace them with taunts or yanks on their ponytails. The boys respected me because I was a formidable athlete in the highly competitive sports of kickball, four square and free form jungle gym.

If I crossed the gender border and skipped rope occasionally, nobody seemed to mind, so long as I kept my skill levels in the boy activities up to par with the rest of them.

Third grade was the year we got to watch a movie called *Free to Be...You and Me*. It was a musical film with animated and live action vignettes about different characters, including a boy named William who wanted a doll. It was so of its time, so Seventies. It preached tolerance and diversity, and it was narrated by none other than Marlo Thomas. I may have been eight, but I knew who *That Girl* was.

Cynthia and I sat together during the screening, holding hands excitedly, smiling until we thought our faces would crack, feeling as if the movie had been made especially for us.

I walked with Cynthia to her house (actually, it was an apartment) one afternoon after school. For some unknown reason, we were in a strange mood and started breaking rules that we knew better than to break.

We opened a can of beer and drank from it, even though it tasted awful. We lit two cigarettes and sucked on them like straws, then coughed and gagged and laughed until we couldn't stand. We threw the barely smoked cigarettes (still lit) into the trash can, then began shrieking as smoke began to rise.

We worked ourselves into an hysterical frenzy of laughter and abandon that afternoon, the likes of which I hadn't experienced before, and haven't since.

The last time I saw Cynthia Nelson I was at school, digging tunnels in the sand beneath the jungle gym. My mind tells me it was the next day, but I'm not sure this is the truth.

I looked across the playground and saw Cynthia, who walked slowly, her gaze turned downward. All I could see were her eyes: they were each nearly hidden in the center of two black and blue rings. The thought that came to me was: "Cynthia Nelson, you look like a raccoon."

She glanced at me briefly, our eyes met, then I slowly turned away and resumed digging tunnels.

She walked straight through the playground, cutting a wide swath. The other kids did not stop and stare. They did the exact opposite, as a matter of fact, just as I had. They kept playing, they went about their business. They ignored her.

I ignored her.

04. My Showgirl, My Self

○

A woman must continually watch herself....

From earliest childhood she has been taught and persuaded to survey herself continually. And so she comes to consider the surveyor and the surveyed within her as the two constituent yet always distinct elements of her identity as a woman. She has to survey everything she is and everything she does because how she appears to men is of crucial importance for what is normally thought of as the success of her life. Her own sense of being in herself is supplanted by a sense of being appreciated as herself by another....

Men look at women. Women watch themselves being looked at. The surveyor of woman in herself is male: the surveyed, female. Thus, she turns herself into an object—and most particularly, an object of vision: a sight."

—JOHN BERGER, WAYS OF SEEING

EXCERPTS FROM DIANA'S "PARENT/CHILD OBSERVATION" NOTES TAKEN DURING RAY'S PRE-K CLASSES:

> Ray seems to be developing more self-confidence.—11/2/70

Ray played with the doll house with Rose this morning. He seems a bit disoriented today.—1/11/71

He doesn't enjoy fingerpainting at all. He says it's 'too messy.'—1/18/71

He's been very quiet—he didn't join in with the songs this morning, or in answering questions. He was moody.—3/1/71

He was very active on the playground today—and played heartily with the boys.—3/8/71

He confidently raised his hand for each question and answered correctly when you called on him. He was also quite attentive to the story today (usually, he's off in a daze).—4/12/71

FACE VALUE

My parents kept their record collection in a brown and white carry case called a Platter-Pak. The Platter-Pak was white with a brown lid that you secured with two latches on the front of the case, and a clear plastic handle on top that you carried it by. The Platter-Pak was decorated with brown graphics of a Treble Clef, musical notes and staff lines, and was designed to hold about thirty albums. My parents' record collection consisted of 15 to 20 albums, a dozen or so 45s and a 10-inch, 78 RPM recording of them getting married in Las Vegas.

My earliest memory of my mother is not my earliest memory, but it is a happy one. We're dancing together in our living room to a song called "You Turn Me On," sung by Ian Whitcomb. My memory takes place during what feels like summer because it's the middle of the day and the sunlight warms the room as it shines indirectly through the windows. My sister hasn't been born, so I'm not yet 4 years old.

The song is upbeat, and Whitcomb sings it in an off-key falsetto. The lyrics are simple, referencing a popular dance of the time called The Jerk, and the last line of each verse starts with a panting, nonsense vocalization that sounds silly, which I respond to favorably.

I'm moving my body with abandon to the music. I'm experiencing complete freedom and joy as I dance. I'm not worried about how I look or if I'm dancing correctly.

My mom is dancing in front of me. Her dark hair falls down past her shoulders and moves in a kind of synchronous yet seemingly self-directed rhythm with her body. She's wearing a collared, sleeveless gabardine top with a few buttons down the front, and a pair of matching cuffed, high-waisted shorts. She's smiling and singing and flipping her hair as she dances. I'm mesmerized by the sight of her. We play the record on repeat and keep dancing.

A few years earlier, after I'd taken up residence inside my mom's belly and was about three months into my gestation era, "You Turn Me On" peaked at Number 8 on the Billboard Hot 100 chart in July of 1965. Since my mom made a point of purchasing the 45, it stands to reason that she would have danced to the song when it was at the height of its popularity that July, six months before I was born, and caught all those happy feelings from it, which made their way into me. It also stands to reason that I absorbed not just all those happy feelings, but the song itself, as a soundtrack to that moment of my existence. It's the first pop song I have any memory of, the first song I remember dancing to, and it's the impetus to the earliest memory that I have of her.

Most memories of my mother are fragmentary and exist as non-linear, impressionistic visuals fused with heightened emotional states. They contrast with those of my father, which tend to have been captured as extended scenes, each containing a beginning, a middle and an end. Memories of my mother and I enjoying each other's' company are powerful but rare. They give me the impression that the moments of pleasure we shared were fleeting. Strung together, however, they create an entire strand of my narrative that has followed me throughout my life.

I live my life swathed in this upwardly spiraling current of memories, as if I'm always surrounded by spirits. Each of them resurfaces occasionally and becomes visible to me, the feelings re-felt, but not linearly and never for very long. They appear, I feel them, then they're gone. I don't fear losing them because I know they're still orbiting me. Sooner or later, they'll return.

What I find interesting about these memories is that the visuals seem to exist only to serve the emotional impacts they've come to symbolize. Moments when I realized something about her that I hadn't known up to that point; moments when she did or said something that ignited an emotional reaction in me; and moments when I experienced the joy and deep satisfaction of connecting with her.

I was conceived when my mom was 17 years old and born just two months after her 18th birthday. While my mom finished her senior year with me in my earliest stage of development, the photo that documents this point on her timeline was taken before my existence entered the picture.

My mom's senior yearbook photo is stunning. She glows. It's a portrait of a young woman who knows how to comport herself, who knows how to present. Her smile is polite and engaging, orienting itself at the equidistance between pliability and steadfastness, while betraying no trace of either.

A diminutive pendant rests just beneath the neckline of her seafoam green angora sweater on a thin gold chain. Her tastefully modest bouffant hairstyle creates a perfect silhouette frame for her face. Her head is tilted slightly, as if she's leaning forward, listening to what you have to say. Her expression conveys warmth but reveals nothing.

My mother's senior yearbook portrait shows a young woman unblemished by life. Her eyes reflect the expansive poppy field of possibilities in front of her. I know nothing about the kind of day my mom was having when she sat for her senior yearbook photo, or how she felt, whether she was happy, sad, both or neither. All I know is what I see.

She radiates poise, optimism, composure and yes, beauty. Her gaze intimates that while she isn't about to brag, she knows what she's doing. She knows where she wants to go, and she believes she can get there. She presents herself in the way that is expected of her at the time. She's coloring within the lines, mostly for your comfort and benefit, but she isn't constrained by them.

Throughout the early years of my life, from my days as a toddler through the beginning of middle school, my relationship with my mom was inexplicably intense, at least on my end. Even as a boy, just barely out of toddlerdom, I expected my mom to engage with me as an equal.

The connection I felt with her ran deep, and whenever she failed or chose not to engage with me at the frequency I expected, I would become enraged at her. I'd be driven into a fit at the thought of her not respecting that connection, which I expected her to acknowledge and inhabit with me at all times.

Some days, I didn't just feel these emotional reactions, I acted on them. On one sunny day, I vented my rage on the sidewalk in front of our house. I had a fairly large collection of Hot Wheels at the time, at least a couple dozen of them, along with racetracks and service stations that I would play with for hours on end. I kept my Hot Wheels in a round black storage case designed to resemble a car wheel.

We also had a beat-up croquet set we kept on the back patio. That day, I went out to the patio and selected a mallet. On my way back through the house, I stopped in my bedroom and picked up the Hot Wheels storage case.

I carried both out the front door and walked to the sidewalk, directly in front of the house. I set the storage case on the lawn, opened it up, selected a Hot Wheel and placed it on the sidewalk in front of me. Then I gripped the croquet mallet with both hands, swung it in a circular motion from behind me, up and over my head until it came crashing down on the car, which was left flattened and shattered into bits.

My mom watched me from the living room window, partially hidden by the drape that hung there. I kicked the parts of the destroyed Hot Wheel out of the way, selected another one, and placed it in the same spot. I looked at my mother. She gazed back, unmoving. I swung the mallet again and smashed the second Hot Wheel.

I knew, as early as the second Hot Wheel, that she would not intervene. She would not stop me from doing this to myself. I also knew that I had to finish what I'd started. I don't remember why I was upset with her that day, I just know that this was how I thought I could hurt her back. I needed to hurt her back because she'd hurt me, and the best way I could think of to do that was to destroy a collection of things she'd helped me curate. I had to make my point. I don't recall what the point was, but I made it. I destroyed my entire Hot Wheels collection.

For the earliest formative years of my life, once I'd reached an age where I had some agency (control over how to behave, what to say, what to express and how to express it), we were engaged in a battle of wills over who would control the emotional intensity of our relationship. My expectation that my mom meet me where I was at, and on my terms, allowed no room for variance or compromise.

As for our battle of wills, she won, because of course she did. Not because she was right, necessarily, but because she was bigger than me. I was operating at a clear disadvantage. I had no frame of reference and very little life experience. I wasn't yet able to discern between authenticity and performance.

From one interaction to the next, my mom was presenting herself to me from more than one internal command center. As a boy, when I experienced my mom looking at or speaking to me, I assumed I was dealing with the same person. And technically, I was. But there were layers that I couldn't see. And though she ultimately won our battle of wills, I've always felt that our relationship suffered as a result.

When I was five years old, I decided to run away from home. I'd probably just watched an annual screening of *The Wizard of Oz* and adopted this idea from its depiction of Dorothy Gale doing the same thing during the sepia-toned sequence at the beginning of the movie. Even at the age of five, I was drawn to (and had an innate flair for) the dramatic.

I wasn't *really* going to run away, of course. But I wanted my mom to *think* that I was. She'd express alarm and concern; she'd do all she could to talk me out of it. She might even, at the end of the day, buy me a treat to express her gratitude to me for reminding her just how wonderful I was and how much she adored me.

I packed my wicker suitcase with the essentials, which consisted of my Snoopy hairbrush and nothing else. I walked into the living room, where she was reclining on the couch watching T.V., and said, "I'm running away, Mommy."

As I approached the front door, keeping my eyes on her, awaiting her expected response, she looked back at me with a vacant expression, shrugged and said, "Go ahead."

Her tone made her statement sound like she was making the dare out of sheer boredom. There was absolutely no emotion, interest or concern in the way she said it. Seeing her look at me that way was, to say the least, shocking and quite upsetting. In my mind, I imagined myself walking out the front door and heading down the block toward wherever I was running away to, which I hadn't figured out yet, because according to my plan, things weren't supposed to get that far.

I'd made the mistake of presenting this provocation to her when it was already dark outside. A few houses down the block, there was a tree that grew quite tall, with several long, leafy branches that hung over the sidewalk. As I stood in our living room, staring into my mother's emotionless eyes and gripping my wicker suitcase, I imagined a winged devil monster that was waiting in the branches of that tree, who would swoop down and grab me as I was running away beneath it.

The winged devil monster would pluck me off the sidewalk, then fly into the sky with me trapped in its filthy claws. As it flew away, I'd be screaming for my mother to save me. But she'd just remain seated on the couch, watching T.V., exactly as she was doing right then.

At the time, it didn't occur to me that I could have avoided encountering the winged devil monster by simply running away in a different direction, a path that didn't lead me directly beneath the branches of that scary tree. But hindsight's 20/20.

Realizing my mistake, and fearful of the dark night outside, I broke into a forced, unconvincing laugh and backpedaled. "I'm just pretending! I'm not really running away! I was just pretending!" She continued staring at me but didn't respond. I, on the other hand, beat a hasty retreat. I returned to my bedroom and tried not to think about what had just happened.

I didn't have the language to articulate the feelings that resulted from being denied reassurance by my mother that, despite this unfortunate misunderstanding, she still loved me. But I still felt them. Needless to say, I was shook. I was never a very relaxed child, but this incident (and others like it) quickly taught me to appear as if I were the chillest little boy you'd ever met.

When you're five years old and you experience your mother disengage from you emotionally; when you see her look at you as if she doesn't know you, and doesn't even find you all that interesting, it instills a deep fear that, if you are not a good boy, or if you do something wrong to make her angry enough, she will abandon you.

I began to fear that she would leave me because what I learned was that her love for me had an OFF switch at her disposal. At least, that's how it felt.

Believing this about your mother at the age of five is terrifying and creates a tremendous amount of anxiety. What it feels like is that you haven't earned your right to occupy the space you inhabit within the family unit (and by extension, the world) as her child.

Once your right to occupy that space is called into question, you're never quite able to claim it securely for yourself again. It's something you must fight for to earn, and yet, you never return to that space and fit back into it the way you once did. Your position within the family unit becomes optional, not foundational. As a result, you find yourself tethered, floating above and a little behind them, following them. Connected but also separate.

Despite this frequently strained relationship dynamic between us, I managed to perform the functions generally expected of me. As I began my social indoctrination, I imagine my parents felt a cautious sense of optimism.

On my kindergarten report card, I was graded on a scale of Yes, Sometimes and Not Yet. I was graded Yes in almost all categories: I played well with others, I tried to control my feelings, I followed directions and I worked without disturbing others. I imagine my future office cubicle was being built for me in anticipation of my dutiful and timely arrival when I attained adult worker bee status.

There were just two metrics on which I received a grade of Sometimes: I Sometimes followed school rules, and I Sometimes finished my work. Two is a small number, but those particular two may have been red flags. My commitment to following rules and producing the output expected of me was tenuous from the very beginning.

In the kindergarten class photo, my head is turned toward the girl standing next to me as if I'm telling her a joke or making a humorous observation; hers is turned slightly toward me as well. She's listening, and we're both grinning. We're relaxed. Our gazes are not directed at the camera. My body language is one of fluidity; I appear to be in the process of putting my hands in my back pockets or straightening out my shirt.

It's a candid moment that captures me being at ease within myself, and it differs markedly from my appearance in the following year's class photo. In that one, I'm standing rigidly, face forward, my arms held straight down to my sides, my gaze aimed directly at the camera, my smile stuck to my face like a gold star.

The remainder of my elementary school career played out the same way. Occasionally, I excelled at something. The rest of the time, the worst I ever did was meet expectations.

SUBDIVISIONS

In 1972 my parents moved us from our home in Bellflower, a post-war suburban subdivision southeast of Los Angeles that was built on farmland during the 1950s, to Orange County, which is further south as you head from Los Angeles toward San Diego. Orange County is a vast sprawl of suburban enclaves built on farmland as well.

Development in Orange County was slow and steady until it exploded in the mid-1950s, when Disneyland became an international tourist destination. Aerospace firms and light industry expansion also brought a significant increase in population and development to the area.

Our new home was in the city of Orange, had three bedrooms, two bathrooms and was closer to ranch style than our previous home had been. The area we lived in was developed throughout the 1960s and 1970s, and built parallel to the foothills of the Santa Ana Mountains, which the suburban sprawl was fast approaching.

In the first half of the 1970s, when she was in her early twenties, my mom worked as an executive secretary at the corporate headquarters of Yamaha Corporation in Buena Park.

The company was in a period of growth and expansion, and they'd recently become major players in the motorcycle racing, off-road racing and recreational motorcycle markets. The energy at the company was that of onward and upward momentum, and my mom was exposed to an affluent side of life she'd never seen before, in an industry that felt young and exciting.

What I didn't know at the time was that before we moved, my mom had talked to my dad about wanting to get a divorce. The monotony of her life at home with my dad was starting to get to her.

Early on in their marriage, they'd both taken night classes, my mom to learn additional secretarial skills, and my dad to get his GED. After he got his GED, though, my dad was good. My mom wanted to keep taking classes, but my dad resented her efforts to continue and became jealous of her male classmates.

Over the years, my mom watched my dad come home every night after work, sit in the same chair, and watch T.V. He didn't have any interest in doing much more than that. She was frustrated by the feeling that if they stayed together, her life was never going to go anywhere, and this made her feel trapped.

When she talked to my dad about wanting a divorce, his reaction was one of deep sadness and grief, and she told me that he eventually seemed close to having a breakdown over the thought of their marriage ending. She'd never seen him in that kind of emotional state, and she was so rattled by the sight of it that she decided to stick with the marriage to try and make it work.

My mom says she never saw my dad cry. I, however, saw him cry twice. The first time was on the day my mom told him unequivocally that she wanted a divorce. We'd lived in Orange County for about a year at that point, and I was eight. We'd just arrived home from a day at the beach. Our skin was still warm from the sun, carrying the salt and aroma of the ocean, and we hadn't showered yet, so we still had sand in our hair and between our toes.

I remember my mom's voice rising above its normal pitch, and she said something to the effect of, "I can't do this anymore!" She disappeared into their bedroom, and when I looked at my dad, he was already crying. When I saw him crying, I started crying. I didn't know exactly what was happening or why, but I knew he was leaving.

Turns out we both left. I lived with him briefly for one or two months right after they separated. He rented a furnished two-bedroom apartment a few miles from our house. For the most part, I liked living there with him. My memory of the apartment is vivid. It felt like my apartment, as if I were a grown-up and had furnished it with my own things.

My dad would sometimes mix himself vodka and orange juice cocktails, which he'd drink from an insulated black plastic Michelob beer mug, and which he'd share with me. I would sing and dance to songs playing on the radio, or goof off for him, as he sat at the dining room table, watching me and occasionally laughing at or with me. It felt good to make him laugh.

That living arrangement didn't last long, and I was soon back at the house we'd all once lived in, staying with my mom and sister.

My grandparents and other relatives doted on my sister and me during this period, to mitigate the effects of the divorce. Even so, my sister and I were expected to soldier on and not complain about anything.

My paternal grandmother would rant to me occasionally, seemingly on my dad's behalf, about what my mom had done, or about the amount of child support he was expected to pay. She spoke to me in these instances as if I were on Team Mom and had not only been involved in deciding the terms and conditions of my parents' divorce, but was also in a position to change them.

◆◆◆

NEW WOMAN

A shift occurred at home during this period, indicating that things weren't right. My mom made a new friend, a divorcée named Pamela who had three kids of her own, and whose ex-husband, a fireman, had physically abused her. Her kids were the same age as my sister and me. We attended the same school, so we hung out a lot.

Pamela was of the opinion that kids shouldn't have much free time to go outside and play, or to stay inside and watch cartoons. She believed they should be put to work instead, and repeated these beliefs ad nauseum whenever she and my mom were hanging out together. I strongly disliked Pamela; she was brash and filled my mom's head with bad ideas. She characterized us kids as obstacles that needed to be overcome, deprioritized, and brought down to size.

My mom became more irritable and began spending less time with us. She began to exhibit overt resentment toward us, and I blamed Pamela for this change. The house began to feel unstable and oppressive. The thought of returning to it would loom over me each day at school. The house also became disorganized, as did my mom's behavior.

One weekend she was on a manic tear, yelling and ranting her way from room to room for a reason I couldn't discern. I had run into the kitchen to throw something in the trash, and when I stepped back out, I saw my mother standing at the far end of the living room, her body racked with sobs.

My mind was not sure what to make of this sight, as I'd never seen her behave like this. The angle of the house seemed to tilt and bend as she stood there sobbing. I was witnessing my mother first shatter, then collapse in on herself. Her shoulders appeared to fold in toward each other and her spine bent as her head lolled down toward her chest, her face in her hands.

She verbalized a long moan of agony that grew quieter until it almost seemed about to fade away. But then it shifted into a deeper register and became something guttural, an angry growl, and the sound she was making didn't stop. It kept growing into something louder and larger until she lifted her head up toward the ceiling and screamed at the top of her lungs for what seemed like hours, filling the entire house as well as, I imagined, the neighborhood and surrounding counties.

I stood stock still, transfixed, horrified by what I was seeing. She'd lost control. She was making noises that sounded inhuman to me, and she was contorting herself with spasmodic jerks as if the rage inside her was fighting to burst out of her body. She'd lost all thought of exercising restraint for my benefit.

I immediately categorized the woman I was watching as Not My Mother, and that's when her head pivoted in my direction. Her eyes met mine, and what I saw in this woman's eyes terrified me: an absence of recognition and a determination to mete out punishment. I'd never seen her before. This woman hated me and didn't care if I knew it. She came at me with no hesitation, no sound. All I could do was brace myself.

I saw an unhinged, violent side of my mom emerge that day. She terrorized my sister and me with extreme mood swings, outbursts of rage and physical abuse over the course of the next few years. Our home became destabilized, and how I felt at home depended completely on how my mom behaved.

I could figure out no rhyme or reason to what would set her off, or when. I lived in constant fear of the Madwoman's sudden re-emergence. At the same time, I hated my mom for her behavior.

I had to separate my mom from the Madwoman so I could mentally and emotionally process what she did to me. This caused my feelings for her to become fractured. I loved the mother I knew until the appearance of the Madwoman, but I also hated her for the things the Madwoman did to me.

These things were always far beyond what the situation seemed to call for; always humiliating and degrading, always a surprise, and always felt in solitude, as I was left alone to process what had just happened to me.

When I was in fourth grade, my mom was at the school attending a parent meeting in the library. After the meeting, she walked past my classroom, chatting with another mom as they headed toward the parking lot.

Some of the girls in my class, watching her walk by, said things like, "Look at Ray's mom. She's so pretty." They were in awe of her, talking about how they wished their own mothers were as pretty as mine.

I looked out the window and stared at her, with her feathered, frosted hair, her fancy work dress, her nylons and her heels, as she walked past the windows, which ran the length of the classroom. She appeared to be listening intently to the other mom, watching her as she spoke and nodding her head periodically. It was a rare moment for me, in that I got a glimpse of her outside the space of fearing she would notice me looking at her. She didn't catch me that time.

I acknowledged to myself that, yes, my mom was pretty. I would give them that. But I felt like warning those kids to be careful what they wished for. They'd never seen the other side of her.

I realized that day, for the first time, the effect my mom had on other people. By way of her looks, how she used her demeanor, how she presented herself in full costume and makeup. I realized how effective she was with her look, because everyone seemed to be entranced by her.

I also realized she saved the ugliest part of herself for me, and I wondered why. Why did she save the most dangerous part of herself for *me* and protect everyone else from it? Why was *I* the one she chose to sick the Madwoman on?

At the same time, I was confused. I felt responsible for her attacks because she blamed me for them; my culpability in causing them was treated as a given.

It's only natural that I would, to some extent, center myself in this new reality I inhabited with her. I was eight years old, still at an age when I centered myself in just about everything. When my mother blamed me for her outbursts, I couldn't help but agree with her, even though I knew at some level that what she did to me was wrong. Once I was at the center of her violence, though, I became its cause and its object.

I never outgrew that sense of myself as the cause of any negative effect I experienced at the hands of another. When others who are not my mother inflicted physical, emotional or mental pain upon me, my default response was to assume responsibility for their actions. My path moving forward was not to defend myself, but to launch an internal investigation into what I'd done to trigger such behavior in them.

The focus of my life at this point shifted from having my own experience of it, to managing it in an effort to both understand why she was being driven to behave this way, and to do whatever I could to avoid creating circumstances that would trigger her to explode and transform into the raging lunatic I'd witnessed emerge on that day that marked the Madwoman's arrival.

When I was eleven years old my mom married an attorney named Walt. Out of an intuitively correct sense of caution, I never bonded with Walt emotionally, and while our relationship was rocky, we got along more often than we didn't.

In June 1977, a few weeks before their wedding, my sister and I were flown to Las Vegas to meet and visit Walt's mom and our step-grandma to be, who let us know upon our arrival that we should call her Grandma Deb.

Grandma Deb lived in a two-bedroom apartment about five minutes off the Las Vegas Strip. She smoked long cigarettes and had dyed black hair that she wore swept up in a gravity-defying flip, which was well out of vogue by 1977 but looked fabulous on her, nonetheless. Her eyebrows were dyed the same color as her flip hairdo, and she wore lipstick in a gash between her nose and her chin, which looked as if it had been applied to both lips with one broad stroke

It was on this short trip to Vegas that I first tuned into the iconography of the Las Vegas showgirl. Up to that point, the only showgirls I'd ever seen were on an *I Love Lucy* rerun. In it, Lucy was given an acting role as a showgirl, which required her to walk down a staircase, gracefully and in time with the music. Of course, Lucy blew it and hilarity ensued. Ultimately, the showgirl element of that episode was played strictly for laughs, so I never got a sense of showgirl magic when I watched it.

My visit with Grandma Deb in Las Vegas, however, was an awakening. She had several tourist magazines on her living room table that contained showtime listings and ads for all the casinos and nightclubs in town. These magazines were filled with showgirl photos. I would study the photos and marvel at the sheer presence these women held, the way they filled up whatever space they were in. They were magnetic.

Grandma Deb told us to pick out a show to see during our stay. I strong-armed my sister into backing up my choice of Tony Orlando and Dawn, much to the disapproval of Grandma Deb, who'd been pushing for Wayne Newton. She begrudgingly relented, shaking her head in disappointment, but the show turned out to be a lot of fun.

We were seated at one of many long banquet tables that were arranged perpendicular to the stage. There was no opening act, but there was an opening number, which was performed by about a half dozen showgirls. The only thing about the show I remember is them gliding about the stage, their towering ostrich feather headdresses and boas trailing behind them, their rhinestones and sequins catching the stage lights and sparkling dazzlingly, even when they stood still.

These women fascinated me. They were beautiful, dramatic, poised and so measured in their movements. The image they projected was one of perfection and composure. I never saw one stumble, or miss a beat, or stop smiling, or allow her chin to drop. I never saw one of them appear to be anything other than in complete control of her performance. I was mesmerized by these showgirls, and I never let go of the feelings they produced in me as I watched them perform: fascination, safety, and distance.

On the day my sister and I were returning home from Vegas, my mom was unable to rouse my maternal grandma from sleep. My grandma was recovering from surgery that removed cancerous growths from one of her lungs, and though she'd been experiencing some headaches, she resisted a trip back to the hospital and told my mom if she didn't feel better by Monday, she'd get it checked out. Other than the headaches, she'd appeared to be doing fine. But that morning, my mom couldn't wake her. She'd slipped into a coma during the night and passed away soon thereafter without ever regaining consciousness.

My grandma's funeral was the second time I saw my dad cry. Before the service, I stood in line to view my grandma in her casket. Many people were weeping, including my dad, but I wasn't emotional in that way about her death.

When I stepped up to the casket and looked at her, I knew immediately that the practically unrecognizable shell in the casket was not my grandma. I never felt that my grandma had ceased to exist. I just knew she'd gone someplace else, and that I no longer had access to her.

That loss was hard, because she was one of the only adults in my life who not only saw me for who I was, but loved me as I was, without any hesitation or inner conflict about who I may become as I grew up.

◆◆◆

Ghosted

The last time I attempted to connect with my mom emotionally, at that intuitive, deep level of connection I'd expected of her when I was a young boy, was when I was in 7th grade. I'd stayed home from school, feigning sickness, but really just to take a break from the bullshit I faced every day from classmates.

At one point during the day, we were having a conversation that felt easy, familiar, and very relaxed as we laughed and enjoyed each other's company. When our laughter died down a little, I said to her, "I really enjoy spending time with you like this."

I was watching her face as I said it, and I could see the veil come down in response, imposing a measure of distance between us that I knew she wouldn't let me breach. She replied, "You need to stop staying home sick from school." The message was that the door was closed and I needed to move on. So I did.

My mother mellowed out when we lived with Walt, but that marriage was short-lived, and when they divorced after only two years, it wasn't long before the Madwoman reemerged. We moved into our new home, which was just a few blocks from the middle school I attended.

My mom's approach to parenting me at this point until the time I eventually moved out can best be described as "hands off." How I did in school, how I did socially, wasn't of much interest to her. For the most part, I was left to figure that stuff out on my own. I was also expected to excel at everything.

My mom was very self-directed when she was in school. She had to be, because neither one of her parents paid much attention to her progress or encouraged her to do well. Despite this lack of attention (or perhaps because of it) my mom was an overachiever: she got straight A's and functioned well socially. Her little brother, my Uncle Fred, was the opposite: he struggled socially and had trouble with schoolwork (turns out he was dyslexic). Measured by the metrics of 1950s America, he was decidedly lackluster. Even so, my grandparents heaped praise and attention on him.

At one point during middle school, my mom was yelling at me about a C- or a D on my report card, and she got to ranting about Uncle Fred. "I'd come home with straight A's, and no one said a word about it! Then Fred would get home, and your grandma and grandpa would go on and on about, 'Wow! Look at that! Fred got a D!'" My mom resented that her brother received so much praise and attention from my grandparents while not accomplishing much of anything, while she went virtually ignored even though her accomplishments were impressive by any metric.

She was determined to make sure that same dynamic didn't occur in her household. As far as my mom was concerned, I'd already won life's lottery by being a boy. I already had all the advantages, and the system was already set up for me to coast to success. I had all the support that I needed: the patriarchy. For me, the rest was all cake.

And she was right about one thing: I was a boy. But I was a queer boy. The system was not set up for me to thrive while being my authentic self. It was set up for me to hide my authentic self or be cast out of the mainstream and relegated to the sidelines. Excluded from the game. Blamed for my exclusion.

I liked learning but I hated school. I hated most of the other kids. They were assholes. Avoiding their attention, which usually manifested in shitty ways and at my expense, got to be so exhausting that I eventually decided, fuck it. I don't care about school; I don't care about my grades. If this was what I had to put up with to be there, then I wanted no part of it.

At one point, the school called my mom in so the guidance counselor could talk to us about my truancy issues and what the problem might be. My mom came in, sat down, and burst into tears, dabbing at her eyes with a Kleenex and lamenting in a choked-up voice about how difficult I was, and how she didn't know what to do with me, and how hard she worked, and how she was just at the end of her rope.

I was staring daggers at her, in a state of disbelief over how she was making this meeting about her. That she would center herself in this instant pissed me off, especially knowing that she was half-assing it when it came to raising me. My predicament became clear: she had no interest in investing any more in me than she already had. She was tapped out.

The guidance counselor spent most of the meeting comforting my mother, and eventually reassured me, almost as an afterthought, that I just had to wait it out, and that things would get better for me in high school, when the assholes would lose interest in me. I didn't believe him for a second.

It was a bummer, but my mom just wasn't that into me. I considered myself a good kid, despite my maladaptive behavior. But others saw me differently. There I was: possibly queer, an introvert, socially inept at times, socially outcast all the time, a frequent truant with a GPA that was sinking like a rock. All I seemed to ever want to do was listen to my music, read my books and be by myself. Nothing I was good at was considered an accomplishment by anyone in my orbit.

My sister, on the other hand, was the golden child: the smart, pretty, popular one that my mom adored. It was easy for my mom to focus on my sister and her many achievements when all I seemed to do was just sit there, disappointing her.

I'm not trying to toot my own horn here (if I could do that, believe me, I'd never leave the house), but growing up, I had no support system. Most queer kids didn't. Like most queer kids of the time who couldn't or chose not to be closeted, I was on my own. And no matter what your gender, race, sexuality, mental or physical health state, not having a support system when you're a kid and adolescent makes those experiences exponentially more difficult than they already are. Forming a healthy sense of self, forging your identity, gaining awareness of your strengths and weaknesses, is hard enough to figure out when you've got family support.

But for kids back then who were trying to figure out that stuff without role models or mentors to provide guidance and perspective, the process of coming up with an effective adult identity was a perilous journey fraught with an infinite array of risks and opportunities to make bad choices. Most kids that age (prior to the internet, anyway) had no frame of reference to help guide their decisions, some of which were likely to affect the rest of their lives.

I wish I'd had adults in my life who could give me the support and perspective I needed to see beyond the social problems I faced at school each day. When you're in it, it feels as if it's always been and always will be that way.

The fact that I was an outcast was treated by the adults in my life as a failure on my part. I was failing to fit in. I was failing to get along. I was failing to attend classes. I was failing to succeed. But I wondered: why should I have to get along with these people when most of them are assholes that I don't give a shit about? Ditching class and being on my own, where I wasn't being harassed or mocked or hassled by my classmates, was good for me. I didn't understand how they couldn't see that.

I was told that solving these problems was my responsibility. My need to be in a school environment where I wasn't an outcast or bullied, and to live in a home where I wasn't abused or treated with indifference, was not sufficient enough to make changes that may inconvenience the adults that were responsible for raising me. I was expected to make it work. And, to a certain extent, I did. I just didn't make it work the way they wanted me to.

In the end, my mother wasn't inclined, or didn't have the capacity, to provide the attention, sustained maintenance and upkeep that's required to effectively raise a child, and this disinterest only intensified after I hit adolescence.

It's unfortunate that in the U.S., we face social pressure to prioritize making enough money to afford an impressive house, nice clothes, a fancy car and whatever other accoutrements can be used to signal professional success and financial wealth, over doing what's necessary to strengthen the family unit, support and empower the family members who need it, and nurture strong, meaningful family relationships that are designed to last a lifetime.

We lived in a nice house on a suburban street populated with tract homes that had been built in the 1960s. My mom drove a Volvo and a string of other nice cars that conveyed a level of affluence that was misleading. We were house poor. My stepdad had financed getting us into the house so that, I assumed, he wouldn't have to pay any sort of alimony after they divorced. It was a tradeoff.

My mom had the trappings of the level of affluence to which she aspired, but the trappings were not supported by her income. The resulting debt and stress these trappings produced over time rendered my mom incapable of focusing on raising her two kids, engaging with us in our lives, and meeting our emotional and developmental needs.

The house became the main reason my mom made money. My sister and I became obstacles to her being able to hang on to the house. She was stressed out and angry because we were impeding her ability to keep it, by costing too much money for her to do both. She didn't get mad at the house for preventing her from building and maintaining good relationships with her kids. It should have been the other way around.

Halfway through my sophomore year, my mom kicked me out after we had an argument. Although "argument" may be too strong a word; it was more like a spat. At one point while I was standing near her, she hauled off and slapped me without warning or provocation. It was a full-swing BAM! right upside my face. I was so startled and infuriated that I raised my fist and leaned toward her as if I were going to slug her.

She flinched and cowered before me in a manner that looked completely unfamiliar and a little rehearsed. In that moment, I got the feeling that she *wanted* me to slug her. My mind extrapolated from where we were standing, and I became convinced that she hit me with the expectation that I would hit her back, so she could then call the cops.

I saw her in my mind's eye, sobbing as the officers comforted her on the sofa, while I sat handcuffed in the back of their police cruiser, which would be parked in our driveway for all the neighbors to see. She'd yammer on about how she just didn't know what to do with me, how I was getting to be more than she could handle.

Then the cops would drive me back to the station and throw me into a cell before commencing with the *Scared Straight* lesson-teaching. Rather than engage further with her, I retreated to my room.

Though she'd failed to bait me into slugging her, she wasn't finished with me yet. She barreled into my room, shouting at me to pack my bags. She couldn't handle me anymore, so I was going to live with my father.

This upset me even more than the slap because it meant I would have to change schools in the middle of the year. I may have hated the assholes at my school, but at least I knew the lay of the land there. Going to a brand-new school in the middle of the school year seemed daunting. Also, my dad lived in a small one-bedroom apartment.

I knew my dad was stiffing her on child support because, one, he would repeatedly tell me that he couldn't afford it, and two, if he'd been paying my mother, and shipping me off to live with him would have reduced her monthly child support by $100, she never would have sent me.

I realize now that she was just trying to make ends meet, but at the time it felt as if she'd just made *Sophie's Choice*, and I wasn't the choice. Nothing I could say would change her mind that day, so I packed some clothes, books and records, and waited for my dad to come get me.

As I waited for him to arrive, something unexpected happened. I realized I was getting something I'd wanted for quite some time: a reprieve from my mother and her crazy, erratic antics, and an escape from the assholes I faced each day when I should have been able to learn without daily harassment. By the time my dad got there, I was guardedly excited and looking forward to getting away from my mother and the mouth breathers at school.

◆ ◆ ◆

MAPS

Most memories of my mom from my adolescence are bad ones, either of me feeling some kind of bad way about or because of her, or of her doing bad things. I do have some fond memories from that time, when we'd laugh together in rare moments of connection that weren't fraught with tension. But these fond memories are the exception, not the rule.

The relative scarcity of what I consider accessible happy memories involving her can be attributed, in part, to my point of view at that age, and what I focused on from day to day. I was in a constant state of high alert, looking for signs that the Madwoman may reappear. Even so, I do have some good memories from the time that are foundational to my identity as a queer man.

The first occurred during the summer of 1980 when I was fourteen. I was outside one night, lying on the cement that ran along one side of the house between the front gate and the backyard. The night was clear because the Santa Ana winds were blowing, and the trees above me from the neighbor's yard were being whipped about as gusts traveled through the yard.

Between my own home's eaves to my right, which extended over the wall of my mom's bedroom, and the trees' wild dance in the neighbors' yard just past the fence to my left, was the night sky, cleared by the wind and blinking with stars.

I was smoking a Marlboro Light, which I'd had to light indoors before venturing out into the wind, and I was feeling deep sadness and loneliness. My heart felt like a stone inside my chest cavity. The stone was an absence of allies, of connection. I wondered if I'd ever feel close to anyone, if I'd ever feel seen, because at the time, I didn't.

As I ruminated on these feelings of isolation and took puffs off my cigarette, one of the stars I was looking at seemed to flare momentarily, shine brighter than the rest, and then I was overcome with the emotional presence of my maternal grandmother, which traveled through my body.

When I realized what was happening, the feelings of surprise and elation, combined with my grandmother's love for me, fused within my chest and seemed to spin there momentarily, like a whirlpool, before rising up out of my body and back into the night, leaving me dazed on the cement, still staring skyward, and no longer feeling alone.

I went back into the house and wrote my first poem that night, in an effort to capture the experience in the best way I knew how: through words. The next day I sat down with my mom at the kitchen table and showed it to her.

She read through the poem once, and her first response was, "I...don't get it." I walked her through the stanzas, line by line, and explained what they meant, what I was describing, what I'd captured. It was a poem, after all. It's a format that lends itself to metaphor and word play.

Once I'd walked her through it, we both relaxed and warmed up for a few moments. We inhabited that shared space I loved so much as we enjoyed one of the first real inventions of my creativity together. It only lasted a few minutes, but it was of great value to me.

I came out to my mom as bisexual when I was fifteen years old in the summer of 1981. My friend Travis had stayed at our house for a long weekend visit, and the three of us were in the car as she drove him home. I was sitting in the front passenger seat; Travis was in the back. It was night, and I remember the faint glow of the dashboard lights within the car, as well as the lights of the suburbs we were driving through, as they shone in the darkness surrounding us.

Despite my fear of rejection, my fear of what her response may be, I never once considered that throwing me out of the house would be one of them. This is a testament to the fact that, even though our relationship was tumultuous, I felt safe enough to share this truth with her without fearing she'd disown me and throw me out in the street. I trusted our connection. I knew that she loved me. My need for her to know me as the person I was, and emerging to be, trumped my fear of rejection and any impulse I had to keep it a secret, or pretend I was someone that I wasn't.

Travis and I had been having a great weekend, getting lots of sex in when there wasn't any adult supervision in the home which, given my mom's work schedule, allowed for some long, unsupervised evenings. I hadn't provided Travis with a heads-up, but I was emboldened by his presence, by my feelings for him, which were strong, and by the time we'd spent together over the previous few days. He sat stock still in the back seat, silent and mortified, wishing that he could disappear into the red velour upholstery of my mom's Mercury Monarch.

The timing of my announcement was also strategic. Travis was my backup. He was my buffer. I knew my mom well enough to know she would never lose her cool in front of company. I seized the rare moment when I would actually have someone on my side in one of these domestic conversations, when most of the time I was outnumbered by my mom and sister.

True to form, and to my expectation, my mom remained calm. After a pause, she said, "Okay." Then she paused again for a moment. "I'm not sure what you want me to do with this information."

It was my turn to pause. "I don't think I want you to do anything with it," I replied. "I just want you to know."

"Okay," she said again. "Now I know."

I don't recall any follow up conversations relating to this topic, but I assume we had some. I do know that I was put into counseling a short time thereafter. If there was an ulterior motive behind me going to counseling, other than just having a place to talk things out, I wasn't aware of it.

The counselor's name was Terry and we had an easy rapport. She succeeded in providing me with a perspective on life that was broader than the one I'd been living under. For the first time, I began to think of myself beyond my role within my family or at school. She helped me think about what I might do after that, in the years that were fast approaching, when I would eventually strike out on my own. However, she wasn't above giving me bad advice.

Of course, context is essential to understanding any situation, and this was the early 1980s in conservative Orange County, CA. In February of 1982, I saw a film called *Making Love* upon its initial theatrical release. It's about a married man who struggles with his homosexuality, meets a gay man who acts as his gateway into "gay life," and eventually comes out.

Making Love was the first movie I'd ever seen that depicted a male couple living happily together as partners by choice. Granted, this image and its message were limited to less than a minute of screen time at the end of the movie, but it was more than I'd ever seen before. I grabbed it and held on for dear life.

The film was controversial, which is probably hard to understand if you were to watch it today. There's a scene early on wherein the main character visits a gay bar for the first time. The scene includes a shot of two men at the end of the bar who begin making out with each other. At the theater I was in, several patrons had visceral reactions to the sight of two men kissing. They made their feelings of disgust known as dramatically as they could, then they got up and noisily made their way out of the theater, voicing their disapproval the entire way.

As a side note, I experienced a similar incident when I went to see *The Birdcage* upon its initial release in 1996. There's a scene with a brief exchange between Robin Williams and Nathan Lane; they're sitting on a bench, having a quiet discussion after an argument they'd had during a previous scene. Williams takes Lane's hand in his, in an act of tenderness. That's it.

Some bitch in front of me made this groaning sound of revulsion and I swear to God, I wanted to stand up and accidentally dump my soda on her fucking head. Give her a reason to make some noise. That I didn't is one of my biggest regrets in life.

I believe these outsized reactions to queer content in public spaces are coordinated and performative on the part of capitalist christians. The louder they clutch their pearls, the more oppressive they are aiming to be. Fuck them. This is not just their world.

Anyway, at one of my counseling sessions I told Terry about seeing *Making Love*, expressed that I was almost certain I was gay, and that I didn't think I'd be pursuing marriage with a woman when I became an adult. She challenged me on my assertion. "What are you going to do?"

"I'll meet a guy," I told her. The answer seemed clear to me. "We'll live together and have a relationship."

"Ray, gay men don't *want* relationships. They don't *want* to live together like married couples do. My gay clients do nothing but complain about how lonely they are, how they can never find a man who wants to settle down. *Making Love* is a *movie*. Those types of gay men don't exist in real life."

I couldn't help but point out the obvious flaw in her argument: "Well, they must exist because some of them come to you for therapy." She didn't respond. I shrugged and said, "There must be people out there like me. I can't be the only one." Granted, *Making Love* was a movie. But if it was in a movie, it was most likely more widespread a sentiment than Terry was letting on.

Looking back, I see how chilling her characterization of gay men in general was, and how that take on gay men erased any version of life moving forward that included a chosen family or a same sex spouse, as options when pursuing a satisfying life. I'm lucky I'd already decided that's what I wanted, expected and would shoot for, before I had that discussion with her. I'm lucky her take on gay men didn't have a chance to take root in my head before I planted my own root first.

My mom made a point of taking me to see two plays in the coming years that were also foundational in my perception of what being gay could look like and mean. The first was the initial Los Angeles run of Harvey Fierstein's *Torch Song Trilogy* in late 1983.

When I saw *Torch Song Trilogy*, AIDS had been named but was still only receiving sporadic news coverage. People knew of its existence, but not its scope. Since I was just about to turn eighteen, my social circle of fellow queer people was small. I did not belong to the larger queer community that, at the time, was centered primarily on queer bars and nightlife.

The play seemed progressive, optimistic and insistent upon asserting the right to build legitimate queer family on queer terms. Ironically, the play was advocating traditional family values for queer people. My primary takeaway from *Torch Song Trilogy* was that I could build a family of my own, a family built on mutual love and support. The play didn't guarantee that things would work out, necessarily, but it did guarantee that I could aim for and possibly achieve them.

The second play was *The Normal Heart*, written by Larry Kramer, which we saw during its initial L.A. run in January 1986. Though I saw this play just over two years after I'd seen *Torch Song Trilogy*, *The Normal Heart* was an entirely different animal: different year, different tone, different message, different world.

The play was brilliant on multiple fronts. There were scenes that took place with characters walking up and down the aisles of the venue, arguing with each other, which put the audience right into the middle of its raw urgency and emotional turmoil. The fluidity in staging dissolved the wall between actor and observer, which helped the audience identify with the characters.

It also allowed the audience to feel not just the presence and fallout of AIDS, but the people whose lives it was shattering and snuffing out in real time, by effectively placing the audience within the world of the production. Which was the world we were living in. The two were the same.

At the time of *The Normal Heart*'s initial run, AIDS was no longer an abstraction in the cultural imagination, especially not to queer people. But its meaning and impact were still up for debate. Politicians argued passionately about whether to fund research into AIDS to find out what caused it, how it was transmitted, how it progressed, and what possible avenues for treatment might be explored.

Right wing conservatives (and especially those who self-identified as christian) expressed the opinion that the gays had brought AIDS (or God's wrath, as many of them preferred to characterize it) upon themselves, and should be left to suffer and die from the disease, as it was of no concern to decent people.

Room temperature take on capitalist christians (one of many I'll express in this collection): when faced with dire circumstances, capitalist christians almost always reveal themselves to be useless when called upon to be of service to the collective good of humanity.

When I refer to capitalist christians in this book, I am not talking about private faith or people who practice compassion modeled after the teachings of Jesus Christ in their own lives. I am talking about the political-religious movement that's rooted in evangelical fundamentalism, white supremacy, patriarchy, American exceptionalism, misogyny and nationalism. It's a bastardized, uniquely American, capitalist form of christianity that's been weaponized against people who don't fit their mold of what's acceptable. For the sake of consistency throughout this collection, I refer to this segment of American christianity, and the people who practice or represent it, as "capitalist christians."

Kramer's play was searing in its depiction of AIDS as it crept into an unsuspecting queer community, and the calculated inaction of government officials who preferred to let their constituents, friends and loved ones die rather than risk losing votes, access to power or political donations.

The Normal Heart forced its audiences to watch what was happening to the queer community, what was happening behind closed doors in political and government spaces when it came to AIDS, and how utterly vile the abandonment of constituents by political leaders was as the pandemic continued to unfold.

Seeing the play at that time, you were learning these things as you saw them unfold on stage. You felt and knew these truths once you'd seen *The Normal Heart*, but these truths were not the consensus of the time. These truths were revealing themselves through subtle channels: through art, stage productions, independent publications and activism. They were not acknowledged or discussed through mainstream news channels or print media. When it came to AIDS, the truth was still up for debate.

In dealing with my queerness, my mom went through a process of reframing her perception and expectations of me. Resources to help her process this knowledge about me were limited, especially where we lived, which was predominantly conservative. Her exposure to media representations of gay men was, like mine, extremely limited. She didn't know any gay people that she could turn to. She also faced social and familial scrutiny and judgment if she was open about me being queer.

Nevertheless, my mom made efforts to do what she could to expose me to gay content whenever she saw an opportunity. If it hadn't been for my mom, I'd have never seen *Torch Song Trilogy* and been exposed to substantive, positive depictions of relationships between gay men. I may never have known that there were more options than just hook ups and sex clubs and back rooms in gay bars, or that there were other gay men out there who wanted what I wanted: a partner to build and share my life with.

I also never would have received the gift of Larry Kramer's unfiltered rage. *The Normal Heart* introduced me to the concept that queer people had a right to equal status within the social framework, status that wasn't relegated to second class, and that wasn't fair game as a target for capitalist christians, or any religious conservatives for that matter, and other bigots who sought to destroy and erase us. It taught me that when queer people are denied the same rights as other citizens but expected to keep paying taxes to uphold the government that is oppressing us, then rage and disruptive activism are acceptable responses.

The days of assimilation and ass-kissing by gays in order to make progress (the history of which I wouldn't even learn about until years later), were clearly over, and had been since the Compton's Cafeteria riot in San Franciso, three years prior to Stonewall. With AIDS destroying the progress queer activists had made over the course of the previous decade, we didn't have time for that shit.

My mom is responsible for shaping me into the adult queer man I became. She did me a great service by giving me access to this content, and I'm deeply and eternally grateful to her for that.

She found meaningful queer content for me to consume when many others may have tried to shield me from it. She showed up for me in ways that didn't announce themselves, but that I'd later look back on and realize, "Ah. Look at what she did."

She also confounded me. But I respected her need to maintain emotional distance. I'd stopped expecting her to change her mind about living in the space of our shared connection. I distanced myself emotionally from all moments between us, even the good ones.

Fast forward thirty years, and I was in Las Vegas attending a conference. I was staying at the Golden Nugget with Monkey, a guy with whom I was very much in love. The hotel was located downtown in an area that had been repurposed as The Fremont Street Experience, which had been updated to include a massive LED canopy over the street, live music spaces, and old neon signs from past casinos and hotels that were displayed outdoors, some (such as the spinning Aladdin's lamp) located at street level like dynamic, flashing museum exhibits.

Monkey and I discussed going to see an old-school Vegas show that not only included, but emphasized, that O.G. variety of Vegas showgirl. After looking into it, we learned there was only one remaining show that included old-school Vegas showgirls: *Jubilee!* at Bally's Las Vegas, which was on the Strip, right across the street from Caesar's Palace.

We also found out that *Jubilee!* was one of the longest-running productions in Las Vegas history, showcased opulent stage costumes designed by Bob Mackie, and made use of elaborate sets for themed production numbers about Samson and Delilah, the sinking of the Titanic, and more. We got tickets and couldn't wait to see the show.

When the cab dropped us off at Bally's we were both giddy, ready for a night of unmatched fabulosity and camp. We chatted as we walked through the casino, following the signs directing us to the theater, and when we arrived it was...underwhelming.

The walls surrounding the entrance were painted white in what looked like basic primer, and there was only one *Jubilee!* poster, hanging in a poster case that was low and off center in a large, empty wall, looking as if it had been put there as an afterthought about 10 years prior.

There was no line of people waiting to get in, just Monkey and me. The ticket taker, an elderly woman wearing a regal, sequined white gown, gifted us with a somewhat detached smile as she tore our tickets and motioned for us to enter the theater.

The theater itself reminded me, as had the ticket taker, that glamour does have an expiration date. The theater had seen better days and was on the verge of looking run down. The house wasn't even half full, and not many more patrons entered while Monkey and I sat there, taking in our surroundings and joking about the tacky delights that awaited us once the show got started.

The stage was cavernous, and I was examining its layout when some movement at its side caught my attention. My eyes darted to an area just past the proscenium where a stage curtain had been pulled back slightly, providing me with a partial view of a sparsely lit backstage area.

Just as my eyes found this pulled back curtain, an adult figure slipped out of sight, and then a young girl peeked out from behind the fabric that was hanging there. I got the feeling we'd caught each other's gazes and stared back at her for a few moments. Then she dipped out of sight, and the curtain fell back into place.

The house lights dimmed. Monkey said, "Here we go," and I chuckled in response.

We sat in the darkness, waiting, until I wondered if they might be experiencing technical difficulties. Then, without a light cue or an announcement, the music began. Three trap doors on the stage opened upward, their undersides mirrored and lit from beneath the stage. In each mirror's reflection was a showgirl.

I became so excited I could barely contain myself. I gasped, sat up straight on the edge of my seat, and forgot to exhale. She wasn't even on stage yet, but she'd already taken my breath away.

I saw her from the elevated angle of the mirror, so I was looking down on her ostrich feather headdress, seeing the sequins on her costume from above, seeing her arms curl in time with the music, and watching her feet move back and forth across the platform in measured, choreographed steps. I was hypnotized by her movements and the ways her costume responded to them. She wasn't even on stage yet, but she was already in motion.

My heart was beating so rapidly I feared it would pop right out of my chest. Her movements made her ostrich feather headdress sway ethereally, and the light from beneath the stage caught the movement of the crystals, beads and sequins sewn into her costume, refracting it up into the darkness. I was so happy to see her again, as if I'd finally made it home after enduring an interminably long separation.

The music continued to swell as she ascended to the stage and into the spotlights. As she rose, she was accompanied by fragments of my memory, surrounding me in their upward spiral, memories of my mother holding court in countless situations with her composure, her radiance, in complete control of her performance. All the times she'd held it together without letting it crack, without betraying that anything may be getting to her. The spotlight beams refracted from the crystals and blanketed the entire darkened theater, creating a galaxy of shimmering lights around us.

Once she was on stage, she stepped off the platform and paused, one foot planted slightly in front of the other, each shoe pointed in a diverging direction. She stood there, bathed in the spotlights, her arms outstretched, standing stock still, her rhinestones continuing to shimmer and glisten, and granting me the chance to observe the gravity of her power.

As I watched her standing there, I began to weep. I was overcome with emotion that I didn't understand. I felt an incredible sense of knowing her, of having been missing her for decades. And being in the same room with her again filled me with the immeasurable joy and relief of being home. All I could do was let my eyes well up and overflow as I sat there, taking her in.

A driving music beat kicked in, and more stage lights behind the showgirl lit up to reveal dozens of other showgirls and male dancers at the top of an ornate staircase located at center stage. They moved in time with the music as well, and began their unhurried, hypnotically choreographed descent down the stairs toward the audience.

Monkey nudged me and whispered, "You okay?"

I nodded but didn't speak. I still couldn't take my eyes off her. I remained entranced by her, and I experienced the entire show in a baffling state of transcendence that I could barely comprehend.

Those memories swirling around me that seemed to rise up from beneath the stage with her were part of a larger revelation taking shape as I sat in the theater that night watching the show. They revealed to me a deeper comprehension of my mother as a woman; not only as my mother, but as everything else she'd been required (and had chosen) to be as she navigated her life.

The appearance of the Madwoman, so long before that night in Vegas, had thrown the Showgirl I'd been living with up to that point into stark relief. The Showgirl was the version of my mom I could rely upon to keep things running at an even keel. My life was ordered when I was in her care.

The Madwoman's arrival taught me that the Showgirl, while singular and distinct, was not the entirety of my mother. And even though I identified her as Not My Mother during my first encounter with her, I came to understand that the Madwoman was a manifestation of her as well. These two were the women with whom I became preoccupied as I moved forward through time.

I viewed the Showgirl as my mother's true, primary self, and the Madwoman as her dark half. Over the years, particularly during my adolescence, they occasionally melted into one another, each strategically adopting elements of the other when necessary, but staying identifiably separate and distinct.

As I grew into adulthood, I needed my mom's reassurance that I was safe to become whomever I was born to be. I needed her to let me be as close to her, for us to be as emotionally interwoven, as I needed us to be, without her experiencing fear that I may become something she couldn't understand or explain to others. I sensed she feared that if we were as close as I wanted us to be, and I ultimately became something she couldn't accept, then the resulting separation between us, the rupture, would be too overwhelming to experience, or even survive.

The Showgirl was strategic that way. Being a parent in the 1970s and 1980s who comes to suspect, or even realize, that one of their kids is queer, could not have been anything less than terrifying.

I imagine it's similar for parents of trans children today. Some react much better than others, but most of these parents love their children, and only want what's best for them. Yet they are cognizant of the world we live in. They're torn between wanting to allow their children to grow into the truest versions of themselves they can be, and needing to protect their children from the predators in society who do everything they can to not only deny, but murder and erase the queer people that have always been and always will be essential components of the human fabric.

At the show that night in Vegas, something new became clear to me. I watched the Showgirl on stage, and I felt the shadow of the Madwoman's presence in the theater, even though by then she only lived in my mind as a phantom. I pondered the reflexive fear of knowing the Madwoman was near me, if not visible, and the frustration of not knowing why the Showgirl refused me entry to our perfect shared space.

Toward the end of the show, my gaze was again drawn to some barely perceptible movement that was out of sync with the production occurring on stage. I saw the curtain, off to the side, just past the proscenium, pulled back slightly like before, and the outline of a small figure peering out from behind it. She *was* observing me. The sounds and commotion of the stage production faded, and my field of vision narrowed as if I were looking through a telescope at the girl peeking out from behind the curtain.

Before I could get a good look at her, the telescopic view extended, its focus moving farther and farther away, more deeply into the past, collapsing time until it finally stopped on my young mother, in our living room, bathed in diffuse sunlight, dancing with me to "You Turn Me On." Her joy was contagious and I felt it immediately. I savored it and felt myself dancing in it for a few exhilarating moments, felt myself being mesmerized by her all over again, until the telescope began to retract.

I came back toward myself, stopping at the sight of my mother, observing me through the living room window from behind the drape as I destroyed my Hot Wheels collection out on the sidewalk. My vision retracted again and arrived in our kitchen as I sat next to her, explaining the meaning behind each line of my poem.

Then I continued moving back toward the future, toward the now of that moment in Vegas, seeing and experiencing the instances wherein she'd allowed herself connection with me, in the way I expected when I was a young boy; or the other instances, in which she'd revealed herself to me, but kept her distance and observed.

As the telescope brought me closer to where I was seated, in Las Vegas, at the theater, watching the production, it moved out from behind the stage curtain and paused, so that I saw her clearly for the first time. I saw the Young Girl, peering out at me from behind the curtain, making sure, before the telescope retracted again, that I was seeing her.

When she knew that I was seeing her, or at least seeing the half of her face not hidden behind the stage curtain, the corner of her mouth lifted into a grin, and the eye that observed me lit up and sparkled in response to being seen.

Then the curtain slid back into place and she was gone. The telescope retracted a final time, past the showgirl at center stage, who was engaged in the final movements of her performance, until I was back in my seat, back inside myself. Elated. Exhausted.

◆◆◆

LET'S MEANDER

After the show, Monkey tells me he needs to find a bathroom. I tell him I'll wait for him until he returns.

Alone, I allow emotion to overtake me again. I lean forward, my elbows on my knees, my hands clasped, my head bowed. I'm not wracked with sobs, but I let the tears flow freely. To anyone noticing me, I probably appear to be feeling ill, or very drunk.

I feel a protective emotional wall I'd constructed as a child breaking apart and collapsing inside me. My tears aren't borne of pain or suffering, but of relief. I can feel myself releasing the rage, confusion and resentment I've been protecting myself with since first being targeted by the Madwoman. I have the impulse to cling to those dark emotions, but they slip through my fingers. Instead, I relax, open up and let them fall away.

The Young Girl backstage had done this. While the Showgirl performed on stage and the Madwoman lurked in the shadows of the theater, the Young Girl revealed herself to me.

It was the first time I'd looked past the spectacle of the Showgirl and the Madwoman, the first time I'd seen the person behind them both, the person I'd never realized was there. She made sure I saw her, and she enjoyed it when I did. She didn't allow herself to be seen very often. She knew this moment would be revelatory.

A young girl her age is vulnerable, unsure of herself, in need of care. But young girls her age are sometimes faced with circumstances that require them to assume the mantle of adult women; to adopt the skills of adult femininity that require them to manage people, behaviors, and the attendant emotions, that young girls are not yet developmentally capable of managing.

Faced with such circumstances many years ago, the Young Girl responded as best she could, not by becoming an adult woman, but by assembling one. She cobbled the Showgirl together using knowledge she'd absorbed from the culture she lived in: what attracted positive attention, what prevented rejection and abandonment, what induced interpersonal engagement in social situations, what invited the interest of men.

This persona served her well for several years, but the Showgirl can only do so much. She's an effective conduit for poise, charm, precision, and composure, but not for emotion. The Showgirl's performance doesn't have room to accommodate sadness, exhaustion, disillusionment, frustration...or rage.

The Young Girl needed another protector, one who didn't fuck around, one who protected her from harm. The Madwoman offered that protection by being scary, chaotic, uncaring and violent. Being near the Madwoman, physically or emotionally, was dangerous. She made sure of it. This kept the Young Girl safe, but at a cost.

When my mom experienced childhood trauma, her mental and emotional development splintered into multiple strands. Some strands continued to develop, others became fixed. The Showgirl as camouflage and the Madwoman as armor were designed and built by a Young Girl who was too young to consider how these constructs might, in practice, harm her own children.

I recognized myself in the Young Girl because I shared a similarly fractured, multi-stranded network of developmental pathways. In some ways, I was a young boy pretending to be an adult male, doing my best to pass as a grown up as I lived my life.

This revelation triggered the first true, undiluted feelings of empathy for my mother that I'd ever had, pertaining to our relationship and how she'd behaved during periods of my childhood. For the first time, I saw past what she did to me. I understood how she could have been capable of doing what she did.

This revelation did not diminish or erase the choices she made that harmed me. What it did was make me know, finally, that none of it was my fault.

Monkey returns and quietly sits down next to me. I appreciate his patience. I wipe my eyes on my sleeves, look over at him and smile.

"Having a moment, I see," he says gently.

"Having many," I reply, chuckling.

"Wanna head back to the room?"

I feel as if I've been wrung out and hung up to dry, but I say, "No. Let's meander."

He cocks his head, still looking at me. I can see him thinking. "What would you say if I told you I could take you to the top of the Eiffel Tower in less than ten minutes?"

"The real Eiffel Tower?" I ask, with the weary tone of a skeptic.

He shrugs. "Real enough."

I smile again, grateful that we're here together. "Prove it."

"Let's go."

05. Red Headed Blanket

Before and after another again
Never to change
Stay always the same
How that must feel
Stagnated
but it's right for you,
amen.

I saw her in a star that flashed
And touched the corner of my eye,
Then dimmed to a presence
I knew from before.
I asked her to come,
I wasn't afraid
Once she arrived.
And here she was again,
amen.

It happened twice one evening.
Afraid to go away,
"Don't you worry," the angel said,
And she sang her song and moved through me,
and was of me even though she was dead,
amen.

When I went in I was willing
To hallucinate them all into perfect being.
Until I resist
The urge to relive
A moment of make-believe joy,
I'll wonder why the fish have died,
     amen.

Verse:
ca.1980, Age 14.
First thing I wrote as personal expression to be shared with others.
After an unexpected visit from my deceased maternal grandmother.

06. Just Like Ricky Did

■

Mona never listened to her father when he warned her not to walk home through the wash. She bragged about it every day on the way home from school, just as we rounded the corner by the beauty shop that had been there ever since we all of us could remember.

Sometimes the door of the shop would open as we approached, letting in or out a woman we'd be sure to make fun of, no matter what we were doing or talking about. And that smell would float out the door through the air and latch onto us. That smell of hot air and chemicals and women. I'd smell it past the beauty shop as it clung to my clothes, past the parking lot, the laundry mat, and two old vacant buildings further along the street, then around the oldest building's side, through a hole in the chain link fence, and onto the trail that led us under the bridge, through the weeds and down into the wash.

A lot of days the rains would leave the wash all churning furious like a landslide, the water mixed with mud and debris. Jim called it a shit stream once and got a laugh, but the next time he called it that we none of us laughed, so he never called it a shit stream again.

There was a giant sewer hole that was big enough to walk in, and we went in there a lot of times, mostly in summer to get out of the heat. But after rains it always spewed out dirty water into the air and down into the bottom of the wash. We'd have to wait 'til things dried up to go back in.

Mona liked to imitate her dad: "Mona, I forbid you to go down into that wash again!" "Mona, if I find out you've gone down into that wash one more time, well, I just don't wanna say!" She'd make fun of him and put him down and laugh her ugly laugh at him and shrink him down to nothing more than a stupid piglet rolling around in a puddle of mud and its own shit. The way she laughed could make you feel like that if she aimed it at you.

And I could never get it, why she hated him so much. I never met the guy, but I saw him a few times, in his yard from the street on my bike, or in town when I was at the bank with my mom. And he was bald and skinny and pale but seemed friendly enough just by looking at him. He didn't seem to have a mean bone in his body.

And I never saw a bruise or a welt or blood on her, and she always wore clothes that looked brand new, and she was always clean, and her hair all styled real nice, so I figured he couldn't be that bad, and I never said to her face what I thought her dad should do to her when she sassed off to him like she said she always did to her stupid father.

Cause then she probably would have looked at me and stayed on me and laughed and said whatever came into her crazy mind. And it would have been something mean. She would have found a way to make me feel like dirt, she always did when she turned it on you. You just had to not let on that what she said got through, and wait it out, and hope she'd turn her sights on something else, on someone else.

I never really liked her that much.

Mona got real mean that year, she got mad and she got mean. She was older than us and wore a bra, you could see the strap sometimes on her shoulder when she didn't make a point of pushing it back out of sight.

On weekends she'd prowl around and pounce if she caught you alone somewhere where no one else would see. I heard them talking about it. She'd get you alone in some dank and dusty place like the field shed where we'd smoke and drink the beers Jim stole from his dad's fridge, and she'd start rubbing up on you and get your pants down and her dress up, and it would all happen too fast to make any kind of sense out of what was going on. If I was a little older, I think I might have liked it some, but I didn't even have hair yet myself and didn't quite know what to make of hers.

So when she left me lying there, sticky and sweating on the floor, watching dust float through the air, I didn't know what to think or feel about it. So I just figured I wasn't telling anyone unless they told me something first, and I needed to avoid being caught alone by her again, and I felt relieved that it was over and done with and pretty much decided to forget about it. Then I went home and took a shower.

Ricky couldn't get enough of Mona, though. Ricky was the oldest, the biggest, the first one to grow moustache and underarm hair, the first one to get zits. He wasn't the only one with hair or zits by the time we met Mona, but he was the first.

In summer he took to making sure he got his shirt off real quick as soon as Mona was around, and stretching his arms out wide, and twisting himself around and cracking his neck, and showing off in other ways like that. He'd laugh at all her jokes about her dad.

And I liked watching him do these things, even though I couldn't figure out what the hell it was he saw in her. To me she was like a junkyard dog, you needed to steer clear of that one, cause if she got you in her sights and her mood was right, you'd better run, get over the fence, before she got to you or deal with the consequences.

But Ricky put himself out there right inside her sights almost every day. Which meant she put them on me less and less, which suited me fine and which seemed to make both Mona and Ricky happy for a while. She'd whine and moan and threaten him like girls always would, but then she'd be smiling underneath it all the whole time, like girls always were.

And even though she told him to knock it off you could tell if he took her up on it, she wouldn't know what to do. In fact, one day he ignored her and walked off and acted like she was a fly buzzing around his head, shooing her away and talking to all the rest of us, but not to her, and we all went along with it and acted like she wasn't even there.

And then Ricky took his shirt off like he always did when Mona was around and stretched up toward the sky, stretched each of his arms across his chest from side to side, and twisted at his waist and cracked his knuckles, and I couldn't take my eyes off him.

Mona fell right off the deep end that time. Mona was beside herself that day, she didn't know what to do, until she finally just did what was left to do, she turned red and clenched her fists, let out a yelp and stomped off away from us in a cloud of dust and grasshoppers.

We all snickered at her as we watched her go, gave Ricky pats on his sweaty back, it was good to see the tables turned for a change. His back was sweaty, it was hot that day, the palm of my hand was wet with his sweat. He acted proud but kept an eye on her as she disappeared, and he didn't say much after she'd gone away.

One day I was walking home from school alone because I had to stay after for Mrs. Wolfe again, and I cut through the fields to save time but wished I hadn't cause the rain picked up too much, the mud was in my boots, a storm was hitting, and I was afraid the lightning would get me if I stayed in the open field much longer.

So I ran as best I could and ducked into the field shed to wait it out. Took my boots off and dumped the mud and water out of them, took off my slicker and hung it on the nail. Turned around to go back to the stash in the back of the shed and see what might be in there, we all said whatever was in there was fair game, if we had smokes or beers or food left over, we'd put it in the back inside an old toolbox and leave it for whoever needed it the next time.

And I turn around and Ricky's sitting on the box and he strikes a wooden match and lights a smoke, and the shadows on his face make him look old, like someone's dad. And he looks mean. He looks how my dad looks right before he gets up out of his chair and takes his belt off. It stops me up short.

I take in a sharp breath, but I don't think he heard it, and I don't want him to see me so easily scared, so I say, "Shit, Ricky." But my throat's all caught up with snot, so I have to clear my throat then start over again: "Shit, Ricky, whyn't you tell me you was in here?"

"Want one," he says. Doesn't ask it, says it. Then says it again. "Want one." And he hands me the one he just lit. I take it and put it in my mouth, the butt's wet from being on his lips, I taste his spit and lick the tip and hit it, breathe him in and taste his spit on my tongue. He pulls another out from his shirt pocket and lights it up for himself. "Have a seat." Sweeps his hand out, like it's his house or something. Like there's a seat. But I do, I sit on the floor, I suck on the smoke some more and take him in.

"Why aren't you at work," I say, not ask, talking like him so we can be alike, and hoping he notices and approves. More than anything else I want Ricky to like me, I want him to approve of me. When I have zits, and hair on my legs and under my arms, I'll act just like Ricky cause that's how older guys act and look, the cool ones, anyway, and that's how I'll act and look, and that's how he'll know we're exactly alike.

"Question," he says.

"What."

He takes another drag off his smoke, the cherry brightens like a meteor then dims, the rain blasts the shed's roof and leaks through in spots. Ricky holds the smoke inside, the cherry hovers, then he blows the smoke back out. It floats over to me, caresses my face, I breathe it in and hold it, then take another hit off my own.

"You fuck Mona?"

This time it's a question. He doesn't say it, he asks it. He raises her name at the end and makes it a question. Like maybe if he asks it and doesn't just say it, it won't be true. He'll get an answer that isn't what he figures it will be. He'll get an answer he doesn't not want to hear.

As for me, my throat closes up and my stomach drops. I can tell the way he feels about her, and I want to protect him from the truth, even if it doesn't mean protecting him from Mona, because I just like it, seeing him happy most the time, watching him feel like that.

But lying's no good cause some of the other guys know, I did end up telling them, and I wonder which ones spouted off at the mouth, those dicks! Lying's no good cause he probably already knows the truth, so I just gotta make it as good as I can.

"Not really. I mean, I don't know. She kinda got me alone once last summer. I didn't mean to. I didn't know what was going on really till it was over, you know? She kinda just made me do it. I didn't know what to do. I didn't mean to. I don't even like her." I hear what I just said replayed in my head and feel lame, retarded, weak. Me blaming her, that's a laugh. I'm so fucking ashamed. What a pussy.

And now he's gonna hate me, and probably kick my ass, and there's nothing I can do but suck on my smoke and hope it's over fast and then lose Ricky, who I most want to be like, just like he is. I wonder why I didn't just lie. It's my word against theirs. How would he know? But it's too late now, I've already gone ahead and done it, so what's the point.

He doesn't jump up and kick me in the face or punch me or tackle me. He doesn't yell. He spits out some smoke and scoffs. Shakes his head. "Jesus, even you, man. Last summer. How old are you again?"

"Almost twelve." Which isn't exactly the truth because I turned eleven in August, so really I'm closer to eleven than twelve. But it gets me mad, being thought of as young. I never want to admit how young I am. I always want to be older.

"It's okay. It ain't your fault," he says. Ricky flicks his lit cigarette over his shoulder into the corner of the shed, gets up and walks to the door. He puts his hood over his head and steps out, no word, no look back, slams the door shut, leaves me in the shed with my smoke in my mouth and his smoke in the corner, which I walk over to, pick up, stub out and pocket, before taking a last drag off mine and flicking it over my shoulder and into the corner just like Ricky did. I save what's left of his cigarette for later.

Sometimes I can see it clearly, the way it happened, exactly the way it happened. I can see her red hair but not her face because the back of his head blocks her face, she's facing me but he's between us facing her, so all I see is the back of his head framed by the dark red frizz of her wet hair, like a tangled wreath around his greased back dirty brown hair. And their hair's wet, it's still raining, which makes it hard to hear them clearly, their voices and her laughs are mixed up with all the other noise.

The rain's coming down on the hood of my slicker and the wash is churning up with muddy water and debris, and she's talking to him I think, and then she's laughing, and I'm hearing her laugh and the water roar, and smelling the hot air and chemicals and women.

And he hauls off and slugs her, slugs her right in the middle of her hidden face. He slugs her and she's knocked off her feet, she's not laughing anymore, but she goes flying backwards on the other side of him and she falls down below the lip of the mound they've been standing on and he's just standing there looking down at her where she fell in. But he doesn't try to do anything to help her, and she never comes back up.

That's the best one I can think of. That's the way it's most real. Cause all the sounds are what they should be, and he looks just like he did and so does she, and when I'm in it I'm one hundred percent sure that's what happened. But when I'm in it never lasts for very long, and it's just as he's about to turn around and see me's when it fades, cause first I can't see his face, and then I can't see nothing at all.

And then I remember that I can't remember anything that happened, and why keep asking me the same stupid questions, anyway? I was in the shed, I fell asleep in the shed, I was in the shed waiting out the storm and smoking a cigarette and fell asleep and when I woke up it was dark outside and the storm had let up. The storm was over when I woke up, and I put my boots and slicker on, and ran home and got the belt for staying out past dark.

After that we all decided the wash was bullshit and started walking home over the bridge after school and throwing things over the rail and seeing how they landed and where.

Ricky ignored me after that, and I noticed but it didn't bother me. I thought maybe we'd find things later that summer, after the wash dried up. Things we'd thrown off the bridge. But nothing turned up.

07. Plugs 1: Dean

*You're like my yo-yo that glowed in the dark
What made it special made it dangerous
So I bury it and forget.*

—KATE BUSH

Plug (Noun):

A plug (or the plug) is a person who has the ability to get or supply hard-to-find items, especially drugs.

—DICTIONARY.COM

Disclaimer:

The Plugs chapters in this collection are works of fiction. All characters, events, and locations depicted are products of the author's imagination. Any resemblance to actual persons, living or dead, or actual events, is purely coincidental.

Also, the plugs' names have been changed to maintain plausible deniability.

—THE AUTHOR

SANDS

My dad was always tinkering with things in the garage. Some of my earliest memories of him are located out in the unattached single car garage of our small two-bedroom house on Van Ruiten Street in Bellflower, CA. He was always working on his motorcycle. It seemed as if he was stuck in an endless process of taking it apart and putting it back together, repeatedly. But it was a process he enjoyed being stuck in. He preferred it to many other things.

My dad had a poster in the garage hanging over his workbench. It was a photo of Dennis Hopper on a motorcycle, a still from the movie *Easy Rider*. He had stringy brown hair, held down against his forehead by a brown headband. He sported a bushy brown mustache over his top lip and was wearing dark, round sunglasses, as bikers tend to do, so as not to collect bugs in their eyes.

His right hand, gloved in thick brown leather, rested on the throttle, which was open and accelerating the bike at a comfortable 55 or 60 mph. Hopper's left hand was not on the handlebar but was thrust forward, at the viewer, its middle finger sticking up out of the surrounding fingers, which were held low and tight to the palm. He was flipping us off. He was saying, "FUCK YOU." This poster hung in the garages of the first two homes of my childhood.

My father was a machine operator. He operated machines. That's all I know about what he did, other than that he wound up working at an aerospace company in one of those enormous production hangars surrounded by gigantic parking lots that were prevalent in working class enclaves south and southwest of Los Angeles throughout most of the last half of the twentieth century.

I loved my dad unconditionally, as I imagine most boys do. He was quiet and confident. He knew what he was doing. He worked on things. He made things work. He liked to smile and laugh but was guarded at the same time. He knew his way around the block.

He enjoyed 1950s rockabilly artists like Chuck Berry and Eddie Cochran. He also listened to the Beatles, which soundtrack some of my earliest childhood memories. My dad liked most of their output, but my awareness of them starts at their final phase: "Come Together," "Let It Be," "Hey Jude," "Get Back."

As I got older, through the 1970s and 1980s, my dad's soundtrack shifted to Los Angeles AOR radio stations like KLOS and KMET. Bands such as Pink Floyd, the Rolling Stones, Aerosmith and Led Zeppelin ruled the airwaves. Those bands and others like them were always playing in the garage while he was working on his motorcycles.

Their songs played when we were on the road as well, traveling the freeways of Southern California together, me along for the ride on the passenger side of the bench seat in his canary yellow and white '67 Ford F150. We traveled the 405 and the 5, connected to or bisected at various points by the 710, the 110, the 605 and the 91, and later, the 22, 55 and 57. Being driven around L.A. and Orange counties was a big part of my kid experience.

My first memory is at night, on the beach. I remember being seated near a huge bonfire with my parents and their friends. Though I know my mom was there, my dad is the only one who appears in this memory. He and one of his buddies walked with me toward the ocean. The waves curled up and crashed on the sand as we approached. The waves, as they rose into the air, and the foam they created after breaking, were bioluminescent, and glowed a light greenish blue in the moonlight.

I remember the moment of confusion I experienced when my dad told me I could go pee now, on the sand, near the water, I could just take it out and pee. And I was thinking: right here on the beach, out in the open, under the stars, in front of the waves, in front of you and your friend? Just whip it out and pee.

I hesitated, not sure about how to proceed. And he reassured me that it was fine, that's what he wanted me to do, and so I did. It was easy and a relief, and he was standing right there beside me, so it was okay.

Later that night, the smoke from the bonfire kept getting into my eyes, which burned, watered, and were hard to keep open. My dad carried me to the parking lot and put me into the back of a friend's truck that had a shell covering the bed, so I could lay down and go to sleep. I was on top of a sleeping bag. It was soft and comforting, and the material it was made of tickled my skin. After he put the door to the shell back down, securing me inside the truck bed, I stayed up for a few minutes more, my eyes watering and stinging.

I watched him walk back to the bonfire to rejoin my mom and their friends, the image of him walking away from me distorted from the water in my eyes. I had no fear of them forgetting where I was, or of them losing me, or of them leaving me behind and choosing something other than me, something else, something that was better. I lay down, closed my eyes, the flames of the bonfire still dancing on the backs of my eyelids, until I fell asleep.

My dad drove the pickup until he and my mom split, at which point he also drove a brown convertible MG. It was a two-seater, a stick shift, exceptionally low to the ground and noisy to ride in. He'd switch between the truck and the MG depending on what kind of mood he was in, I guess. I've never had more than one car at a time, myself. In the 1980s he drove a Mulsanne Blue 1970 Camaro. He drove the Camaro until he was arrested and went to prison in the mid-1980s. I don't know what he drove after he got out.

In the 1970s, at the height of the motocross craze, there was a movie called *On Any Sunday*, a documentary about dirt bike racing that originally came out in 1971 but was re-released every summer. Everyone I knew went to see that movie multiple times over the course of summer vacations. I remember it as a loop because I can't tell you the beginning, the middle or the end of the movie, but I remember its imagery as if I'd seen it yesterday.

At the age of nine I was lucky enough to have my own dirt bike, a Yamaha YZ80, which my mom got from work at a significant discount. It had a yellow gas tank with YAMAHA in black lettering on it. We'd take road trips to the deserts of California and Arizona in my grandparents' motorhome, towing a trailer that was carrying our dirt bikes. My dad frequently entered enduros, off-road motorcycle races, and performed quite well in them.

The first time we arrived at our lodgings in Arizona, a small apartment in a building situated at the edge of the vast Arizona desert, I asked my dad questions about what I was allowed to do. How far could I go? How fast?

My dad said, "You've been trained on how to ride, haven't you? You took lessons, right?" I said yeah. He said, "Then you know how to ride responsibly. Right?" Again, I said yeah, a little less certainly. "Well then, I don't care how fast or how far you go. You go as fast and far as you wanna go, Ray. Just be back before the sun goes down. You don't want to be lost in the desert after dark."

I had a backpack with a compass, water, and a small collection of basic supplies. I got a fluttery feeling in my stomach as I realized how fast and how far I went was up to me. I rode my dirt bike off-road in the open desert, reaching speeds my adult brain wouldn't dare allow me to even attempt today.

The exhilaration of opening it up and moving with the bumps and slides of the bike as I drove it through the open desert produced intense feelings of excitement, freedom, and agency that I don't think most kids that age have the opportunity to experience. Those feelings were deeply embedded into my psyche and my heart. They've never left me.

When my mom ended their marriage, he didn't take it well. While my mom had ambitions to ascend to new heights in life, my dad was already where he wanted to be, the only place he'd ever considered being: married with kids, a good job, a mortgage, and a garage to tinker in on weekends. He was devastated and never fully recovered, at least not during the following decade or so in which I still interacted with him. His anger became the core of who he was. It eventually drove everything he did.

He resisted paying my mother child support, and while she eventually took him to court over it, and prevailed, he always managed to get out from under paying what he owed. After my mom's court victory they attached his wages, but he was so committed to denying her financial assistance that he quit his job and went to work for a friend who paid him under the table. The court could issue its orders, but there wasn't really anyone to enforce them, as far as I could tell, because he continued to get away with shirking his financial responsibilities toward my sister and me.

This was back in the days when divorced parents could freely trash talk each other to their kids and complain about all the adult ways in which they were proceeding daily to fuck each other over. There was never a sense back then that talking to your kids about your ex-husband or ex-wife in this way might have a damaging effect on them (the kids).

I quickly assumed the role of peacekeeper in my family and, as a result, was saddled with constant feelings of dread, failure and anxiety, because the peace was never kept between them, at least never for very long. I failed unequivocally in my efforts to keep them on good terms with one another. I don't know if the role of peacekeeper is something I took on as a result of my own initiative, or if it was foisted upon me by them because I was the oldest. I don't remember. It may have been a little bit of both.

After the divorce, my dad partied and hung out with his friends more. At first, weekend visits with my dad often evaporated on Friday nights before they'd even started. He'd stop at his friend Gordon's house to get high before driving out to pick me up at my mom's. Then he'd blow off or forget about our plans for him to come get me. He just wouldn't show up.

I'd wait on the couch for him, stubbornly ignoring my mom's suggestions that I go to bed, resenting it when she told me that she didn't think he was coming, until I couldn't stop sleep from overtaking me. I'd wake up the next morning feeling disappointed, empty and alone. But as time went on, my dad flaked out on me less and less. He'd pick me up first thing on Friday nights, then take me with him to Gordon's house to hang out with the other kids while he got high with his friends.

My dad and his friends would spend hours on end, entire nights, out in Gordon's garage, "working on the boat." The boat was the beginning of a speedboat they were building so they could enter the races held at Lake Elsinore, which we would sometimes drive out to and observe on weekends in my grandparents' motorhome.

On Friday and Saturday nights, when my dad was at Gordon's "working on the boat," the kids would hang out in the house, unsupervised, roughhousing, playing games and watching late night T.V. until we eventually fell asleep to the sights of early James Bond or Hammer horror movies.

While my dad, Gordon and whatever other buddies were there might have spent a good portion of that time working on the boat, they were also doing copious amounts of cocaine and crank, depending on the night. I knew they were all capable craftsmen of one sort or another, so their lack of progress on the boat at the time mystified me. That boat never even came close to being finished.

On a Saturday morning following one of these nights, my dad was supposed to take me to a Webelos function; a pancake breakfast, a trip to the mountains, or some other similar event for boys and their dads to engage in. Webelos were the highest level of Cub Scouts who, in theory, were preparing to graduate to a Boy Scout troop. The Webelos den I belonged to was a diverse, awkward group of boys just about to hit puberty.

It was early that morning; the sun was up enough to light the sky, but not high enough to be seen. We had a couple of hours to kill, and my dad pulled his truck into a church parking lot on LaVeta Avenue in Orange, parked it facing a row of 1960s ranch styled suburban tract homes, and killed the engine.

He told me I had time to sleep if I wanted to, so I lay down, resting my head on his thigh underneath the steering wheel. I breathed in the scents of my dad: the denim of his jeans, the grease from his job, and the slightly chemical smell of his sweat, before falling asleep. This is the last memory I have of my dad that isn't tied to feelings of confusion, anger, disappointment or fear.

◆◆◆

CAUGHT

My dad made a point of trying to observe me while I was masturbating. I know this because I caught him doing it twice. Once, when I was thirteen, I was in the bedroom I shared with my dad's girlfriend's son, Kyle. We slept on bunk beds whenever I was there for an overnight. I was sitting in a swivel chair with my shirt pulled up and my shorts and boxers pulled down around my ankles, tugging away.

The bedroom had two doors: one that entered the room from the adjoining bedroom, which belonged to Kyle's older sister, and which I was seated with my back to. The other door was on the side of the room, which I was facing, and led to the den. The house was designed so that you could make a circuit through it if you wanted to.

I was going at it when I heard a floorboard creak in the adjacent bedroom behind me, just on the other side of the bedroom door, not more than three feet away. The sound informed me that the person who made it had been making a concerted effort to avoid being heard. It wasn't the sound of someone casually walking into the room, like Kyle, his mom or sister would have done. It was the sound of someone sneaking, carefully, so as not to be detected. I knew someone was there, and I assumed it was my dad.

I jumped out of the chair, pulled up my shorts, bolted through the den and dining room into the bathroom, where I tried to button and zip up my shorts over my erection. I waited for a couple of minutes, flushed the toilet, then casually walked

81

out of the bathroom to greet him, doing my best to conceal my hard on.

My dad usually didn't arrive home from work for another hour or so. But there he was, standing in the living room, and when we looked at each other, he grinned and asked me what I was up to. The question was loaded, and we both knew it. I said, "Not much," playing it cool. We left it at that.

The second time I caught him I was twenty years old and living with him in his mobile home. I was in the shower, going at it again, not paying much attention to anything else. After I nutted, I turned around toward the shower nozzle to rinse the soap off and my dad was in the bathroom with me. When I saw him, he pivoted, opened the medicine cabinet and rummaged through it as if looking for something. I stood still beneath the stream of water, staring at him until he left.

In January of 1980 my dad picked me up for the weekend in his M.G. When we got out to the car and settled into our seats, he started it up the way he usually did. But instead of releasing the clutch and pulling out into the street, he reached behind my seat and produced two glasses and a bottle of wine. He handed me a tumbler, filled it with white wine, filled up his own tumbler, handed me the bottle, told me to put it down between my feet and make sure it didn't spill, then said, "Here's to getting to know you better."

We toasted with our tumblers, and I took a swig of the wine, which tasted bittersweet. I didn't know what to say to him. My dad also got me stoned for the first time that night. I guess this was his way of welcoming me into manhood. That night, I got the feeling we were going to relate to one another on a different level moving forward. Man to man. I certainly wasn't against this development; getting an alcohol buzz felt fun, and being stoned wasn't so bad either.

On the drive back to my dad's, we were listening to one of the AOR stations he always listened to. We were on the freeway when, out of the blue, they played a Carly Simon song called "Vengeance," which was the hardest (and close to the only) straight up rock song she'd recorded up to that point. I was surprised to hear her on one of my dad's stations, and I was excited too. I asked him if I could turn it up.

I started singing along with her as she belted out the song, and after a while I asked my dad, "Do you like this song?" He smiled at me and said, "Sure. It's rock and roll, isn't it?" I could tell he was being diplomatic, but I appreciated the gesture. My dad found some of my musical tastes, which included Carly Simon and leaned heavily into ABBA, Olivia Newton John, Blondie and several emerging new wave bands, puzzling, to say the least.

We both took another swig of our wine, and I enjoyed the moment as my dad drove us through the night. It felt synchronous, which was a feeling I wasn't accustomed to. It seemed I'd hit the jackpot. I was getting high and drunk with my dad, Carly Simon was rocking out on the radio, and he was treating me as if I were one of his buddies. I was excited, and curious about what lay ahead for me. I felt like I was finally growing up. I had just turned fourteen.

My dad was a small time plug in the 1980s. He sold to his friends, a few co-workers, and a small group of clients he cultivated through other people he knew. He sold black beauties (pills that contained amphetamine), which I had no interest in, and weed. He was insistent on not providing me with weed to take home because he was certain my mom would find it and have him arrested.

This was extremely frustrating for me because who wants the ability to get stoned whenever you want, as long as you're with your dad each and every time? I mean, I loved him, but getting high with him was strange. We didn't have much in common when it came down to it, especially as I got older. I wanted to get high with people my own age so I could relax, cut loose and act like an idiot. Smoking out with my dad was fine, but I felt trapped. There are some things you just can't say or do in front of your dad.

My dad's version of teaching me how to be a man consisted of giving me two pieces of advice. First, he told me to follow his lead: if I got a girl pregnant, that was her problem. Second, before you do anything else, get high. We smoked weed just about every time we got together. It was fun for a while, but it started feeling like whenever we had plans or spent time together, I was expected to get baked before we got there. Sometimes I liked being high, but other times it made me self-conscious and paranoid. If I didn't partake, he'd give me a look that said, "What the hell is wrong with you?"

The turning point came when my dad took a friend and me to see Tom Petty & the Heartbreakers at the Inglewood Forum in Los Angeles. My dad moved up to an empty seat in the row behind us, having noticed that in the row behind that there were two teenaged girls. He sparked up a joint and started smoking it. The girls chatted him up, came down to sit next to him, and before long they were getting high together, laughing and bobbing their heads to the music. For me, it was just another night out with my dad.

I looked over at my friend Dan. Dan was of Chinese descent. He was studious, intelligent and family-oriented to an extent that I could barely relate to. His parents were first generation immigrants. When you have parents like mine who rarely show much interest in you, it's a trip meeting other kids whose parents are actively engaged with them and hold influence over their lives.

Dan was turned slightly in his seat, looking up over his shoulder, sneaking glances at my dad getting stoned. The look on Dan's face was one of pure shock and mortification. It startled me, the way he looked at my dad. His reaction was so genuine and unfiltered that I had no doubt of its authenticity.

I found myself reflecting, for the first time, on what my dad's behavior in my presence might look like to an outside observer. It was the first time I thought critically about the fact that my dad and I got high and drunk almost every time we got together. I was suddenly observing this behavior with some distance, beyond the point of "Wow! I have access to free weed and beer!"

A few days later, Dan had a serious talk with me and told me he was concerned about my well-being. The concern he expressed for me was, again, so unfiltered and genuine that I had no choice but to take him seriously. He told me he'd discussed the matter with his family, and they'd concluded that the best route forward for me would be to join the military as soon as I was old enough.

No one had ever expressed this kind of concern for me before. I was confused because I didn't think my situation was all that bad. I was also touched, because it meant a lot to me that he cared enough to have this conversation.

This occurred during the summer between my freshman year in junior high and my sophomore year in high school. It was before I came out, so Dan didn't know I was queer. I assumed he was straight, and while I didn't know for sure, there was never any sexual tension between us. We were just good friends.

I sensed that my confusion about my sexuality, which I hadn't sorted out yet, was not a good match for the military, but I appreciated his concern and told him so after thanking him for taking the time to talk to me about it. I assured him that I was okay, and that I would take care of myself and cut down on getting high with my dad. It was at this point that I decided I'd pull back from my dad some, and maybe not party with him so much.

◆ ◆ ◆

SWEAT

Halfway through my sophomore year is when my mom sent me packing. The Monday after I moved in, I strolled onto the campus of Bellflower High School, walked into the main building and approached a woman who exuded an air of authority. She was standing behind a long wooden counter and watching me as I approached her. I said, "Good morning. My name's Ray, and I'd like to enroll."

She gave me a bemused smirk. "Where are your parents?"

"I live with my dad. He's at work."

"Well, you'll need to come in together before we can enroll you here. There are documents your father needs to sign. In person. I'm afraid I can't enroll you without an adult guardian present."

"Oh," I said, surprised. I'd expected this process to be completed by me alone and without a hitch, today. "Okay. Well, I guess I'll see you tomorrow, then."

"I look forward to seeing you."

I turned around and left. As I exited the school grounds I studied the buildings, which were older than the ones at the high school I'd left behind in Orange. Those buildings resembled shoeboxes and were painted an ugly mustard brown.

My soon to be new school, however, appeared to have been built at a time when builders put in enough time and effort to construct buildings that were aesthetically pleasing,

86

with unified design elements. The outside walls were painted an unassuming off-white, which contrasted effortlessly with the dark-leafed trees and foliage that surrounded the buildings and common areas. The walls were accented with red brick at building entrances and around their bases, which lent the campus an air of history and gravitas that encouraged a certain amount of respect for what it represented.

Living with my dad started off well, but soon devolved into constant tension, shouting matches, threats of violence and physical altercations. Living with my dad in a one-bedroom apartment was awkward. I was extremely aware of my physicality at the time: I was doing sit-ups every day, lifting weights, trying to look athletic. I was a good-looking kid, even though I didn't know it at the time.

Being at the new school and away from the cohort I'd grown up with suddenly reframed me in a way I wasn't accustomed to. I got a lot of attention from boys and girls, as well as men and women, so I had an innate but still undeveloped awareness of the currency my physical appearance afforded me. I had the air of someone who was being observed at all times when out in public, even when no one was looking (which was most of the time, I'm sure). But I was always on.

I was also horny. All the time. Jacking off as many times a day as I could manage, confused and conflicted over who I was horny for. There were a few instances I had with girls where we'd be hanging out at her house and arrive at a moment of pensive silence. I knew that was my cue to move in for a kiss. But I hadn't engaged with these girls, pretty and interesting as they were, in an effort to score with them sexually. I found them interesting, and I liked their company, but I wasn't looking to fuck them, and it made for some awkward moments.

I did have a girlfriend at Bellflower High, a christian girl named Sally. We'd attend weekly lunch time bible study groups together, and I accompanied her family to church on a few Sundays. Her pastor tried to save me one Sunday after I'd been moved by his sermon to raise my hand when he asked if there were any people present who wanted to be saved. So I walked up to the front with the others, but once I got up there, I didn't know what they were asking me to do. It was as if I was expected to have memorized my lines, but I'd never been given a copy of the script.

I turned to the pastor and said, "I don't know what to do." He chuckled and said, "That's okay," and motioned for me to go back to my seat next to Sally so he could focus on the congregants who knew what the fuck they were doing.

Sally was a good sport about it. She was a very chill christian. Not like one or two others I dated, who were hellbent on saving my soul from damnation and who outed queer boys to their parents on more than one occasion. After Sally graduated from high school, she got married, had some kids, and eventually came out as a lesbian.

So there I was at the age of fifteen, hormones raging, my sexual libido at the forefront of my consciousness, working its way into my emergent young adult identity. Meanwhile, my dad was fast approaching middle age. He'd gained weight and sported a sizeable beer gut, which his drinking did nothing to mitigate. He was suffering from male pattern baldness and maintained a carefully sculpted combover that I hated.

I found his combover to be an offensive sign of weakness. Just shave your head, I would think to myself, mentally heaping piles of scorn on him. One of the coaches at Bellflower High sported a shaved head; he was virile and fit in a way that my dad couldn't touch.

It's crazy how harsh I was when it came to evaluating my dad's masculinity. I really did feel a level of contempt for him, based on metrics I barely understood. I judged him harshly for not being manly enough for me, to an extent that I could aspire to be like him. At the same time, I was afraid of him. Afraid of what he might do to me. It was a weird contradiction.

Harsh as I was about the combover, it didn't seem to get in the way of him scoring with ladies at the bar. They'd stumble through the front door shortly after two a.m. and "sneak" past me as I lay there in a sleeping bag on the cot I slept on. They'd be whispering loudly, trying not to awaken me (too late), bumping into furniture and knocking shit over until they got into his room, at which point they'd shut the door and get to the business of fucking, often quite noisily.

On weekends I let it slide, but if it happened on a school night and I couldn't fall back asleep I'd barge in on them while they were fucking. I'd just walk past them, pretend I wasn't paying attention, and go into the apartment's single bathroom to take a piss.

I'd often see the shape of his erect penis silhouetted against the white bed sheet as he pulled out and grabbed for the sheet or the blanket to cover up their nude bodies, but it was always too late. I knew he made these efforts to cover up more for the women he was fucking than he did to hide them from me.

For some reason, my dad didn't care if I saw his dick, and he didn't go to any great lengths to hide it from me. Another time, we were arguing through the closed bathroom door when he yanked the door open and stood before me, bare-assed naked and sporting a hard on, which I struggled to avoid looking at. It was jarring and awkward. I think he may have won that argument by default because he managed to shut me up.

Once I moved in with him, my dad became an angry, aggressive bully, prone to uncontrollable rages and outbursts of physical violence. To the rest of the world, he was the quiet, though affable, hardworking father who never complained about anything. To me, he became a constant threat. This was the flip side of the good times roll version of himself he'd introduced me to right after my fourteenth birthday.

My dad would get into moods where he would berate and threaten me for what seemed like forever. In most instances his tirades would only last for about ten or fifteen minutes, but ten or fifteen minutes is a long time to sit there and listen to your dad tell you what a piece of shit you are, and how you'll never amount to anything, and that you think you're so big and such a bad ass, and you really think you're hot shit, don't you? And you know what, maybe you just need your ass kicked, you little punk. Maybe you just need someone to beat the shit right out of you, maybe that's what you need. How do you think that'd feel, asshole? Hey! Dipshit! You listening to me?

Despite the tension and conflict between us, which went from bad to worse during my stay with him, I enjoyed that time period a lot. At school, I got along with the kids. I didn't make any enemies. I didn't get called fag. I performed well in sports (especially basketball) like I knew I could. I auditioned for the lead role of Mortimer in their Spring production of *Arsenic and Old Lace* and made call backs (much to the indignance of the department's resident theater queen, a cute guy who threw me shade any chance he could get until he was ultimately cast in the role).

Even though things went well for me at Bellflower High, I was expecting things to be different because I'd been socially conditioned to expect my peers to treat me a certain way, a way that triggered anxiety. Whether it was a teacher who intimidated me, or the subject matter, those small factors could trigger a domino effect that blew up all the rest of my anxieties about being at school. I couldn't escape the feeling I was being targeted. When the school finally caught up with me and called my dad to let him know what was happening, he was blindsided.

He came home from work that day, and it didn't go well. He shoved me backwards in the chair I'd been sitting in, leaned over me as I lay on the floor, and started berating me. Every time I tried to get up, he'd hit me in the chest, knocking me back down to the floor.

Having dropped out of high school himself, my dad frequently told me he wanted me to do better than he had. But using bully tactics and threats to get me there wasn't an effective strategy. Those tactics didn't stop me, even if they did often frighten me into promising I wouldn't ditch any more classes. I couldn't control my impulses to leave. They overrode everything else.

On the last day of school, the attendance lady told me she'd called my dad at work to verify a bunch of absences I'd accumulated over the course of the previous week. My dad had warned me a few days earlier that if the school called him one more time and told him I'd ditched another class, he was going to beat the shit out of me so bad that I wasn't ever going to forget it.

I told my girlfriend I was in deep shit and asked her if she could drive me down to my mom's place in Orange County. Mom didn't know it yet, but I was moving back in. We blew off the rest of our classes that day, rushed to my dad's apartment, packed up all my stuff, and she drove me down to my mom's.

He was PISSED, of course, for leaving the way I did. No doubt he was gearing up to give me the ass kicking he'd promised and felt I deserved. But when he got home from work, I was gone. No note. No phone call. Just gone.

He caught me on the phone at one point shortly after I'd left and read me the whole "I'm gonna kick your ass," riot act. I sat there on the phone, staring into space while I listened to him, playing it incredibly bored and acting like I didn't give one flying fuck about what he was saying.

I was fifteen. I was in my disaffected, bored to death teenaged prime and he fucking hated it. It would enrage him when I wouldn't act frightened of him, and he'd escalate his threats and promises to fuck me up the next time he saw me to ridiculous levels that almost made me want to laugh.

Of course, on the inside, as I was listening to him, my heart was pounding, my mouth was dry, my stomach was tied up in knots and my roiling emotions were caught somewhere between hurt that he would even *say* any of this shit to me; ashamed, because I figured he was probably right about the kind of person I was; and pissed off that I didn't have the balls to just hang up on him.

Instead, I listened to him rant and rave, occasionally interjecting with phrases like, "Oh really?" "Is that what you're gonna do?" "Whatever makes you feel better." Pissing him off more, not understanding why his temper was boiling over, or why he was letting me get to him the way that he was.

By that time, though, I knew the first rule of having dickhead parents: never let 'em see you sweat. I was good at playing it cool, no matter what was going on.

ERASURELESS

I returned to school at the beginning of my junior year with a new take on myself and my cohort. I'd learned, from being at another high school for a semester, that I was not a worthless piece of shit unworthy of social inclusion. I just knew that the assholes I went to school with had chosen to treat me as if I were, and that they'd done the best they could to convince me they were right.

I knew I was still an outcast, but I also knew my outcast status had been dictated to me by the other students, not created by anything I'd done (except, you know, failing to fit in). Conforming to their expectations, trying to blend in (thereby effectively erasing myself) and operate within the lines of what they deemed to be acceptable, would not win me any favor with them. They'd already made up their minds about me. So why bother trying to please or impress them? I decided it was time to do what I wanted.

The summer before my junior year was the summer MTV arrived like a glitter bomb and completely changed the fashion landscape for people my age, seemingly overnight. The kids all gravitated toward the bands and looks they felt best represented them, or looked the coolest, or whatever. Unlike the conformist kids who adopted the looks of the rockabilly and mod scenes (which were rooted in and reinforced heteronormative gender roles), I went the New Romantic, gender bending route. It was the obvious choice, and the one that resonated with me most. For the first time in my school/social life, I was adopting a persona that would *invite* attention, rather than one that would blend in and go unnoticed.

I embraced my queerness with the same ferocity with which I'd been suppressing it up to that point. I felt my queer power for the first time and aimed it back at all the assholes who'd weaponized it against me for so long.

At the same time, I wore eye makeup, bought most of my clothes from thrift shops, and experimented with fucked up hair styles that defied categorization. You'd be surprised by how creative you can get with a full head of hair, a tub of Dep hair gel and a blow dryer.

When any of them insulted or tried to intimidate me at school, I was ready for it. I'd stand there wearing one of my androgynous shirts from Judy's that buttoned up the front diagonally; tossing back my blown-out, spiked up, Siouxsie-inspired coif; really FEELING my eye liner, and call them fuckin' faggots right back to their faces, in front of other people, who didn't know what to make of the spectacle. Not one of them ever escalated these encounters.

In English class I wrote a story about someone getting sexually assaulted at a house party, and it's revealed, at the end of the story, to be male on male rape. The teacher read it to the class. She didn't reveal the author, but I got some alarmed, WTF looks as she read it.

I also went to school drunk a lot of the time, as I managed to keep a relatively stable supply of room temperature Olde English 800 in my bedroom closet. An acquired taste, to be sure. And I admit, not a healthy practice. But it got me through the day when I needed it to.

The counseling office called my mom and arranged a time for us to meet with a counselor to address my ongoing truancy issues. We arrived at school for the meeting, and she was bitching at me as we walked toward the counseling office. She was settling into her role as the respectable, at the end of her rope matriarch, making sure I was feeling my role as the fucked up, lazy, delinquent loser that she just didn't know what to do with.

We walked into the office, and I let the secretary know who I was and why we were there. Without any hesitation, the secretary said to my mom, "You know, you should just let him take the proficiency exam. If he passes, he'll be free to pursue a job, or take community college classes. He won't have to keep coming here. This obviously isn't working for him."

My mom and I stood there for a few moments, stunned. Me, because I'd never heard of such a thing, and because I was being offered a way out of this god forsaken place. And her, because she'd been insisting for years that I had a duty to stay in school, put up with all the bullshit, and ride it out until graduation, because that's the way it was, that's what people did, and it was the same for me as it was for everyone else.

This woman had stuck a pin in that balloon and popped it instantly. We stared back at the secretary without saying anything, then she gave me a slight smile before leading us back to the counselor's desk. The cat was out of the bag. And I was going to make damn sure no one tried to unring the fucking bell.

My mother enrolled me in community college during what would have been the Spring semester of my junior year in high school. I'd taken and passed the Proficiency Exam (the equivalent of the GED) and was out of high school hell. But my study skills were poor, my social skills were worse, and the anxiety and depression had become more entrenched in my psyche, which impacted my behavior.

I eventually dropped out of community college because I was struggling to keep up, which was unacceptable. I had to know what I was doing, or I was failing. At the time, my limited perspective didn't allow for things such as practicing, studying or learning as I went. I was succeeding or failing. I knew it, or I was stupid. My mom considered her obligations met in the education department. She'd given me a chance, and I'd chosen to fail.

I worked a variety of jobs that didn't last. While living with my dad at one point, I had a meltdown when I realized both my parents intended to drop me like a hot potato into the work force without any further support for college. The reason this pissed me off was because I'd been operating as peacekeeper for them under the mistaken impression that there was going to be a payoff for the time and energy I'd put into it. When it became clear to me that no such performance bonus was coming my way, I flipped out.

I called my mom and told her I'd been putting their shit ahead of my own since they split, and now I needed some payback. I needed a car, and fast, so I could get a job and start making money. I guess I struck a nerve. Instead of arguing with me, my mom, resourceful as ever, even though she didn't have extra money lying around, secured the $1700 it took to buy a car I'd found in the Auto Trader: a 1967 Ford Mustang. It had a V8 289 engine, power steering and a new paint job (navy blue). It was gorgeous.

Once I got my car, I worked for a video and record store chain called the Wherehouse. In due time, I worked my way up to the position of Assistant Manager. I was always eager to take on additional responsibility, and I found the mechanics of the operation interesting, so I got in with management's good graces pretty fast. The hours at the Wherehouse were flexible, and I made further attempts at college, although my attempts failed and wouldn't succeed until many years later.

The last time my dad invited me to party with him was around April of 1986. I was twenty years old. I lived with him and my stepmother off and on, depending on where I was working and who I was dating.

My girlfriend and I were hanging out at the mobile home one Friday night when my dad brought out a fancy wood box from the bedroom. He opened it, pulled out a baggie full of cocaine, dumped a mound of it on the table and then started cutting out big fat lines. He invited us to join him with a generous smile on his face.

My girlfriend did a few lines with him, but I declined. As much as I may have been tempted to partake in the fun, I just didn't want to give in to my dad with that kind of compromise. He knew how I felt about doing drugs with him, and yet he repeatedly persisted in trying to get me to partake. I think he figured my girlfriend being present would make me feel pressured into joining in, because why would I pass up the chance to hang out with such a cool dad?

But I didn't feel safe getting lit around him, not with my girlfriend there. I was afraid he'd try and get something started, and I didn't want to have to deal with that situation high on coke if it happened.

The following month my youngest stepsister confided to me that my dad was molesting her and her sister. They were seven and nine at the time, and it turned out he'd been doing it for years. My dad was arrested less than three months later, the girls were removed from the home, and the fallout from these revelations, his arrest, and the resultant destruction of our family unit forever changed the course of my life.

METABOLISM

It's hard to love a man unconditionally for so much of your young life, only for that man to slowly turn against you.

I looked up to him when I was a kid because I didn't know any better and he hadn't given me any reasons not to. But my memories of him are all contaminated in some way by things he did later. It's hard to separate the two.

As I entered young adulthood, he tried to steer me in a different direction, getting me high, getting me drunk, offering me coke.

He sexualized me, which was something I couldn't understand or figure out how to respond to.

My father expected me to adopt the life he lived: doing an honest day's worth of working-class work five days a week, earning a skilled laborer's salary, with full benefits and retirement savings, and bringing home enough bacon to support a family and pay a mortgage.

The more I declined to adopt his habits and worldview, the more I became fixated on pursuing a college education, the less interest he had in me.

He wielded the threat of violence to keep me in line, and to prevent me from developing a sense of adult self that was too far removed from his own.

He'd sit in the living room and clean his guns slowly and deliberately, glaring at me until I left.

My fear and loathing of him grew just as large as his denigration of me did. We had an uneasy truce to keep it unspoken, but the truce could be shattered if one of us triggered the other. And when it came to us, we both had hair triggers.

During this time, behind closed doors, he engaged in behavior I only became aware of after receiving a desperate cry for help, from a seven-year-old girl, who trusted me enough to make what was happening to her stop.

I'm lucky I can remember him the way he was when he loved me, at a time when he wasn't afraid to show me and tell me so. I'm lucky he gave me reasons to love him back and look up to him before he gave me so many reasons not to.

I'm unlucky as well, because he took his love away from me and replaced it with something else. He blamed me for what he replaced it with. He convinced me that I deserved it.

I don't think he knew how to metabolize a queer son into his worldview or life, in a way that was good for both of us.

◆◆◆

By Design

It's harder to live without something once you've had it. When you have something, then it's taken away, you really do feel its absence. You're left with an empty space in your heart and your psyche where that missing thing once lived.

You try to figure out a way to get it back. Failing that, you try to fill the space it once inhabited with something else, so you don't feel so empty. You try as many times as you can, for as long as it takes. And if at first you don't succeed, you try again.

I'm hard wired to love men who remind me, at an intuitive, subconscious level, of my father.

When I meet these men, involuntary impulses kick in: to win him over, to make him warm up to me, to get on his good side.

To lower his guard.

I achieve this by erasing any part of myself, when interacting with him, that can be construed as a threat. I meet him head on, in conversation and body language, but without challenging him. I make sure he sees me doing this.

It's closer to deference than submission. It's a portal to access. Once closer, I can level up and seduce him with the hint of a promise of care.

Until we reveal more than we intended, and we're pushed up against one another, uncomfortably close, not sure if the space we share holds enough room for us both. Nothing's been decided yet.

He might like me. He might fuck me. He might love me.

You never know unless you try. That's why I'm always compelled, when I meet these men, to do what I can to find out.

Getting close is never easy. He's reliably hard on the outside, sharp and jagged around the edges. Like my father, he's tougher than most other men, because he's had to be.

Once I get past his armored exoskeleton, there might be soft tissue beneath: kindness, intimacy, emotional connection, sexual release. Or maybe there's just sexual release. Depends on him.

These men are fortified with moats, electrified fences and twenty-four-hour surveillance systems. He's designed to keep people out.

What I've learned, over time, is that maintaining a fortress burns a lot of energy. He becomes anxious, exhausted, and starved.

He's anxious because he's exhausted, and yet he can't take the fortress offline. Exhaustion makes him want to rest his head on someone's lap from time to time.

He's starved for someone trustworthy, someone who'll see him and not bolt. Who'll take care of him until he no longer needs to be taken care of. Who won't try to stop him when it's time to disengage.

Being alone with these men. Saying and doing things that we both know can't leave the room. It's exciting, exhilarating, an honor, scary, and can lead to unpredictable outcomes.

Outlaws. Bandits. Thugs.

Guarded. Reserved. Unreadable.

Strong. Solid. Disciplined.

Dangerous. Tough. Immovable.

The problem with most men is that they don't let you in.

Which isn't a problem for him. In fact, it tends to work in his favor. He's usually designed that way.

But the men who are rocks. The men who are metal. The men who snap crackle and pop.

I live in my strength with him. He lets me.

I embrace what most people loathe and fear about him.

I want what he brings.

There's a way to behave once you've made it past this man's guard. Contained and deliberate. Respectful and humble. You don't gloat. You don't behave as if you're putting one over on him, because you're not. You focus. You give. You remain.

Revere it. Be grateful. Relish that shit. Savor his sweat and his fur and his scent as you swallow him whole. Breathe him in and keep going until he can't help but make noise about what you're doing.

I look up at him and see him from an angle that most others don't. I watch him give that to me, knowing I'm trusted to bear witness. I meet him where he's at because I can. I'm built for it.

There's no recklessness in my pursuit of these men when I happen upon them. Many of them have been damaged beyond repair by life. They've lost touch with what makes them human.

But the ones who haven't forgotten. The ones who didn't give up. The ones who long to feel grounded and seen by someone like me. He's quiet and confident. He knows what he's doing. He works on things. He makes things work. He likes to smile and laugh, but he's guarded. He knows his way around the block.

He knows he can bring his authentic self to me in its truest, undiluted form, because he knows I can match and accommodate it. He knows I'm designed to withstand what he gives.

He doesn't need to protect me from it.

He can relax.

There's no catch.

We come to an agreement. We follow through. It's a promise that none of us break.

That's the reward, that's the end game.

And for as long as it lasts, nothing's missing.

08. Henrietta

*

Up close, the street looked buckled, as if it had been trampled on too many times. Countless wheels and feet had weathered the asphalt down to a pale, lifeless gray, and the tired buildings that lined it leaned against one another for support. On the rolling sidewalk, a figure ambled up the street with considerable grace, gaining momentum with each harried step.

Her breath came in short, labored gasps as she hurried up the battered sidewalk, her gaze held incessantly downward while she skirted the cracks, gouges and unexplained height differences that the sidewalk had to offer. To keep her mind off the fact that her lungs felt close to exploding, she'd begun counting the weeds that grew out of the cracks in the sidewalk, valiantly reaching for the sky.

Two voices babbled on inside her head. Her own-best-friend voice was wheezing in agony, "Sixteen, seventeen – oh, God, this hurts! – there's another one, is that nineteen? Twenty, twenty-one...come on, you can do it, just one more block. Come on, we don't want to miss the bus," and on and on. The other voice, the critic, wasn't as loud but snuck in between weed counts with, "You've already missed the bus, you fool.

Why don't you just give up? Better to be a bit late than to drop dead of a heart attack trying to make it on time!"

As she approached weed number twenty-six, the sound of the bus rumbling past the bus stop on the boulevard ahead crept into her brain before she even had a chance to stop running. She slowed to a resigned walk and attempted to catch her breath.

As she approached the bus stop, with its token wire mesh trash can and dilapidated fiberglass bench, the presence of her own-best-friend voice was nowhere to be found, leaving the critic to fill her head with smug silence. She checked the bench for fresh bird droppings or any other unpleasantries that might await her and, seeing none, sat down heavily and let out a long, woeful sigh.

Like her mood, the sky was gray and growing rapidly darker. The dense rain clouds loomed overhead, threatening to open at any given moment and soak her and the entire neighborhood through to the bone. The shabby buildings seemed to cower in the clouds' presence, and she found herself pulling the collar of her frayed raincoat tight around her neck.

She couldn't help but reflect on how her life had become worn and haggard, much like the neighborhood in which she now lived. When she was young, she never had to worry about working. Her calloused hands had once been immaculately manicured, her brittle, close-cropped hair once long and vibrant. She could feel herself tossing her head back and letting out a practiced yet convincing laugh as the photographer yelled, "Smile!"

A flash of lightning startled her back to the bus stop just in time for a roaring clap of thunder to drown out the sounds of the approaching bus. She looked up to see the bus's headlights dipping and bobbing as if they were at sea, and when the bus came to a squealing, painful halt in front of her, she climbed on board without a second thought about her past. The door wheezed shut, the bus pulled away from the curb, and the clouds opened up and wept.

09. Agent Orange

I'll give you some wood
Yeah, I'll give you some fire
I'll give you myself
And I will show you my desire

-CARLY SIMON

◆ ◆ ◆

1980

1980 was a memorable year for me when it comes to music. New Wave had emerged as an additional album section in most record stores that I frequented. Being a more palatable and mainstream offshoot of punk, New Wave incorporated pop sensibilities and produced songs that actually got played on the radio.

American bands like Blondie and the Knack had hit the big time, scored number one singles and become household names. Their feisty lead singers portended an edgier, more adventurous pop landscape that broke out of the stranglehold album-oriented rock and disco held on mainstream radio for the second half of the 1970s.

In 1980, Seventies stalwarts Billy Joel, Donna Summer, Carly Simon, Alice Cooper, Paul McCartney and Linda Ronstadt all released New Wave albums. Or at least, that's how they were marketed at the time. Devo and the Police scored big hits and joined the mainstream. The B-52's released *Wild Planet*, which revealed a darker, paranoid energy that was unexpected but just as intriguing as the effervescent vibe of their debut. The Cars disappointed me with *Panorama*, which I wouldn't come to appreciate the genius of until decades later. Talking Heads, Pretenders, Pat Benatar and AC/DC released albums that were perfectly self-contained masterpieces and sounded like nothing else that was out at the time. My obsession with Bowie, which would last a few years, began in 1980 with his release of *Scary Monsters*. I discovered the Motels via *Careful*, XTC via *Black Sea* and X via *Los Angeles*.

Music in 1980 was all over the place, just like I was. It felt like anything could happen, just like I did. I absorbed it all like a sponge and I'm still soaking in it. It smells like fresh vinyl to me. I hear it the way I did back then: it sounds new and exciting, even (and sometimes especially) when it sounds dated. It was an exciting time for pop music in the U.S., and to have that formative, transitional part of my life be soundtracked by such innovative singers and bands is a gift for which I'll always be grateful.

Between May of 1979 and June of 1980, when a lot of this music was being played on the radio and in record stores, a man named William Bonin abducted, raped, tortured and murdered at least twenty-one boys and young men who ranged in age from twelve to nineteen. Before he was caught, the media dubbed him the "Freeway Killer," and his murder spree was something straight out of a horror movie, before horror movies about that kind of thing were made.

He drove around Los Angeles and Orange Counties in a beat-up old van, usually with one of four young accomplices he'd recruited to act primarily as drivers, and he'd pick up guys who were hitchhiking, hanging out or just walking along the street. He'd lure them into his van with promises of alcohol, drugs, some kind of good time, or just a ride to wherever they were going.

The insides of the van's passenger and back doors had been stripped of their door handles to prohibit the victims from escaping. He'd proposition them for sex, and whether they agreed to it or not, they'd wind up stripped and bound in the back of his van, where he would sexually assault, beat, torture and eventually bludgeon or strangle them to death, before dumping their bodies along the many roads and freeways that snake their way through the Southern California landscape.

I was aware of the Freeway Killer by way of the news stories that appeared on T.V. at the time, but I didn't know many details about the murders until much later, as details, especially those kinds of details, were much harder to come by back then. I don't recall ever having a conversation with either one of my parents about it.

◆◆◆

ATTENTION

I engaged in a phone conversation with a stranger one weekday afternoon, right after I'd arrived home from school. It was the winter of 1980, which means the weather was brisk but still sunny. I was fourteen years old and in the ninth grade. Mom was at work, and my sister was off cheerleading somewhere, so I had the house to myself for the afternoon, as was usually the case.

Back in those days, when the phone rang you answered it. I hardly ever avoided answering the phone. Avoiding phone calls never occurred to me unless I was avoiding my dad, but I was conditioned to always pick it up. It might be something important, it might be an emergency, or it might just be one of the few friends that I had.

The guy on the phone sounded older than me, but not by much. He had a deep, friendly voice that put me at ease the first time I heard it. He asked if my mom was home, and I said no. He asked if anyone else was home, and I said no. He told me he'd done some carpet cleaning for us and was checking in to make sure everything was okay. I said, "I guess so," unaware of any recent carpet cleaning activity in the home but doing what I could to move the conversation along and get to the point where I could hang up.

We continued to chat, though, about random things like going to the beach, what kind of music we were into, the Big O (a nearby skate park) and other topics that piqued my interest and warmed me up to the guy. Eventually, the conversation moved away from carpet cleaning to me. How old was I? What did I look like? Did I play any sports? How much did I weigh?

As we continued to talk, I paid more attention to his voice. He sounded like the kind of guy who always knew the right thing to say to keep the conversation going. The kind of guy who didn't allow any pregnant pauses to occur. Since I could barely make it through placing an order at Burger King without stuttering or stumbling over some of my words at least once, I admired that about him.

There was also a sexual element creeping into my experience of his voice, and the conversation, which was emphasized and eventually drawn out with the questions he posed. After we'd discussed my physical attributes, the conversation got around to sex: any experiences I'd had, what I liked to do, how it made me feel.

He eventually told me his name was Damon. I liked the name Damon. It was a cool name. We'd chatted about so much within the space of about ten or fifteen minutes, and we seemed to have so much in common, that it felt as if we were already friends.

Ninth grade was the first point in my life when I consciously allowed myself to experience sexual attraction to a guy. For years, after having been teased, bullied and dismissed as Gay Ray, the school's token faggot, my emerging sexual attraction to men as I entered adolescence was a source of great inner turmoil. I'd be damned if I was going to let all those asshole classmates of mine be right about me: I REFUSED to entertain the possibility that I might actually be gay. Wasn't gonna happen.

Then one day in Mr. Johnson's algebra class, I was sitting at the desk nearest Mr. Johnson's as punishment for having ditched for several days over the course of the previous few weeks. I looked out the classroom door and saw one of the varsity football players there. He was one of those guys who'd already completely filled out by ninth grade: he had a muscular, adult male body, dark brown hair, and the beginnings of a mustache on his upper lip, which he didn't shave.

He was at his locker, just outside the open classroom door, so he kept moving in and out of the frame afforded by the doorway as he changed his shirt and conversed with someone I couldn't see. He was wearing a pair of red jogging shorts that had side slits, which afforded a perfect view of his tanned, hairy, muscular hamstrings, not to mention the lower portion of his glutes.

The sight of this guy's bare torso, muscular legs and partially exposed ass, covered in fur and seeming to exude the brute essence of masculinity that I seemed to be lacking with my skinny limbs, barely there leg hair and complete lack of facial hair, created overwhelming feelings of envy and sexual excitement that hit me like a bolt of lightning. I couldn't stop staring at him.

My dick hardened fast without asking for permission, as usual. I was confronted with the realization that I couldn't control my sexual attraction to him or deny its existence. That day after school was the first time I jacked off and allowed myself to fantasize about another male's body while I was doing it. That day was the beginning of my sexual awakening. It was a breakthrough.

Damon managed to enter my life and strike at precisely the right moment to get the reaction from me that he was looking for. I didn't know all that much about him: he was a self-employed carpet cleaner, he'd cleaned our carpets for my mom (a claim I found dubious but let slide), he had red hair, and he was twenty-three years old.

In my imagination I created an image of Damon as a good-looking, All-American type. I imagined he was athletic, muscular, and had feathered red hair that framed his handsome face just right.

This image, which I assigned to the voice on the phone, continued to titillate me with talk of sex and how horny guys like us could get. My dick was hard already, which I admitted to him when he asked me about it. He asked me if I could go someplace in the house where I could be in front of a mirror, so I moved from the kitchen into my mom's bedroom, where she had a pair of closets with mirror-covered sliding doors, as well as a phone extension that I could use in front of the mirrors.

Damon asked me if I was in front of the mirror and I said yes. He asked me if I was still hard and I said yes. He asked me, "How horny are you right now?" and I said, "Pretty horny." I chuckled, somewhat embarrassed.

He egged me on. He asked what I usually did when I was horny. I said, "Jack off, I guess." He asked me if I wanted to jack off right now, and I said, "I could, I guess." Then he told me I should take my clothes off. I told him to hold on, put the phone down and removed my clothes. Once I'd gotten them off, I picked the phone back up and let him know I was naked. He told me to look at myself in the mirror and describe for him what I saw.

I was incredibly turned on at this point, rock hard, barely able to contain myself. But I waited for him to tell me what to do before I did anything. He was the adult; he was in charge. By the time he told me to touch myself my dick was already leaking precum, and once I started masturbating it didn't take very long before I was ready to cum.

I was making all the usual noises I made when I did this alone, and I felt free to verbalize my pleasure and make the noise because the entire time I was pleasuring myself, he was speaking right into my ear, encouraging me to keep doing what I was doing, telling me to not stop until I finished, complimenting me on how hot I was even though, as far as I knew, he'd never seen me before. When I nutted it was epic, although, to be fair, back then almost all my nuts were epic.

After I'd cum, he talked me down until I caught my breath and my head cleared. He asked me if I'd be interested in maybe getting together and hanging out. I said sure. I didn't expect to ever hear from him again, but I was grateful for the experience, which had been hot and exciting.

I was also grateful for the attention he'd paid me. I felt flattered that someone was showing an interest in me sexually, especially someone like Damon, a twenty-three-year-old who could have sex with anyone he wanted, but who was interested in me. It felt good to know I was on someone else's radar for once.

To my surprise, he asked if I could meet up with him that night. I said sure. We agreed to meet in front of Thrifty Drug Store, which was about half a mile from where I lived.

My mother at that time had two jobs: one as a legal secretary on weekdays and the other as a bartender three or four nights a week. The law office job was local, but the bartending job was in the city of Artesia, which was a good thirty minutes away in Los Angeles County.

My mom bartended at an Italian restaurant called Ramboni's, which had been built in the 1960s and had never been redecorated. It was dimly lit by hanging lights ensconced in orange, sunset-colored glass orbs that cast a deep orangey-yellow glow over the dining area. Each table had its own candle burning in a frosted glass candleholder. There were no windows, and the place was dark and smokey, but the food was reliably delicious.

Occasionally, I'd accompany her on nights that I didn't have school the next morning. I'd hang out playing tabletop Pac Man or feeding quarters into the juke box while she served drinks to the clientele, who were pretty much older locals who got drunk on the daily and enjoyed flirting with her while she worked.

My mom was working at Ramboni's on the night I first met up with Damon in person. I was nervous about meeting him for a couple of reasons. First, I didn't know what would transpire between us, but I had a feeling something sexual was going to occur, and I didn't have any sexual experience with guys. Second, I didn't know Damon, and the specter of the Freeway Killer, as well as everything else I'd ever heard the adults in my life say about homosexual men, loomed large.

But Damon's attention made me feel seen, desirable, appreciated and turned on, all things I very much wanted to be and feel at the age of fourteen. I was curious and eager to get more sexual experience under my belt, especially since I'd never done anything with a guy. Damon had pretty much fallen into my lap; how could I pass up the chance to take advantage of this opportunity?

I had a pair of jeans on, along with a T-shirt, and over that a ski sweater that'd been handed down by one of my cousins. I took a standard hunting knife with me, a folding knife with a blade not more than two and a half inches long that my dad had given me, "for protection," he'd said.

This was the first time I'd done anything where I felt protection was warranted, so I brought it. Even though I had no idea what was going to happen, the possible payoff seemed worth the risk. Before I left the house, I told my sister I was going to meet a friend and that if I wasn't back in two hours to let Mom know something was wrong. She didn't know what to make of what I was telling her, but she went along with it.

I arrived at Thrifty Drug Store and lingered near the entrance, scanning the parking lot, looking for a sign of Damon. As I waited impatiently, feeling more conspicuous than I wanted to, cars and trucks came and went, swallowing or spitting people out depending on what their drivers and passengers were doing.

After about ten minutes, a van slowed down in front of the store, but it was just a couple of guys, no redhead. The guys in the van were looking my way, but then a car pulled up behind the van and honked its horn. The van pulled away and the car behind it coasted to a stop in front of me.

I saw Damon at the same moment he called out my name. His car was a boxy, dented, oversized American brand from the early 1970s that was in no way fashionable or retro cool like an old 1950s or 1960s car would have been at the time. Damon was most definitely not the hot, sexy, All American college jock with feathered red hair I'd envisaged.

Instead, he was a pale, skinny, somewhat goofy-looking guy with a mess of kinky orange hair on his head that emanated from his skull like jagged electric bolts. Though I was disappointed that he didn't meet my fantasy expectations, he wasn't unattractive or off-putting, and he didn't appear to pose a threat to my safety. I got into his car and he drove away from Thrifty Drug Store, slowly navigating the parking lot until he pulled out onto the street.

We hadn't driven more than two blocks when we hit a red light. Suddenly, police lights were flashing behind us. We both turned to look out the back window. Sure enough, a police car was right behind us, and we were clearly the object of its attention.

Damon pulled over and a male police officer sauntered up to Damon's window while a female officer approached on my side, hanging back at the rear of the car while her partner spoke with Damon.

Damon, whose license was suspended. Damon, who didn't have the car registration in the vehicle. Damon, who had an active warrant out for his arrest. As each of these previously unknown facts were revealed to the officer (and to me, since I was sitting in the front seat right next to Damon), I realized my chances of getting some dick that night had dwindled to nothing.

Before long, I found myself standing outside the car on the sidewalk in the flashing red police lights, being questioned by the female cop.

Had I had anything to drink? No. How did I know the driver? We were friends. How long had I known the driver? Not too long. Where did I meet the driver? Through friends at school. What were you doing? Nothing. Just hanging out. Do you live with both of your parents? No, just my mom. We need to call your mom so she can come pick you up. She's working.

I can just walk home. No. You need to have an adult come pick you up. Do you have someone else you can call?

I didn't know what to do. I had a cousin that lived nearby, but I didn't want this to get around to our extended family. My mom already made me out to be a problem child, I didn't want to fuel the fire of that narrative.

I did have a neighbor's phone number in my wallet. I had agreed to feed her pets while she and her family were out of town for a weekend. Her name was Brenda, and while she was sweet, and had never been anything but kind to me, she was also the neighborhood busybody.

Our house was the source of much neighborhood gossip for various reasons, many of which stemmed from my sister and I living like kids who, being largely unsupervised and left to their own devices, would tend to live. During the summer, my sister had a knack for throwing house parties on nights my mom was working. They'd materialize out of thin air like flash mobs, but remember, we didn't have the internet back then.

I don't know if she used smoke signals, two-way radios, or carrier pigeons, but I could leave the house for a stroll to the liquor store to pick up a pack of Marlboro Lights, and I'd return to find that the house had popped off: jam packed with middle and high school kids who were drinking, smoking pot, blasting music and carousing in a way that shattered the neighborhood's suburban sense of calm and order.

I was trying to think of an alternative plan to having the cops call Brenda, but I was out of options and I knew it. I didn't have much choice, so I gave the cop Brenda's number while the other cop arrested Damon and deposited him into the back of the police cruiser.

Brenda picked me up about ten minutes later, barely able to contain her excitement. She peppered me with questions, and seemed disappointed when I didn't offer her any juicy details in return. She told me apologetically that she was going to have to tell my mother about this, and I said I understood.

The incident resulted in my mom calling Walt over to the house a few days later so he could assess the situation and give me a manly talking-to. Walt was about thirty years old at the time. He'd always had a hardheaded, no-bullshit approach to dealing with me, and this time was no different. He didn't waste any time fucking around.

Walt grilled me with questions, which I answered, some truthfully, some not. The only thing that was indisputable was that I'd been with Damon when he got arrested. My version of events boiled down to me meeting Damon through some friends at school, how he'd be there sometimes when we were hanging out.

If they'd bothered to dig a little deeper by asking which friends, my lie would have unraveled, but they didn't. I didn't have many friends, and it wouldn't have taken much investigating to determine that I was lying. I didn't elaborate further. I played dumb at any implications Walt made relating to there being absolutely no reason for a twenty-three-year-old to be hanging out with a fourteen-year-old.

During this interrogation, I adopted the stance of a person who couldn't understand what all the fuss was about. Luckily, I pulled it off. I can be good at playing stupid. I promised I wouldn't hang out with Damon, and that was the end of it.

INSTINCT

Of course, that wasn't the last time I saw Damon. A few weeks later we agreed to, like before, meet up at Thrifty Drug Store. When he pulled up this time, he said through the window,

"Shall we try again?" We laughed as I climbed into his enormous, ugly 1970s car. This time, no cops intervened.

Damon drove us to Hart Park, with its sprawling greenery, baseball diamonds and paths lit by old-fashioned streetlamps from the 1940s. He parked in the deserted lot and killed the engine. I was apprehensive, he was horny; I played it somewhat hesitant, he assured me that we could stop at any time that I wanted to.

At one point, in an effort to convince me, he asked, "Have you ever heard the saying, 'If it feels good, do it?'" I hadn't, but I knew it was a lame, ineffective line; a relic left over from the free love era. But I was horny too, and about to get my dick sucked, so there was no way in hell I was gonna play harder to get than I already had. Pretty soon he went down on me, and I was enjoying my first blow job from another guy.

As the car windows fogged up, we eventually took our tops off, pulled our pants down, and worked our way into a position where each of us had the other's dick in his face. Damon's dick was rock hard, thick, white, and veiny with a purple head. The light scent of sweat from his fire crotch didn't do much for me at first, but I'd come to love it as I gained more experience.

When I slid his dick into my mouth, it felt like it belonged there. Blowing and getting blown by Damon felt totally natural, and I experienced none of the awkward fumbling I'd struggled with while having sex for the first time with a girl at the age of thirteen. In Damon's crappy car that night, I felt as if I'd read the entire instruction manual for this, and I let my innate understanding of what I needed to do, and when I needed to do it, guide me through the experience. Neither one of us came away from the encounter disappointed.

Damon was a bit of a nomad. He rented rooms in apartments and houses that seemed to change almost every other month. One day I spent a couple of hours riding the bus to the general area he lived in, then walked a couple of miles to his apartment building to meet up with him. His two roommates, a pair of dark-haired college guys, seemed surprised and curious about the fact that I was there to see Damon. They stared with bemused grins on their faces as I followed Damon past them and into his bedroom.

Early that summer, he was living in Garden Grove with an older roommate, the homeowner. I'd somehow managed to orchestrate an overnight stay with Damon with my mom, probably by telling her I was staying someplace else, knowing she was unlikely to check up on me. When we got there, I was introduced to the homeowner and a younger guy who was Damon's age. This younger guy's name was Paul, and I was instantly attracted to him.

Paul had an easy smile, a moustache, dark hair that was feathered and parted in the middle, and a gold lightning bolt necklace that looked fantastic against his deeply tanned skin. We drank beer and got high, listened to music, played pool and horsed around, just having fun roughhousing and letting off steam.

Our antics reached a fever pitch as we blasted *Back in Black* and *Women and Children First* on the stereo, and there was a lot of flirtatious sexual tension brewing between Paul and me. While I knew I was there to see Damon, I had trouble hiding my attraction to Paul. Paul noticed and responded in kind.

At one point, I found myself in the bathroom swapping spit with Paul, getting a taste of his tongue and his mustache by way of a few rushed, furtive kisses. Before Damon and I went to bed for the night, when Damon had gone to take a leak, Paul asked me for my number, and I slipped it to him.

Though I'd lost my virginity with a girl one year prior, it was Damon who popped my cherry that night. And though my fear and anxiety about taking a dick up my ass was palpable during the hours leading up to, and including, the point that he actually got it in me, once it was in and I moved around a little, adjusting position and adapting my hole to its presence, I knew I was going to be fine. Damon's fat ginger purple-headed dick in my hole felt great, it felt right, and when I came with it still deep inside me, I knew I'd arrived.

My intentions that night were two-fold: to get off, first of all, because when was there ever a time back then that I didn't want to do that? But I also wanted to get the sexual experience under my belt. I needed to figure out if this was what I wanted, if this was what turned me on. If this was what I wanted to build my identity around.

I knew that, once I walked down this path, there would be no turning back. The mysterious act of being gay, which I had no clue how to navigate or pull off, was a life changer once committed to. It meant a life path that was largely unforged. I would be on my own, in the wilderness, without the comforts of social norms to navigate my way.

I knew I wanted to be paired up with someone in a committed relationship that was akin to straight marriage, but I had no way of knowing how to make that happen. I foresaw my life as an adult the way I'd foreseen it before deciding to accept the fact that I might be gay. I just foresaw it with the female role of wife or girlfriend being filled by another man instead, at least in the best-case scenario.

I spent the next day in my backyard sunbathing and waiting to hear from Paul. I was overcome with sexual desire at both the memory of the night before, being fucked by Damon, and of fantasies about what would happen when I had sex with Paul. I was certain that sex with Paul would happen just as soon as he called and we figured out where to do it and when.

But I waited for his call in vain. All day long, taking breaks from sunbathing only to go inside and jack off to try and relieve my sexual tension, I waited for the phone to ring. All day long, it didn't.

I called Damon late in the day to see if I could find out what might be going on. I skirted around the subject at hand, but Damon finally cut to the chase. "Paul's not gonna call you. He threw out your number. I told him if he fucks you, I'll kick his ass. Friends don't do that to each other. You're with me." I was disappointed but didn't say so. So long, Paul.

RUMOUR HAZZIT

A short time after my deflowering by Damon, I was confronted with what I would soon learn were some harsh truths, certainly about young gay men, but also about gay men in general, at least most of the ones I ran into for the next several years: they were horny, they had trouble keeping their dicks in their pants, they were fickle, and they had very short attention spans. Don't get me wrong: I shared these qualities with the rest of them, just not to the same extent as most gay guys I met. I was looking for love, and love was being an elusive bitch.

For most of my life, I've generally approached sexual encounters as the possible beginnings of an ongoing relationship of some sort: not necessarily a romantic relationship, but because I don't tend to have sex with people I haven't established some kind of mental or emotional connection with, I rarely consider the sexual encounter itself as the desired end result.

I've largely treated any sexual encounter I've had as a possible bridge to something more: friendship, fuck buds, boyfriends, whatever. Why waste a mental or emotional connection with another person? They weren't that easy to come by.

That summer, Damon picked me up one afternoon and informed me that he was taking me to a gay bar in Garden Grove called Rumour Hazzit. He knew the people who ran the place and was going to try to get them to let me in.

I was feeling myself that day for some reason, and I'm not sure why, because most of the time I was ruled and guided by my feelings of insecurity and inadequacy. But on that day, I was feeling correct.

I had on a pair of Levis 501 button fly jeans I'd scored at a thrift store. I'd spilled bleach on them, so they had that DIY bleached out look that, in some circles, was quite edgy, forward thinking and British, according to me. I had on a white wife beater, and the whiteness of my ensemble highlighted my summer tan, which I'd worked on diligently. My hair was spiky and high, styled in a way that was messy and put together at the same time. My shoes were a red pair of Converse high tops that provided a small pop of color and contrast to the rest of my ensemble.

Damon pulled into the Rumour Hazzit parking lot, told me to wait outside and vanished inside the bar. Through its entrance I could hear the thumping beat of the music and the raucous sounds of what I supposed was a building filled with gay men having a great time. I leaned against Damon's car, lit a Marlboro Light and took languid hits off it, waiting for Damon to come back out and retrieve me, enjoying the warm summer afternoon.

Just then a tall, dark-haired guy with a beer belly, decked out in jogging shorts and a Hawaiian shirt, sauntered out of the bar and lit a cigarette of his own. He tossed his match onto the ground, looked over while taking a hit, and saw me. His eyes widened as he finished sucking on his cigarette, then he removed it from his lips and his face broke into a grin. Blowing out the smoke, he said, "We-hellllllll! What do we have here? Look at you!"

I knew he was addressing me, but since he hadn't seemed to ask me a direct question worth answering, I just stared at him, smiled half-heartedly and took another drag off my own cigarette.

"Well, aren't you adorable!" he continued.

What could I say to that? I mean, I wasn't gonna disagree with him.

"What's your name, hon?"

"Ray," I said, giving him a chin up, taking another drag, holding it, exhaling my own cloud of smoke.

"Ray!" he said, chewing on it to see how it tasted. "What's a cute little thing like you doing out here?" he asked, spreading his arms a bit and cocking his head to the left, to the right, indicating the crowded Rumour Hazzit parking lot. He seemed amused by the fact that he was having this interaction with me, and I wasn't sure what to make of it. Was he making fun of me?

"Waiting for a friend," I said, throwing him a little bit of shade because it sounded like he was implying that I didn't belong there, and I hadn't even made it in the door yet.

"Oh!" he said, breaking into a drunken laugh. "Waitin' on a friend, huh? Who might that be?"

"Damon," I replied. "You know him?"

"Can't say that I do," he answered, but with a less engaging tone in his voice. "How old are you, anyway?" he asked, narrowing his watery, bloodshot eyes at me.

"Why?" I countered.

"I'm just trying to figure out if I should buy you a drink," he replied. His smile was still there, his demeanor was still drunk and friendly, but his curiosity was waning. I could tell.

"Seventeen," I lied.

"Ohhhh…too bad," he said, "Why'd your friend leave you out here all alone?"

"I can handle myself," I said, grinning, showing off.

"Better watch out. You'll end up in a dumpster somewhere."

"No I won't," I said, annoyed that he was trying to scare me, thinking *This guy's wasted*.

"Well, you be careful now. I'm goin' back in," he said, then belched so loud I laughed at him, I couldn't help it. It was a good one.

He threw what was left of his cigarette to the ground, then stepped on it, and as he turned back toward the entrance he said, "Have fun, little man." And that was it, he was gone.

I was alone again. I looked around at all the cars, listened to more cars out on the street driving by, and wished there were at least one or two people out there so I'd have someone to talk to. I'd have even settled for the drunk guy again. What was taking Damon so long?

After what seemed like an amount of time that bordered on offensive, Damon emerged from the bar's entrance and waved me over. When I walked up to him, he said, "Okay: I told them that you have to use the bathroom. You can only go in, use the bathroom, and walk straight back out. DO NOT stop. DO NOT linger. In and out. Got it?"

"Sure," I said.

"Okay: when you walk in, the bar will be on your right. Walk around the bar and the bathroom is at the other end. Straight in. Straight out. Got it?"

"Yeah," I said.

He waited for a moment as I stood there staring at him, then he threw his hands up and said: "Go!" I went.

My first gay bar! I walked in and noticed how crowded the place was. People were talking and laughing and smoking. The air was thick with smoke. Music was blaring. Dance music, disco. I didn't know the song.

When I walked through the door, the first person I got a good look at was this young guy with blond hair, who was sitting at a high top, smoking a cigarette and chatting with the other person at the table. His hair was in the New Romantic style, parted on the side, flipping up and hanging down over his right eye. His eyes were blue, and he had a long face with amazing bone structure.

As he took a hit off his cigarette, I noticed his wide mouth and full lips, which reminded me of Carly Simon's lips. I recorded and stored this information in a matter of seconds, filing it away in my memory bank as I walked past his table and headed around the bar toward the bathroom. Nothing else notable occurred; I took a piss, buttoned up, turned around and walked back out of the bar.

When I got outside, Damon told me to wait by the car while he ran back in to say goodbye to his friends. A few minutes later, he exited the bar once more, this time accompanied by a guy with dark, shoulder length hair that made me categorize him as someone who still listened to Led Zeppelin and Pink Floyd. We all piled into the car, and as Damon was driving it out of the parking lot, he informed me there'd been a change in plans: he was taking me back home.

Now this, *this* was a predicament I had not foreseen. But it didn't take long for me to put it together. Damon was dropping me off so that he could go back to his place and fuck this guy instead of me. I was being thrown over for this douchebag, right in front of him, while he sat next to me, avoiding eye contact.

I was outraged! This was unacceptable! All the way home, I was stifling my anger and fighting my desire to start talking shit at them both, but I didn't want to risk being dropped off somewhere without a way to get home.

When Damon pulled into my driveway, I asked him to come inside with me for a minute. I said I had to talk to him about something important, I promised to be quick about it.

Once inside, I asked him what the fuck was going on, and he tried to explain that he was never going to have another chance to get with this guy, it had to happen now, and he was sorry but I just couldn't be included.

In my head, all I could think about was what a fucking CREEP he was being, and how I was pretty much done with him. But at the same time, it was critical that I not be treated like this, especially in front of the guy that I was being replaced by, who was sitting in Damon's car out in the driveway, with that smug expression on his face that I eventually learned guys get when it's been determined that they're the ones who get to fuck your man tonight, not you.

I began to kiss Damon and grope his dick through his jeans, undoing his belt and unbuttoning his pants until I had his dick in my hand. Then I got down on my knees and started blowing him. Damon, bless his heart, didn't have a chance. He made no effort to stop me or push me away. I had him right where I wanted him, and I'd be damned if I was gonna let him dump me out of his car and take off without making sure I got him off first. I hoped he wouldn't be able to get off again with that dickhead waiting out in the car.

Soon, we were both on the floor with our jeans around our ankles, sucking each other's dicks with horned up ferocity. I was swallowing his dick, using my hand to supplement my mouth as I went, and bringing him to the edge before he even knew what was happening. As he nutted in my mouth, letting out gasps and groans, my replacement out in the car began blaring the horn in an angry reminder to Damon that he was still out there.

I didn't care. My work here was done. "Have fun," I said with the taste of Damon's cum still in my mouth. We pulled our pants up, I opened the door for him, fighting the urge to tell him, "Don't let it hit you on the way out." He left without a word.

AT THE DRIVE-IN

The next time I went out with Damon, he had a new car, which wasn't new, but was much better than the shit heap he'd been driving up to that point. The new car was a used Chevy Vega hatchback. The front passenger seat had been removed, however, so I sat in the back seat on the passenger side while he drove.

He took me to a drive-in theater on Beach Boulevard in Westminster where a movie called *Humanoids from the Deep* was playing. It was a Roger Corman creature feature about amphibious humanoid monsters that come out of the ocean to rape the women and murder the men of a quaint fishing village. I was big into slasher films at the time, movies like *Terror Train*, *Prom Night*, *Schizoid*, and *Friday the 13th*. *Humanoids from the Deep* wasn't really up to par, which is really saying something..

Despite the Rumour Hazzit fiasco, I still considered Damon special because he was the possessor of the dick that had taken my anal virginity. I expected us to connect that night on a somewhat deeper level, perhaps even romantically. Not become boyfriends or anything like that, just be closer than last time, when he'd spent the entire afternoon in the bar, and I'd waited in the parking lot for him to come back out.

Gay guys weren't so easy to come by back then. I didn't want to give up on him yet. I was considering this outing a date, and while I wasn't thrilled with the quality of the movie, I did enjoy being together again.

As soon as the movie began, Damon had his hands on my crotch, finding my dick, getting it hard and then taking it out of my jeans and going down on it in short order. He crawled out of the driver's seat and laid flat on his stomach in the space where the passenger seat would have been. I wondered if this was the reason the passenger seat was missing. Had Damon converted his Vega into blow job mobile?

I wasn't really into it, though, because we were in a drive-in theater lot filled with cars, and in the cars were people. People who were walking by at any given moment to visit the snack bar or use the restrooms. Damon's car windows were not tinted, and the graphic carnage on screen was not conducive to creating a mood for hot sex.

I tried to go with it at first, but I became too uncomfortable during a particularly screamy and bloody moment on screen, so I pulled away from him and buttoned my pants back up. After our last encounter in a house, in a bedroom, in an actual bed, this awkward fumbling in a car at the drive-in wasn't cutting it for me.

Damon became frustrated when I told him I didn't want to do it here, there were too many people around. "They can't see!" he insisted, which was bullshit and we both knew it. Anyone could see if they glanced through the Vega's windows.

I asked if we could go back to his place, and he told me it wasn't an option that night. When he realized I wasn't going to put out, he gave up trying to talk me into it and pouted in the driver's seat while the movie continued to play.

At the end of the movie, when (spoiler alert) a character who was impregnated by a humanoid "birthed" a baby humanoid, which ate its way out of her stomach on the delivery room table, our "date" had pretty much come to an end as well. He drove me home in silence. The closer we got to my place, the more I regretted stopping him. Now I wasn't gonna get off, either.

But I didn't understand why he thought he could just expect sex from me whenever and wherever he wanted, even if I wasn't into it. Up to that point, our sexual activity had been mutually agreed upon, even if non-verbally. Tonight, he was putting pressure on me, and I resented his assumption that that was something he was free to do.

I soured on Damon that night. I didn't feel compelled to chance another encounter with him, now that I knew there was a very good chance our encounters would end badly

My relationship with Damon ended the same way it began: with an unexpected phone call. It was four years later, and I'd just moved in with my first official boyfriend. We shared a one-bedroom apartment in North Long Beach.

I was alone when the phone rang, not doing anything in particular. I picked up, said hello, and was greeted by the sound of Damon's voice, which I didn't recognize at first. "Hey, Ray, guess who?" I couldn't place his voice and said so. "It's Damon!" he exclaimed, as if I'd been waiting for him to call with bated breath. Surprised, I said, "Oh! How's it going, Damon?"

I was uneasy about being on the phone with him at that moment. I was unsettled that he'd tracked me down and called me at my new boyfriend's number, after not having spoken to me in four years, and was now talking to me as if we'd just seen each other last week. "How'd you get this number?" I asked as the question came to me, not really thinking about whether or not I should ask it. I was genuinely curious.

He told me he'd called my aunt, explained that he was an old friend of mine who'd lost my number and was trying to track me down. I didn't find this explanation believable, but I didn't say so. How would he get my aunt's number in the first place? My aunt knew better than to give my number out to someone she didn't know.

Besides, I hadn't even given her my new number yet. In the time since I'd last seen Damon, my mother had been stalked by a crazy guy she had the misfortune of crossing paths with, so my aunt would have known not to give my number out to a stranger, if she'd even had my new number to begin with. The only people who had my number were my parents.

Our conversation didn't last long. He said he'd been thinking about me a lot lately and thought we should get together. I told him I didn't think that was such a good idea. When he asked me why, I said, "I don't think my boyfriend would like it."

Damon exploded. Screamed at me. "YOU DON'T THINK HE'D LIKE IT? WELL MAYBE I'LL JUST HAVE TO TAKE CARE OF YOUR FUCKING *BOYFRIEND*, SO WE WON'T HAVE TO WORRY ABOUT HIM! YOU! ARE! MINE! YOU BELONG TO ME! YOU GOT THAT?!"

I was stunned. I'd never seen or heard Damon behave this way. We hadn't spoken since I was practically a kid. His call was out of the blue. The fact that he was screaming these words at me was frightening. My heart was beating loudly in my chest, and I was frozen, unsure about what I should say. Clearly, he was unhinged, and I couldn't think of an appropriate response.

Instead of saying anything, I hung up. He didn't call back, and we never spoke again.

◆◆◆

LOOKING BACK

Making sense of what happened between Damon and me is...tricky.

He holds prominent space on my timeline, but that's because the node he inhabits contains milestones, not because he brought anything of lasting value to my life.

Damon was a vehicle I jumped into so I could visit some destinations I'd never have been able to get to on my own at the time.

Things I needed to try out.
Red flags I needed to learn how to recognize.
Decisions I needed to make.
Dynamics I needed to familiarize myself with.
I was ready when he found me
To take that first leap.
Damon got me there.
That was his function.

I was a lonely, isolated queer boy,
Hungry for attention.
Damon offered me what I sought,
But his attention was never about me.
His attention bought him access.
That access bought me experience.
My approach was strategic.
Transactional.

At the dawn of my sexual life.
I was young and innocent and horny.
I never fell in love with the guy.

Authentically queer people are as diverse and varied
As a group of human beings can be.
But we all have one journey in common.
We forge our path out of safety and into the wilderness,
Out of the placid, lazy comfort of fitting in.
Out of complying with societal expectations about
Who we're supposed to be,
How we're supposed to look,
What we're supposed to do,
When we're allowed to speak,
Why we're here,
And who we serve.
We don't need permission
To discover ourselves.
We don't ask for it, either.
Because we already know what the answer will be.

There are memories I've avoided for years,
Fearing I lacked the strength to withstand them.
I finally looked back and saw that kid
Navigating life
In a world not designed for him
To survive, let alone thrive.
Jumping into massive waves,
From cliff to peak,
Hanging on for dear life,
Dangling up there in the sky
Above swamps and lakes of fire
That hoped to devour him.

Targeting his spot to land
Timing when to let himself drop
Calculating risk
Strategizing
Jumping swinging running flying dodging.

I look back and watch that kid
And marvel at his agility
His uncanny instinct
His ability to focus
His capacity for love
And my fear dissolves.
I'm proud of that kid.
That kid is brave as fuck.
My strength is forged from his.
That kid is my foundation.
Combined, our strength is fortified.
I feel its depth, and how far back it goes,
And use it to propel me further into this experience.
It's the reason I don't cave.
It's the reason I'm still standing.
It's the reason I'm not driven by hatred or fear.
It's the reason why,
No matter how hard they've tried,
Or how many times,
It's the reason they've never destroyed me.

10. We

*

Ray, Travis and then Alex. This is the order in which I'd list us. I put Alex last not because of her gender (which was closer to male than either Travis or me), but because she didn't last as long as we did. Travis and Alex, if asked, would probably each list themselves first, just as I do. That was one of the problems with us: we each thought of ourselves as the leader.

Alex was the toughest. She stood only 5'6" or so, but she carried herself with more confidence and swagger than any man I'd ever met. She had bleached white hair that was spiked on top, shaved on the sides and back. She didn't wear lipstick. She had a tattoo, though, a scorpion on her tricep, headed north toward her shoulder as if it would move in for her jugular given the chance.

When we drove to the projects to buy sherm, Alex was the one who brought a gun and went in to perform the transaction. Travis and I waited in the Ghia, wondering what we'd do if shots rang out, if Alex didn't come back or, worst of all, if the guys she was buying from came after us. The danger was palpable. We relished it.

Travis was in beauty school, always on the verge of flunking out. I once wondered aloud how anyone could flunk out of beauty school, but Travis's outraged reaction shut me up immediately and I never asked the question again. Travis was the driver, and I think this is why he would consider himself the leader. We would ride all over Hollywood and the South Bay in Travis's dented white Ghia, which was the color of coffee-stained teeth.

But Travis's reckless driving led to too many near misses. Once, in Palos Verdes, he missed a curve and we slid off the road sideways. I was crammed into the back seat, and all I could see were silhouettes of the backs of their heads up front, Travis in the driver's seat, Alex in the passenger's seat, their heads bobbling from side to side as we slid over bumps in the dirt, then came to an abrupt and unexplainable halt on the edge of a canyon.

The Ghia, like our eyes and mouths, was filled with dirt from the cloud it had kicked up as it slid off the road toward the canyon. When we got out to inspect the damage, we saw that the only thing stopping us from flying into the canyon was a small mound of packed dirt located along its edge. If we'd been driving my Mustang or Alex's raised pick up, we would have slid right over it. But then, if Alex or I had been driving, we'd never have missed the curve.

Which brings us to me, and why I consider myself the leader. Well, I was the one with the people skills. I was the persuader, the bargainer, the convincer. I was the one who got us in. I could get us the Southern Comfort, the Olde English 800. I was the one who could talk.

Things were a lot more lax back then. Doormen and liquor store clerks were a lot more flexible. They would listen to reason, they'd negotiate. I got us into all the places we weren't supposed to be. I got us all the stuff we weren't supposed to be able to get.

11. Heavy Metal Lover

○

I was working at the Wherehouse in Lakewood, CA the day we met.

The Wherehouse was a chain of record stores that had gone from being a neighborhood head shop in the 1970s (according to one of the O.G. managers I worked for) to being a regional behemoth specializing in videotape rentals in the 1980s. The catchphrase in their radio and T.V. spots was "Where? At the Wherehouse!" During the week-long management training program I completed at one point during my employment, they told us their goal was to be "The McDonalds of the video rental industry." It was the 1980s. We aimed high.

It was an interesting time to work for that kind of retailer because media consumption was going through a lot of changes and growth. I worked there when CDs came on the market. They were packaged at the top of long containers that were made of clear plastic, or of cardboard, which were preferable because the cardboard containers were usually imprinted with a variation on the album's original artwork. Their packaging was designed to fit into existing vinyl album display cases.

We also had a small software section, which took up a total of about four shelves. My brain did not tune into the frequency inhabited by personal computers until about 1989. When I worked at the Wherehouse, I would look at the computer software and game boxes, and my brain would shut down. Half the time I couldn't process the information provided on the product packaging. It just seemed so complicated. I was fine working with our DOS-based point of sale system, but that's as far as my tech savviness went.

The first time I saw Glenn, I was manning the cash register, which was located on a raised platform, an island in a sea of vinyl, cassettes, CDs and videotapes. I was gazing out the window, and he caught my attention when he rapped his knuckles on the counter. I looked down and saw the kind of guy I would usually avoid just because I tried to get through life without being verbally harassed or physically assaulted. He had a long, curly mane of dirty blond hair, a mustache, earrings in both ears and tattoos on his arms. He was a headbanger.

He asked me if I knew when the new Iron Maiden was coming out. I relaxed a little because I knew the answer to his question, since that was my job. My knowledge about pop, rock, new wave, synth pop, funk, soul and all points in between from the last fifteen years or so was just shy of encyclopedic. When it came to straight up metal, though, I only went about as deep as Iron Maiden, Judas Priest, the Scorpions, Accept, Queensryche and Def Leppard, which were bands I knew about but didn't listen to all that much.

The glam metal onslaught of bands like Ratt, Mötley Crüe, Cinderella, Poison and the like was in full swing as well. It seemed like most of those hair metal assholes talked shit about gays in the press every chance they could get. Which was rich, coming from a bunch of guys whose lustrous, teased up, blown out tresses and use of makeup often made them prettier than their girlfriends.

By the mid-1980s, the reputation of headbangers as a whole had gone from an image of laid-back stoners chilling out to Led Zeppelin, to druggies and messy blackout drunks who were notoriously homophobic and rarely had anything nice to say to or about gay people. I'd met a few nice ones over the years. But the nice ones were the exception, not the rule.

I gave him the release date.

He flashed an easy smile at me and said he'd noticed me the last time he was in here and thought I was cute. And if I ever wanted to go out some time to give him a call. Then he handed me his number on a piece of paper.

I was thrown off guard and a little confused. There was no way this guy could possibly be gay. But here he was, giving me his number. I smiled back and thanked him. I'd been so fixated on his look and what I thought it communicated that I hadn't taken the time to get a good look at him as a person beneath all the headbanger stuff. He held my gaze for a few seconds before he turned around and strode out of the store, the heels of his black leather boots making clunking noises that faded after the door closed behind him.

I called him. He invited me over. We got baked, listened to albums and fucked in short order. Then I moved in with him for about a year and a half. It was the 1980s. We went for it.

Glenn grew up on the outskirts of Las Vegas in a trailer park. No air conditioning. Glenn had tattoos at a time when they still signified a class of people that most other classes chose not to associate with. People could use your tattoos as a reason to look down on you with quiet confidence. They (tattoos) also weren't associated with gay men. That wouldn't happen until the 1990s.

That Glenn presented as a headbanger was very unusual in the gay community. Gays were obsessed with upward mobility; they usually chose to present as preppies. If they didn't have money, they did their damnedest to look like they did, just like almost everyone else did back in the 1980s. Glenn's look was decidedly different: masculine, working class, somewhat dangerous and hot as fuck.

When we were out together in public, rocker chicks flirted and tried to pick up on him all the time. He always flashed his smile and had a funny response that would make them laugh. I got so worked up knowing these girls had no idea that as soon as we got back to the apartment, he was going to fuck my brains out.

And fuck my brains out he did. Glenn was hung and he knew how to use it. He liked rough sex. He'd hold me down and fuck the hell out of me. No one ever heard me complain about it, because I didn't. The sex kept us together for much longer than we should have lasted.

One day, Travis was over at the apartment. We'd smoked half a sherm stick, were listening to records and laughing our asses off at every other lame thing each of us said. Glenn came home on his lunch hour to say hello. He was a dispatcher for a trucking company his dad owned. Sometimes he drove trucks. After he ate lunch, I was chatting with him in the kitchen when he put his hands on my shoulders, shoved my back up against the wall, moved his face in so close to mine I could feel his breath, and said, "If you fuck around with him, I'll kill you."

His aggression (and the fact that he was dead serious) turned me on. I thought: "Wow, he really loves me."

We had a good run, especially for a couple of eighteen-year-old kids. Who were gay. In the 1980s. After about a year and a half, he moved in with his dad and I moved back in with my mom. Our last six months or so were miserable for me, in part for reasons that had nothing to do with Glenn, and in part because our relationship was disintegrating.

A few of our arguments descended into physical violence. It seemed like a natural progression. Toward the end, Glenn could get quite mean. He'd say things he really had no business saying to me. One night our argument moved out into the front yard. It was the middle of the night.

I can't remember what set me off that night, but Glenn was taunting me and seemed to really be enjoying himself, which pissed me off even more. At one point, he got into his truck, then closed the door behind him and locked me out. He was giving me a fuck you look and grinning. He was being cruel. My temper boiled over.

With some of the boyfriends I had when I was younger, there came a moment when things got physical. And with each of those boyfriends, before things got physical, there was a moment when they realized they'd gone too far and were about to find out what me wailing on them looked like.

I don't consider myself a violent person, really. I avoid violent confrontations. But sometimes, when you've been with someone for a certain amount of time, and you've given them the benefit of the doubt, and you've let it slide the few times they've already crossed the line, and then you get into it, and they're saying things designed to hurt you, and they dishonor your relationship by crossing lines that no human being crosses unless they're a fucking abuser, well, it becomes the time to take action. At least, that's what I thought at the time.

There's a moment each of those guys had in common: the moment their eyes widened when they realized I was about to kick their asses. I'm not saying it's the right thing to do. I'm not proud of myself, necessarily. It's just what I believed I had to do in those situations. Sometimes, when you go too far, you get your ass kicked. It works both ways.

Glenn was sitting in the passenger seat of his truck, looking smug and safe. But I had a key to his truck, which he apparently forgot about. I took out the key, inserted it into the slot, turned it, watched the lock inside the truck pop up, and watched Glenn's eyes pop too when he realized I was about to drag his ass out of the car and fuck him up. Which I did.

To be honest, it wasn't that bad. It was more like we were fucking each other up, really. We were evenly matched. Neither one of us drew blood. It was a power struggle. He was fighting for dominance; I was fighting for respect.

His dad's house had a converted garage that was made into a den, and Glenn's room had a back door that opened into the den area. I would sit in the den late into the night at a wooden dining room table, the sides of which were folded down because it was just being stored out there

I was journaling about what was happening with my dad, how lost and alone I felt, what it meant for my family, what was happening in my life, trying to wrangle some amount of control over the events and my feelings about them. Glenn used to say I was "writing letters to myself," and he didn't mean it in a good way.

He befriended some twinks from Placentia and had them over a couple of times while I was there. I didn't care for them. They were provincial in their thinking but thought they were sophisticated. They offered Glenn what he was looking for at the time: fun, nights out, adventures. They knew I was on the way out, so they made a point of lording it over me whenever they came over.

When Glenn finally ended it, he told me it was because he was young, and he wanted to have fun. All the stuff happening with my dad had turned me into a morose, withdrawn, moody downer of a person. It was too much for Glenn to handle. I was a moody downer of a person, I won't deny it. I was in a deep depression, while at the same time experiencing unprecedented (for me) levels of anxiety that shot through the roof.

I can't say I blame Glenn for not wanting to go through it with me. Nevertheless, I expected him to, at the time. I thought that's what boyfriends did for each other. I didn't expect him to bail. I'd fallen into a deep depression before my dad even got arrested, as the situation came to a slow boil, and I waited for the authorities to do something. I had also quit the Wherehouse, been hired by a competitor (Music Plus), but then quit that job as well on a day when I just couldn't leave the apartment due to how much anxiety and futility I was feeling.

After we broke up, I'd awaken each day and be fine for a moment. Then I'd remember it had ended, that Glenn had thrown me over for some dumb ass twinks from Placentia, and I'd get a knot in my stomach that would linger for a few hours. Waking up like that lasted for a couple of months. It stopped, eventually.

Glenn and I went our separate ways and did not keep in touch.

The last time I saw him, I wasn't sure if I actually saw him. I'd rented my first apartment in Long Beach, a studio near 4th and Cherry, and I was at the beach one Saturday, on a towel, soaking up rays. I'd put my towel down at the edge of the sand farthest away from the water, which wasn't my habit because I enjoyed being near the water.

When I was with Glenn, I'd let my hair grow out longer than it had ever been or ever would be again. But when I got my own place, I tried to make myself over into someone I could be proud of.

I was no longer some scrawny, long-haired little runt who got bossed around and insulted by his heavy metal lover all the time. I'd joined a gym, I had a new buzz cut. I'd adopted a masculine new look more in keeping with the decade, a look I was proud to be able to pull off. Things were good. I was young, I was hot. I had no complaints. I'd moved on.

I opened my eyes and sat up to take a look around the beach, and straight ahead I saw Glenn, rising up over the crest where the sand sloped down to the water, walking in my direction. He still had long hair, he still wore lots of earrings, he was still rocking that furry torso and those tats.

My stomach dropped, and so did I. I laid back down, closed my eyes, and waited. I half expected to hear his voice say my name. After a few minutes, I opened my eyes and sat back up. He was gone. I looked in front of me, at the beach, along the water, then behind me at the parking lot, but he was nowhere to be found.

That isn't really the last time I saw him, though.

We reconnected decades later by way of Facebook. Before I left L.A., we got together several times to see concerts. The first time we saw each other after breaking up was in September of 2012 at the Hollywood Bowl. Twenty-six years later, for anyone who's counting. Because there was so much distance between what had happened back in the 1980s and where we stood that night at the Hollywood Bowl, we had nothing but good feelings about each other. The painful ones had faded away.

The event was a "Totally 80s" line up of the Go-Go's, the Psychedelic Furs, the Motels and Bow Wow Wow. I was attending the concert with an ex-girlfriend from the 1980s as well, so the whole night was one big throwback to that era.

The crowd was filled with binge drinking Gen X ladies in shiny mini dresses stumbling around on their high heels and probably eager to find some Gen X dick. I wasn't drinking at the time, so I got to observe the entire hot mess from the sidelines.

The bands all performed stellar sets and I was reminded of the propulsive drum beats that were so prevalent in music at the time. The drums were the driving force behind all those bands at their live sets. At least that's how I remembered it, and what it felt like that night at the Bowl.

Glenn and I also met up in Vegas to see Britney when she had her residency at Planet Hollywood. He paid for the tickets, and I got the room. I loved the show.

It took me a while to warm up to Britney. What cinched it was *In the Zone* and most of her subsequent releases. It was when "Toxic" was out that I finally came around, but the song that did it was from her previous album. I was in a dance club one night and heard a remix of "I'm a Slave 4U" and thought, *Oh my God, this song is a fucking masterpiece. I must reevaluate my blanket dismissal of Britney and her body of work.*

I didn't realize that by the time we saw her in Vegas, she was basically being trafficked by her father, forced to perform in the shows, record albums and earn a fuck ton of money, which he then took from her while keeping her under house arrest. I mean, that's one fucked up example of prioritizing capitalism over family. We should all take a lesson from Britney's experience.

Glenn apologized to me for how and why he ended our relationship back in 1986. He said he regretted it. He felt bad and knew he made a mistake. He just wanted me to know.

It was a nice thing to say, and I appreciated it, because I know that Glenn doesn't like to admit mistakes. But it was water long under the bridge, and how it ended back in the day didn't matter anymore. What mattered was our relationship moving forward.

We remain friends to this day.

12. Super Cupid / Thru the Ringer / Until I Forget

Super Cupid

You've been shooting it all wrong
Let me aim your arrow
I'm tired of having hard times
Just a shoot and a fake name
They never call me tomorrow
Let it not be the same thing
This time...

Hey Cupid, I'm warning you
I've been wanting it all my life
How do I find love?

Nobody want me a little boy
So little something so sacred
But worth pretending a little while
A little while inside my bed
In my car, behind the bar
Is this what I do to be worth your time?
No I don't mind, I don't mind

Hey Cupid, I'm telling you
I've been wanting it all my life
Maybe death would have changed it
They're still wanting a lone night
How do I find love?
Is this the price?

They're gonna wonder, "Why me?!
Have I been so bad, Daddy?"

I'm Super Cupid now spread my love
Out in every direction
Has death changed me?
I point my arrow straight at you
(You hit me with it first)
Hey, easy target, you don't move
I point my arrow you stupid fools
Bullseye!

Thru the Ringer

I was sitting in my car
Left unchosen at the bar
My ego felt black and blue
Nothing happened til I saw you
Sitting in your car

All I have to do is stare
You're on your way over
I was looking good to you, it showed
I was lonely so I brought you home

Counted to three, took a leap
Put myself
thru the ringer
Nothing like putting myself
thru the ringer again.

Wonder what it is, what's this need
Feeling pain doesn't suit me
Setting up to fall back down
Kissing dirt and licking the ground

All I do is bitch and complain
How I'm gonna make it work someday
But for now I'm rolling on glass
Being happy's just a pain in the ass

So I count to three, take a leap
Put myself thru the ringer
Nothing like putting myself
thru the ringer again.

When the time's right I open my eyes
I accept it, this is my life
And I try to stop making mistakes
Try not to feel like I woke up too late

Feeling good's nice, feeling good works
When I'm there, not so sure
Feeling right don't feel familiar
Wanna know I'm good
Just not sure

"You're not worth your weight in dimes!
You'll be dead before your time!"
Wicked wicked me,
Oh wicked wicked me
I don't wanna die right in front of your eyes
Wicked wicked wicked little me.

Until I Forget

One more year, one more time
They happen more and more
Getting deeper into my life
It's never like before

Habits change and people change
Wish you'd stay the same
I'm through a door then another door
Still inside your maze

Every time I wanted you
To know just what to say
You'd get quiet suddenly like
With that look on your face

And every time I wanted more
I went and got more
Then wondered why
I'm feeling bad
And what I did that for

Are you remembering me
Or do you choose to forget?
Am I really alone in this thing
Until I forget?

Thru quiet times and other times
I drive my own life
It's so strange without you there
To defend and decide

Questions here and whispers there
Slither thru my mind
But back on Earth
They're distant now
We're better off this time.

Verse:
ca.1986, Age 20.
Post Glenn, pre anyone else.
Early AIDS years.
Negotiating safe sex. Realizing some men lie so they can sleep with me.
Watching capitalist christians and conservative leaders weaponize AIDS.
Written in the middle of the night.

13. Surprise

*

In the summer of my twentieth year on Earth, dread hung over my head like an anvil. I could feel it up there swinging, spinning slowly, hanging by twine and a paper clip, casting its shadow and dripping its sweat down the back of my neck.

I refused to look up and acknowledge its presence. I refused to look down and see its shadow. I stared straight ahead and kept my chin not quite up but parallel to the ground. No matter the ticks, the itches, the cramps, the spasms. If I unlocked, the twine would give way.

There wasn't much time left (they kept assuring me). It was just a matter of solidifying their case, gathering evidence, finalizing paperwork before they could move in and arrest him. My girlfriend and I were in it together, trapped in the dead space of stopped time.

We drove to an industrial park in the Grenade; her mom's car, a Ford Granada on the verge of throwing a rod or spontaneously combusting at any moment. We parked next to the railroad tracks at two o'clock in the morning. We snorted crank drank vodka from the bottle smoked cigarettes and fucked in the front seat for hours because the crank made it difficult to cum.

A freight train cruised down the tracks and passed us in the night while we were fucking and smoking, it kept going past, its cars kept clanking and banging along at a lazy rhythm. That train was in no hurry. We didn't stop or try to hide, we didn't care. We sat naked and sprawled in the front seat, passing the vodka back and forth, feeling its sting, hearing its steel wheels roll over the tracks, watching it creep toward wherever it was going, and waiting. Sleep was no good, it might drop.

Sitting in the Grenade with crank in my nasal cavity vodka in my blood and smoke in my eyes was a moment that lasted for weeks while they got it together.

She called me right after it happened. I was living in Vegas with my boyfriend's sister. In a large mobile home with wood paneled walls and brown carpet. She dealt meth and slept all day. Her little girl slept on the floor in one of the bedrooms on a pile of blankets. The crib had been sold before I got there. I paid my rent by getting up in the morning when the baby did. I'd give her a bath, help her get dressed, fix French toast and Farmer John sausage links each morning while her mother slept. Then I'd plant her in front of the T.V. set to watch *The Smurfs* and *He-Man and the Masters of the Universe* while I smoked cigarettes and stared straight ahead with my chin parallel to the ground. I got a part time job bagging groceries.

It happened outside the bar he frequented just as he was heading toward his car, he'd had a few. He had a momentary impulse to bolt, he quickened his pace as they approached him. Then he thought better of it. They took him away in the back of their car and my girlfriend called to let me know it was done.

Relief paid a brief visit then left. The anvil stayed. I realized that while one part of this process had just ended, a new one was beginning. I pummeled myself for not having the foresight to see past his arrest until that moment. The thought of doing so hadn't even occurred to me and I was speechless, dumbstruck, high on illegally obtained prescription painkillers my boyfriend's sister had given me, furious that it wasn't over, wouldn't be for I didn't know how long.

I was in a 7-11 parking lot in Vegas at four in the morning, not a big deal since nothing ever closes there. I got out of my Mustang and called my mom and asked her if I could move back home until I sorted shit out and got a job. I told her my boyfriend's sister was dealing drugs so she wouldn't say no. She made me promise to behave but said okay.

I got back in my Mustang and suddenly knew I was gonna puke. There were people right next to me standing alongside their car, talking and laughing, so I leaned over my gear shift and threw up onto the passenger side floor.

I drove back to the mobile home, stumbled in and passed out on the bed, forgot to leave my car windows open. When I woke up the next afternoon it was well over 100 degrees outside and my car had been stabbed by the sun for hours, just outside the anvil's shadow, filled with the stench of baked vomit.

14. Write Down the Dream / One More Time

Write Down the Dream

Best be quick to discover it
Or I'll miss my appointment
If I forget how to get there
Have I ever really been there?

I remember there's a sun up above
That can penetrate even my deepest fear
And I'm feeling its shine deep inside
Am I feeling it here?
Did I really forget?
When I remember it
I remember it best
But I was quite young then.

I can stray off my path within reason
So long as I cover my tracks
Can't be too careless
Can't be too safe
Once that feeling takes flight
There'll be no turning back

Suppose, just suppose time's not linear
There's no perfect moment to capture
Did I take the right action?
Am I feeling the right feeling?
Can this be where I am?
I'm not certain

Anyone knows where I came from
Knows where they need me to be
Exactly
They allow themselves freedom
To decide where I'm going
When I arrive I'll be making life happy

And while this little path still unbroken
Is all too familiar to me
It's faint, but that little voice
Is telling me something
Am I feeling it? Am I feeling it?
Or am I just remembering?

One More Time

Loved your little token
Wonder when I'll get the next one?
You don't give me much to go on
I'm not in control, but it's fun.

I want you to remember
Just like I'm remembering.
I don't want to shake this feeling.
I'm glad you're the matter with me.

I don't wonder how you do it.
I'm just liking how you get to me.
Touch me once and I'm insane.
Make me harder when you say

When you coming back?
I can't wait a lifetime.
If you're open to persuasion
I'll drop dead for one more time.

Verse:
ca.1987, Age 21.
Brief Vegas epoch.
Isolated. Rudderless. Trouble distinguishing memory from fact.
Waiting for police to arrest my dad.
Obsessed with a guy named Billy.

15. Jared

Jared faces himself in the mirror, his eyes wandering over the reflection of his nude body, his legs spread out on the floor, thighs nicely rounded, not too skinny or fat, the upper thighs doused in a light layer of blond down, his legs carelessly muscular, not bursting at the seams, but firm and holding strong, solid and filling his milky white skin just so. They are nice enough to induce lust in anyone looking at them while he is in this position with his legs spread out on the floor, nice enough to induce lust in himself. He's got the legs, there's no doubt about that.

He studies his calves and admits to himself that they could be rounder, sturdier, but they are good, they are fine, they'll do. He's still growing, he's still expanding, he's still a boy, despite the fact that he has just turned twenty-four. There is still time to build up his legs, if necessary, still time to sculpt them into bigger, better, manlier appendages.

Jared's gaze floats past his penis and balls, moves up his torso, his eyes narrowing as they speculate. He definitely needs some work up here: he has no washboard abs, although his waistline is Size 30, and his pecs protrude nicely enough; not a hair to be found, and there's a cleft between them. The arms are soft but nicely shaped, the biceps and triceps are distinguishable, the forearms taut, sporting veins that he hasn't even earned, really, not until recently when Tyler made him start working out every day at the gym.

Jared sighs, lets go of his half hard dick and stares himself down in the mirror.

Jared speaks to himself.

Jared listens.

16. Study You

I like to study you,
And my response to you.
The ways I'd like us to touch
And spend our minds together,
I think about it so much.

With states and miles between us
My thoughts are all I've got.
I'm hardly ever soft.
Well, the fear don't stop the feeling
But the feeling can't stop the fear
From creeping up.

I like to study you
But there's a dark cloud over my head.
I like to think about touching you
But there's a dark cloud over my head.

What about the past?
You know I think
I've felt this before.
And what about the men you've had?
Could I love you
Just to lose the war?

Guess I should find out
If all this worrying
Is for nothing.
Go down and take it, just take it.
But it might show something.

I like to study you
But there's a dark cloud over my head.
I like to think about touching you
But there's a dark cloud over my head.

There's nothing more to my fear
Than fear.
There's no guilt behind my fear.
Exiting undignified
Then no longer here.
That's what's trying to catch me.
I'm not ready to face that fear.

Study my own life
And study where you come from.
Study where I've been
As time and again I had my fun.
Study how I might feel
If I should have to go.

Verse:
ca.1988, Age 22.
I've embarked on my 2nd year of clubbing but the scene feels like a ghost town. Deserted. The men who remain look like ghosts. Shell-shocked. Some are ill.
Dance floors are almost always at less than half capacity.
On the hunt for love, that's my number one goal. Most other guys, not so much.
Realize I don't fit in with the gays, either. Huge disappointment, but I keep going.

17. In the After Hours

I am not a slut.

Santa Monica Boulevard has been devoured by the middle of the night. The bars have regurgitated the very last of the canines, who are making their way up and down the street. Toward their cars, toward their apartments, lingering, awaiting some eye contact or an approach from behind.

"How's it going?"

"Got a light?"

"Wanna fuck?"

I am sitting in my car, which is parked in the lot of a prehistoric mini-mall (built before they were called mini-malls) that includes a 7-11, a laundromat and a Mexican restaurant that never closes. I don't venture this far up Santa Monica Boulevard very often, it can get a little dicey in this area. It reminds me of when my standards were this low, and all I wanted was confirmation of my sex appeal from anyone who would deign to give it to me.

Ignorance, that's what it was. But I'm enlightened now. Above it all. Looking down on all the dogs rolling around in the dirt. Tails wagging, tongues lolling as they curiously sniff each other's assholes. I'm looking down on them with disdain in my mouth and mind, disdain and envy, because I long to frolic in the dirt with the rest of them.

The 7-11 is really hopping now. I fidget and avoid eye contact with each passing man on the prowl while at the same time trying to catch someone checking me out. I don't have much luck.

I am not a slut.

I'm waiting for someone I met off a 976 line at 1:30 in the morning. Lots of gay men meet friends on 976 lines. I'm no different than anyone else. His name is Earl. Yes, Earl. He's meeting me here with his buddy Clem. That's what he said. "Me and my buddy Clem."

I imagine he'll drive up in an old model Ford pickup with chicken cages in the back and Louisiana license plates. He and Clem will hop out of their truck and mosey on over to my little red Subaru hatchback. He'll be a beautiful, butch slab of country beef, packed into a plaid flannel shirt, tight faded jeans that don't leave much to the imagination, and leather cowboy boots.

This is Earl I'm imagining. I haven't spent much time imagining Clem. Clem is just as butch and manly a name as Earl, possibly more so. But Earl's the one I'm focused on.

I'm not even sure why Clem is coming. Do they want a three-way? Are they straight good old boys out to bash themselves a fucking faggot? I'm not sure. I'll see when they get here. I'm excited and a little bit nervous. The possibility of danger has me on edge, but hot at the same time. Hot and bothered.

They pull up next to me in an impressively new oversized American made sports car, like a Firebird or a Corvette or something like that. I'm not into cars, though. If I ever witness a getaway, the cops will probably beat the shit out of me for not knowing my Firebirds from my Corvettes.

Earl gets out (I know it's Earl because he said he'd be driving, and this guy was driving) and I'm thrown a reality check as I realize the country beefcake from Louisiana fantasy was just that. He's got blond hair, he's fair-skinned, he has a slender build, but he's a bit heavier than I am. He's not that bad.

He smiles at me as I roll down the window. I'm stretched across the passenger seat, trying to look cool, not smiling too much, just enough to let him know that so far, I like what I see.

He asks me if I want to ride with them. I say sure, always agreeable, not really pondering what might happen should he drive me up into the Hollywood Hills to the end of a deserted road and pull a gun on me. Such thoughts have no place in this moment of potential future fun to be had.

I get out of my car and lock it. I look around at all the people milling about, as if it's Sunday afternoon in the park. All these barflies, cruising, schmoozing camping it up, riding out their drunkenness and trying to get laid. I have a second thought about leaving my car here, unprotected in the jungle. What if it gets towed? Vandalized? Stolen even?

I look back over at Earl. He's politely holding his car door open, smiling at me but failing to hide the "C'mon, just get into the fucking car and let's get out of here," twinkle in his eyes.

I cancel all worrisome thoughts about my car. That's what insurance is for, right? I let go and let God handle it, knowing He'd never let me down. I decide that Earl is cute enough to pursue this evening, and crawl into the backseat of his car.

I'm sitting (more like reclining) in the back seat of Earl's car. It feels like I'm about two inches off the ground, I'm so fucking low. Earl and Clem look harmless enough. Certainly not what I had in mind for an "Earl and my buddy Clem." What names! Here I was imagining Louisiana country beef delivered from Central Casting. I was practically expecting them to be chewing on stalks of hay when they arrived. These two look like software engineers. Unless they pull a gun on me, I'm sure I can handle them both if push comes to shove.

We take the 101 into North Hollywood, right over the hills, past Universal City and boom! We're there. As we approach the club, I see a huge sign with the name and logo of a bathhouse I've seen advertised in local gay news rags. I feel a moment of panic as I wonder what the fuck they expect me to do when we get there.

But then I see the sign, much smaller, of the after-hours club just a few doors down from the bathhouse and relax. Whew! Anyway, I'm titillated that I'll be dancing in a somewhat disreputable after-hours club just doors down from a bathhouse where who knows what may be going on. Group sex? Fisting? Any of those other mythical gay sex rituals from the 1970s that you read about? I mean, Jesus! Were they on drugs or what?

18. Cracked Xmas

■

There's an ever-increasing sense of trepidation that permeates each and every one of my thoughts as I tiptoe into my twenty-sixth year. I find myself questioning everything I say, everything I do. Every question I ask is in turn questioned by a strange yet familiar voice that has recently taken up residence somewhere in the back of my head.

I assume this voice is me, although if it's me it's a part of me that I don't like. In fact, I detest it. It's doggedly persistent and sounds very sure of itself. If I was one of your run-of-the-mill born-again fucktards, I'd think it was the devil. Or at least a demon. But I'm not, so I don't.

It's just a knowing voice in the back of my brain that always says the exact thing about myself that I don't want to know, at the exact moment that I'd least like to hear it. It's the voice of my enemy. It's stalking me. Its mission is to get me to agree with it.

I'm not all that interested in myself anymore, so the voice doesn't have much pull. One day maybe it'll realize this and give up, go elsewhere, find another head to haunt.

Until then I'll let it yammer on about how nothing I'm doing is amounting to anything, how I'm totally blowing it with Alan by not being more receptive to the whole open relationship concept, and how I must look really disgusting because it's been at least a couple of weeks since I last worked out. And on and on. Like I said, it never shuts up. At least this morning it's only just poking lightly. I can barely hear it.

It's Christmas Eve and I have a lot of things to do before I head down to my mom's. I'm lying on the bed in a stupor, trying to gather up some energy to go in and begin mixing the cookie dough and melting the chocolate for pretzels and strawberries.

But I'm beat, I can barely move. My brain doesn't want to allow it. I choose to just shift my head into a cold spot on the pillow, close my eyes and let go of last night as if it never happened. *But it did happen.* But it will never happen again. *That's not the point.* Whatever the point is, I'm just lying here, not thinking about it. That's all. No big deal. We all have dark moments in our lives. I'm not going to sweat it.

The fact is, I'm no longer able to live as I have been for the eight or so years that make up my adult life. There are certain events in adulthood that remind you that you aren't a teenager anymore, and no matter how drunk you tell yourself you were, you are always going to remember this. And you will cringe inside when you do.

I prefer to think of these moments as revelatory; positive moments in time that mark a queer man's personal growth spurts, his increasing intelligence, his deepening integrity. Of course, the voice has a name for these moments in time. The voice calls them EMBARASSING FUCK-UPS. The voice can be extremely annoying when it's right.

Alan is in Florida this week spending the holidays with his family. I wasn't invited, and I wouldn't have gone anyway. We're too new. We're not even engaged, ha ha. We're just sort of living together and getting a feel for each other as we prod through our individual "lives," for want of a better word.

We've been living together for about four months now. I love it. I don't know what else to say. Nothing compares to togetherness. Cuts the rent right in half. We turn on the space heater right before we go to bed, and then once we're in bed we get all tangled up in each other's arms. By midnight we've kicked the covers off and our sweaty bodies are sticking to each other. Neither one of us minds. He works breakfast shift at the Dandelion Café, so when I come home from work, he's usually here, lying in bed, waiting for me to get home.

We go shopping together, do laundry together, wash dishes together, take showers together. Of course, there are times when we don't do things together, but those times are rare, and when they do happen, it seems as if we're both ready for time apart, so everything seems to work out fine.

I feel very much in love with Alan. But I'm not sure if it's love or something else. I don't trust myself anymore, especially in the love department. I've fucked myself over too many times. No big deal. I tend to set myself up for disappointment, that's all.

But I'm not going to do it this time. I'm leaving my options open. I mean, if he ASKS me to marry him, then maybe I'll consider it. But until then I am not going to delude myself into thinking that this is anything of the sort.

Anyway, it's just like that song by Deee-Lite when they keep asking, "What is love?" and saying, "I think I know what love is." But they never give you the answer.

And why should they? It's a stupid question. Love is what you make of it, I guess. Unfortunately, I've been making mud pies and eating them wholeheartedly, thinking that's what great love tastes like. Sometimes it takes a while to catch on.

I don't know what I was thinking last night. Well, that's not exactly true. I know what I was thinking. I just don't know why I was thinking it. I'm sure part of it had to do with the fact that

I'd been drinking. I'd had about five or six beers by the time I left the bar in Santa Monica and began the drive to West Hollywood.

The bartender had made last call, and there wasn't one possible sexual encounter left in the place, so I decided it was off to WeHo. I decided it was time to do something I'd never done before. Something kinda dangerous and, I had to admit, pretty sleazy. But fun! And relatively cheap. I was going to pick up a hustler.

This seemed rational to me at the time. It's like, I had the alcohol in me, I had the urge to get laid, yanking it wasn't going to suffice, so I decided to just do it. I figured that doing it with a hustler for money would somehow relieve me of any responsibility I had to my relationship with Alan. Not that I have any responsibility to remain monogamous with Alan at this point, which I have been. Had been, I mean. I thought, I'll be paying for a service, I'll get the service, it'll be done, I'll go home, that'll be the end of it. No strings. Easy peasy.

And besides, it's a rite of passage for men. Isn't it? The first time you hire someone for sex? They make movies about it.

I got to that part of Santa Monica Boulevard where things start getting industrial and the side streets are lined with studios, warehouses and other large, nondescript buildings. I'd never picked up a hustler, but I saw them all the time. I'd wonder where they were from and what brought them here.

It was almost three o'clock in the morning, though, and I was driving around blocks in circles, not finding anyone. Finally, I came around a block, turned onto a side street, and saw a guy standing at the corner under the traffic signal on Santa Monica.

I slowed down and stopped at the light, close to the curb since I was about to turn right. He was a skinny white guy about my age with long blond hair. He wore a folded-up bandana over his forehead that was tied in the back like a doo rag. He had a white sleeveless tee shirt on, black jeans and boots, a leather studded belt and studded black fingerless gloves. He had bandannas hanging from a couple of the beltloops of his jeans, and his wrists each had a few silver bracelets. He looked like a young Axl Rose.

"Hey, what's up?" I asked through the open passenger side window.

He squinted a little as he approached my car, leaned down to the window and peered in to look me over. "Not much. Wanna get high?"

"Sure," I said. "You got a place?"

"Yeah," he said. "Few blocks away. My roommate might be there, but he's cool."

"Okay," I said. "Let's go."

He trotted a few steps away from the truck and bent over to pick up his backpack, which was leaning against a fence that enclosed a large parking lot. He got in and told me how to get to his place. At one point he noticed me checking him out and asked, "What?"

"Nothing," I said, smiling. "You look like Axl Rose."

He laughed. "Call me Axl, then."

"All right, Axl."

I turned onto his street and parked. He led me to an old, two-story American Craftsman style home on a big lot. The house was pitch black inside. We walked up the driveway, which ran along the right side of the house, through a gate and into the backyard, then around the back of the house.

On the other side there was scaffolding that only went as high as the top of the first floor. We climbed onto a piece of scaffolding that was placed at a slant so we could walk up to the top of the first-floor level, which went halfway along the length of the house. When the scaffolding ended, he told me to jump onto the flat roof of a room that was built out from the main house. It must have been a laundry room or something. From there we stepped up onto a ledge, where he led me forward a few more steps until he stopped in front of a large window. He lifted the window, bent over and ducked inside the house. I followed.

The house was dark, like I said, but my eyes adjusted easily since it was the middle of the night. He lit a couple of kerosene lamps, and their light blanketed the room in a muted, yellow glow.

"Relax," he said, sitting down on a lumpy, beaten-up red velvet sofa. "Get comfortable."

I sat down next to him and we looked at each other. "Come here," he said. I leaned over to him, and we kissed. He was a good kisser. "I don't get fucked," he said.

"That's fine," I said.

"You can suck my dick, though," he said.

"That works."

"Wanna get the money outta the way?"

"Yeah," I said. I pulled cash out of my pocket and handed it to him. It was more than he asked for but I figured he needed it more than I did. He set it on the arm of the sofa.

"Wanna get high?" he asked me again.

"Yeah."

He reached over the arm of the sofa and poked around in his backpack before coming back up with a glass pipe and some stuff in a plastic bag. He sparked a lighter and heated up the pipe, then started hitting it when it began to smoke.

"Speed?" I asked him.

"Crack," he answered.

"Crack?," I said. "Crack is whack." We chuckled. He handed me the lighter and the pipe so I could hit it, and we kept that up for a while. "Where you from?"

"Portland," he said.

"Oregon's cool," I said.

"Yeah," he said. "Too rainy, though. I like it down here."

"You in a band?"

"Nah, not right now. I'm lookin' around."

"What do you play?"

"Bass," he said. "But I had to hock my bass." He took another hit, held it in and passed the pipe back to me. "Gonna get it out soon, though."

I hit the pipe again as the crack plowed like a raging bull through the china shop of my system. Crack is never my first choice, but I don't turn it down if it's the only option. As soon as it hits me, crack makes me feel like I've been strung out for three days. It's that kind of high. It also makes me super horny.

I took another hit and leaned toward Axl until our lips were touching, then blew it into his mouth. Our tongues found each other and moved together for a few seconds before I pulled back, and he blew the smoke out. "Why don't you take your pants off?" I asked him. He did. The skin on his legs was white like coconut meat and covered in dark blonde fur. I got hard pretty fast after that.

When I get high with someone like this, I can connect on a deep level in a very short amount of time. We don't need the getting to know each other, the mating ritual, the back and forth, all that time. Our desires rise to the surface, we show ourselves to each other, we're intimate and sexual, we agree to go there together via shortcut.

But we're not vulnerable, because we're high. We aren't worried about holding back out of fear. The fear has gone up in the crack smoke we exhale after we take hits off the pipe. We're free to engage with one another and be in the moment without any fear. Last night I was lucky. In addition to his furry white gams, Axl had a big, dark blond bush and a nice thick white boy dick on him, too. I wasted no time getting down on it.

We smoked and talked, and I blew him on and off for a few hours. At one point this other guy appeared out of nowhere. He came in and looked at us, me on the floor between Axl's legs, him reclining on the couch smoking his pipe. We were laughing about something.

The guy wasn't very friendly. He grunted at both of us, raising his arms up in a gesture that implied a question like, "Who the fuck is this, and why are you in here partying with him?"

Axl hit the pipe again, and as he exhaled, he said to the guy, "Oh, no, it's okay. He's cool. We're just partyin'. He's cool, we're cool."

The guy came closer to the couch and grunted again with a raised inflection at the end of it. He was asking Axl another question.

"Yeah," Axl said. "Backpack."

The guy reached down, picked up the backpack, and left the room.

'Who's that?" I asked.

"My roommate."

"Is he mad?"

"Oh, nah. He's cool, he's cool. He don't mind. He'll leave us alone. Want some more dick?"

After more dick, the room began to fill with faint light as the sun came up. We'd had fun talking about stuff. Him getting his dick sucked, me getting a mouthful, and both of us taking turns blowing smoke into each other's mouths and kissing. Eventually, his roommate reappeared and hovered impatiently at the door for a few moments, then turned and left the room.

"Guess that's my cue," I said. I grabbed my underwear and my jeans, which had come off at some point, stood up and put them on while Axl did the same.

"Hey, thanks, man. I had a good time," he said. "Really."

"Yeah, me too," I told him.

"Most fuckers out there are just..." and he scoffed without finishing the sentence.

His roommate came back, walked over to the window, opened it and waited for us to crawl out. I followed Axl like I had before. We walked back along the ledge, jumped over to the small roof, then onto the scaffolding, which led us to the back yard. We left through the same gate we'd used to come in, walked down the driveway to the street and stopped on the sidewalk.

"Can you give us a ride?" Axl asked.

"Sure. Where to?"

"Hollywood and Highland?" he asked.

"Yeah. Come on."

We walked to my car and piled in. Ten minutes later, I was pulling over to let them out at Hollywood and Highland. His roommate got out first but didn't move once he was out of the car, so when Axl got out and stood up, he couldn't go anywhere. I could hear them having an exchange, and then Axl leaned back down into the car and said, "Can you spot me twenty bucks?"

I knew he was asking me because his roommate told him to. I wondered if this guy was his pimp or something. Did gay hustlers have pimps? I always assumed they were independent contractors. I said, "Yeah," and reached into my pocket. It was Xmas Eve, I was glad I had it to give.

"Thanks again, Axl. Take care of yourself."

"You too, man," he answered and smiled. Then he lifted his head out of my car and shut the door. They walked off down Hollywood Boulevard together like they had someplace to be.

Now that I'm lying here thinking about it, I realize it wasn't that bad at all. Axl was hot underneath all that metalhead gear. It was nice being with someone on the night before Xmas Eve instead of being by myself all night. And it was fun getting lit and sucking Axl's dick for a few hours.

Now I've gotta make cookie dough, melt chocolate, dip strawberries and pretzels in it, take a shower, get dressed, make sure I've got everyone's presents ready and drive all the way down to Orange County. I need to get up if I'm going to get all that done and make it down there on time. It's almost noon.

Five more minutes.

19. Blue

The night is crystal clear, freed of L.A. smog by the warm Santa Ana winds that have managed to reach the city this year. I am sitting in my convertible MG, which is parked in a red zone at the corner of a brightly lit intersection on Santa Monica Boulevard. I have my emergency lights flashing to give the impression that I am experiencing car trouble to anyone who may care to wonder what I am doing here.

I wait patiently, my hands in a loose grip on the steering wheel, my eyes fixed on the doors of a crowded gay disco across the street. I do not fidget or squirm or think about leaving. A good thing is coming to me, and so I wait.

When I see him exit, I will find my eyes glued to the back of his body as he saunters up the boulevard toward his car, which I know is parked up a side street three blocks away. I'll notice the expanse of his broad shoulders, housed in skin that is beautifully tanned for the summer. I'll notice the curves of his muscular arms as they sway slightly, in time with the rhythm of his gait. I'll notice the white muscle tee that he is wearing to show off his powerful upper body; how the thin cotton clings to his skin, having absorbed the sweat that has run down his back along the spine.

I do not fear that he will see me. He will be too drunk to notice me at this distance, should he even glance my way. To him, I'm invisible.

I will follow his car as he navigates winding, treacherous Sunset on the way to the freeway, then follow him home as he swerves drunkenly within the slow lane of the 405, heading up over the Hill and into the Valley. I will watch him pull into his designated parking space behind the apartment building that he lives in, then marvel at how he avoids falling as he stumbles up the stairway that leads him out of my sight and to his front door.

Although I won't be able to see, I know he'll fumble with the front door key, perhaps even drop it once or twice, before finally finding the slot, turning it and going inside. He will close the door behind him, stumble to the bedroom skirting furniture and piles of dirty laundry, collapse onto the bed, and fall into a deep, drunken sleep.

I will quietly go up the stairs to his front door and probably walk right in, as I doubt he'll have remembered to lock it. But just in case he does, I will use my copy of the front door key, which I secretly had made before returning the original to him the day he dumped me.

I'll walk silently through the living room and into the bedroom, which will be bathed in the soft blue glow of the cheap lava lamp that I bought him for his birthday last spring. It's been plugged in and turned on every night that I've visited. Isn't that sweet?

I will gaze down upon his muscularity and once again become envious, wondering how God decides who gets the right metabolism. I'll recognize the quiet snores he makes as he sleeps soundly in alcoholic oblivion, and I will long for the nights when I would fall asleep to their sounds.

I'll lie down next to him and nuzzle my face up against his bared neck, my head resting on his vast shoulder, and breathe in the aroma of his sweat. I'll tenderly kiss his neck, taste his scent, let my tongue linger on his delicate, vulnerable jugular, and experience a painful thirst for him that ties my stomach into knots. I'll thank God that my life was blessed with his presence, even though it was just for a short time.

Then I'll get up without a sound, creep out of the soft blue underwater glow of the lava lamp, and promise myself once again that I'm leaving this place for the very last time.

But I'll keep the key.

20. Gutter / Man This Coat's Big

Gutter

Anytime is overcome and me
Is just a little one
In favor of my picture
My binoculars are fine

I'm the one in saying no
To put the other under
So I'm laying it to rest
You'll be thanking me in time

Loving mother from the gutter
All she did was look at me
So I'm trying to rise above it
More I like the less I see

Somebody keeps asking
What about it what you want?
Never never said I had to know
You worry me with your love

I'm the one in my inside
And I could always let it show
By how it is I live my life
And yet you claim you didn't know

Love you mother from the gutter
All you do is look at me?
Watch me rise myself above it
More I like the less I see

And in once upon a future
Remember how I called
Raising up a muddy hand
For a hand to grab is all

There's another muddy gutter
Homes another dirty boy
When I see him I'll come running
Pull him up and out the void

Man This Coat's Big

There are so many dreams I've had,
The real vivid ones are still there.
My head, The Dream Factory, never lets up.
I've got 10 new ones for each one I drop.

Don't give me ideas, I got plenty.
May I be excused? My brain's full already.
Chug chug chug—out pops a new baby...
Got my name written all over it!
I'll keep it protected from what it might be like.
That way I won't have to
Chalk it up to experience.

But this isn't about keeping dreams locked inside,
Bottled up in child proof jars.
My pockets got so full,
I started dropping dreams right out of my coat.

They'd shatter all over the street,
All over the bus,
Or wherever I was.
I'd try to pick them up
But the ideas, they slipped through my fingers.
And I knew that what I'd tried not to waste
Had been wasted by not being used.
Pretty soon I stopped wearing that coat.

Now I can't say I became an adult
Because I don't recall ever being one.
One day I woke up, I was six feet tall
With hairy legs and a deep voice.

And I realized my thoughts were so dumb!
I'd sweat over rent and debt and flesh,
I'd sweat over what someone I didn't know
May be thinking about me as I walked to my car.
"So this is how people die," I thought,
And my awareness shrank down to a
Three foot high open mind.

I spent the whole day
Getting into this man's closet,
Putting on clothes, trying to feel
What it feels like being a man.

When I tried on his coat and looked into the mirror,
I thought, "Man this coat's big."
And I noticed how the pockets bulged.
Somewhere a voice from the past or the future said:
"Now don't you go digging through that nice man's pockets!"
But did the mirror bother hiding my mischievous grin as,
Being a kid,
I followed my instinct
And went digging.

Verse:
ca.1989. Age 23.
Bending to the forces of capitalism. Still resisting contortions of conformity.
Method acting my role as an adult male.
Time sharing my life concurrently with my inner nihilist demon.
I need to prioritize school, but survival requires work.
Work moves school to the back burner. Tick tock.

21. Jesus H. Christopher

"He's my boyfriend, I guess. I don't know. I mean, what is a boyfriend, anyway? I've always thought that when you had a boyfriend, that was it. But that's not true, at least not right now. Not with Christopher. When we first met, it seemed as if we were meant for each other. We hit it off immediately. I fell hard for Christopher. He said all the right things. He really drove me crazy in the beginning. I was in love and I thought, 'This is it!'

But lately, I have doubts about whether I could be happy with Christopher in the long run. I could kick myself for doubting our ability to have a successful, long-term relationship. I was so sure of it once. But there you go. Hopefully, counseling will help me deal with my fear of getting close. Because if I don't figure my shit out, it won't stop with Christopher. And Christopher and I are just so ideally suited for each other, or at least I thought we were.

Like, if Christopher is my life partner soul mate thing, why do I feel such animosity toward him? Why do I feel so trapped when he's around? I think about breaking things off, but I'm afraid that I'll be making a mistake. But then, how can I

be making a mistake if this is how it feels when
we're together?

I'm scared by the fact that I once felt so sure that
he was the one. And now I don't feel like that. I
can't conjure up any of those feelings. Why can't
I? What happened to me? I can't feel for someone
past a certain point. And not only that, but once I
get to that point, all feeling that I had leading up
to that point is lost as well. What does this
mean?"

SIGNALS

Alan and I moved from his place to an apartment in Venice
Beach, which we rented with a straight couple. Before the year
was half over, both couples had broken up. The male half of the
heterosexual couple moved out, but the three remaining
roomies stayed until our one-year lease was up. It was while I
lived in Venice, after Alan and I had split, that I met
Christopher.

We found each other at a party thrown by a woman
named Jane. Our social circles overlapped. My entry into the
circle we shared was a friend and occasional fuck bud from
Silver Lake. He was a graphic designer who worked on movie
posters. Jane was his best girlfriend.

They'd grown up together in the Southeast and moved to
L.A. to see what they could make happen. My friend was a
creative and ran primarily with other creatives socially, but
because his best girlfriend was a social worker, the parties
they threw (and there were many) had a diverse mix of social
workers and creatives in attendance.

Christopher worked with Jane. She rented an old house in Mt. Washington that had a good-sized backyard, and there was a firepit on the patio where many of the partygoers parked for most of the night.

Christopher was hot, had a worked-out physique that I could aspire to, had a college degree, a sensible job, and like all of the other social workers (and creatives) who attended Jane's parties, he drank a lot.

We crossed paths at the party when we entered a group conversation separately, noticed each other during said conversation, decided we were intrigued, then broke off from the group conversation to have our own. We sat by the roaring fire and started getting to know each other. Like me, Christopher came from a family that was dysfunctional and struggled financially.

He put himself through college and was proud of that achievement. He was the first person in his family to graduate from college, so the accomplishment was of significance to him. He was charting new territory in the course of his family's history, while at the same time making a conscious effort to be the endpoint of certain dysfunctional and toxic family dynamics he'd grown up having to deal with. I related to all that.

I fell fast and hard for Christopher, which is something I tend to do, not because I'm reckless but because I pursue relationships based on intuition and my gut feelings about a person. There are a lot of other things that factor into it as well, but when I click with someone at a romantic and personal level, I don't hesitate to pursue it.

More often than not, my relationships have been worth it. I've learned more about myself, and achieved more personal growth and improvement, through my relationships than I have through any other means. I have also experienced the happiest times in my life with significant others, who, by their sheer presence, enrich and deepen the emotional resonance of those memories.

Toward the end of the lease on the Venice Beach apartment, Christopher asked me to move in with him and his roommate, a straight guy named Andrew. Andrew was nice, but he creeped me out. He and Christopher had a relationship that appeared to run more deeply than a typical roommate relationship usually did. When they bantered back and forth, I could sense a married couple or boyfriends vibe that often confused me.

I'd spent the night with Christopher one weekend, and he'd left the next morning to run some errands alone so I could sleep in. I got up to make myself some coffee, and a few minutes later, Andrew walked into the kitchen completely naked, except for a towel. He didn't even have the towel wrapped around his waist; he was just holding it in front of his crotch in a way that was showing full bush.

When I saw him, I turned around and said, "Oh, shit!" because I assumed he just didn't know I was there. But he was all smiles, saying, "It's okay, it's okay, don't worry about it," all chummy and shit. I mean, what the fuck?! My boyfriend's straight roommate comes out practically naked in front of me when Christopher isn't there? What did he think I was gonna do, get down on my knees and blow him? I mean, he was hot and all that. Tall, muscular, blond, Italian...you do the math. It got me thinking about the dynamic between Christopher and Andrew, and how mysterious it was.

There were other aspects of my relationship with Christopher that I didn't understand. He was a walking contradiction. He would pester me to commit to a monogamous relationship with him, but he also demonstrated, on several occasions, that he had trouble keeping his dick in his pants.

He would make sex connections with other guys on nights that we went out. There had been a night we'd gone out with my friend Travis, when Christopher had disappeared for half an hour. Travis found him getting blown out on the bar's patio.

There'd been a night when he'd gone out with Travis and one of Travis's tweaker friends. They all wound up back at Travis's apartment, naked and sweaty and fucking all over the place. Christopher confessed to these transgressions, but only because he'd had to. He'd been caught, or he'd done things I would inevitably find out from others, so he'd nipped it in the bud with awkward confessions.

HELP

A perfect example of this was when we took a road trip to New Mexico. It was an excellent getaway, and we were having a great time. We'd gone through Santa Fe, then to Bandelier National Monument, where we'd done the whole cliffside dwellings and caves hike. We got some great pictures. After that, we hit Taos, where we stayed at an old retro motel just outside of town.

Christopher was harping on me at the motel about wanting to go to some hot springs place in Taos. He said a friend recommended it, and I'd really like it. I told him I didn't bring a bathing suit, and he said, it's okay, you don't need one. And I was like, what do you mean I don't need one? And he said, you've got underwear, don't you? Which made some kind of sense, so I finally said fine, let's check it out.

We got there and it was this strange, mid-century styled lobby building, which was built in the shape of a rectangular box, standing, near the base of a rocky mountain. The lobby had a front desk and a small seating area with a couple of sofas and chairs arranged just so. There were locker rooms off to each side of the lobby, and the back wall of the lobby facing the mountain was dominated by two very large sliding glass doors.

We paid to get in and went to the men's locker room to undress. Of course, Christopher decided he wanted to go commando underneath his towel, but I kept my boxer briefs on because I didn't know exactly what I was getting into.

We walked back through the lobby and out one of the sliding doors onto what looked like a residential patio, just larger. There was a big white brick wall, just standing there in the middle of the patio. The brick wall was built parallel to the lobby building's wall containing the sliding glass doors, and it blocked anyone in the lobby from being able to see the pool on the other side of it.

Because the people in the pool were naked, just like Christopher. The wall blocked most of the bright patio lighting, and because there was no pool light, the people in the pool weren't much more than silhouetted body shapes without discernible features.

The pool was rectangular and had a ledge built into its sides around the perimeter, so everyone had a place to sit when they were in the water. It was a wading pool, only about three feet deep, and there were a lot of people in it.

Beyond the wading pool, closer to the mountain, there was a plunge you could jump into, but the water was freezing cold. Christopher told me that was the point; that it was like *so* cleansing to plunge into a freezing cold natural pool of water, under the stars at the foot of a rocky mountain. Up the mountain there were hot springs as well, but they weren't accessible at night because there weren't any lights up the mountain.

All those people in Taos were just *so* spiritual. Yeah. It didn't take long for me to figure out that this was just a glorified bathhouse, only it was outdoors and up against a mountain. With men and women! These spiritual Taoseños were swingers!

I hesitated on the patio as we approached the wading pool, but Christopher couldn't wait to get in. He ditched his towel on a lounge chair and hurried over to the pool, his dick bouncing in the night air like it was dancing a jig.

I got into the pool with my underwear still on, feeling a little awkward because, clearly, just about everyone else in there was naked. I chatted with a few people but mostly stuck close to Christopher, who was going on and on about how it was *so* relaxing and beautiful under the stars, and how it made him feel *so* centered, and how he could feel his chakras getting *so* aligned in the moonlight and the night air and the water, and all this other new age bullshit. He loved to act like a Zen master when he got around other people who were like that.

I just relaxed on the perimeter ledge, my back against one of the sides of the wading pool, and figured, whatever, do your thing, Christopher.

It was interesting watching the men and women interact with one another in the wading pool. And it was weird to see women walking around naked. That's not a sight I'm accustomed to. Eventually, the crowd thinned until there was hardly anyone left.

I told Christopher we should get going, they were about to close for the night, and I was going to rinse off and get dressed. He said, "I'm right behind you."

I went to the locker room, slid my wet boxer briefs off and headed to the showers. When I returned to the locker, expecting to find Christopher getting dressed, he wasn't there. I dried off, put on my clothes and walked back out to the patio, which was extremely quiet. All I could hear were the night sounds and the hum of the pool's water pump somewhere nearby. I didn't hear any voices or chatting.

I got a weird feeling in my gut, the kind you get when your instincts tell you you're about to make an unpleasant discovery. I walked around the wall and couldn't see anything at first. But then I saw a pair of figures near the center of the wall: there was a guy sitting on the edge of the pool resting back on his hands, and I could tell this guy wasn't Christopher.

But there was also someone down in the water who was blowing this guy. I couldn't identify that person in the darkness, but I had a pretty good idea of who it might be.

I said, "Christopher," and they both jumped. Christopher's reaction was so abrupt that he made a big splashing sound. I said, "Time to go," and walked back to the other side of the wall.

A few seconds later, Christopher came hurrying around the wall, shaking his head as if to rid himself of some awful thought he couldn't stop himself from having. He passed me by, and I followed him back to the locker room.

As soon as we were out of the lobby, I said, "What the fuck?!"

"I know, I know. I'm sorry," he replied.

"What do you mean, you're sorry? What the fuck did I just see?"

"I'm sorry! It just kind of happened," he sputtered as he dried himself off.

"You keep bugging me to move in with you, but almost every time we go somewhere you wind up fucking some random stranger!"

"I didn't fuck him!" he corrected me.

"You know what I mean. Jesus, Christopher!" I spit out. "Give me the fucking keys."

He fumbled in his jeans pocket, then handed them over.

I turned on my heel and stormed out of the locker room.

The guy he'd been blowing was walking toward the lobby and he was well lit by the patio lights. Of course, he had to be hot. He was a light skinned Latino-looking guy, or maybe he was Native American, fuck if I knew. We were in Taos, after all. Probably some fucking shaman with the dick of an Apache warrior. He had tattoos on his arms and shoulders, his skin was smooth, and he was jacked up like a West Hollywood gym bunny. I became more enraged as I exited the lobby and headed out to the car.

On the drive back to the motel, I sat silently and fumed, my hands clenching the steering wheel as if I were trying to strangle it. Each time Christopher started to speak, I told him to shut the fuck up and leave me alone.

When we got back to the room, I got a beer from a six pack we'd bought earlier, went into the bathroom, sat down on the toilet and chain-smoked cigarettes. I didn't cry or anything, but I was so pissed off!

I felt helpless. And the feeling of helplessness was ten times worse than having caught Christopher blowing a guy in the pool. I mean, Christopher getting his dick wet was nothing new. But why did I feel helpless?

Probably because I was sitting in a roadside motel outside Taos, New Mexico in a bathroom covered in pink and black tiles, sipping on my beer, chain-smoking cigarettes, slogging through *The Secret History*, and feeling like Judy Davis in *Husbands and Wives*. Stranded in that motel room on a fucking road trip with Christopher!

I was in there for a couple of hours, but eventually I calmed down and got sleepy. When I came out, Christopher was sitting on the bed with his back against the headboard.

"I'm sorry," he said. "I don't know what came over me. He was just there, and he was hot, and...." He didn't finish the sentence but shrugged his shoulders instead.

"Forget it," I said, taking my clothes off. "We'll keep it open."

"I don't want to keep it open," he said.

"Tough shit," I answered, signaling that we were done with this conversation. But when he didn't respond, I said, "You can't insist we be monogamous and then fuck whoever else turns you on." I waited for him to agree with me, but he just sat there, his eyes staring straight ahead at the wall.

I got under the covers, rolled on my side so my back was to him, and reached up to turn out the lamp. I didn't say anything else to him. Just got down in bed, closed my eyes, and willed myself to fall asleep so I could dream about something and not be thinking about this.

Part of me wanted to tell Christopher to fuck off. It wasn't working. I didn't want a boyfriend who couldn't keep his dick in his pants. I knew gay couples who had open relationships, but my feeling at the time was that, if I was in an open relationship, what was the point of being in a relationship?

I'd come of age in the shadow of the AIDS pandemic and felt a duty to reject some of the less traditional aspects of gay life that had contributed to its rapid spread and deadly outcome: casual promiscuity, open relationships, an emphasis on instant sexual gratification as the primary driver of our behavior. I wanted to be with a guy who allowed me to feel relaxed and safe. I wanted to be able to take for granted that he wasn't still on the prowl for sex with other men every goddamn waking moment we weren't together.

But another part of me was coming from a mindset that considered those expectations of restraint to be naïve and unrealistic. "After all," that other part of me said, "Christopher is hot, and you do love him, and you've been together for a while now."

"But what if I come home one day and find Chrstopher fucking someone in our bed?" I asked that part of myself. The thought of it gave me anticipatory anxiety. I got no answer.

I wasn't sure what to do, and time was running out. The lease was up in six weeks, and I hadn't done shit to find a new apartment or a room to let. I'd been putting it off. I was gonna have to be out by the end of the following month and I didn't know what I was gonna do.

Of all the guys I'd gone out with since living in Venice Beach, Christopher seemed like the logical choice. Compared to the rest of them, he was the safest bet to keep me on the trajectory I was trying to navigate. He drank too much and too fast sometimes, and when he drank too much, he'd fuck just about anything that walked.

Maybe if we just focused on being home a lot, and working out, and spending time together, and not hanging out in bars, we'd do okay. At the end of the day, Christopher wanted the same things I did. He was fucked in the head about certain things, but who wasn't? I knew I was.

Maybe we'd be good for each other.

RELIEF

Christopher and I found a one-bedroom apartment in Mar Vista, about a half mile off the 405 near Venice Boulevard. It was your standard West side apartment built in the 1960s. Nothing fancy, but cute to look at.

Living together was easy to adapt to. I was working at the same customer service job in Santa Monica and Christopher was doing social work for the same agency he'd been at since we met.

There was friction in our relationship not long after we moved in, though. I told Christopher I wanted to go to school full time once I got laid off. I figured this was doable since we were sharing a relatively cheap one bedroom. I wanted to get school done before I got any older so I could start making some real money.

I was still bad at doing school, though, and needed to give it the attention it required. Taking night classes while working full time was difficult. If I had to do it, I figured I would, but it would be so much better if I could make school, instead of work, my top priority until I got a degree.

Christopher opposed the idea. It was important to him that we both had full-time jobs so we could each pull our own weight. I understood his logic: he didn't want to end up being a sole breadwinner with an unemployed boyfriend.

But he already had his degree, and it felt like he was becoming an obstacle to me getting mine. I told him I could wait tables and take mid or evening shifts so I could have mornings free for classes, and if I got into a good restaurant the tips would bring in more than my salary at a full-time desk job would.

Christopher wouldn't budge. He didn't consider waiting tables a real job. "And what about benefits?" he asked me during one of our conversations that had escalated into an argument. "They don't offer major medical for slinging hash!"

I resented him for his unwillingness to consider my position, but what I really resented was that I'd moved in with Christopher without hammering out these details first. I felt trapped, and that usually meant an inevitable path for me had been forged: a path that would lead to my escape.

There had been some nights when Christopher got home from work late in the evening without letting me know ahead of time, which went against my expectations, based on what we'd agreed upon before moving in together. He claimed he was going out with coworkers to have a couple of drinks, but I realized (again, belatedly, now that we were officially a couple and living together) that I didn't trust him.

Christopher thought he was a good liar. And he was good enough at it so that people rarely questioned the veracity of what he was saying. I knew better, but I didn't let on. I considered him an amateur.

On one of the nights Christopher didn't show up at the usual time after work and hadn't called to let me know where he'd be, I decided fuck it, I'm getting laid. We'd lived together for no more than a couple months, and it wasn't going well, at least not for me. That I was already faced with unexplained disappearances by Christopher made me angry.

I called Voice Male and browsed the messages on the main bulletin board. One guy caught my interest: he had a deep, friendly voice and his profile said he was six feet two inches tall, muscular, and had a large endowment.

I responded to his post, and he got back to me within fifteen minutes. His name was Eric. He lived in the Valley but was willing to come pick me up. We chatted for about ten minutes more, then I gave him my address and directions. The plan was to go have dinner in Santa Monica. His ETA was one hour.

After I hung up, I was torn between the excitement of meeting this guy and possibly having sex with him, and worry that Christopher would decide, on this particular night, to cut it short with whomever he was with and arrive home before I headed out to meet Eric. I took a quick shower to freshen up. Fifty minutes later I walked down to the driveway and waited for Eric to arrive, hoping Christopher wouldn't get home before I left.

Eric pulled up about five minutes later, driving a Mercedes-Benz. As I approached the car, the passenger side window slowly came down all by itself, and Eric said hello as he pushed a button that unlocked the door. I said hello back. "Get in," he said, smiling. I got in. I'd never ridden in a Mercedes Benz before. Eric told me the model but I never retained the info.

He drove us to Santa Monica, and we ate at a restaurant that looked pricey. He insisted on buying dinner, because he'd been the one to make plans. Eric was personable, polite and made funny jokes. He was humble, which appealed to me. He didn't give off any arrogant or entitled vibes, even though he looked like the type of guy that usually did.

As we prepared to leave, Eric asked me if I wanted to come over to his place for a little while. I told him I couldn't stay out too late, and he promised to have me back home by eleven. He drove us over the hill into the San Fernando Valley. The neighborhood looked a little sketchier than the West side, but his apartment was great. He co-owned the complex with a woman named Gwendolyn who lived in the apartment next door to his.

The one-story complex only had four units. Gwendolyn's was in the back and the apartment in the front was rented out. Eric had joined the two middle units, a one-bedroom and a two-bedroom, to create a large living space for himself. The front door brought you into his living room, and there was a guest bedroom, a T.V. room and a bathroom off to the right, with a kitchen straight ahead. He'd installed a door in the common wall between the units, and through that door he'd turned the adjoining apartment's living room into the master bedroom. He'd converted the other rooms on that side into a laundry room and a workout room.

Eric decorated his apartment as if he were an old lady. It looked colonial, with wing backed chairs upholstered in dainty floral prints, and white curtains with lace trim.

To add to the grandma's house vibe of the place, Eric stocked the curio cabinets and shelves that dominated the living room with white and blue chinaware of all shapes and sizes. There were plates (some stacked, some displayed in the upright position), teacups, butter trays, pitchers of various sizes, and even a set of egg cups. All of these items were white and covered in blue patterns or images: blue flowers, blue country houses, blue maidens, blue cows, blue sheep and blue farmers pitching bales of hay.

After giving me a tour of his place, we lingered in his bedroom. He was asking me questions about myself that I answered freely. He came close, put his arms around me and moved in for a kiss, which I readily accepted. He was a good kisser.

We got down on the bed and made out for a while, but none of our clothes came off. While he was on top of me, he eventually used his knees to push mine out so he could put his weight on me, then he pressed his crotch up against mine. I could feel his erection through our jeans, and it was big. I reached down and rubbed it through the denim just to be sure I'd felt what I thought I had. Yep.

He picked me up again the following week, and that night I lied to Christopher and told him I was going out with a friend. Eric drove us straight to his place. As soon as we arrived, we got down to it.

After kissing each other for a while, on the lips and down our necks, Eric reached down and pulled my shirt off over my head. When he took his own shirt off, I got to see his beefy upper body for the first time. I was already stiff; seeing him shirtless just cemented it. I got to work on his chest and nipples until he unbuckled my belt, undid my pants and pulled them down to my ankles.

He didn't wait for me to remove my shoes so I could take my pants and underwear off. Instead, he pushed me down on the bed and got on top of me, shoving his tongue into my mouth and gyrating his hips against me. Due to his size, I wouldn't have been able to get out from underneath him if I'd wanted to. Luckily, I didn't want to.

Before long, he managed to undo his pants and pull them down to his own ankles without ever getting off me. I felt his hard dick against mine as he continued to dry hump me, and pretty soon, he moved his hips down onto my thighs briefly, sucking on my neck and then my nipples, until his dick fell down between my legs. Then he came back up and planted another sloppy, open-mouthed kiss on me while he pushed his dick up between my legs so that it pressed against my taint and ass crack. It was huge. It was the second biggest dick I'd ever encountered in the wild (Wade from Sydney still held the top spot).

As we made out, I was toggling back and forth between excitement and trepidation. On the one hand, my reaction was the same it was every other time I'd encountered a monster dick in the wild: unsure if it would fit, but willing to give it a shot. A lot depended on whether he knew how to use it.

I managed to extricate myself from beneath him, enough so that I could roll us over and get him onto his back. I got down to the floor and untied his shoes. I removed the rest of his clothing in short order. Then I got between his legs, reached up and grabbed his dick.

I examined it closely for the first time. It was uncut. It curved downward and had a big head. I stroked it a few times, then scooted up and licked his balls as I continued to do so. Then I worked my tongue up to the tip of his dick, opened my mouth and swallowed it whole.

When it came time for him to tell me he wanted to fuck me, I helped him put on a rubber, but I didn't know how to proceed. His dick was so big, I didn't want it to hurt me to the point that I couldn't enjoy it, then make him stop when it got to be too much. He told me the best way would be for me to sit on it. That way I could guide how deeply it went in, and I could go down on it as little or as much as I wanted to.

I took his advice. I stood up and removed the rest of my own clothes while he arranged himself on the center of the bed with his shoulders and upper back raised on a couple of pillows, which emphasized his beefy tits.

I straddled him with one knee on the bed, standing on the foot of my other leg to keep me high enough above him so I wouldn't just slide straight down and bury it balls deep in my hole. Once I got it in, I maneuvered myself until it felt positioned correctly, with a straight shot all the way to the back of the house. I eased down on it, accommodating myself to its girth and length, until I was down on both knees.

I leaned forward and kissed him, and he started moving it in and out. After I got used to that, I raised myself up and arched my back so my ass could go all the way down on it. Eric's dick was a shock to my system at first because it felt like it hit me so deep that I almost wasn't sure what to make of the sensations I was feeling. But once I knew the end point, I started riding it. And once I started riding it, I opened up more. That's when he started fucking me in earnest.

We stayed in that position for a while, but my legs eventually got tired, so he sat up and put his arms around the small of my back, then somehow lifted me up just enough so that I flipped onto my back.

Eric was suddenly on top of me. My ass was now facing upward, his dick was down in it, my ankles were over his shoulders, and his arms were resting on each side of me. We looked each other in the eyes as he bore down on me, his muscular shoulders and arms bulging in the air above me.

There was an extended moment when all we did was stare into each other's eyes. He brought his face down to mine and kissed me, long and slow. He stopped the kiss, kept still for a few quiet moments, staring down at me. Then Eric proceeded to bang the fucking hell out of my ass.

By the time he came about ten or fifteen minutes later, we were both covered in sweat, and I was in a daze, having been fucked into such a state of delirium that I had no control over the noise I was making or the words I was saying. I did have the presence of mind to discern that he was into it, though.

Eric pulled out. I hit the bathroom to throw out the condom and wipe the lube out of my ass crack, then I rejoined him in bed, where he helped me get off. Once we figured out the logistics of fucking, our sexual compatibility was instantaneous.

He drove me home and I was buzzing the entire way. I thought to myself that if I was ever going to have an affair with someone, Eric was the perfect guy to do it with. I was already anticipating seeing him again, and I wasn't even home yet.

We got together a few more times, and each time the sex was better than the time before. Eric's dick was big, but when he fucked me, it felt like a perfect fit. My body accommodated it without any problem at all.

Eric also fucked me so hard that once he got going, I lost control of myself. He'd be pounding away at my ass and I'd be hooting and hollering so loud, I'm sure the entire neighborhood figured out that someone nearby was getting some dick and getting it good.

In spite of all the shame and embarrassment I had about letting people see or hear the real getting-dicked-down me, when Eric was doing it, I didn't care who heard me. In fact, when Eric fucked me, my brain was incapable of thinking about anything else but what he was doing to me with that dick. Nothing else mattered.

◆◆◆

THINK FAST

He surprised me one evening when he called and said he needed to talk to me. He picked me up, and not five minutes later he said, "I like you, but I don't want to be with a guy who's living with someone else. I don't want to share you with anyone."

My heart sank. We had such a good thing going! And now he wanted to end it. "Okay," I said, and looked out the window to avoid looking at him.

"Okay, what?" he asked.

"Okay, I'm not gonna argue with you?"

"Argue about what?"

"I mean, you want out, right?"

"Not exactly," he said.

"I don't get it."

"Your job winds down at the end of December, right?"

"Yeah..."

"I'm thinking you should move in with me. When it winds down for good you can get a part time job and go to school. You said that's what you want, right?"

"Yeah, but..."

"But what?"

"What about Christopher?"

"I don't know. You can't see both of us. You have to decide. Him or me."

I couldn't believe he was putting it to me like this. It was so unexpected, and he wanted me to make up my mind right then, in his car, before he dropped me off and went back to the Valley.

Eric was hot but didn't appear to know it. We shared a childhood history of being outcast and bullied, which I think kept him humble. I could relate to his wariness of other people, and his drive to work out until he got to be the size of a person most people wouldn't fuck around with.

He was a pale white guy, about 6'2" with light brown hair and a solid build. I envied him his full head of straight hair that looked amazing and fell down perfectly on his head no matter what he did with it. His hairline was flawless, too. Eric was four years older than me and weighed in at about 210 to my 170. He was beefy and muscular, with big guns, thick thighs and calves, a broad set of back and shoulders, and an impressive pair of pecs. He also had a bit of a belly, which was sexy and added to his charm.

Eric's size meant he commanded attention wherever he went, but at the same time he gave off the vibe of a gentle giant. I guess I had a thing for deceptive appearances because one of the things that got me so hot and bothered about being with Eric was knowing that, behind closed doors, that gentle giant's great big dick of death was waiting for me, and there was nothing gentle about it.

Since he was expecting me to make a choice, I considered my options. Christopher, while good-hearted and a nice enough guy, also had some notable flaws. I don't know that I characterized him as an alcoholic back then, but he was certainly headed in that direction. He drank too much, and he had trouble keeping his dick in his pants whenever he drank. He'd also demonstrated, on more than one occasion, that he didn't have to be drinking to whip it out.

Christopher was also an obstacle to me attending school full time so I could get a degree, and a college degree seemed critical to my ability to reach the professional level of employment I wanted to achieve. Christopher had also given me HPV at one point, which I'd minimized and let slide when it happened, but which came up as a deciding factor in this soon-to-be-made decision.

I couldn't shake the feeling that if I played it safe and stayed with Christopher, my life was never really going to change that much. I was approaching the age of thirty, and my clueless twenty-seven-year-old brain was convinced that at age thirty, all my youthful vitality, all the opportunities that were waiting for me, would evaporate.

The choice seemed obvious that evening, as I sat there and pondered it with Eric waiting for me to decide. Given the gravity of the decision I was making, it didn't take very long. "Okay," I said. "I'll move in with you."

Shit was about to get real.

◆◆◆

INTERIOR: DIVE BAR

That night, after Christopher got home from work, I suggested we go to a local dive bar over on Robertson Boulevard that we frequented when we wanted to get drunk on the cheap and didn't feel like dressing up and preening, which would have been required on a trip to WeHo.

We ordered beer and played a game of pool. I ordered two more beers, and we sat down at a table in the back. I knew there was no easy way to do what I was about to do. In my relationships, I was almost always the good guy. There were exceptions, of course, but overall, I treated my boyfriends well and didn't make a practice out of fucking them over.

But that night, I knew I was about to do just that: fuck Christopher over. There was no escaping it. I felt bad, but I had to think about what was best for me. And dumping Christopher so I could move in with Eric was what was best for me.

One of the unfortunate circumstances of this scenario was that Christopher had moved out of the apartment he'd shared with Andrew for several years. They'd had some cozy type of arrangement of convenience that I wasn't privy to but could sense. I reminded myself, as I prepared to stab him through the heart, that Christopher had fucked numerous other guys on occasions when we'd gone out together, or when he'd gone out with Travis, and who knew what other times he'd done it that I didn't even know about.

The bottom line was that, when it came to getting a college degree, which Christopher already had, I didn't have very many options to help make that happen. I returned to the mantra I'd been repeating to myself ever since Eric left that day: I must do what's best for me, at least every once in a while. This opportunity was a fluke. I'd lucked into it, and I'd be a fool to turn it down.

I gave it to Christopher straight. I'd met someone. He'd offered to let me move in with him and work part time so I could go to school full time. I wouldn't be under pressure to keep paying rent when my job wound down in December. I was being pragmatic, is what it all boiled down to, and there were already too many cracks in the foundation of my relationship with Christopher.

Christopher sat there, his mouth agape, but I bit the bullet and continued. I reminded him that he made a practice of getting drunk and fucking other guys, and that he'd been doing that since before we moved in together, while at the same time saying he wanted us to be a monogamous couple. If he didn't want to be monogamous, why was he characterizing our relationship as a monogamous relationship? He was sending me mixed signals, to say the least.

I told him I'd decided to take Eric up on his offer and move in with him. I did my best to let him know that this decision was primarily based on what was best for me, and not in reaction to any specific thing he'd done. In other words, I said, "It's not you, it's me," but without actually saying that.

Christopher appeared to go through the seven stages of grief within the span of about forty-five minutes and three more Bud Lights. I sat back and gave him the floor, because I'd done the horrible, difficult thing that I'd come here to do. I was off the hook.

The rest was just paperwork.

22. Earthquake Weather

○

I moved in with Eric while still working in Santa Monica, but they were winding down operations soon and I'd be out of a job by the end of December 1993. The timing was perfect; I enrolled at Los Angeles Valley College and started my college education journey (again) in January 1994 at the age of twenty-eight.

When I landed at Eric's place, I was provided with the first opportunity to breathe a sigh of relief since I'd been living on my own. I'd been flying without a net, without any savings, and without a home to return to. Not having a safe place to land created a tremendous amount of pressure on me to avoid homelessness. Every decision felt like a high stakes, do or die situation. If a job didn't work out, it could throw my life into turmoil very quickly.

When Eric opened his home to me and allowed me to make school my top priority, I felt like I had an opportunity to exhale and redirect my energies. I almost felt safe, which was not a familiar feeling. Then an earthquake showed up unannounced and shattered any sense of relief I may have felt about my new living arrangement with Eric and the opportunity it afforded.

On January 17, 1994, just after 4:30 a.m. PST, I woke up screaming, with my hands over my ears. My first thought upon awaking was that a passenger jet had fallen out of the sky and landed on us, because that's what it sounded like. It was a massive crash and roar. Then the world began to pitch and shake. The room jumped and lurched in the dark. The bedroom's corners pitched up and down, rising and falling in a range of at least two to three feet. All of Eric's tchotchkes flew off the shelves and crashed onto the floor.

Eric made a habit of wearing ear plugs to bed and would have slept through the whole damn thing if I hadn't hit him on the shoulder to awaken him so we could experience the terror together. The shaking lasted for only ten to twenty seconds, which doesn't sound like very long, but it's a long time to wait and see if the building you're in is going to collapse on top of you, or if the ground beneath you is going to crack wide open and swallow you whole. It was that kind of major big ass earthquake.

The epicenter of the earthquake was about eight miles from where we lived. Less than a minute after the initial quake, the first aftershock hit. It was a terrifying feeling of déjà vu all over again, before we'd even had a chance to catch our breath.

When the pitching and lurching stopped, we got up, put some shoes on and examined the damage. The apartment was in a shambles. The T.V.s and stereo equipment were knocked to the floor, several pieces of furniture were upturned, and Eric's chinaware was tossed about the rooms. The kitchen cabinets had been thrown open as well, and their contents shaken out onto the kitchen floor. Thankfully, the building suffered no structural damage.

The night was eerily silent after the shaking stopped. There was no power. We were engulfed in a thin fog of earth dust that had been kicked up by the quake. I could feel it coating my mouth and my lungs with tiny particles of God knew what that had been shaken loose and kicked into the air by all that movement.

I was about as close to panic as a person can be without losing their shit. I was on a huge adrenaline rush and felt like I'd been struck by lightning.

On the day of the quake, we drove around the area to view the aftermath. The damage seemed random and without reason. Buildings that remained standing and unscathed sat next to buildings that had been pulverized and were in various stages of collapse. Before any authorities could get to damaged apartment buildings, tenants were packing their vehicles, trying to save as many of their belongings as they could before their buildings got red tagged or condemned.

At one point, Eric and I were waiting for a traffic signal to turn green at the intersection of Nordhoff and Reseda, when another aftershock hit. The traffic signals, the streetlights and the buildings surrounding us swayed and creaked above us as the Earth rumbled below. Eric's Mercedes and the other vehicles surrounding us rode the waves that traveled through the asphalt, and I pushed a button on the car's console, causing the sunroof to slide shut, in a ridiculous effort to protect us from any potential falling debris.

The aftershocks continued and became a daily feature of life for the next several months. I hated the aftershocks because my body and brain reacted as if it were the original quake all over again. My instinct was to bolt in any direction, didn't matter which one, to try and escape the shaking. The sense of panic I felt at the arrival of each new aftershock was instantaneous and I had no control over it. Gradually, as the frequency of aftershocks lessened, and over the course of several months, my panic response subsided.

The Northridge earthquake measured 6.7 (and the first aftershock 5.9) on the Richter scale, which is considered moderate by geological standards. But the quake had an immense impact because it occurred beneath the densely populated and built-up urban area of Greater Los Angeles. Even though it was a blind thrust earthquake, which means the fault it occurred on didn't reach the Earth's surface, it was *close* to the surface, which resulted in a severe amount of ground movement and in many areas, liquefaction.

Uplift, or the ground's displacement and deformation that resulted from the shaking, was significant throughout the region. The Santa Susana Mountains, a moderately sized range just north of the epicenter, were permanently pushed up from anywhere between 15 ½ to 20 ½ inches. The Santa Susana Mountain range is sixteen miles long.

Depending on the source, between 57 and 72 people died as a direct result of the earthquake and its aftermath. Over 11,800 people suffered injuries, and about 1000 were hospitalized. An estimated 80,000 to 125,000 Angelenos were displaced from their homes due to earthquake damage.

Five major freeway interchanges were closed due to collapse or structural failure. These closures, in addition to more than 170 damaged freeway bridges, disrupted traffic patterns, which resulted in months of traffic jams on streets across the city. When adjusted for inflation, the Northridge earthquake caused more than $40 billion in damage, making it the costliest earthquake in United States history.

Like everyone else in the city, I was just trying to live my life. Trying to manage my panic response each time a new aftershock dropped in on us. I remember sitting in class one day when a moderate aftershock hit. We remained seated at our desks, silent and still as the floor shifted back and forth, demonstrating a surreal malleability that undermined my ability to consider the ground I walked on as solid, as safe. The light fixtures hanging from the ceiling dangled above us on their taut supports, so that they jerked to a chaotic, rhythmless beat that only they could hear.

We all waited to see how bad the shaking would get before it stopped, and when it was over, the professor returned to giving her lecture, and we all pretended it hadn't happened. The aftershocks felt like monsters that thrived on our fear and attention. If we ignored them, perhaps they'd lose interest in us and let us live.

The symbolic significance of the event was crystal clear. The universe was saying, in no uncertain terms: *Don't get lazy and comfortable, bitch!* Thinking I would be given at least one meaningful or profound reason for what the universe had just said, I waited for a follow-up statement, ready to pay attention and take copious notes. I waited in vain. Apparently, the universe didn't have anything more to say.

My relationship with Eric wasn't an easy one, even though much of it was good and I got a lot out of it. Eric was extremely generous to me. By affording me the opportunity to make school, instead of survival, my top priority, he changed the trajectory of my life. It took me a while to acclimate, learn how to study effectively, find my path, and succeed. But eventually I did.

I also struggled with demons I'd been carrying since my mid to late teens. I was a periodic binge drinker. I was out of control during certain time periods, usually around Father's Day, and other dates I associated with one or both of my parents. I'm lucky I didn't get arrested, injured or killed, or injure or kill anyone else.

I was self-destructive. I was chasing something. The earthquake ruined my expectation of accomplishing my educational goals while feeling safe enough to succeed. I appreciated that I was making progress in school, but I didn't feel safe. I didn't feel like I was really being taken care of. I feared that, like most others in my life who had at some point been important to me, Eric would realize he'd made a mistake, that I was unworthy of his love, time and attention, and eventually abandon me just like everyone else had.

Even though I carried a deep hatred for myself that manifested in compulsive and self-destructive behaviors, I was accomplishing personal growth and development during the same time period. Working out, passing classes, writing my novel *forever ago*. But I was in a mind space of extremes: full-tilt discipline, self-improvement and positivity, or full-tilt sex, drugs and nihilism.

I wanted good things for myself, and when I lived with Eric, it felt like I had many of them. But I didn't, not really. I had access to them. But they weren't mine. I felt temporary in Eric's life. I also had the compulsion to be reckless, flirt with danger, break rules, and dare the forces of all that was pure and good to stop me from defying them.

After we'd been together for a while, Eric just seemed to lose most of his interest in me, except for when we needed to socialize as a couple, or when he got horny. Eric and I had great sex. Even when we weren't getting along and our relationship was hitting the rocks, the sex was almost always stellar. It was a language we could return to using that allowed us a form of connection when nothing else in the relationship was functioning. The sex kept us running on fumes and made the relationship last longer than it would have if we didn't have such good chemistry, but eventually something happened that caused Eric to break up with me.

I lived with Eric for a total of four years, and we were a couple for roughly three of them. But the facts are these: Eric was a bit of a cold fish, and I was a hot mess of compulsive and self-destructive behaviors. We just got to a point where things weren't going anywhere that was good.

I moved into the guest bedroom and got to work planning my final exit.

I also had time to think about the trail of failed relationships that littered the landscape I'd traversed to get here, fading away in the distance the farther back they went. My relationship with Eric, behind me but still closest in proximity, appeared as one of those random, unfortunate apartment buildings that had been pulverized by the quake a few years back. Surrounded by others that remained intact, untouched, inhabitable.

There were all kinds of reasons a building might collapse when the earth pitched and shook beneath it. Maybe it was faulty design or construction, or a weakened foundation, or a lack of maintenance and upkeep. Maybe it was just how velocity, thrust, and the waves moving through the earth beneath the building came together and worked in tandem when the quake hit.

I had fleeting feelings of panic and fear come over me, but strangely, my strongest feeling was one of relief. I didn't have to live here anymore and keep waiting for the other shoe to drop. Yes, I was again flying without a net. But this was something I was good at, something I knew how to do. It was a grind, but I had muscle memory embedded in my body that hadn't let me down yet. I could do this shit in my sleep if I had to. Why be upset?

I'd known I wasn't safe, and I'd been upset and angry about it for practically the entire time I'd lived with Eric. Not all that much was about to change, really. I would just keep going. Keep going, and while I was at it, stay alive, housed, sane, and yes, safe.

Despite what the quake had taught me, it's what I had to aim for.

Nothing less would do.

23. Bandages (an awakening)

∎

In the dream, my face is still hidden behind the bandages that are wrapped around my head. The gauze makes my skin itch, and though my eyes are open, I can see nothing but darkness. I am unable to tell night from day. I feel no sense of time. The hospital that I am in is devoid of any doctors or nurses or confused visitors wandering into my room by mistake. I am alone in the hospital, as if it is my very own. As if I am free to recover for as long as I wish from whatever horrible trauma it is that I have suffered. As if I am free to decide when I am well.

In the dream, I decide that this is the day to remove the bandages. I rise from the hospital bed, somewhat unsteadily, not accustomed to the simple task of standing on my own two feet or taking steps across a room that I am not familiar with. I feel my way around the room, groping at the air like a blind man without a cane. Because that is what I am, and that is why I've chosen this day to remove the bandages that blind me.

I knock over a glass of water, which shatters on the floor and cuts my bare feet as I grope for something to lean on and save myself from a fall. But the pain in my bleeding feet (I can feel them bleeding, even though I can't see them) does not phase me. I am too worked up. I am too excited. I am shivering in antici...

...pation. If I could see, I wouldn't be able to see straight. This is how excited I am! Excited and afraid. For when I think about the moment that I see myself in the mirror for the first time since the accident, I wonder what it is that I will see. Will I see the same face that I was? Or will I see a once-attractive face that has been rejigged and damaged beyond repair? A butterface? What is it that I'll see?

But the fear is not enough to hold me back. Not today. "I've waited long enough," I think to myself in my dream. I've waited for the scars to heal, I've waited for my face to be beautiful again. I've waited and I've waited and I've waited, until I can't wait another day.

I stumble forward, with no sense of direction, and suddenly I know that I am in front of the mirror, which I've never seen, which I've been looking for with only my hands and my mind to guide me. I am standing in front of a mirror that I cannot see, yet I feel its presence and know it is there, just as surely as I know that my feet are bleeding and that I've waited long enough to heal.

I begin to unwrap the bandages with great care, ever so slowly, so as not to rush tragedy should I be mistaken and be facing my face too soon. I yearn to have a nurse or a doctor doing this for me, talking reassurance and giving me a meaningless pep talk about how everything that can possibly be done has been done. About how I've recovered so quickly and thoroughly and impressively. About how there's absolutely no need to worry about anything, because everything is going to be just fine. About how I'm sure to be looking just as good as new!

But I am alone. Unwrapping my head more quickly now, because the light is coming in, and I'm catching a glimpse of the wall out of the very left-hand corner of my eye. Now I can see the bed behind me, reflected in the mirror that I am standing in front of. I am scrutinizing the room in the reflection, the room that is behind me, in the mirror. I'm noticing every detail about the room, because now the bandages are off. All the way off. And I cannot bring myself to look at my face. Not just yet. I study the room, and the chair, and the TV hanging from the wall, and the shards of glass on the floor, and the dark crimson color of my blood that looks like it's been fingerpainted on the linoleum.

I have noticed everything in the room that there is to notice, except for my face. Well, not exactly everything. I've forgotten to notice the rest of my body. I begin with my feet. They're fine, the same as they were the last time I stood in front of a full-length mirror and studied myself intently. Just a little bloody, that's all. My calves are fine, my knees are fine, my thighs, my balls, my dick, my abs, hands, arms, chest, shoulders, neck and...my face!

It's fine! It's me! I'm back! Just as I was and have always been! I'm beautiful! My tan's faded a bit, but they don't have tanning beds in the hospital. They do have exercise bands, however, and I'm just now remembering that I've been working out while staying here, so my muscles are all in place and looking better than ever.

Ah, my face! It's beautiful, just as it's always been. I turn my head slowly from side to side, examining my features, drunk on the beauty of my face. I heave a giant sigh of relief. I am filled with relief and gratitude. Thank you, God! Thank you from the bottom of my shallow heart. I am filled with joy and gratitude and relief.

I am full of myself. All I can see is my face. My face, and something else. Catching my sight. It's moving steadily upward. It's an erection, it's my cock. I haven't beat off since the accident. I've been terrified of what my face might look like. The thought of masturbating with my head wrapped in bandages that were possibly hiding a butterface was enough to kill any horniness I may have felt during my hospital stay.

But now I am wicked hard. I'm so hard it hurts. So hard that I grab it and tug on it and go for it in front of the mirror, so happy to be alive and well and unscarred and jacking off in front of myself with such wild abandon. I am completely full of myself. I am completely at peace with joy and gratitude. I am cumming.

And I wake up cumming. Not even touching myself. Cum splashing onto my stomach, my entire body covered with a light film of sweat, and my lungs gasping desperately for breath. I awaken and I wonder where I am all of a sudden. Still filled with joy, still full of myself, still in mid-orgasm, still grateful for the beauty I've beheld in the mirror.

And then I remember. It's only a dream. It isn't real. It's my sick brain playing a cruel prank on me, every night. Every fucking night. There's no mirror in my room. I refuse to have one. Because I am scarred. I am rejigged. I am a fuckin' butterface! I am gone. I've been replaced with something that I don't know how to be. A scarred up, rejigged, motherfucking butterface MESS with the heart, mind and soul of a fierce, raging beauty queen stud.

I am fucked.

24. I Really Do Like You / Bubblehead

I Really Do Like You

Entertained but alone
All the way down the rabbit hole
I can never guarantee
Your amusement or well-being

Under ordinary circumstances
One can talk and one can listen
But a little number three
Never hear and never ask me

Many times are memorized
And many very much alive
Forever greeting the future
Time turns inconvenient

You say inhale truth
You say exhale lies
Pierce my wounds before they've healed
Rearrange my insides

Is this over yet?

Meter and rhythmless
In adulterated matters
I've a dripping throat to harbor
And a soul that might explode

Shaved smooth
Like velvet next to you.
I prefer not to think about
This moment as it happens

Are you almost done?

Just give me your number, I'll call you.

Bubblehead

I've been a bubblehead
Nothing but trouble there
Nothing but trouble
When your head goes pop!

There's something,
Something I'm missing.
But life is so clear!
I can see you, smell you, hear you
When you walk right up to me
And yell in my face.

Life is clear, it's oh so clear!
Everything I see, that is…
My eyes, they open just so much.
Just so much but not too much…
I don't wanna burst my bubble.

The T.V. and the video machine
And my sofa and table and chair
Are what I accept for myself right now.
Compared to what I had before
This is so much more!

But there's something,
Something I'm missing.
And it's coming to me.

Oh my bubblehead,
Kept you protected.
Didn't want to rock the boat.
Didn't want the wind to blow.
Bubbles are so fragile...
What if it broke?

I'm floating over the street.
On my way to work.
Looking down on me.
Look at that jerk.

Hear a little voice call,
Hear it call my name.
A little boy voice calls
My little boy name.

And I try not to listen
Cause the wind is really blowing
And the walls are really bending
And I can't let the air in.

But suddenly I'm falling
Out of wind too weak to hold me
Now that my bubble's broken
By some faceless, nameless kid.

Verse:
ca.1995. Age 29.
Playing by the rules yields mixed results.
Performing adulthood on a minefield drains my energy.
Wracked with imposter syndrome.
Sex as sport (when in Rome...).
The faster I go the more removed I become.

25. Plugs 2: Victor

Repetition compulsion is the unconscious tendency of a person to repeat a traumatic event or its circumstances. This may take the form of symbolically or literally re-enacting the event, or putting oneself in situations where the event is likely to occur again. Repetition compulsion can also take the form of dreams in which memories and feelings of what happened are repeated, and in cases of psychosis, may even be hallucinated.

-JAN GRANT & JIM CRAWLEY, *TRANSFERENCE OF PROJECTION: MIRRORS TO THE SELF*

From one day to the next,
I can't change my mold

-THE VERVE

◆◆◆

SHOWMODE

I called my friend Aric and he invited me over.

Aric was a tall, lanky guy from New Jersey with dark hair, long limbs, freckles and a dick as thick as his New Jersey accent. Aric and I had hooked up a few times and become regular fuck buds.

Aric was only a few years older than me, but those few years meant he'd experienced a gay scene that I'd only heard about, and that had been wiped out when the AIDS bomb detonated. His stories of free Boomer love and decadence were fascinating, and the world they depicted was the stuff legends and myths are made of.

When I got to his place, I walked in and there was this big, menacing guy I'd never met sitting at the dining room table. This man exuded dark energy. He was built thick and wore a black tee shirt, board shorts and backwards baseball cap.

He had a deep tan, and I couldn't tell if he was white or Latino because his features weren't clearly identifiable as one or the other. He had black hair, a salt and pepper goatee, tattoos on his arms and eyes so dark I couldn't discern the pupil from the iris in either one of them. His gaze was laser sharp and whenever our eyes met, I felt like a deer in the headlights.

I was instantly attracted to him. Aric introduced us and we chin-upped but didn't shake hands. His name was Victor.

A few minutes later Victor left the room. Aric lowered his voice and asked me *is it okay that he's here?* and I scoffed and was like, yeah, because who was I to dictate who Aric had at his place? Then he asked *you wanna do a line?* and I said yeah. I was relieved because sometimes I go to Aric's and we do a couple lines and sometimes I go to Aric's and we don't. That night I was really in the mood for it.

Aric got his swirled marble tile out, which was 12x12, gray on white, with the tina and a razor blade on it. He brought it over to the coffee table and cut out a few lines, then handed me a black straw and nodded and smiled as I snorted a couple lines, one up each nostril.

Aric and I were on the couch. Victor came back into the room and sat down on a chair opposite us. He smiled at me and asked, *You get high?* I said yeah, so he took out a pipe filled with weed, took a hit and passed it to me. I took a hit and passed it to Aric.

Aric offered me some more lines before hitting the pipe, which I did, then I took another hit off the pipe, handed it back to Victor and realized I'd forgotten to buy cigarettes on the way over. So I got up and said, "Be right back. I need to go get some smokes."

Aric jumped up as I walked past him and asked, *will you really be back?* I gave him a weird look and said, "Yeah. What, you think I'm gonna ditch you?" Aric didn't answer so I said, "Come on, Aric! You know me better than that!" I was keeping it light, but I was confused and a little offended that he was implying I might just take off at this point in the evening, when we were barely just getting started. I was also curious to see what kind of heat Victor was packing and was hoping to find out. "Be right back," I said and headed out the door.

At the gas station up the street the tina hit me full tilt boogie and it was intense. I could feel it dripping down my throat and I was sniffing repeatedly to keep my nose from running. I felt just like a coke queen with big hair in some bad 80s movie, and I could barely inhale without feeling more particles of it drip down the back of my throat. I drove back to Aric's, found the same parking space out front and went back up to his apartment.

There was more tina ready on the tile so I did a couple more lines and smoked some more weed and drank some beer that Aric offered me. Aric disappeared into the bedroom, so I had a few minutes alone with Victor.

I found him intimidating above all else. He had the air of someone who'd seen some shit and lived to tell the tale. He had the confidence of a man who knew how to take care of himself and had no doubts about his ability to do so.

Whenever our eyes met, I got a feeling in the pit of my stomach that I couldn't identify as good or bad. Was it fight, flight, or was it just intense sexual attraction? Hindsight would eventually fill in that blank for me, but that night I couldn't tell what I was feeling. He turned me on, I knew that much. But I didn't consider him a prospect because what could a guy like that possibly want with a lightweight like me?

I pegged Victor as criminal but wasn't sure about the extent of it. I was comfortable enough with him to hang out that night, and the uneasiness I felt only served to enhance the sexual tension that was growing between us as the evening progressed. He was a type of man I was all too familiar with, but not in this context. I hadn't mixed the areas of my life that contained criminals and homosexuals.

My dad's world was peppered with people who had questionable character traits, dubious values and criminal records. While not all the homosexuals I'd met in my life were of high character, there weren't any who were criminals either, as far as I knew. Mixing the criminal elements of my dad's world with what I knew at the time of the homosexual realm seemed like an oil and water situation. I didn't realize at the time that they could, and often did, mix.

My limited exposure to the criminal element in my life gave me an overinflated sense of my street smarts. At the same time, Victor was an anomaly I hadn't yet encountered. I didn't really know what to make of him.

Aric came back out a few minutes later wearing a pair of boxer briefs and a cut-off tee shirt that exposed his midriff. He sat down next to me on the sofa. All my nerve endings seemed to be tingling from the tina. Each time my knee brushed up against Aric's leg I would feel a little shock of electricity, which would course through my body for several seconds before subsiding.

There was porn on the T.V. at that point, something called *Rear Entry*, with leather and dildos and hairy muscle men doing it to each other in all different manner of ways. Aric had a leather cock ring in his hand, which he was fondling and playing with in an overly obvious way, so I finally asked, after some more lines and another hit off the pipe, "Are you gonna put that on or what?"

Aric grinned and said, *i wanted to put it on you* and *why don't you get comfortable?* meaning take my clothes off or whatever.

"No thanks," I said, "but do you have any shorts I can wear?" Aric got me a pair of mini boxer shorts, and I went into the bathroom to change into them. I stripped down to my wife beater, put the mini boxers on, and looked into the medicine cabinet mirror, grinning, and thinking, Man, I haven't been this high in I don't know how long, maybe even ever, but I'm so glad I'm tweaked out right now.

My reflection in the mirror, still grinning, said to me aloud, "This is how I'm supposed to feel."

My reflection didn't mean I'm supposed to feel high all the time. It meant I should feel unburdened. By the inhibition, the policing of myself, the guard that was implanted in my head and kept watch over everything I said and did.

This guard interjected itself into whatever activity I was engaging in, to sound the alarm when something I was doing was either too gay or too sexually satisfying. She was the inner manifestation of the homophobia and Puritanism that's ingrained in American society, and that I grew up in.

My brain felt so good after a certain point that the guard was just like, fuck it, whatever, have fun. My brain and the guard were both high as fuck that night, just like I was. They were so high, they forgot to police my thoughts and actions.

I was about to feel what it feels like to be who I really am. No guilt, no shame.

I returned to the couch, sat down next to Aric and we talked about random shit. I made a few jokes, enjoyed their laughter, listened to them talk about the early 1980s and how wonderful it all was back in the day.

Victor cut out more lines, I snorted more tina and thought to myself, this night can't get any better. Victor left the room for a few minutes, I did another line at Aric's request, lit a cigarette, enjoyed the moment. Aric was grinning at me and I chuckled because I could tell we were thinking the same thing.

Victor came back into the room and we snorted more lines, then Aric said, *can I put this on you?* He was referring to the cock ring he'd been so preoccupied with for the past half hour or so, and I said, "Sure."

He smiled, said *come here*, so I stood up and went over to him. We were standing there, and I said, "I don't wanna be the first one to strip." So Aric took off his boxer briefs and tee shirt, then I took off Aric's mini-boxers and my wifebeater, then Aric started to put the cock ring on me, tried to separate my balls with it and stuff. It was one of those black leather rings that snaps closed and he was having trouble. It was cumbersome and uncomfortable.

Victor said, *Here, this is better.*

He came over with a leather string that looked like a shoelace. Victor kneeled in front of me, surprised me by taking my dick in his mouth, started sucking on it expertly, all the while using the leather shoelace to separate my balls and wrap it around the base of my dick so that when he was done and moved back to examine his handiwork, everything was standing at attention and separated and looking quite meaty and fine.

We moved over to a mattress that was set up in the middle of the living room just beneath the T.V. screen and the porn. I lay down and they were on me like white on rice, keeping my dick hard, sucking my tits, licking my balls, and Aric could suck dick good, but Victor could suck dick excellent, which meant he was keeping me good and hard despite the tina.

He worked my dick, balls and ass all at the same time, made it feel like there was a motor running down there, and it felt so good I couldn't help but moan and writhe and exclaim, "Fuck!" more than once.

Then I was sucking Aric's dick, then I was sucking Victor's dick, and we were all just going at it in this tina-induced liberated sexual free for all, and everything was good and nothing was wrong and I felt really fuckin' happy to be alive.

At one point I was playing with Aric's ass, since he'd asserted his role as the bottom of the group, and sucking Victor's massive uncut dick, since he'd asserted his role as the top of the group, (and by the way, Victor's monster dick replaced Wade from Sydney's at the top of the Biggest Ever list) and while I didn't know exactly where that left me, I didn't really care because it stood to reason that whatever happened, I'd be taken care of.

It felt so good being naked and hard and bouncing around and being so utterly fucking free of the self-consciousness that dogged me throughout every waking moment of every waking day. It'd been like that for as far back as I could remember. But that night, the guard bitch was gone, okay?

I was making out with Aric when Victor suggested, *Why don't you fuck him?* but we were all so far gone that we kept getting distracted by stuff and never got around to finishing anything we got started.

We fucked around for a few hours before Victor said he had to get going. He handed me a business card before he left and said, *Call me.* When I drove home that night the streetlights all had halos around them.

I called Victor, of course. I was fascinated by his dick, first and foremost. Coming across a monster dick in the wild feels like hitting the jackpot. Ding! Ding! Ding! Ding! Ding! Wade from Sydney's had been in the top spot for several years, with Eric running a close second. Dicks didn't usually get much larger than Eric's or Wade's, and yet here was Victor, packing even more heat than either one of them.

And you may find yourself asking, "But why, Ray? Why did you feel compelled to pursue the largest dick you'd ever encountered in your life?"

I don't know. Because it was there?

I knew I wanted to see Victor again because if I wasn't mistaken, we had good sexual chemistry. He was assertive, bordering on dominant, when he was fucking around, and pretty much called all the shots, which I got into.

It was almost a case of fangirling because I'd categorized him upon our first meeting as a person of interest who was most likely unobtainable.

Having sex with him and Aric that night was an awesome bonus, but I didn't expect anything more to happen. It's not that I considered him out of my league. I just figured he wouldn't have much interest in someone like me.

STUNLOCK

Victor lived in an apartment on Cahuenga, just inside the pass off the 101. It was in a forest green apartment building that hugged one of the hills and was built vertically to accommodate the hillside. The first night I arrived he buzzed me in, and when I got to his apartment door it was open behind a thick metal screen. I knocked on it and he yelled at me to come in, which I did. Then he told me to take a seat and offered me something to drink.

I sat on the sofa and examined the apartment. The living and dining spaces were combined to create a large, open room with two sliders: one at the dining room end and the other at the living room end, both of which opened onto a single balcony. They shared that wall with some floor-length windows that, combined with the sliders, provided a nearly unbroken view of the night outside.

The view was decent, but since the building was fairly low on the hill, it only offered a view of the neighborhoods below, not the vast city beyond. Considering the direction I was now facing, I figured that if I did have a view of the city, I'd be looking down past the 101 into Hollywood, Hancock Park, Miracle Mile and beyond.

Victor handed me a bottled water and we chatted for a few minutes. Then he excused himself and told me he'd be right back.

The sofa faced the sliders and floor-length windows in the wall separating the apartment from the balcony. To my immediate right was the front door I'd come through and a small hallway that led into the living room I was now sitting in. Where that hallway ended was a wall to my right which ran toward the balcony. In that wall to my right was a doorway, which Victor exited the room through.

As had been the case at Aric's, there was a mattress on the floor between the sofa and the T.V., which was located in front of the windows and facing me. The T.V. was tuned to a cable show I didn't recognize.

I sipped water and kept checking out the room. Between the sofa and the T.V., right next to the mattress, was a smoked glass cube table with rounded corners and chrome trim. It was very 1980s and had the air of a relic. I could see vague, distorted reflections of other things in the room on its dark, smoked glass surface. Behind the glass, it looked like there was movement within the cube, fleeting shadows cast by the light from the T.V.

A few minutes later, Victor came back out the door to my right, followed by a middle-aged man I'd never met before. We shook hands as Victor introduced us. I instantly disliked the guy because he leered at me as if I were a piece of meat hanging in a butcher shop window. By the time we were done shaking hands I'd shifted from politely meeting a stranger to throwing shade at a creep.

He didn't seem to mind; though. He just kept looking me over and then smiled as he left. Victor turned the light off, but instead of the room going dark, it sank into soft violet-blue light, as if shimmering off pools of water, that made Victor's apartment feel as if we were in a dramatically lit cave. The lighting cast a surreal, constantly shifting violet-blue glow over us both. It felt like we were swimming in it.

Victor sat down and stared at me. His gaze burned into mine, and as I felt it sweeping up and over my body, I broke eye contact and looked out the windows to regain a sense of perspective. I could see Victor from the corner of my eye, though, and his gaze didn't waiver. He remained silent while I struggled to think of something funny to say. Right when it was about to get more uncomfortable, he moved in on me.

His kisses were tentative at first, as if he were tasting me. I responded to them with a measure of restraint, leaving the door open just in case he changed his mind at the last minute. Instead, the energy between us intensified as we continued to make out and pretty soon, we were down on the mattress.

We partied hard that night. Whenever I came up for air, panting and sweaty, he'd offer me another line, which I'd accept, recklessly trusting him to manage our tina intake as we had wild sex and found things out about each other that can only be discovered through this kind of interaction

I was still fascinated by his monster dick, of course, and showed him how fascinated I was every chance I got. He wasn't selfish about my attention, though. He reciprocated to an extent that surprised me, to be honest, because a lot of these guys hold the opinion that all they need to do is show up in these situations. They tend to leave the rest of the work to whoever else happens to be there.

As the next several weeks passed, we continued to get together at his place for these chem sex extravaganzas. Had they been Hollywood musicals, I'd say they had the spectacular scope and choreography of Busby Berkeley, along with the hyperkinetic disorientation of Baz Luhrman. As wild as our nights could sometimes get, I grew to feel comfortable in his presence, even though he still cut an imposing figure. He was very welcoming whenever I went over, and he always had a bounty of party favors.

I didn't feel guilty about using the tina he offered up because he was very clear about wanting me to come over for the express purpose of partying together and fucking and having a good time.

When I offered him cash, he waved it away and insisted it wasn't an issue. When I brought my own favors, just to show him I could and would, he was dismissive. He said he preferred his own source. He said it was quality shit and, based on how fucked up it got me, I didn't doubt it.

The routine I went through on nights I hooked up with Victor was that I would prep at home first to get things on the right track. Once I got to Victor's place, we'd get high, we'd watch porn, we'd make out, get naked and do everything but fuck. Then he'd tell me to go to the bathroom and do a spot check. Better to be safe than sorry, and considering the size of his dick, making sure everything checked out was a good practice to have prior to him dicking me down.

This practice had become a habit because of Eric's big dick. It seemed at the time like I was constantly under pressure to be ready for action on a moment's notice.

I know. Size queen problems.

◆◆◆

GANK

The night things changed took place about two months into our recurring hook ups. Things unfolded as they usually did. He'd cut out a few lines for me. There was porn on the T.V. I was high as fuck, we were making out, I was going down on him, he was liking what I was doing, it was all good. He told me to go do a spot check and I did. Everything was good.

I came out of the bathroom and sat down on the mattress. He offered me another line and I snorted it. We got back to making out.

Pretty soon I was on my back, and he was on top of me. I was rushing fast, he was kissing me deep and hard, his beard was scratching the skin on my face, I was totally turned on, and he was maneuvering himself in between my legs.

As we continued making out, he got one of my legs up over his shoulder, then did the same with my other. He was rubbing his dick up against my taint and balls, thrusting as if he were fucking me already.

Then he stuck the tip of his dick right on my hole and started pushing it in.

I broke away from kissing him and said, "Hold on, Victor, wait," panting as I said it.

What?

"We didn't put the rubber on yet."

We don't need a rubber.

A pause as that sank in. "Come on, Victor. I don't even know if you're HIV."

I expected this conversation to unfold in a certain way and was waiting for us to just clear up this little misunderstanding and get back to fucking. He stared down at me. Then he said, *Ray, I would never fuck you without a rubber if I was HIV.*

"But Victor…."

He stared me down again as he adjusted his weight, putting less on his legs and more on his torso. He pressed down harder on the backs of my legs, which were up in the air but coming down, my knees getting closer and closer to my ears.

Come on, he said, and shoved the head of his dick into my hole.

"Ow!" I exclaimed, squirming beneath him, not because it hurt so much, but because I couldn't believe he'd stuck his dick head inside me without putting a rubber on first.

Come on, he repeated. *That doesn't hurt. I know what you can take. We're just getting started.*

The energy between us had shifted. Victor transformed into someone else. It was Victor, but not who I thought Victor was. He wasn't the Victor I'd come to know over the course of the past several weeks. Victor's dark side reemerged in the violet-blue light as he glared down at me.

I was on my back, I was high as fuck, I was ass up. I'd allowed myself to be contorted into this vulnerable position based on my past interactions with him. I'd made assumptions about Victor based on those interactions and how we behaved together when we were fucking.

While part of my initial attraction to Victor was tied up in his menace, he had done nothing when we were partying but behave in ways that showed me I could trust him to treat me well and be responsive to what I said or did.

I looked into his eyes and squirmed some more as I said, "Come on, Victor," but I could barely move. He was locked down on me. I didn't have room enough to move beneath him.

His eyes looked different. The charm and affability I'd become accustomed to seeing in them were gone. What I saw now was calculated determination. He'd worked us into this position and from it he saw no way for me to escape. I was faced with the fact that Victor was doing what he'd planned, what he wanted to do.

I was trapped under his glare. He observed me with an air of remove, and indifference to what I was saying. He wanted to see what I would do next. If I put up a fight.

My mind extrapolated telling Victor to stop again, struggling to get out from under him, managing to do that, gathering my things, getting dressed and leaving. I knew anything past me saying stop in that extrapolation wasn't going to happen, at least not until he was done.

I performed a cost/benefit analysis to determine what likely outcome fighting him would produce. He was bigger, heavier and stronger than me. He was a fighter. He had weapons. He was at home in his violence.

I hadn't applied Victor's potential for violence to my own interactions with him because he was friendly and charming and he liked me. I enjoyed his attention. He kept asking me to come back and party with him. He spoke highly of me when I was there. He flattered me, is what I guess you could say. It worked. It got him to where he was. Where we were. The adage about flattery getting you everywhere rang through my head.

All this shit running through my mind occurred within the space of about three seconds while we stared at each other, he pressed his dick deeper into my ass, and I tried to figure out what to do in this situation that I wasn't prepared for and hadn't even entertained as a possibility.

When I realized he wasn't going to change his mind, I decided the thing to do was to let him fuck me. Ride it out. Get it over with. Hopefully, I'd avoid any resultant physical attack he might inflict on me should I resist.

He maintained his eye contact as he shoved his dick even deeper into my hole. He didn't wait for me to say it was okay. And I didn't.

I said, "Don't cum inside me."

He broke our gaze, got down on me so that his face was next to my head but out of my range of eyesight, and proceeded to fuck me harder than he ever had up to that point.

Usually when we partied and he fucked me, he'd only go at it for maybe five or ten minutes before we'd move on to something else for a bit to give my ass a rest.

That night, he stuck with it. He fucked me for about five minutes with me on my back. Then he pulled out, rearranged me on the mattress, and shoved it back in without any of the politeness or concern he'd afforded me on the previous occasions he'd fucked me.

About fifteen minutes later he put me on my back again, lifted my legs straight up in the air, shoved his dick back inside me and had at it with full thrusts. He came back down on top of me, forced my legs back over my shoulders and my ass back up toward the ceiling, and fucked me more.

I made a lot of noise because it fucking hurt.

He pulled his dick out. *Shut up.*

He grabbed my legs, flipped me onto my stomach, shoved his dick back into my hole, and fucked it that way until he came. He blew his load deep inside me.

He collapsed on me, panting, sweating, drooling on my head, neck and shoulder blades. I stayed still.

He pulled it out again for the last time that night and trotted off to the bathroom to clean up.

I got up, put on my underwear, sat down on the couch and lit a cigarette.

Victor seemed to be taking his time. I had the feeling he was hoping I'd be gone when he came out of the bathroom.

I moved over to the spot he usually sat in on the sofa and leaned back on the cushions with my legs spread, taking up all the space I could.

I lit another smoke as soon as I was done with the first.

Halfway through that cigarette he still hadn't come out.

I refused to leave without making him see me first.

I walked over to the table, cut myself two fat lines and snorted them.

When I was halfway through the second line, he popped out of the bathroom, bright eyed and bushy tailed. Fully clothed. Grinning. Not a care in the world.

Oh, hey! he said, as if he were surprised to see me. I guess he really had expected me to leave. *You need to use the head?*

"Yeah," I said. "I need to shit your load out of my ass."

Yeah, he said. *Right. You told me not to cum inside you. Sorry about that. You were so hot, though.*

What a fucking piece of shit, I thought.

I hit the bathroom, took care of business quickly, returned to the living room and got dressed.

Victor didn't say anything until I was heading toward the door.

Call me.

That was it.

COOLDOWN

I tried to stop thinking about Victor. I was pissed off at him. I was upset by what had happened, but I didn't know if I had a right to be. It felt like something had been done to me, but I wasn't sure. I had feelings about how it went down and struggled with a hunch that he'd planned all along for it to go down like that. I didn't know why I was having so many feelings about it.

I wrote Victor off and decided to forget about him.

Then I came down with something. I couldn't tell what it was, but it started with a sore throat that got progressively worse until I had to call off for a couple of shifts at Cali Pizza, where I waited tables. I was exhausted and sore. My throat was raw and felt like a cube of lye was lodged there, eating away at my esophagus.

Then I broke out in some kind of rash and was worried that it might be measles. I called my doctor's office, described what was wrong, and he agreed to see me the same day.

After checking me out and taking my vitals, my doctor suggested I might be in the process of seroconversion. I asked him what that meant and he said it might mean I'd been infected with HIV. Had I engaged in any unsafe sexual activity recently?

"No," was my automatic response. "There's no way," I insisted.

I was in denial, of course, even though I was in my doctor's office, and he was telling me that it looked like what it looked like. It certainly wasn't measles.

He told me he could refer me to a colleague at Cedars Sinai who specialized in HIV, who could evaluate me and perhaps give me some treatment options that hadn't even hit the market yet.

"Just call him," he said. "It can't hurt."

That's what you think, I thought to myself.

"Sure, yeah," I said. "Thanks."

I called his colleague from the front desk because my doctor's office, located in Sherman Oaks, was about halfway to Cedars Sinai from where Eric and I were living by then, in the outlying suburb of Santa Clarita.

The colleague's office asked me a few questions, got my doctor's information, and told me they could see me at 3:30 p.m. to take a blood draw, make a record of my symptoms and open a file on me. I drove over the hill against afternoon traffic, knowing I'd be stuck in it all the way home.

About a week later I drove back to Cedars Sinai, where I was informed I'd been infected with HIV.

Even though this outcome, given the circumstances, was close to inevitable, I was stunned. Not exactly surprised, though. The feeling of inevitability had set in as soon as my regular doctor had told me what it looked like. But my denial had successfully overridden the inevitability. *Anything is possible!* my denial kept telling me. Keeping hope alive. Keeping the truth at bay. Until it wasn't.

I drove home knowing my life was now a different life. Not just different, but a different life. I'd become something unacceptable. I'd become it through unacceptable behavior. I knew the rules. We all did. How could we not? I'd played by them for practically my entire adult life.

The acceptability of being queer was still up in the air at that point, being debated and decided by society. But having HIV? That closed the door on acceptable, honey. Both within and outside the community. The only people who didn't seem to give a shit if you were HIV+ were people who were HIV+.

So, this was my new life: a big red "A" branded on my forehead from this point forward. And while I was optimistic that I could rock that "A" better than Hester Prynne (or at least give her a run for her money), this was going to take some getting used to. The gravity of my situation, once it became clear, never escaped me. But by the time I was halfway home, I was already making plans.

When you're always thinking three or four steps ahead, part of your strategy is accepting current facts as they are. Without acceptance of the current facts, any foundation you lay as you build a path forward will be unstable.

I'd heard the words I'd feared and dreaded for the entirety of my adult life. I still had some processing to do, but I hadn't spontaneously combusted upon hearing the news. I wasn't dead yet. I still had time to get shit done. I got home, determined to keep moving forward with my life. No detours. No delays. I had things to do.

The first thing to do was call Victor. Any fear I had of him was gone. The oppression I felt when he was bearing down on me that night was ever-present. I wondered if I'd be stuck with it forever.

I picked up the phone and went out to the garage. I sat down just outside the door and lit a cigarette. I called Victor.

I was being somewhat performative when I did this because I didn't expect him to pick up. Victor never picked up.

But once I called, I'd be able to tell myself I'd been brave enough to call him, even though I hadn't reached him. I could live in the righteousness of what I'd intended to say had he picked up, or of what I'd said, but to his machine. I could point to my attempt to confront him as evidence of my bravery.

I was feeling quite satisfied with my effort as the phone rang once, twice. Then Victor picked up.

I was thrown momentarily. I paused for a moment as I wondered again whether I had the right to be mad at him. But it passed, and my anger took over.

I took a deep breath and let him have it.

"You told me you'd never fuck me bareback if you were HIV positive," I said.

I wouldn't, he said

"You looked me in the eye and said that."

It's true.

"Bullshit! I just found out I got HIV. It happened within the past few weeks."

Well, you didn't get it from me, he declared. *You must've got it from someone else you fucked!*

"I haven't been with anyone else," I said.

There's no way it's me.

"There's no way it's anyone else."

You had to have been with someone else, he said. As if that someone else had just slipped my mind. He wasn't taking me seriously. He was amused.

"It's you. You're the only person it could have been."

Victor left me hanging in silence.

"Victor," I said.

It wasn't me, he said.

"But I haven't been with anyone else."

You must have. Come on!

"Victor, I haven't been with anyone but you since September."

Well, I don't know what to say.

He was still looking for a way out. His tone had shifted to defensive.

"You don't have to say anything. But you did this."

I would never do that.

"But you did."

No I didn't.

"Who did, then?"

Again with the silence.

"Victor!"

It wasn't me, he repeated, his voice cracking.

"Bullshit, Victor!" I said. "You fuckin' raped me!"

Victor got his voice back real fast.

I did not rape you! Jesus! That did not happen. I would never do that, Ray! Victor's tone had shifted from dismissive, to defensive, to unsure. Then he circled back to dismissive. *You must've been with someone else,* he insisted.

"I HAVEN'T BEEN WITH ANYONE ELSE!" I yelled at him. "FUCK! Do you think I'd call and say this if I didn't know it was true? You're the only person I've been with, Victor! I HAVEN'T FUCKED ANYBODY ELSE!"

Okay, okay, calm down. Just listen to me.

Victor was having to think fast on his feet. He scoffed, though, then said, *I can't believe you think I would do this. We're friends. I would never do you like that, Ray!*

"Then what?!" I replied. "What the fuck happened?"

It's gotta be someone else, he repeated. He said it reasonably. He said it like he was trying to talk some sense into me.

And at this point, he also sounded as if he were on the verge of panicking.

He seemed genuinely upset by the fact that I thought he would intentionally do what he'd done. I'd expected him to deny it, but I didn't expect him to get this upset. Getting this upset was not something villains did, as far as I knew.

I thought maybe he'd be angry at me for confronting him, but the way he was reacting at this moment didn't seem right for someone who'd done what I was accusing him of doing.

I was confused by his change in tone, and I suddenly doubted myself, even though there was no other explanation. The only other person I'd had sex with during the past few months was Aric, on the night I'd met Victor, but that had occurred too long ago for resultant symptoms to be showing up in late December. And none of us had actually fucked that night anyway. The only other person I'd been with since then was Victor.

Out of nowhere, everything I'd been through since I'd last seen him caught up with me. Body slammed me. I was exhausted. I felt like I'd been pulverized.

I'd been fucked against my will, then gotten sick, been told what I had looked like HIV, had my blood drawn, then time had slowed down to a crawl. I was in limbo while vials filled with my blood were sent to a lab and tested by humans I would never know or meet.

For that week when my blood was out there in the world being analyzed, I was a man who didn't know he was HIV positive. The days slowed down and dragged, and everything around me moved so sluggishly that I felt half asleep and could barely detect movement. Things may as well have stopped moving altogether.

Right when I was about to get comfortable with the idea of living in limbo, it sped back up. The test results came back. I drove down to Cedars. I listened to someone tell me what I most feared hearing. Now, here I was. Now I knew.

But my anger dissolved, and I was overcome with doubt. My certainty that Victor was the villainous piece of shit responsible for adding this new dimension to my life was the only thing that had been powering me through it. Without the anger to fuel me, I collapsed.

I started crying into the phone without any restraint. I had nothing left in me. "Stop fuckin' lyin' to me, Victor!" I said, sobbing. I was trying to regain some composure, but I couldn't stop what had already been unleashed. "I'm just trying to figure out why. Why would you do that?"

He didn't say anything.

After a few minutes, I got the sobbing under control. I latched on to a remnant of the anger that had driven me to call him in the first place and pressed forward. "Why, Victor?"

You should come over, he said.

"What?" I asked.

You should come over. We'll hang out.

"Why?"

In the language between Victor and me, come over and hang out meant getting high and fucking.

Because you need to hear me out.

This time I stayed quiet.

All I wanted to hear from Victor at that point was an apology and a reason why. It didn't seem like much to ask for.

What else could he have to say to me? Did I even want to know?

But I also felt compelled to accept his offer. Maybe he'd come clean. Let me in. Provide me with the explanation I needed. Maybe he'd grant me access to the truth.

"I gotta go," I finally said.

Call me, he said.

I hung up.

SIDEQUEST

The second thing I did was tell Eric. When he got home from work that day, I gave him some time to get undressed and settle in for the evening before I approached him. I couldn't help but feel that I was ambushing him. My concern over how he might feel about it distracted me from my fear of how he was going to react.

His reaction was subdued, pragmatic, and decisive.

He told me that this would mark the end of our relationship as boyfriends. He expressed compassion for me and for what had happened with Victor. He emphasized that I was under no pressure or imposed time frame to move out, but that I should move to the guest bedroom and start sleeping in there.

He didn't say: GTFO! or I never want to see you again! or You're a filthy tramp and I hate you! To be fair, it was well within his rights to say any or all those things to me. But Eric wasn't that kind of guy.

His reaction tracked with the state of our relationship during that time. We cared for one another, but it wasn't working out. Until that day, having a conversation about ending our relationship seemed bigger and scarier than just allowing things to keep going as they'd been, living a life together that we were accustomed to.

But disclosing that I'd had a drug-fueled, sexual affair with another man that had resulted in me becoming HIV positive was the catalyst we both needed to finally face facts and act accordingly.

I moved into the guest bedroom and stayed there while I recalibrated and tried to determine next steps. The day after we broke up, I was at the house alone, watching a movie, when the phone rang. I looked at the caller I.D. and it was Eric, calling from work.

My heart started beating at an accelerated rate. I was excited. Eric never called me from work. He couldn't be bothered. But for him to be calling me from work in the middle of the day, of his own accord, and without any prompting from me, it must be something really big.

I suddenly had hope that maybe this course I'd been on was about to be turned around. Perhaps he'd changed his mind after having some time to think about it. Maybe he loved me after all.

But Eric just called to ask me how I was doing. As a courtesy, because he knew I had a lot to process and he cared about me. He wanted to make sure I was okay.

Being faced with the unfiltered reality of my circumstances, which included there not being any option available to me that would turn back the clock, correct my mistakes, and give me a do over, gutted me. I'd fucked up. I'd created these circumstances. It was a tough pill to swallow about my behavior, about cause and effect, about consequences.

I kept working. I kept going to classes. I hit the gym full force.

I avoided Victor and ignored his calls.

I started asking around about him, at bars or clubs I'd go to, just to see what I could find out.

The biggest concern the tweakers had was that I was saying these things about Victor. Because Victor was cool. Victor was a good guy. Victor would never do that to anyone, especially not me. Victor really liked me. He was hurt that I'd accuse him of doing something like that to me.

Aric reached out and asked me what the fuck was going on. Victor was Aric's plug, and Aric was experiencing a reduction in access to Victor due to him being the one who introduced us.

I told Aric what had happened, and he couldn't seem to understand what my problem was. I said, "Well, first he fucked me without a rubber, then I got HIV. Figure it out."

but you were partying, Aric said.

"So what?" I asked.

so you knew he would fuck you, he replied.

"How?" I asked.

well, he gave you tina, right?

"Yeah..." I said.

so you knew what was gonna happen, he said.

Despite myself, I understood Aric's logic. It seemed reasonable, almost inevitable. It was ingrained in me: If A then B. But now that I was seeing that equation from the inside, I knew it was bullshit. I never tried to put one over on Victor. I wasn't trying to get something for nothing.

"I agreed to party with him, Aric. I didn't agree to go over there and get fucked against my will without a rubber."

Aric warned me to lay off talking about Victor. He reminded me several times that Victor had connections to the Mexican mafia. I didn't want to get on Victor's bad side, did I?

On the contrary, I still wanted to get in with Victor's good graces. If I could get his approval, win his confidence, get him to let me in, I would know that I mattered. I'd know I wasn't disposable. But I couldn't return just for a do over.

Time passed. I integrated my HIV status into my life as just another component of who I was. As I got more comfortable with it, I felt less of a need to villainize Victor. I came to an acceptance of my own role in the incident and was no longer obsessed with holding Victor accountable for what he'd done.

FOOZLE

I ran into him at the Hollywood Spa one night. He invited me to his room and we partied together. I played it cool, as if I'd forgotten what went down. He acted respectful and contrite, without ever apologizing or copping to anything he'd done.

We fucked around and had more fun than I expected. He embraced me that night, wrapped me up in his mass, his beard, his tats, his gravity. It's true that when Victor and I were together, I felt outmatched. But I also knew he was someone who could give me what I craved. If he wanted to. How could I make him want to? We set a date for me to go back to his place to spend a night partying together.

I know it's fucked up and hard to understand, but the role Victor played in my seroconversion became something that bonded me to him. It was rare for a person to know how they'd contracted HIV. Not only did I know who I got it from, but I knew and remembered the night that it happened.

One of the reasons I decided to start fucking with Victor again was the result of a simple question I asked myself the night we ran into each other at the Hollywood Spa: what was the absolute worst thing that could happen?

The worst that could happen had always been the same thing: I could catch HIV. But I'd already done that. The worst had already happened. That's what I thought, anyway.

I also believed that if I returned to Victor's apartment and partied with him, I could handle the situation differently. I could maintain control, manage it correctly, and walk away again, knowing that this time I'd conquered it. I wouldn't have this specter of victimhood hovering over my head for the rest of my life.

I returned to Victor's apartment several times and we partied. But the experience changed in numerous ways that all happened concurrently. It was a lot to notice, so I didn't notice it all at once, but I did come to notice it all over time.

We had a routine: I'd show up, we'd party, we'd watch porn, we'd get naked, I'd hit the bathroom to do a spot check and freshen up if necessary, and then we'd fuck, in that order. After I returned, though, we didn't always follow the same routine.

I'd show up, we'd party, we'd watch porn, we'd get naked, I'd go hit the bathroom to do a spot check and freshen up if necessary, and then maybe we'd fuck, or maybe we'd just fuck around.

Then Victor would leave the room to go do something else but tell me to make myself at home and get comfortable. Sometimes I'd wind up masturbating by myself, other times when I didn't, he'd come back into the room and we'd get back to fucking around, but then he'd leave me alone again and I'd keep going by myself.

I began experiencing side effects I'd never had before.

I heard men's voices reacting to sexual activity we were engaged in, as well as noises in the apartment that I couldn't make sense of. I'd hear things, and look for the source, but nothing was there.

One night I arrived and Victor was wearing a white doo rag wrapped around his head that hung down over the back of his neck. He almost looked like a sultan. We partied, watched porn, got naked. I hit the bathroom to do a spot check and rejoined him on the mattress.

Then I was standing up, facing a young Latino guy who didn't look any older than twenty or so. He was nude like I was and wearing the same doo rag Victor had been wearing. I had my hands up on each side of my face, and was wiggling my fingers, making noise like you do when you make faces at a little kid.

The guy made a different face and sound, performing different gestures with his hands. He stopped and seemed to be waiting for me to imitate what he'd just done. But I didn't imitate him. I was looking at his face, thinking, who is this guy? It wasn't Victor.

I saw the moment the guy realized I'd snapped out of it because his eyes widened, then he got down on the floor in a fetal position with his head resting in his arms and his face hidden from me. The door to the bathroom area opened, but no one came through it. Instead, the guy on the floor got up and darted through the door, which closed again.

I stood there, looking around the living room, disoriented, not knowing what time it was or what had been happening or who that guy was. The door swung open again, and out came Victor, smiling, with his white doo rag on. *How's it going?* he asked me.

"Who was that?" I asked.

Who was who?

Another night I was caught up in all the usual stuff, partying, porn, sex. I opened my eyes, I was facing the television, and I saw a guy to my right, retreating into the corner of the room, crouching down more and more until he shrank and faded into the corner. Then Victor stepped between us and said, *Look at me, Ray,* as he moved slowly in the opposite direction.

And I did, for a moment. He was asking me a question, and as he did, I glanced back into the corner at the silhouette still crouched there and stared at it. Victor said my name more sharply. *Ray!* Drawing my attention back to his face, asking me another question, and I pretended to listen, but I was thinking, there must be other people here. And realizing, this isn't the first time I've noticed that.

Things had become nonsensical. I couldn't explain what was happening. It was like dream logic had taken over. And yet, my impulse was not to wake up from the dream, remove myself from it and walk away, but to instead keep returning to Victor's and try to manage the dream until I managed it correctly.

I kept respawning into Victor's apartment with the same mission each time. But I kept getting killed. It got to where I told myself that the goal would be to just make it to the first checkpoint without passing out. To stay awake until I could find out what was happening.

I started suspecting something else might be going on. How could I pass out while high on tina? It made no sense.

On my penultimate visit to Victor's, things started off as usual. Partying, porn, fucking around. Then I opened my eyes, I was making noise. Victor was fucking me hard, he was gripping my face, sweating, panting, saying, *Ray! Shut up! You're being too loud.*

The last night I saw Victor, I decided to do something I knew would stop anything weird from happening. I didn't freshen up before I went over there. When he told me to go do a spot check, I went into the bathroom and rinsed out once, but that was it.

We got back to watching porn, and then he was telling me to go back into the bathroom and rinse out again. I did, but only once, which wasn't enough. Again, I sat down on the couch to watch some more porn.

Then I heard Victor's voice saying, *You should clean up and get dressed. It's time to go.*

I wasn't usually asked to leave Victor's place before I'd had enough time to sober up, but I guess that night I'd worn out my welcome.

I was too fucked up to drive home, so I drove down Cahuenga to Hollywood and got a room at the Hollywood Spa. I went to my room, laid down, and passed out. I was in and out of consciousness for a few hours, seeing all kinds of things each time I came out of it.

I called Victor the next day. He didn't pick up. After the beep, I left a long, rambling message on his answering machine. I told him don't call me again. I told him I didn't know what the fuck was going on, but I was done trying to figure it out. I told him I didn't want anything to do with him.

He called me back immediately.

What's wrong?

"You don't think very highly of me, do you?"

Of course I do. Come over tonight.

"Why? So you can knock me out?"

Tonight'll be different.

"Every night's different."

Tonight'll be more different.

It was unheard of for him to ask me to come hang out on two consecutive nights. I always had the impression Victor's calendar was very full, planned out weeks in advance. My instincts told me something was afoot and that I needed to steer clear of Victor from that point forward.

"Don't call me anymore." I hung up.

AFTERCORE

He'd used me, deceived me, assaulted me, fucked with me, and I was still on the outside looking in. I had no idea the extent of what he may have done to me, or who he may have done it with. My attempts to crack the code and get in with Victor had failed. But I was done hitting my head up against this avatar for what I eventually realized was my dad.

My feelings and compulsions for Victor felt outsized and unexplainable at the time. They hit me like sledgehammers, leaving me broken, crippled and unable to achieve any sense of balance. Even though I saw, interacted with and recognized Victor as Victor, subconsciously I was engaging with my dad.

Victor was intoxicating to me because he was all the things my dad had been: unreadable, intimidating, dangerous.

But this time he was choosing me. That's what it felt like, anyway. That's how bad I needed that feeling.

Victor remained five steps ahead of me the whole time I knew him. If we'd been playing the same game, I might have been able to catch up with him. I might have had a chance.

Victor was a blind spot. He managed to get past all my gatekeepers, all my strategic thinking, all my lines of defense. And once he was in, he could do whatever he wanted.

I didn't realize he'd made it into the control room. I didn't even think to look for him there. The call was coming from inside the house, but I was outside, chasing my dad up the street.

Victor knew what I needed from him, and he dangled the promise of it in front of me, just beyond my reach. He used it to lure me into his game and then watched as I frantically tried to grab it. I was stuck in a game I didn't even know I'd fallen into. The longer he failed to deliver, the harder I tried to win.

For years, I felt gaslit by gay men I told about what had happened between Victor and me. I find it strange now that in almost every conversation I had with other gay men about it, none of us used the word "rape." It was like we were honoring an unspoken homo code that said we never say the R word about another homosexual.

The fact that I'd gone over there with the intent of partying with Victor seemed to justify his actions, as far as most people I told were concerned. They characterized it as an unfortunate life lesson that needed learning. Or as a consequence of my lapse in judgement. They dismissed my strong feelings about it as overblown, melodramatic and misplaced. After all, what did I think was going to happen?

The only exception to this gay male conventional wisdom was Travis, who had no qualms about calling it what it was. Travis had his own gothic neo-noir adventures in tweaking to recover from, so this was something we could bond over.

We'd stay up late into the night, watching 1980s sci-fi horror movies, drinking beer, regaling one another with tales of all the surreal tweaker nightmares we'd survived, and hammering out the details of our revenge fantasies.

None of them panned out.

26. Hit It Early, Hit It Hard

I disliked Dr. Foley from the moment I met him, and it's not just because he was the person who eventually broke the news to me that my HIV test came back positive. Although, if I'm being honest, I'll admit that his being the bearer of bad news probably magnified my negative feelings toward him. But they were already there, and he did nothing to stop them or keep them in check.

My hatred of Dr. Foley stemmed, in part, from his vulture-like appearance: the way his shoulders curved forward, the way his Adam's apple bulged sharply out the front of his neck, the way his curly hair hugged his skull so tightly, and at such an odd angle, that his head resembled an unmanicured chia pet.

He also had a robotic communication style, which left the impression that he had been trained in how to communicate verbally with other humans, had then failed the final, but passed the class anyway because whomever he'd been learning from couldn't wait to get him out of there. As time passed, his actions seemed designed to do nothing but fan the flames of my disdain for him. What became most maddening was that it was obvious to me that he didn't care.

I had been so good, so responsible, so careful, for so long, that entertaining the idea that my one indiscretion, with the same person (theoretically), would result in the outcome I'd been successfully avoiding for the past thirteen years, seemed absurd. I'd become so disoriented by my experience with Victor that the outcome I was now faced with seemed not only grossly unfair, but impossible to process.

Dr. Foley's handling of the Big Announcement was indicative of his approach to me as a patient. I sat in that sterile doctor's office, waiting for him to see me, recalling what had happened with Victor, insisting to myself that what was about to happen could not possibly be about to happen, the reality of what had occurred between Victor and me finally starting to sink in.

My head was swimming in a feverish fugue state. Images of Victor on top of me, images of all the times I'd forsaken truly undaunted physical connection with people to avoid this, thoughts of what I was going to tell Eric, relief that we hadn't slept together since I met Victor, disbelief, despair, confusion, panic...I was lost in a raging sea, a storm of mental and emotional chaos, barely listening to Dr. Foley's half-assed attempt, after he finally graced me with his presence, to sound sincere when he said, "Well, unfortunately, your test came back positive."

And not any care to pause here. No time to allow me to catch my breath, gay gasp, burst into tears (not that I would ever display such naked emotion for him, but still), react in some naturally human way.

And then, without even waiting to see what I would say or do, he continued.

"However, this presents us with a *very* exciting opportunity, because we are rarely in a position to catch someone while they are still in the process of seroconversion."

A very exciting opportunity, I heard him say again, in my head, but in slow motion.

Then he laid out his big sales pitch on why I should begin a cocktail regimen immediately; how we needed to hit it early and hit it hard, in order to stop the virus in its tracks, before it replicated and mutated and delivered me, on a silver platter, like a pig with an apple stuffed in my mouth, to a painful, lingering, rotten death so horrible that I couldn't even begin to imagine how awful it would be.

I'm paraphrasing.

His nurse, Cindy, stood silently with her arms folded, trying to appear relaxed and concerned at the same time, guarding the office window as if I might try to throw myself through it upon hearing this news in Dr. Foley's shallow, tinny, pencil-necked voice.

I craved some sort of emotional release. Something on the spectrum between a laugh and a scream, that would only take a moment, but I was unable to decide on one. Then the moment passed.

I sat there, guarded, knowing already that he had his own agenda, which he was too stupid or too insensitive to hide from me. Dr. Foley wanted to make a finding, any finding, a discovery of some sort, any sort, to get his name published in a medical journal, which was something other doctors would see, be impressed by, and heap praise on him for.

At the same time, he and Cindy were throwing me a lifeline, and I knew it. It's just that the conditions of taking it were unclear to me. But there were some things I did know. I knew I'd need to stay alert whenever I dealt with them. I knew I'd be wise to not take anything they said at face value. And I knew that neither one of them was doing this for me.

There we were, facing one another in the examination room at Cedars Sinai that Dr. Foley used when he wasn't working at USC. There we were, sizing each other up. I knew the lines being drawn were permanent, and having been drawn wouldn't shift once I'd signed the consent forms they placed in front of me.

Like I said before though, they were offering me a lifeline. Of course, I grabbed it. The medication could not only possibly save my life, but it was paid for by the study. I'd return every six weeks or so for a blood draw. They'd track my viral load and my CD4 cell count as indicators of what the virus was doing to my body, and what kind of effect the medications were having on me.

My seroconversion occurred at the same time several drug cocktails were just about to hit the market. The previous treatment for HIV and AIDS, AZT, had run its course with mostly ineffective and deadly results. This new round of treatment options provided a glimmer of hope, and there I was, poised to jump in, ready to ride that cutting edge of a treatment wave to see where it took me.

I was given Saquinavir (a protease inhibitor), Ritonavir (a "booster" protease inhibitor) and Lamivudine (a nucleoside reverse transcriptase inhibitor), each to be taken twice a day. The prescriptions were written at such high doses that my body eventually rejected everything I put into it.

I would wake up in the morning with a toxic feeling of having been irradiated. As if I'd just been cooked from the inside out in a microwave oven. I had an awful, metallic taste in my mouth at all times that prevented me from tasting any type of flavor in food or beverages. Even drinking water was unpleasant.

And though my food intake greatly decreased, because it was just too unpleasant an experience to eat, my body eventually became a diarrhea factory. I don't know where it came from because I wasn't eating very much. But I'd have onslaughts of explosive diarrhea where I'd be sitting on the toilet while what felt like gallons of shit came shooting out of my ass. I didn't know my body had the capacity to hold that much of anything. And there was no margin for error when these attacks occurred; if I didn't find a toilet immediately (and a few times, I almost didn't) that diarrhea was happening whether I was ready for it or not.

Blood draws could be a nightmare if Cindy wasn't there because I'd get sent to some neophyte who would stick me repeatedly, trying to get the blood to come out. My veins were easy enough to find, but for some reason once the person taking the blood draw found a vein and stuck me with the needle, the vein would roll out of the needle's path. Other times, they'd get the needle into the vein, but it would close before they'd had a chance to draw the amount of blood they needed.

Cindy always managed to get it on the first try. I don't know what she did differently, but she was an expert. I nominated her for Nurse of the Year at one point for some nurses' association, and she won. She was Aussie, married and had a child during my time in the study at Cedars. I always liked her a lot. She made up for what Dr. Foley lacked in the human interaction skills department.

One day I was skimming through the newspaper Eric subscribed to and came across an article about current HIV treatment efforts. In it, Dr. Foley was featured as a leading provider of HIV treatments that were on the cutting edge of HIV care. He stated in the article that they didn't have any evidence that "hitting it early, hitting it hard" had a measurable impact on how the disease progressed, or whether it was of any benefit to the patient to start treatment early, given the possible long term side effects that the medications often caused.

This statement was the exact opposite of what he'd told me on the day he'd pitched the course of treatment to me.

Outraged, I called Cindy and asked her what the hell was going on. I told her what he'd said in the article contradicted what he'd told me the day I agreed to take part in the study. Cindy insisted that I'd misunderstood what Dr. Foley said when he pitched me on the drug cocktail, and that I must have been in a confused state of mind with everything I was dealing with at the time.

When doctors recommend a course of treatment, they always present it as the best possible course of action. The patient, often ill, feeling desperate, needing guidance, usually goes along with what the doctor recommends. After I saw that article and called Cindy, I knew my instincts about Dr. Foley (that he had his own agenda, that I had to think for myself and not take everything he said to me at face value) were correct.

Cindy, who I'd come to think of as some kind of surrogate friend, was obviously given the task of circling the wagons if anything like this occurred. I guess I couldn't blame her, but it was still disappointing. I had to make a decision, all by myself, because what was best for me wasn't necessarily taking medications at doses that were causing severe side effects and impacting my ability to function from day to day.

Dr. Foley had prescribed this method of treatment to a patient (me) to track its outcome as a method of treatment, and to see what effects it may have on my body, and observe how the course of treatment played out. Whether the outcome was good or bad for me was beside the point. I withdrew from the study and stopped taking medication.

I stayed off HIV medication for close to seven years. I was sexually active during those years but, for the most part, I only hooked up with other HIV positive men. On hook up sites I always identified myself as HIV positive.

I avoided chance in-person hook ups because I knew that I'd always have to disclose and then have that awkward moment when the other person decided whether or not they wanted to risk having sex with me. Men had several approaches to making this decision and how they informed me of that decision: sometimes not wanting to hurt my feelings, other times not giving a shit if they hurt my feelings, and sometimes even going out of their way to hurt my feelings.

There never seemed to be a right moment to disclose my HIV status to men I'd just met, because right after meeting someone, I didn't know if I even wanted to hook up. But after some time together, chatting and flirting and getting to know each other, I felt guilty, as if I'd reeled them in only to spring it on them, putting them on the spot. There was no easy way to have that conversation. It was unpleasant, to say the least, and hooking up online, where I could just put it out there up front, was much easier.

I finally went back on treatment after a subsequent primary care doctor expressed frustration with me for refusing to go back on it even though I was still sexually active. My viral load had been creeping up, but I only slept with other HIV positive men, so I wasn't all that concerned about it.

However, there was speculation at that time about reinfection being a thing, and that reinfection could result in an HIV super bug, a strain of HIV that would be impervious to all known methods of treatment.

My doctor told me that being sexually active with the viral load I had was irresponsible. She was visibly upset with me for having turned down her offer to start back on treatment, and I was taken aback. What her reaction implied was that I had become a risk to public safety. I certainly did not consider myself a risk to public safety because I practiced safe sex and slept primarily with other HIV+ men. But her reaction also triggered some guilt in me: I didn't want to be irresponsible.

I didn't want to feel like I'd been irradiated, either. I discussed treatment with her further, and she explained that the new treatment options had by that time become much less taxing on the bodies of the HIV+ people who took them. Reluctantly, I went on a medication called Atripla, which brought my viral load down to undetectable, where it stayed.

Since I became HIV+ more than twenty-five years ago, treatment options have expanded, as has knowledge about HIV strains and the behavior of the virus.

If there's anything I can thank Victor and Dr. Foley for, it's being major catalysts in my life that forced me to examine my assumptions about being queer, about the queer community as a support resource, about queer male hook up culture, about my behavior within those realms, and my beliefs about the type of queer man I thought I should be, and why. All of which led, eventually, to greater acceptance and understanding of my queerness and myself.

The queer people who perished from AIDS-related illnesses didn't have access to the drug cocktails I've come to rely on to extend my life far past the point once expected for a person with HIV. We can thank the activists among them for pressuring the U.S. government to get those treatment options to the public. They fought like hell for all of us, even though many of them died before they could reap the benefits of what they sowed.

The only reason effective treatment options became available when they did is because a broad coalition of queer, feminist, and allied activist groups banded together, shared information, agreed upon plans of action, and carried out those plans.

Queer activists and their allies drew attention to the U.S. government's shameful failure to act, the pharmaceutical companies' price gouging of treatment options, and the bureaucratic dereliction of government agencies that used the ruse of adherence to proper procedures as an excuse to justify their lack of responsiveness.

Activists disrupted and often halted (if only temporarily) several operations, with actions conducted at the New York Stock Exchange, the Centers for Disease Control, the National Institutes for Health, Burroughs Wellcome (the pharmaceutical company that offered AZT as a treatment method, then charged astronomical prices for it), the Democratic and Republican National Conventions, and a controversial action that interrupted a mass at St. Patrick's Cathedral, which generated international press coverage. Activists also shut down the Food & Drug Administration with a targeted action that is considered one of the most effective single acts of civil disobedience in the history of advocacy for American health care.

As a result of some of these actions, the price of AZT was significantly reduced. The FDA changed its policy on how they managed experimental drug access and implemented faster drug approval processes. The CDC expanded the definition of HIV/AIDS, which was initially defined by symptoms experienced by queer men. This limited focus on symptoms in males led to women with HIV/AIDS being systematically excluded from diagnosis, from drug trials, and from disability benefits, because women often had a different set of symptoms. The expanded definition also resulted in women with HIV/AIDS gaining access to treatment and disability benefits, as well as more accurate numbers of HIV/AIDS infections and deaths being reported.

Queer people and their allies did that. It wasn't politicians or CEOs or billionaires who made it happen. It was us. That's how effective queer and allied activists can be when they work together. We as a collective forced the government to act at a time when it was hell bent on looking the other way. We forced the government to act on our behalf. That's how much power we flexed.

From 1982 (when I turned 16) through 1996 (when I turned 30), over 375,900 people in the U.S. died of AIDS. That's roughly the equivalent of the entire population of New Orleans. Every person. Every neighborhood. Wiped out in the span of just 15 years.

Any impact I can make, any good I can help bring to the world, will always be in memory of my queer brothers, sisters, siblings and allies who didn't survive the plague that the U.S. government refused to acknowledge, and made no attempt to stop, until those same queer people and their allies forced them to.

They tried to kill us off, but they failed. It's a recurring theme in queer history.

27. Spin

■

LAUREN:

She's in her mid-40s. Straight red hair in a pageboy cut. Friendly, always smiling. Leads spin class on Monday and Wednesday nights. She doesn't use a microphone because she doesn't need to. Her voice is loud and clear and heard by everyone in the studio.

Lauren mixes it up a lot, music-wise. She also employs a lot of variation in her routines. She's not just phoning it in. She's probably one of the original graduates from the Jane Fonda school of aerobics instructors, only she pivoted to spin class when she needed to. She thinks ahead. You know the type. She's hardcore without being obnoxious about it. She makes you feel good about being there.

Lauren broke a mirror during class this week while repositioning an exercise bike, and she said the gym would probably take it out of her paycheck. Was she joking or telling the truth? It wouldn't surprise me. This gym really seems to be cutting corners lately. She got right back on her bike at the front of the studio and told us to keep going.

◆◆◆

Vanessa:

She's in her late 50s. She's as tall as I am and has an impressive pair of tits that'll knock you on your ass if you don't see them coming. Vanessa's tits were her calling card back in the day. She's a former first runner up in the Miss America pageant circa the early 1970s.

She has an impressive list of television guest spot appearance credits from an era when television meant something to people: *Harry-O*, *The Rockford Files*, *Fantasy Island*, *CHiPs*, *Mannix*, *Starsky and Hutch*. Vanessa even starred in an episode of *Kojak*. In her guest spots, she usually played a temporary love interest or a hooker. Her IMDB page does not disappoint.

She sat next to Johnny Carson on *The Tonight Show* once and chatted with him, charming the pants off Johnny and even getting a few hearty laughs from the audience.

Vanessa eventually created a line of exclusive jeweled handbags that became all the rage on red carpets during the mid-to-late 1990s. She has a portfolio filled with dozens of photos of actors and other celebrities posing on red carpets, adorned with or holding the jeweled pieces from her line.

She's still in the game but having to fight tooth and nail to stay there. She's fallen prey to that scourge that befalls many designers of clothing and accessories these days: knockoffs. There are merchants in New York City who have fancy storefronts that are filled with "discounted" items, including Vanessa's jeweled handbags, but the items on their shelves are cheap, unauthorized knockoffs, manufactured in China and imported at prices so low that it would be more scandalous if they weren't such great deals.

Vanessa has filed civil suits against several businesses who sell knockoffs of her work, as well as distributors who help get the pirated items to market.

On the verge of bankruptcy, she sometimes can't pay the migrant workers she employs when payday rolls around. These workers sit in the work area of her Beverly Hills office and help fulfill orders by painstakingly applying Swarovski crystals by hand to the items that have been ordered. She finds herself having to rob Peter to pay Paul, and the stress is getting to her. She's prone to dramatic fits of sobbing and angry outbursts about the unfairness of it all.

Even so, her items on eBay still cost a mint. On the rare occasions they appear on the site, they get snatched up before you can even place a bid. I sometimes wonder if she lists them herself.

She's a proud and accomplished woman, still beautiful, very fit, a Republican and born-again christian, though you'd never know it from having a casual conversation with her. She's genuinely friendly and pleasant, and she doesn't appear to have an ill-intentioned bone in her gorgeous body. For someone who is hanging on to the edge of a cliff for dear life by her exquisitely manicured fingernails, she manages to put up an admirable front of bravery and determination. I admire her for it.

NICK:

He appears in a grainy video of poor quality, in images that appear to stretch out and then jump forward on the screen. He's just a kid, although at one time in my life, when I was much younger, I would have considered him over the hill.

They stand behind him and keep talking in what I assume is their native Arab tongue. I don't know what language or what dialect it is. They keep talking, though, blah, blah, blah, like I give a shit about what they're saying. Their message must be important, though. Important enough to have done what they're about to do.

The ending of the video is inevitable. It's already happened. It's been broadcast and uploaded to YouTube, discussed and analyzed on cable news shows, argued about by various talking heads who self-identify as experts. The act is done, there's no changing the outcome. Even if I pause the video to delay my bearing witness to the incident, even if I stop the video and don't watch it at all. It's done. I can't change that.

I look at his face staring back at me through the camera lens, through my computer screen, through time. The young man I'm observing is alive in the video. Does he know, in these moments I'm watching, that this is it? Will it come as a surprise? Why is he so calm and why does he keep shrugging his shoulders, as if it's a nervous tic? Did they give him some kind of drug so his guard would be down, so he wouldn't fight back? So he wouldn't care as much about what was happening.

I watch the video because I have to. It's the least I can do. I can at least glimpse a small piece of the horror that is happening over there every day. The horror that we're inflicting upon them. Everyone I know has watched the video or plans to watch it. It's a thing.

The sound is down low but still audible. The sound is always the worst part. Whenever I watch horror movies, I cover my ears, not my eyes. The sounds are often worse than the images. And in this video, it's no different.

After his captors finish speaking, they tackle him to the ground, out of frame, but he's screaming. He's screaming for his life. It's the first time I hear the real sound of a man screaming for his life. He's screaming for longer than I expected him to scream, if I expected him to scream at all. I didn't know what to expect. But the screams go on for longer than I expect, and then they stop just as abruptly as they started.

And then before I have a chance to wonder what's about to happen, his severed head is lifted into the frame by one of his captors, who speaks some more in what I again assume is his native Arab language, as the head dangles and spins, slightly off center in the frame. Whoever's holding it is holding it by the hair.

Nick's head looks like a prop. I have a quick, hopeful thought that maybe it's a prop. Maybe Nick is okay, maybe this is all some elaborate prank. But it isn't. The image becomes distorted, gray blade-shaped lines shatter the image on the screen, and then it goes black, and the video is over.

I sit, unmoving, staring at the screen.

JUNO:

Juno is of Asian descent, that's about as specific as I can get. If I had to guess, I'd say he's probably Korean. He's in his mid-30s, lean and muscular like a runner, and wears black bicycle shorts when he heads up spin class on Tuesday and Thursday nights. He uses a microphone on a headset and speaks broken English, but he gets A's for enunciation and enthusiasm. I admire anyone who comes to this country of assholes and has the temerity to make a life for themselves.

Juno favors long, steady climbs and classic rock. The warm-up song is Pink Floyd's "Breathe." In case we miss the point, Juno implores us to "Breathe! Breathe!" during the song's vocal breaks.

I'm here because this is what I do. If I don't do it, I'll be consumed by all the things I have no control over and sink back into a deep depression that I can't even flirt with at this point. The last one was so deep, there was a period of time that I couldn't see a way out of it. I had no hope that I could get back. I had no concept of what getting back could be or look like.

I refuse to sink back into that pit. I refuse. He's dead, I'm alive. Maybe when Nick saw what was happening over there, and his reaction was to see it as an opportunity to generate some profit from it, and to go there in pursuit of financial gain, maybe that wasn't the correct response to have. I'm sure he knew the risks. But how much money could be worth that much risk? Anyway, he's dead. I'm alive. Maybe I'll do something meaningful to justify my existence.

I notice that the broken mirror has been replaced since Monday night's spin class. Juno says "Up! Up!" and we all raise our asses off our bicycle seats and pedal in standing positions to the sound of "Sweet Home Alabama."

I breathe and I pedal and I sweat.

What else can I do?

28. BRAD!

○

MEETFUCK

Brad and I met late one night at a North Hollywood dive bar. We were getting drunk and chatting each other up, talking about music, movies and the college experience. He'd entered college at a later age than was the norm, just like I had, so we had quite a bit to discuss.

One thing quickly led to another: when you know, you know. You both give the green light and it's not even a matter of when, but where. I told him he looked like Vince Vaughn (who was young and goofy-hot at the time), and in between a couple of rounds, we went out and fucked in the back of his Astro minivan. We decided we were meant to be and hit the ground running heads first into our relationship.

Brad had already graduated from college when I met him. His degree was in film and media studies, and he lived in Burbank with a couple of roommates with whom he'd gone to college. They all had studio jobs and were starting out on the bottom rung, hoping to work their way up through the ranks.

Brad's roomies, as well as all his former classmates, were straight. Brad had never come out to them, but to my surprise and delight (lucky me!), he decided to come out after we started dating. Being the First Gay Boyfriend to someone's family or social circle really did suck back then. I played that role in a few relationships and became the target of some people's ire as a result.

The ones with the biggest problem with it all focused on me as the outlet for their homophobic feelings when the guy they thought they knew and loved turned out to be a fag. Brad's straight roommates all went through their requisite period of pearl clutching, when they reevaluated their friendships with Brad and calculated all the times Brad may have had the opportunity to see their dicks in the locker room or whatever, and having feelings about that.

Brad and I started off on the right foot. We always managed to have fun together. We'd rent 1970s movies from a video store in Toluca Lake near his apartment. We watched great movies from the era like *The Ritz* (a mob comedy that takes place in a gay bathhouse*)*, *Kansas City Bomber* and *Mother Juggs and Speed* (both starring Raquel Welch), *Can't Stop the Music* (starring the Village People) and many others. We developed script ideas together, and while we never finished any of them, we had great fun putting scenes together and doing everything we could to make them funny.

For about six months I tried to birth a screenplay I called *Femalien*. It was an updated take on 1950s science fiction creature features like *Tarantula*, *Invaders from Mars* and *Invasion of the Body Snatchers*. It centered on a voluptuous beauty named Veronica, whose body is taken over by an alien that turns her into a bloodthirsty mantrap who feeds on all the hot but chauvinistic and rapey male humans in her small Arizona town.

Aside from Veronica, the primary characters were a Black mayor who was always looking for ways to bring in tourists to increase the town's revenue, and a pair of local good old boys named Booger and Hoss, whose homoerotically charged relationship was a running gag. There was a big set piece finale in the ancient lava caves just outside of town, where our heroes save the day by figuring out how to cause a contained volcanic eruption, which kills the alien inside the caves. I intended to make it so that Veronica survived her ordeal, but I never got around to writing that part.

I later learned the title had already been used for a movie in 1996, and while I managed to complete a good opening, some great scenes and about forty-five minutes of screen time, I never finished it. I had a great time working on it, though, even if I did come to realize that screenwriting is not my forte.

Brad and I were a great team when we got along. Brad ushered in some of the most stable, productive, and fun years of my life. He also had a habit of disregarding personal boundaries and baiting me into arguments that could escalate and turn physical. Eventually, the question became, is there any way on God's green Earth that I can actually make this dumpster fire of a relationship work? It would take me a while to find out.

◆◆◆

Y2K

It was the New Millenium. The age of blogs, Occupy, MySpace, Britney, and eventually, the emergence of Gaga. On top of all that, the fight for marriage equality was raging full force.

Brad and I co-owned a house in Reseda. I was on the mortgage, even though my income was significantly less than Brad's. Still, I contributed the same percentage of my income to the household that Brad did. I had my first job after graduating with my B.A. It was a luxury to have a day job and work Monday through Friday, with evenings and weekends off, after so many years of juggling multiple part time jobs that rarely afforded me even a day off, let alone a weekend.

Despite a good amount of compatibility, as daily companions and in the bedroom, Brad and I were prone to messy arguments that could escalate quickly. Brad, like my last two long-term boyfriends, came from an upper middle-class background, and he often felt entitled to inhabit a space within our relationship that subjugated me to second class status.

His digs at my background, my family dynamics, and my insecurities as I tried to function properly in the L.A. social circles we ran in (which were industry-centered and filled with numerous twenty-somethings from affluent families) were triggers that could set me off in an instant.

When we argued, Brad expected me to cave up front, but instead, I'd push back, refuse to back down, and throw insults back at him, matching him shot for shot. A former drag queen and activist from Seattle, Brad was, by his very nature, dramatic. When he was on my side, things were wonderful between us. When he turned on me or tried to demean me into submission, things got ugly.

While in college, I held down several jobs simultaneously to get by. I delivered the *L.A. Weekly* newspaper each Wednesday, picking them up in Santa Clarita and delivering them on a route that covered parts of Burbank, Toluca Lake and North Hollywood. I had to make 3 trips to get it done, and the heavy loads I carried effectively destroyed the light pickup truck I drove at the time.

I worked server shifts at a Cali Pizza located in Burbank, and on weekends I provided in-home care for a wheelchair user by helping him get out of bed, showered and dressed for the day. On top of all these shifts, I was also attending classes full-time at L.A. Valley College and, eventually, CSUN.

Part of our problem was that we socialized in bars a lot. I also worked at a couple of gay drinking establishments in the Valley during this period, working my way up the slippery ladder from barback to cocktail waitress to bartender.

Even outside my bartending shifts, we'd meet up with friends for karaoke or just to hang out and get drunk. Brad and I used to recite a line from the 1970s T.V. sitcom *Maude*, starring Bea Arthur (Dorothy from *The Golden Girls*), which Maude herself delivered to her husband: "We're a drinking couple, Walter!" And so were Brad and me.

By this time, I'd curbed my binge drinking and could better pace myself, but it was still a coping mechanism to smooth out the edges of my social anxiety, as well as a release valve that helped me manage the pain and trauma baggage I was still carrying. For many years, drinking did the trick and helped get me through life without completely self-destructing.

I'm lucky I had a taste for draft beer more than anything else. Though I'd occasionally consume mixed drinks, or throw back the random shot, I pretty much limited my drinking to beer most of the time. It filled me up, it got me happy drunk and didn't cost as much as liquor.

Brad and I weren't mean drunks, but we could both be hot heads, and we both refused to back down; Brad because he was stubborn and felt entitled to win every argument we ever had. And me because I was right.

But I must sing Brad's praises, as well. It wasn't all drunken arguments and misery! Brad was excellent at managing money, much better than I've ever been. I handed my paychecks over to him and he'd manage finances. Our bills always got paid, we were able to take pleasure trips at regular intervals, and whenever things fell into a slump, we could take a spontaneous shopping trip somewhere and, even though we bought stuff, we didn't have to worry that we were breaking the bank. Brad was very good at being frugal in certain respects, and that frugality allowed for a lot of trips and purchases that more careless spending would have deprived us of.

Regular jaunts to Vegas and Palm Springs were standard fare. We'd stay at a new hotel each time we went to Vegas, progressing from the Stratosphere to Treasure Island to New York, New York, to Luxor. Not the fanciest joints in town, necessarily, but fancy enough for me.

Brad took me on my first trips to New York and London, as well. The New York trips were great fun. Brad was a musical theater queen through and through. He LOVED Patti LuPone (probably still does) and modeled much of his behavior after her diva antics, I've no doubt!

One of the reasons for our trip to New York was to see her in a revival of *Sweeney Todd*. The staging was minimalist, very artsy, and LuPone was LuPone. Brad loved it, I got through it. The other production we saw on that trip, *The 25th Annual Putnam County Spelling Bee*, was more my speed.

The London trip, while marred by some drunken arguments I'd rather forget, had many more high points than low points. I gained like ten pounds from chocolate, bangers, mash and ale, but it was worth it.

While out drinking one night with our hosts, I got the hots for a blond bartender who took a liking to me after we discussed the favorable reputation Americans enjoyed in Europe for giving good head.

That night, after the pub closed, I blew this Australian bartender from a London pub under a bridge that crossed the River Thames. I asked Brad if it was okay before I did it, and he said it was fine. We didn't make a habit of having sex outside the relationship, but we could, and sometimes did, let things happen on the fly, if we gave each other the courtesy of asking for permission first.

Brad also got me into karaoke, which I loved, because I'd always wanted to perform for a crowd, and karaoke made that possible. Even though Brad would get up there and belt out some Broadway show tunes every time we went out, he wasn't just a Broadway diva. One of his favorite songs to perform was "One Week" by Barenaked Ladies. It was a crowd-pleaser, and he always performed it quite well.

My favorite numbers to perform were "Buffalo Stance" by Neneh Cherry and "All I Wanna Do" by Sheryl Crow. I sang "Buffalo Stance" while inhabiting the most oblivious white guy persona I could muster, to great comedic effect as far as I was concerned. Some people got it. I sang "All I Wanna Do" straight and had a great time with it because it's such fun to sing. I loved it.

◆◆◆

FOCUS ON THE FAMILY

When I was in my twenties and thirties, I gravitated toward men who already had their shit together or were just about to get there. Two of them eventually became attorneys, so they were ambitious, disciplined and strong-willed. These are qualities I felt I needed to develop in myself, so it stands to reason that I was attracted to men who already seemed to possess them.

I had three major relationships during that period of my life, including the ones with Eric and Brad. All three came from affluent, upper middle-class families. Their fathers were corporate executives, none of their mothers worked outside the home, and none of their parents were divorced. Also, each of their mothers suffered from some kind of severe behavioral, mental health, or substance related disorder that caused them a significant amount of mental and emotional anguish. From what I could tell, it was kinda the norm.

My concept of family at that point was what you might call "minimalist," save for some time being involved with my sister and her two sons when they were young.

When I was brought into these guys' family environments, it was a shock to my system, and something to which I had to work very hard to adjust. Eric's parents disliked me from the get-go because I was the first boyfriend he'd ever introduced them to or lived with.

In their eyes, I was the young homosexual who swished into their lives and, with my wicked fairy wings and mad cocksucking skills, forever corrupted their cherished first-born son. I was treated accordingly. Not with overt hostility, mind you, but they made it clear they were merely tolerating my presence until Eric came to his senses and cast me out.

Though Eric had been raised upper middle class, his parents' roots were decidedly blue collar. His parents had married young, his Dad had co-founded a business that took off, and pretty soon, they were set for life. They'd been living the capitalist dream ever since.

Whenever I accompanied Eric to their home for a family gathering, I may as well have been on Planet Jupiter. I had no frame of reference for how they lived or behaved, and I was too crippled by insecurity and social anxiety to do much more than hang out at the perimeter of the room and wait until Eric was ready to leave.

Brad's parents were different. They gave off airs of having been born into the upper middle class and knew how to navigate its spaces effortlessly. I never got to know them very well. His dad was affable, his mom, high strung and volatile. After the first time they came for a visit, and were safely on their way to the airport, I told Brad, "Oh my God. I understand now why you are the way you are." I steered clear of his dramatic mother, who was frequently at the center of family crises and dramas. I didn't want to engage with her because I knew she'd turn on me as soon as she found a reason to.

I also got to know Brad's sister, her then-husband and their three kids. They had a family dynamic that was very grounded. Whereas Brad had emerged from the family home, taking with him his mother's flair for drama and his father's ambition, his sister appeared to have decided to go in the opposite direction. She allowed her kids to grow into who they were without putting them under pressure to meet performance standards, socially or at school, as her own mother had done to her. She was extremely kind to me. From day one, she treated me like a member of the family. At the time, that type of treatment by family members was a new experience for me. I enjoyed it immensely.

I got the sense that when Brad's and Eric's parents looked at me, all they saw was some trashy bitch from the wrong side of the tracks, an interloper who was clearly out of his element. Both their fathers seemed to have sized me up upon meeting me and determined that engaging with me in any meaningful way would be nothing but a waste of their time, so they didn't. The same went for both their mothers. At the time, I attributed their mothers' lack of interest in me to the fact that they both pretty much always did what their husbands told them to.

Both their fathers held sway over their respective families in a way I'd never witnessed in my own. They held all the financial power, which meant Eric and Brad were beholden to them. As strong-willed and confident as they could be on the stages of their own lives, they both knew when it was time to bend the knee to their fathers and didn't hesitate to do so if it would get them what they needed. Their egos didn't factor into those moments, and I admired them for that because I couldn't imagine doing it myself.

Over the years I spent being the live-in boyfriend of these guys who came from upper middle-class families, I recognized the familiar feeling that I was pretty much couch surfing through their families' lives, never gaining much traction or being integrated into their family structures the way my heterosexual counterparts were. It was similar to the dynamic between me and my own parents. They were indifferent to me, and I didn't expect anything more, so I wasn't disappointed.

When I expressed my observations to Eric and Brad regarding their family dynamics, and how I fit (or didn't fit, as the case appeared to be) into them, and how I was pretty sure it was due to me being working class, they heard me out but were dismissive of the notion that there was any manifestation of class disparity, or even consciousness, occurring. I don't think they could see it because they'd never been excluded from it. They didn't know what it looked like from the outside.

With the sole exception of Brad's sister, my relationships with Eric and Brad didn't enjoy the cachet or legitimacy in their families that the heterosexual relationships did. Same-sex relationships at that time did not yet have, in most heterosexuals' eyes, the patina of legitimacy their own relationships enjoyed. At best, gay relationships were treated as uncharted territory, a curiosity. At worst, we were treated as imposters trying to destroy the sanctity of marriage from the hands of upstanding heterosexuals. It was like being your boyfriend's coming out boyfriend to his family, but ramped up to a thousand.

◆◆◆

Stepping Out

The problem with Brad was that he was too quick to hit me below the belt, and this is a common thread that ran through several (though not all) of my relationships back then.

When I'm in a relationship with someone, I expect us to operate in accordance with a code of conduct, a set of ground rules, lines that are not to be crossed. This is a baseline of mutual respect that we both should be able to take for granted, since we've agreed to be partners.

Me, I'm the type who will give that person the benefit of the doubt. Perhaps it was a slip up. He might have been a bit drunk. Maybe he was just having a bad day. The problem is, once it happens the first time and you let it pass, if that's the kind of guy you're with, it begins to occur repeatedly, and with more vitriol.

Brad and I had a lot of great times together, and that sustained us for most of the relationship. But we were a highly combustible mix, and eventually, to me anyway, the arguments became pointless and just seemed to be exercises in trying to inflict mental and emotional damage on one another.

When he was angry, Brad had no problem with saying things designed to make me feel devalued and worthless. Each time that happens in a relationship, it erodes the bond between the partners who are in it. Unless you're a masochist (and I am not), you can only stand so many transgressions. After that, all bets are off.

By the time I was out trolling on hook up sites again, I had pretty much checked out on Brad and was formulating exit strategies. The cracks in my relationship with Brad were real gapers, and we'd soldiered on for as long as we could. I admit, I made this decision unilaterally. But as far as I was concerned,

Brad had pissed away any additional second chances I'd set aside for him. By the time I told him I was moving out, it was already a done deal.

Having struggled my entire adult life to climb out of my house-poor, trailer park origins, I was overly sensitive to Brad's efforts to keep me in my place, not only within the bounds of our relationship but also in a way I believed was motivated by an unconscious need to reassert class norms.

Still, my fight for upward mobility was real. I was trying to achieve something that was more than what I'd known. What I'd lived in my whole life felt decidedly subpar, but I still wasn't sure exactly what I was aiming for, and I had to admit, I hadn't even reached the level my parents had been living at when they raised me.

I wanted a partner and a home. I wanted to be happy. The jury was still out on whether I could obtain those things in a way that meant I had a stable, fulfilling life. Was that even allowed for someone like me?

29. Cool (Former) Sk8er Guncle

■

WIPED OUT

"Are you okay Uncle Ray?" he asks breathlessly, his hands on his knees, his blurry face coming into focus. His voice is at a pitch halfway between panic and delight, and I must suppress my urge to howl like a wounded animal. I must blink back tears that threaten to flow from my eyes, which are stinging and feel like they've been pounded into their sockets with a hammer.

I want to be the boy right now, but I can't be. I give him the best smile I can muster. "Ouch."

He accepts my smile and "Ouch" as a sign that everything is okay. "Wow! You really shoulda seen that! Wow! You really flew!" He's bursting with pride for me. I have once again proven myself worthy of his seven-year-old attentions.

"I did see it," I tell him, struggling to get up.

"You're bleeding," he says, pointing to my right leg, which, from knee to ankle is a colorful mix of torn skin, blood and algae from the shady inlet that I landed in. My devastated shin howls. It may as well be on fire.

"Wow, your leg's bleeding a lot!" he exclaims, impressed.

I grit my teeth instead of saying, "No shit," but bite my tongue in the process, then say it anyway. "Ow! No shit!"

He giggles, excited by my use of profanity. "No shit!" he exclaims.

"No S-word," I manage, and yelp when I try to put weight on my injured leg in an effort to stand up. Sensing the level of pain that I'm in, he complies.

I remain seated, gingerly, on what's left of my ass, not able to feel where it begins or ends, because after I slid across the cement and over the edge of the inlet, I tried to save myself by twisting around and landing on my backside, hoping it would absorb most of the impact.

He sets his hand on my knee, and I flinch violently, pushing him away and saying, "Don't touch! It hurts."

It hurts, yes. But the blood. That's the issue. It's an issue I'm not prepared to deal with.

"Sorry, Uncle Ray. I'll get your board."

WALL OF DECKS

I bought the board, on a whim, at the outlet mall after walking into Phoenix Skate & Surf. The minute the door closed behind me, I was free of the outside world and dropped into an adolescent hellscape that was dipped in angst and packaged to sell as many units as possible. I responded to it immediately. I felt thirteen again. *Damn*, I thought to myself with a flutter of excitement in my belly, *these kids today are off their meds*.

The music was loud and obnoxious: heavy metal with guitars that sounded like they'd been processed through a computer, and staccato vocals ("WAH-AH-AH-AH!") that sounded like they'd been surgically inserted into the song. The vocalizations were short bursts that sounded completely out of context but were implanted seamlessly into the track so that it sounded like a well-oiled machine of mechanized rage.

The clothing was covered in skulls, reapers and a wide range of evil-looking cartoon characters. It also appeared to only be available in shades of black, dark grey and a deep, bloody crimson that I half expected to drip down and collect in puddles on the floor.

I was drawn to the back wall of the store as if following a beacon because I could see all the decks on it, arranged vertically to showcase their artwork. As I walked toward them, I took notice of two clerks, each at an opposite end of the store, both of whom behaved as if I wasn't there, which was fine with me. I didn't want to be bothered. I reached the back counter and rested my elbows on it, leaning forward to examine the wall of decks.

◆◆◆

ANT

When I was thirteen years old, way back in 1979, I had a friend named Cody that I'd known since fourth grade. Our shared history as classmates was the main reason we remained friends, but by the time we were in 9th grade, we didn't have all that much in common.

Cody got straight As, was an alarmingly proficient guitar player, and excelled at basketball, track & field, and just about any other thing he decided to do. I envied him for his discipline and his output, be it class work, music or athletic prowess. But I could tell I bored him.

I didn't view the world or think with the same kind of intellect that he did. He could grasp the big picture or dive down into the detailed minutia of any project to which he had committed himself. I just wanted to hang out at the Big O and not think about anything.

Cody's older brother Ant had become much more interesting to me than Cody. Ant was so cool. He was tall and lanky, lean and muscular, with big veins that popped out on his forearms and biceps. Like most of us, he had a deep, rich tan from countless days by the pool or at the beach during summer vacation. His blond hair was almost dark enough to be brown, and whenever he took his shirt off, I enjoyed seeing the fur that was growing outward from the center of his chest.

There was also the patch of fur just beneath his belly button that led down to a mysterious place beneath the waistline of those loose board shorts he was always wearing, which always hung so low on his hips that they seemed to be teasing me with the possibility of seeing some bush if I was patient. I'd been patient for a few weeks that summer but still hadn't seen any.

Ant was leaving for college in the fall, and Cody called me to let me know Ant was looking to sell his board because he was about to be a college man, and college men didn't ride boards. Ant's board was primo, just like Ant, and I knew everything about it as if it were my own. It had an Alva deck that was scratched and scuffed up pretty good since he'd bought it at the end of his sophomore year, right before summer. Ant used to skate at the Big O a lot and I would make sure I was near him whenever he was there.

He talked about his board all the time right after he got it. Eventually his buds told him to stick a sock in it, they'd heard enough. But I could have listened to Ant wax poetic about his board all day long. He and his friends were a few years older and had no interest in hanging out with me, but whenever I had a chance to interact with him one on one, I'd just ask him about his board and that would usually get me about ten minutes with him while he sang its praises.

I enjoyed those short one-sided conversations with Ant. As he spoke, I'd let that lazy, baritone California drawl pass through me while I studied his face and the rest of his body for details I hadn't noticed before: how blonde the hair on his forearms was when lightened by the summer sun, and how good it looked standing out against his tan; the way his hair fell down around his skull and seemed to always frame his face perfectly; and his enormous feet. They were huge! I snuck a peek at one of his Vans once when I was hanging out with Cody to see how big they were. The fading tag on the insole read Size 16.

Ant's deck had black grip tape on top, except where it was cut to frame the shapes of the letters that spelled out ALVA in red and gold script. It was fitted with Gullwing trucks, Kryptonics wheels and Bones bearings. Since he'd had it for a couple years, the wood at the tail of the deck was dinged and scratched up, there were dents around its perimeter, and the wheels showed their age, but none of that bothered me. It was an awesome board. It was infused with Ant's energy, and I had to have it.

I'd earned money over the course of the past couple months by mowing lawns. But then, on an impulsive shopping binge at Record Trading Center, I'd blown a good chunk of it on *My Beach* and *Candy-O* (both new), used copies of *Meet the Dickies* and *Nervous Breakdown*, and the "Gidget Goes to Hell" 45, so I only had fifty-seven bucks left.

I asked Ant if he'd take fifty-seven for it and he laughed as if I were joking. My face must have fallen, because when he finished laughing and took a look at me, he said, "Well, I don't know. Let me think." He put a finger to his chin, looked to the side and squinted.

I could tell he was acting stupid, so I shrugged. "No biggie," I said. "Don't worry about it."

But he said, "No, no…I think I could work with you. Unless you aren't interested anymore…."

"I'm interested," I told him.

"Why don't you pay me fifty-seven now and pay me twenty-eight more before I leave for school in August?" he asked. "That work for you?"

I thought he'd miscalculated, so I said, "That's eighty-five dollars, though."

Ant said, "Yes! I'm letting you pay less to me now, when I could be getting more from somebody else. Ten bucks is how much it's gonna cost you to have the board you want without paying the full amount for it up front."

I wasn't gonna argue with him. Ant had paid more than a hundred and fifty bucks for that board. It was fuckin' rad, there was no way I was passing it up. "That totally works," I said.

Ant held out his hand, palm facing upward. I looked at his palm, then up to his face, then back down to his palm, then back up to his face. He rolled his eyes, then it hit me, what he was waiting for. I fumbled for my wallet, pulled on the Velcro flap that kept it shut, plucked the money out and handed it to Ant.

"Follow me," he said, turning and leading me to his bedroom. His board was leaning against the wall next to his closet. He picked up the board, walked toward me and handed it over. "It's yours," he said.

I held it tightly in both hands, feeling its weight, looking at the stickers on its underside: one a black and yellow tracker trucks decal, the other featuring a pineapple with the words "Hawaiian Delight" surrounding it in chubby yellow letters. When I looked back up at Ant, I was beaming.

◆◆◆

VEGA

"Can I help you find something?"

She was pierced, she was tatted up, she had blue hair and side-swept bangs. Her make up was heavy on the eyeliner, light on everything else. Her nails had been painted black about three weeks prior and hadn't been touched up since. Her nose stud made its point, and the earrings that lined her outer ear all the way up to the top were impressive, if for no other reason than the sheer number of them.

She went by Vega, according to the nametag hanging sideways on her black shirt, which sported the word *glassjaw* on it, all lower case in red font, beneath a red silhouette of a woman in a seated position, facing front and leaning back on her hands with her legs spread. Vega gazed at me with curiosity in her eyes, as if she'd never seen a real man in his thirties before.

"I'm checking out the decks," I replied, smiling.

She waited to see if that was all I'd give her, but not for very long. "Which ones do you like?" she asked, turning back to look at them.

I couldn't help but feel I was being tested. I scanned the wall of decks just to see which designs, if any, jumped out at me. The variety and intensity of the designs blew my mind. It was a far cry from the options I had in 1979.

"That one's cool," I said. "F6."

Each deck was tagged with an alpha numeric identifier. One of the reasons the deck I pointed to stood out was that its only colors were black and white. On a black background there were white stars at the top, and some barely visible black and white stripes beneath them, so it was an American flag hanging down.

In front of the flag was a woman with long black hair and bangs like Bettie Paige. She had a cigarette hanging out the left side of her mouth and was wearing a deeply cut V-neck garment. She appeared to be looking down her nose at us, as if she were somewhat elevated above us, and a black line was drawn across her face, right where her eyes would have been if we could see them.

It was like those old photographs from the 1950s, where they'd put a black line over the eyes of the people in the photo so you couldn't identify them. This method of hiding the photo subjects' identities indicated they'd been photographed committing sordid or criminal acts. Toward the bottom of the deck, the word ZERO was stamped across it in crooked letters.

"Okay," she said. She stepped to the wall and removed the deck. "What other decks do you like?" she asked.

Another one caught my eye. "That one," I said. "B3." This deck had a red and white background, white covering the top two-thirds of it, and red covering the rest at the bottom. The white area denoted a wall and the red area a floor.

On the left side of the deck a skeleton was on the red floor, sitting on a skateboard with his arms crossed and resting on his knees. The skeleton was wearing a black baseball cap and appeared to be grinning, his smile being wider than the average skull's usually is by default. On the right side of the deck, the word MUSKA hung vertically. The letters were all caps, each one made of bones colored bright green with bright yellow trim.

"Nice," she said as she retrieved it from the wall. She walked back over and placed them on the countertop in front of me.

They looked even better up close. My eyes darted back and forth, taking in the details, sussing out the feeling I was getting from each board. "How much are they?" I asked.

"Punk Girl's sixty. Muska's seventy-five. But that's a really decent price for it."

"It is?" I asked with the tone of a skeptic.

"Oh, yeah. Wasn't a big run. We're lucky we even got any," she said.

I looked at the Muska deck, then the Punk Girl deck, then the Muska deck again.

"It's the only one we have. The rest sold as soon as we put 'em out."

"Did they now?" I asked, looking up at her and smirking.

"Oh, yeah," she said, nodding. "You know, this is an outlet, so most of the stuff we get is mass produced, not that special. The Muska deck is not that. Punk Girl's cool too, but that Muska deck is sick. It's funny, out of all the decks on the wall, you chose two that only got limited runs. Which one do you like best?"

"Muska," I said.

She flashed her first genuine smile since I'd walked through the door. "Right." She lifted Punk Girl off the counter and returned her to the wall. "You're getting Indy trucks, right?"

"Oh," I sputtered. "I guess. I mean, yeah."

"It's such a tight deck," she said. "Be a shame to put crappy trucks on it."

I hated the idea of her upselling me into bankruptcy, but I just happened to have a brand-new Visa card in my pocket. As far as I was concerned, money wasn't an issue that day.

She led me toward a register but sauntered right past it, then stopped behind a glass display case and waited for me to catch up. "What about wheels?"

As I approached the display case I saw racks of wheels to my right, hanging from metal rods in clear plastic packages of four. I assumed the wheels in the case were pricier than the ones I was looking at. I saw a brand name and said, "These Spitfires are lookin' pretty good," as I walked toward them.

"Spitfire Classics. Solid choice."

"I think so," I said.

"But you might wanna check out these Bones SPFs or DTFs over here if you want wheels that don't flat-spot so much," she countered.

Vega just won't let up, I thought to myself. But I stood my ground. "Yeah, I bet. I'm partial to these Spitfires, though" I said.

"Okay," she said, letting it go, walking over to me from behind the counter.

As she helped me pick a size, I marveled at how much smaller wheels were now than they'd been back in 1979. The difference was almost comical.

We'd finally made it over to the register, and I breathed what turned out to be a premature sigh of relief because I thought Vega was done selling me stuff.

"Okay, so we've got your Shorty's Muska deck for $75, your Indy trucks for $40, Spitfire Classics for $40, Bones bearings for $20."

"Bones bearings?" I asked, not remembering when that part of our exchange, the part where I'd bought Bones bearings, occurred.

"They're the best bearings. They're the ones you want," she replied. "You want me to put this together here for free, or do you wanna struggle with it when you get home?"

"You're the expert," I said, smiling.

"What about grip tape? You want me to do that too?"

"Please," I told her, trying to get to the end of this.

"Sure, I got you. How do ya want it?"

I needed to regain the upper hand. I could not allow Vega to dominate this exchange. "I was thinking a diagonal split," I said, raising my eyebrows at her.

"Sure," she said, nodding, and not missing a beat. "I can do that. Don't blame me the first time your foot slips, though. Mob grip tape. $15. And I assume you'll want a skate tool, just in case," she added, in a way that didn't really allow for anything but an affirmative response.

"Yeah, sure. Good idea," I replied, shrugging my shoulders and shaking my head no, even though that's not what I was saying.

"You won't regret it," she told me. "It'll save you a world of trouble."

"I'm sure it will," I said. "Are we done yet?"

"Last, but not least," she began, but I groaned. "What?!" she asked, irritated. "That's it," she said. "Relax. I just thought you might want one of our shop tees. Only ten bucks."

The black shirt, which was designed to look distressed, had the shop's name at the top and Skate & Surf at the bottom, both in old-fashioned lettering. In the center was an orange phoenix, stylized like an engraving, with the underside of a skateboard off to the side. I'd been prepared to reject it outright, but despite myself, and swept up in the moment of purchase, I loved it.

"I'll take one. Large. Okay, Vega, what's the damage?"

"Merchandise total is $215, tax brings it to $232.74," she said, extending her hand so that I could place my credit card in it.

About thirty minutes later, she presented me with my new board. I took it in both hands to inspect it and had the same feeling I did the day Ant gave me his Alva.

I took a moment to check the cut of the grip tape, which looked fantastic. "Outstanding," I said, nodding my head. I took out my wallet and plucked a twenty from it, which I handed to Vega. "I appreciate your help today. I love it," I said, turning my attention back to the board. I was beaming.

"Thank you, sir," she said, trying to hand the twenty back. "We're not supposed to take tips, but I appreciate it."

"What do you mean you're not supposed to take tips?" I asked her. "Who's gonna know? Fuck 'em. Keep the damn tip."

She smiled at me and pocketed the twenty. "Thanks."

"Thank *you*," I said. "Well, Vega…it's been real."

She chuckled. "It's a tight board, man. Your son'll love it."

She walked away and left me standing there, gripping my new board with a puzzled look on my face.

GEAR

"Uncle Ray brought his skateboard!" Noah had cried when he answered the door upon my arrival to pick him up. He'd run into his room at full steam, near to bursting with his seven-year-old combustible male energy, leaving me to face my sister, his mom, who stood silently in the doorway, holding the door open and judging me.

"That's yours?" she'd asked, more annoyed than anything else. I'd nodded. "What are you gonna do with it?" she'd asked, incredulous.

"Bond with your son," I'd answered, trying to deflect what sounded to me like an accusation.

"You've got to be fucking kidding me!" she'd hissed, so Noah wouldn't hear her cuss. "When was the last time you rode a skateboard?" Again, like an accusation.

"It's been a while," I'd admitted. "But it's like riding a bike. You never really forget."

"Jesus, you are just like Dad," she said, shaking her head. "You're not a fucking kid, Ray!"

The sounds of Noah returning (still at full speed ahead) had made her relax her body language, which had been coiled spring tight, and resume the appearance of someone who wasn't seething with rage nearly every waking moment of every waking day.

"Ready!" Noah had shouted as he pushed past his mother to get out the door. "Where we going?!" he'd demanded, grinning up at me and gripping his own board, along with a mesh bag that contained his helmet, plus knee and elbow pads.

"I don't know, sport. Where do you usually ride your board?"

"We could go to the Big O," Noah had suggested, looking at his mother and raising his eyebrows into question marks.

"You are *not* going to the Big O!" she'd declared, her rage peeking out again from behind the mask of suburban apathy she usually wore. "You're not taking him to the Big O, Ray. It's been shut down for years. It's condemned and half demolished. Homeless people live there. Drug addicts. I don't want my son anywhere near it. Understand?"

"MOMMM!" Noah had protested.

But she'd been having none of it. "Uncle Ray forgot to bring his gear. I think you should both wait until next time to do this," she'd said, nodding her head in the affirmative while looking at me, trying to use that non-verbal communication b.s. she'd learned in college.

Nice try, I'd thought. "Oh, it's ok. I'll be careful," I'd replied. "Unless you *really* just don't want us to go," I'd added, placing the decision squarely back into her lap, knowing she didn't want to deal with Noah's reaction if she prevented us from going, and smiling at her sweetly as she'd glared at me, wishing me dead.

"C'mon, Mom, we'll be careful. Promise," Noah had implored, still playing it sweet, not yet finding it necessary to move into tantrum mode, although now that he was older the frequency of his tantrums had trickled down to practically never.

"Where are you taking him?" she'd asked me.

"I'm not sure," I'd said, "but we'll find someplace. Probably just a school or something. An empty parking lot." I'd stared at her blankly.

"Are you sure it's a good idea to go skateboarding without any gear on?" she'd asked, changing tack to a sweet-smelling, concerned tone fabricated for Noah's sake.

"Oh, we'll be fine," I'd answered, smug in my confidence that this was safely within my wheelhouse of skills and talents. I was quite adept on a board, and she knew it. I had a long history of it and didn't buy into my sister's attempts to make me feel insecure or nervous about picking it back up with Noah that day. Even though I hadn't been on a board in years.

As we drove out of their neighborhood, I was thinking about my sister with what I now realize was unbridled arrogance. About how she'd become a weirdly mutated version of our mother, one that could manage rage more effectively, but didn't seem capable of experiencing any happiness with everything she'd achieved. Our mom could be a lot of scary things, but when she felt it was warranted, and couldn't think of any reason not to, she'd access that part of herself who still knew how to be the tom boy she'd been when she was a kid. My sister hadn't relaxed in years. Since before Noah was even born. She didn't seem to have any interest in it.

HEATHER

Back then, my sister and I were closer than we are now. As young adults, we'd bonded over our shared experience of being raised by parents who'd had two kids when they were still teenagers and couldn't help but have second thoughts about what they'd done.

But it being too late for them to change anything, and since they were more or less stuck with us for the time being, at least until we aged out of their obligations to feed, clothe and house us, our parents soldiered on with a mix of obligation that they more or less managed to live up to, and resentment that they didn't bother to hide.

And of course, on top of all that ambivalence was the trauma baggage they each carried, the mental health issues driving their erratic and sometimes frightening behavior, which framed our experiences growing up with them. Nothing that isn't normal for 99% of families, I would guess. When it comes to parents, you eventually get a taste of everything: the good, the bad and the ugly.

My sister was adept at managing situations. She had a plan of action figured out before anyone else had even decided if they were capable of handling any given set of circumstances. The day I told her I was HIV positive, her first reaction surprised me because it was visceral, not strategic.

She burst into tears, her face a naked illustration of her revisiting, in that moment, everything she'd ever heard or seen about AIDS and the people who got it: the emaciation, the hollowed-out eyes, the dying young men who looked like ghosts of the former selves they'd just very recently been. And the social stigma, no doubt.

We were having lunch at El Torito on a Sunday afternoon in suburbia. The conversation felt out of place, and I was self-conscious, feeling guilty that I'd traveled into her realm and dropped this messy life bomb on her without warning. But I figured this *was* the warning. I wasn't going to keep it a secret and then just shrivel up and die out of the blue, without an explanation.

She asked me, "What happened?" Because she knew me well enough to know I wasn't stupid about that stuff, or at least I hadn't been, previously. She also wanted to make some kind of sense of it. I knew that feeling.

I just shrugged and said, "I trusted the wrong guy." Which was the truth, kind of. I liked characterizing it that way because, on the one hand, I owned my mistake. But on the other hand, I didn't shoulder all the blame. There was another guy involved. There always is.

"I just don't get it," she said, shaking her head as if to clear it. "You're such a cool guy. I mean," and here she laughed, because I think she knew how silly her logic was, just about as quickly as she'd said it.

"That didn't factor into it, I guess," I said.

My bitterness over my predicament had been tempered already by a level of acceptance that I'd reached fairly quickly, but only after being realistic about needing to hold myself accountable. Not exactly slut shaming, but tough slut love. Sluts gonna slut, but if the bill comes due, you gotta pay it.

I couldn't blame Victor forever. I mean, I could always remember what he'd said, then done. But to keep going, I had to be strong enough to own the mistake I'd made and move forward with that mistake being a part of who I was and who I would be from that point forward.

"Well, you know what you have to do then," she declared, all brisk determination, like a life coach. "On the anniversary of that date next year, you need to go sky diving. Jump out of a fucking airplane. Plummet through the fucking sky without knowing whether or not your fucking chute is gonna open. Make the date about THAT. Not that fucking asshole who did this to you." She removed the straw from the nearly full margarita glass she'd been nursing, raised the glass to her lips, tilted her head back and gulped it down until she finished it off.

I was thankful she put it the way she did, because I was having trouble accepting my situation as anything other than something I had done to myself. As shitty as Victor had been, I'd still felt compelled to shoulder the blame for my behavior while excusing and explaining away his.

I also knew there was no way I'd ever be jumping out of an airplane. "Or maybe I'll go shopping and buy something very, *very* expensive," I answered.

"That's not exactly the kind of adrenaline rush I had in mind," she said.

"Trust me," I said. "It'll hit me when I get the bill."

TRANSPORT

Noah walked me back to the car with the patience of a saint, as I couldn't really perform the task of what anyone would call "walking." I was of half a mind to hand him the keys, tell him to bring the car around and hope for the best, but thought better of it. The pain was a cunt.

Once we got to the car, I had to figure out how to bend my leg at the knee so I could drive it, which was a challenge all its own that lasted almost as long as our painful journey (well, mine painful, his patient) back to the car.

I had Noah get a towel from the trunk, poured some bottled water on it, then washed his hand thoroughly. I didn't think I needed to worry; he had no open wounds on the hand that had touched me, and there wasn't anything left on the towel once I'd washed his hand off. He'd probably rubbed it on his shorts or something, and he was impatient with me for taking the time to do this, not understanding why we were falling down this rabbit hole of washing his hand when I clearly needed to get my leg taken care of.

When we got to the ER, which was practically empty, he broke away from me once we entered the building and approached the desk, telling the nurse, "My uncle needs help. He fell off his skateboard and hurt himself."

The nurse didn't miss a beat. "Oh, I just hate when that happens," she said to him, then looked up at me. "You got an insurance card, uncle?" I limped over to the desk and handed her my card.

She told me to take a seat.

NOAH

Now I find myself lying in a hospital bed, my leg in a splint, stitched and bandaged, the edge of the pain dulled by a pharmaceutical I can't remember the name of, and my sister standing at the foot of the bed with her arms crossed.

"Where's Noah?" I ask, so she'll stop staring me down.

"He's getting something to eat. How do you feel?"

"Little groggy, I guess. Better. Sorry you had to come down here."

"What's wrong with you?" she asks.

"Well, the bone isn't broken or anything. Just bruised. I might get some tendinitis, but they said it probably won't be too bad. I'll have a killer scar, though."

"No, Ray. I mean, what the fuck is *wrong* with you?"

"What," I say, not liking where this conversation appears to be going.

"What the fuck were you *thinking?* That fucking skateboard! Why did you take him down to the *river?*"

"It's a wide-open space. It's a lot of concrete. We were just riding around. It wasn't dangerous," I tell her. "There was no one else around, no cars, nothing. We had the place to ourselves."

"It wasn't dangerous but you're sitting here in the fucking E.R.!" she says. Her fury, which I'm very well acquainted with, is building, and I'm trying to just find a way to diffuse it.

"I know, okay, but it's not like Noah was doing anything dangerous. I was just showing off. Or trying to, anyway. I just got stupid."

"Why do you act like such an *idiot* around him? You regress to a point where I don't even recognize you!"

"I'm just having fun with him, Heather. I'm not regressing," I tell her, in a calm, measured tone designed to dismiss her concern. It doesn't land, and we both notice.

"Ray, you're supposed to be his uncle. His grown-up uncle. I'd like to think you're a role model for him. You're supposed to try and raise him up to your level, not sink all the way down to his."

"I'm just having fun with him, Heather. I'm showing him you can be a grown up without shutting all the fun parts down."

She looks at me like I'm crazy and scoffs. "Fun?! Putting my son in danger is not required for you to have fun."

"He wasn't in danger. I just want him to have a good time, Heather. We hardly ever did, and it sucked! Why can't he just have a good time with me now, when it won't cost him anything?"

"Ray, you hurt yourself today! How the fuck do you fall into a fucking inlet at the river? What the fuck were you doing?!"

"I was—"

"What if you had landed differently? What if you had landed on your fucking *head?*"

"Jesus, Heather, come on!" I say.

"Ray, you were out of control on that skateboard. You need to put that shit down when you're in charge of my son."

"I was not out of control!"

"You ate SHIT!"

I close my eyes. She's winning the argument (she's won it, actually) but I don't respond. Instead, I remember the moment of panic I experienced when Noah put his hand on my bloody leg. I've just realized something for the first time, something that I guess I should have known all along but didn't. I can't claim to be an effective protector of Noah if I'm the type of asshole who will injure myself and bleed all over him just so I can keep being the cool guncle.

But when we were out there together, we were having so much fun. I was thinking about all the tricks I used to do, and how much I got off on impressing Noah with what I could do, even if I hadn't done any of it for more than twenty years, and even though I couldn't really do it anymore.

It was not like riding a bike. It felt very different trying to do it now. All I managed to pull off for him today, before I ate it, was an ollie, and a mediocre one at that. I approximated it, perhaps just enough to pass muster as someone who knew his way around a board once, but that was about it.

I realized things were very different; my body was different, not limber like it was when I was a kid, not fluid in its moves as I rode around on my Muska. But I wanted to show

Noah that I could ride it. I wanted to share my skill set with him and show him that we had this in common.

I realize what I did today was stupid, though. What if I'd really injured myself and hadn't been able to get back to the car? What if I'd knocked myself out and he'd tried to help, and got my blood on him and had somehow ingested it, and it got into his bloodstream? I couldn't handle something like that happening. I'd never forgive myself.

There was nothing I could say in my defense when confronted with the fact that my first priority, whenever I'm with him, needs to be ensuring that he's safe and that I'm capable of taking care of him. I can't just show up and hope for the best. I can't continue to not think that far ahead.

"You're right," I say. "I'm sorry. It won't happen again."

She exhales a long, deep breath I didn't realize she'd been holding. "Damn right it won't happen again."

An hour or so later, we're in the parking lot, me discharged, my sister and Noah both glad that I'm okay but eager to get on with their lives. We've wiped down the driver's seat as best we can with the towel from the trunk, and folded me into the car, which wasn't as difficult as it was earlier. It was still painful enough for me to consider calling off work tomorrow, though, just so I can lie on the couch in my underwear and let my body recuperate.

"Call me when you get home," she tells me.

"Okay," I say. Then, "Oh..." as I think about the board for the first time since arriving at the hospital. I check the back seat but don't see it. I can't remember what we did with it.

"Oh, what?" she asks.

"My board. I don't know where it is."

"Oh, it's fine. I'm taking it home for safe keeping," she tells me.

"Bye, Uncle Ray!" Noah pipes up from somewhere near the back of my car.

"Bye, Noah!" I call, waving a hand. I look back at my sister. "You're gonna keep my board at your house? Why?"

"Cause if you pull some shit like this again, I'm gonna smash your fucking head in with it," she says. "Bye!"

30. The Roosterfish

■

Transcript of a found conversation between three drunk homosexual men sitting at the next high top. The conversation was overheard (and possibly recorded) at the height of a boisterous Sunday afternoon Beer Bust at The Roosterfish in Venice, CA.

-cat's got a real flatulence problem.

Really?

Yeah. Well, it's not a problem for *him*. He'll just let one rip and go on about his business without a care in the world.

I didn't even know cats farted.

Me either!

Does it stink?

Kinda…but sweet.

Kitty farts smell sweet?

I didn't say I liked it.

You guys are getting *way* too into that cat. Can we just refocus for a minute and get back to figuring out what *I'm* going to do.

You'll do what you always do: cry for a few days, quit grieving in time for the weekend, then go out and find the next one you're gonna latch onto.

Excuse me? I do not *latch onto* anything.

Girl, you're like a bad case of crabs. Can you even name the guy you were hung up on six months ago?

Hmmmmmm...yeah. That was Frank, I think. The rugby player? He was hot.

Kinda doughy, if you ask me.

He was an animal in the sack.

Of course he was.

Wait a minute, let's circle back. How do you deal with the cat problem?

Cat problem?

The farts!

Oh, well...the cat's not the one with the problem, really. It's the people who happen to be visiting the studio at those moments. *They're* the ones with the problem. They look at me like I'm the one who farted!

Again, with that fucking cat! You guys, I'm having a crisis. And you, my supposed 'best friends,' are just too self-involved to listen!

You're right, boo. We are your best friends, okay? But there's a cap on how many of your crises we're obligated to deal with in any given six-month period.

A cap? On my crises? I hardly think I have more crises than the average person.

Bitch, please! You've had more crises lately than a suicide hotline. At some point, you gotta just deal with that shit on your own.

Since when is there a cap on the amount of support I can ask of my best friend?

Which best friend?

Friends. I meant to say friends.

It might have something to do with the volume of guys you go through.

Yeah. It's kind of a lot.

It is not *a lot*. Listen to you guys! Fucking puritans! At least I'm out there, meeting people. All you two ever wanna do is sit at home and play video games all day.

An activity that is sounding more and more appealing to me with each passing minute.

Yeah, me too.

Fine, forget it! Excuse me!

Oh, come on now. Settle down.

No! I'm really sorry! I didn't realize you were too busy discussing your cat fart problem to be bothered!

Oh, for fuck's sake. Will you stop with the theatrics and just tell us what's wrong? Jesus!

No, never mind.

Just tell us what's wrong!

No. It's nothing.

I swear to God, if you don't tell us what's fucking wrong right now, I'm leaving.

Yeah, me too.

Well...if you insist.

Christ on the motherfuckin' cross...

You know that guy Kevin I've been seeing?

Kevin...is he the clown guy?

Mime, babe...he's a mime.

Oh, right. Mime. I remember him. From Des Moines. Wanted to be the first gay porn mime.

No, it's not him.

Went on an audition and wouldn't blow the director. Got black balled. Started a JustMyFans instead. Making a fortune! Still active on it.

Is he now?

Well, that's what I heard...

That was Alain, not Kevin!

Oh, right. Alain. Whatever happened to Alain?

It's like you said: Palm Springs, JustMyFans, and burlesque shows now, too. Now will you please shut the fuck up and listen to what happened with Kevin?

Kevin's that corporate guy, right?

Oh yeah, that HR douche bag. Clawing his way up the ladder!

Kind of a dick, if you ask me...

Yeah, I never really vibed with Kevin.

So ANYWAY, he got promoted. And they're sending him to New York. They're paying all his moving expenses and setting him up in a new place. They're even paying his rent for three months after he gets there!

No shit!

Wow! That's impressive!

I'm in the wrong profession.

But the bastard dumped me! He said he loves me, but he's just not up to having a long-distance relationship.

Oh, I'm so sorry!

And they're paying his rent for three months? That's awesome!

And then I told him, well, maybe we didn't *have* to be apart. And that, what I was getting at, was that we could *both* move to New York. I meant together. Do you know what he said?

I don't know, but I'd do that in a heartbeat if they offered to give me a promotion, *and* move me to New York, *and* set me up in an apartment, *and* pay my rent for three months!

That's not the point!

Shit, I'd move to Bakersfield if someone offered it to me. I hate this fucking town.

You guys!

Just sayin'...

Do you know. What he said. When I suggested. We both move to New York?

Okay, I'll bite. What did he say?

He said, 'I'll see you when you get there.'

(Exclamations and laughter.)

Ouch!

Shit!

Well!

(Laughter dies down.)

I'm glad you find my dead relationship so amusing!

I'm sorry! But face it: you knew he was a dick going in.

Yeah, but he was a dick to *other people*. Not me!

Well, it was bound to happen eventually.

Yeah, don't take it personally! He's ascending to a new socioeconomic level. He's moving on.

And up.

Yeah, and up. You represent the *past*. What *was*.

Mmm-hmm, back in L.A. when he was just a lowly branch manager. Now he's gonna be a...what's his new job title?

Oh, who knows? Director of Fuckery Relations. Some stupid corporate bullshit. I don't remember! My ears were still ringing from him saying he'd see me when I got there.

Well, you can't really blame him, honey. You knew he was ambitious.

And a dick.

Yeah. And if it isn't meant to be, better to find out now than to move all the way to New York.

Yeah, and have it fall apart in the big city—

The OTHER big city—

—yeah! And so far away from home...

A whole *country* away from home! Not to mention being so far away from your friends and your family...

Yes! And with no one there to help you pick up the pieces every time you faceplant right into the gutter.

(Laughter)

Oh, great. Fuck you both! For real. I'm spilling my guts out all over the table and you're ridiculing me!

Oh, come on…you know we love you.

No pouting!

If this is love, I'm fucked!

(Laughter)

Remember that porn guy you dated?

Which one?

Fuck you, which one! I've only dated maybe half a dozen porn models.

Is that all?

Jealous?

He was big and tall with dark hair, and he could self-suck.

Alain?

No, not Alain. The guy who was *actually* in porn. The felon.

I don't think I know who you mean…

Bullshit!

Don't you lie!

The dude with all the tats. What was that guy's name?

It started with an F.

Felix maybe?

The guy who went by Dick the Dick.

Oh, you mean Fitz!

Fitz! That's the guy! Whatever happened to Fitz? He's so hot! And his scenes are fucking crazy!

No shit!

Ohmigod, the first time I ever saw him was on that Mantrap compilation? *I'm Straight! But I Like to Suck Dick and Get Fucked In the Ass! But I'm Straight!* He topped that one guy and then they flipped. I came like a dozen times the first time I watched it.

My favorite one is *Nuts In Space*. 'In space, no one can hear you nut.'

The effects in that one are pretty good, actually.

Yeah, considering...

That zero gravity cum shot, though!

God, what a dick on that guy!

Oh, anaconda right there, honey!

Did you really let him fuck you?

Only once. That was it.

Did it hurt?

What the fuck do you think? Yes, it hurt! By the time he was done I was afraid the back door would never close again.

I can't get fucked by monster dicks like I used to. I don't want to get all loose and stretched out.

Why were you looking at me when you said that?

Don't worry, honey. You can do Kegels. Get yourself back to nice and tight.

That's just an urban legend, girl. Ask any old queen who's a bottom. She'll tell you.

She won't have to tell you. You just listen for the wind tunnel when she swishes by.

Well, not if she's had anal rejuvenation surgery.

Fuck you, that's not real!

Yes, it is!

Remember how every time he finished fucking a guy, they'd show a close-up of his dick sliding out?

Their holes were so wrecked!

Yeah, that could get pretty gross sometimes.

I think it's hot.

God, you're a pig.

(Snorting sounds)

So, whatever happened to Fitz anyway? I never see him anymore.

Oh, he moved back to Florida. Got married, had a couple kids. Got fat, got arrested again. Last I heard he was serving two to three years at Pensacola. He got all twacked out one night and beat up some guy for checking out his wife.

For real?

Yeah! It was on *Cops*. He put up a fight and everything. They had to taze him twice before they could tackle him on the front lawn. His wife's in a bright red teddy and a pair of black sweatpants.

No shit!

Oh my God!

Yeah! She's totally shitfaced, stumbling around on a pair of high stripper heels and screaming at the cops the whole time.

A bright red teddy, black sweats and *stripper heels?*

Yeah!

She musta put the sweats on when the cops got there…

I don't know when the fuck she did it, honey, I just know it was WRONG.

No shit!

Pick a look and stick with it, bitch.

Word. So what happened?

Oh, it's epic! Fitz is shirtless when they tackle him, by the way. Nothing on but a loose pair of boxer shorts. I'm pretty sure he flashes some nut at one point.

How does he look?

He looks great! He's flashing nut, what more do you want?

Yeah, but how fat did he get?

Well, he's got a beer gut in that *Cops* episode, but he's still beefy as fuck.

God, if only I could be his cellmate for one night. I bet he pumps iron in the prison yard all day. Comes back to the cell all sweaty and stank.

Settle down, princess.

What? I can't fantasize? He could bounce that belly up and down on me as many times as he wanted!

Can I get you some lube? A tissue, perhaps?

I think it's still on Xtube. Vevo kept taking it down.

I'll have to check it out.

So, whaddya say? 'Nother round?

31. Married Alive

○

I DID

For many queer men who are, or were, married to the man of their dreams, their true origin story is a tale of love at first hook up. It's a meet-cute that probably included sucking dick and, if he was really the one, eating ass too. Those memories will always remain so precious.

Elio and I met online, and our first meeting came about as the result of our desire, based on our profile pics, to fuck each other. Elio was Latino, originally from west-central Mexico. After we were married, we agreed upon a stock answer whenever someone asked us, as someone invariably did each and every time they found out we were married, "So! How did you two meet?"

We'd tell them we met at church. If the person asked a follow up question, we just chuckled knowingly and left it at that.

Though our story ends in divorce, I only have good things to say about Elio as a person. When we met, he lived in an old apartment building on Cahuenga Boulevard, only a few blocks from Victor's place. I was working at a law firm in Century City, so on the nights we got together I would drive across town to Hollywood at the height of traffic, which was no mean feat.

Like I said, I found Elio on a hook-up site in the year of our lord 2005 B.A. (Before Apps). In 2005, our phones were still appendages, not the centers of our existence. For online activity, we had to sit down at a computer, point and click with a mouse, then wait.

I fell in love with Elio the way I usually do: quickly, and with an air of certainty that can often surprise or unnerve people, especially the ones I fall in love with. He was the first adult relationship partner I ever had that treated me like he truly loved me (for a while), and he was dynamite in the sack (again, for a while).

I'm pretty sure I hit my sexual peak at right around the age of 40. I was unstoppable. We enjoyed each other's company tremendously. After breaking up with Brad I rented a house in North Hollywood for a year while my dog Hunter and I recuperated from the relationship, and I acclimated to my new job at federal court.

When my lease was up in North Hollywood, I moved into Elio's one bedroom apartment in Hollywood. The purpose of that move was so I could save money, pay off my debt and try to get ahead for a change. We had an additional roommate, Leonidus (Leo for short), who was Elio's best frenemy. It was a fun time.

We got married right when it became legal for us to do so in 2008. The City of West Hollywood organized marriage ceremonies at a city park. I have video of the day we got married and it's great. Before the ceremony, we waited in the park's community building. I have video files of us waiting for our names to be called, and we both look a little nervous, but you can plainly see that we're in love and very happy.

Our officiant was a kind woman who looked just like Rachel Maddow. We were so nervous that when it came time to put the rings on our fingers, we put them on the fingers of our right hands (wedding bands are worn on the left). Elio got nervous and had trouble getting through a part of the vows in English, and though he became flustered for a few moments, he recovered quickly and we got through it.

It was a magical experience, and it's a singular kind of elation and happiness that I'd never felt before and haven't since. If I ever get married again, maybe I will.

After I'd paid off my debt, saved some money, and done all I could to clean up my shitty credit report, we started thinking about buying a house together. After a false start looking at properties in Oregon, I called the realtors that found the house in Reseda that Brad and I had owned. Elio and I spent a few months searching for a house we could both afford and enjoy living in.

It was a strange time to be house hunting. The market was in the shitter due to the 2008 financial crash, and the majority of homes we were checking out were in foreclosure. Many still had families living in them.

We felt weird walking through these lived-in homes. Our realtor would call whatever realtor had listed the property, and if the residents still lived there, their realtor would call them to let them know some prospective buyers were coming to check the place out.

We'd walk through the front door, and there would be traces of the family that lived there, who'd just left in a hurry so we could come look at it: plates with toast on them at the dining room table, a television left on that was tuned to a cable cartoon network, a ceiling fan left running in one of the bathrooms, where steam still clung to the medicine cabinet mirror. You could feel the presence and the energy of these families in their homes.

Elio and I felt weird about these circumstances because we didn't want to take anyone's home right out from under them. We believed that doing so would be cruel, so we never considered buying any that were in foreclosure and still occupied.

On a sunny Saturday morning, we piled into the realtor's car, weary of the process by that point and not very hopeful that we'd find a house we'd deem The One. After a couple of false starts, the realtor drove us to a home in Granada Hills that he'd never seen but had added to our list that day because it seemed possible that it might check enough of the boxes for us.

When we first saw the house on Verada Avenue, we were ambivalent. It had been foreclosed upon and vacant for more than a year. The grass in the front yard was brown, as were most of the bushes that backed up against the house.

On the other hand, the floor plan was fantastic, and the house had a lot of natural light. We spent more time there than we had at any other, inspecting rooms more than once together, commenting on what we'd need to fix, and other things we could do to make it fabulous.

There were some aspects of the house that bothered us: the cottage cheese ceilings, the originally exposed brick fireplace, which some genius had decided to paint fire engine red, then worsened by painting the grout white. The floors throughout most of the house were covered in the saddest, cheapest looking linoleum I'd ever seen.

The remnants of bad design choices made by the previous owners were numerous, but we knew we could fix those things ourselves. We both sensed potential beneath the surface.

We walked out to inspect the backyard, and it was in a sad state, just like the rest of the house. But the water in the pool was clean and blue, reflecting the sun on its rippling surface as if to flash a friendly greeting in our direction.

The backyard was almost all cement, except for some squares of dirt that had been left in the patio to house tall Italian Cypress trees along one of the fences. The trees stood proudly in their patches of dirt, their dull, brown foliage absorbing the sunshine. Despite their parched and uncared for appearance, they grew high above the backyard, with each of their points topping out at between twelve and fifteen feet.

Elio and I discussed how we'd be able to transform this cementified back yard into a more welcoming space. We'd get large planters for succulents and other desert plants that would have no trouble withstanding the direct sunlight, and we'd build raised beds to place at different locations, which we could use to grow tomatoes and peppers. We could also fill the flower bed areas that dotted the backyard with chaparral landscaping plants that would grow voluminously but stay close to the ground.

What reaffirmed it for both of us was Cherry Forever. She smiled up at us from the pool wall, on the slope between the shallow and deep ends. She had feathered blond hair that was parted in the middle, bringing Farrah Fawcett and Cherie Currie to mind. If she'd been in human form, she'd have been on her knees, with her forearms outspread, as if to maintain her balance while hovering in the water. But Cherry wasn't in human form. She was in mermaid form. The top half of her body was unclothed, and her ample breasts looked magnificent.

The remarkable things Elio and I noticed about Cherry Forever that day were the light in her eyes and her beautiful smile. She was radiant. Looking at her created an emotional reaction within me, beautiful waves of happiness and of feeling loved. When I saw her for the first time, she left a vivid impression on me that hasn't faded or diminished. If anything, it's grown stronger. She lives in my awareness, and she gives me so much love whenever I think about her.

Gazing up at us from the pool with that smile and those beautiful eyes, Cherry Forever looked happier than just about anyone I'd ever seen being happy. Her happiness and her love were contagious. They still are.

The instant we both saw Cherry Forever smiling up at us, emanating love and happiness, we knew she was the deciding factor: we'd found the house we were looking for.

It was built in the early 1960s, was around 1780 square feet, and had a specific mid-century modern, slightly Japanese aesthetic in its design. The living room was open from one end of the house to the other, with the kitchen, laundry room, master bedroom and master bath flanking it on the left side of the house, and the guest bedrooms and guest bathroom flanking it on the right. We emphasized the mid-century aesthetic when we decorated the place, but not to any extreme. The furniture had mid-century design elements, but all the pieces were contemporary.

My favorite feature of the house was the fireplace. It faced the front door and was the first thing you saw when you entered the house, Off-center in its wall, its bricks protruded individually, by about ¾" and ran the width of the hearth, rising up in a straight line all the way to the ceiling. The bricks were designed to be exposed but had been painted over, like I said, so we had a guy come out and remove the paint from the bricks with a high-pressure blaster. Once exposed, the brick was beautiful just like I knew it would be. The fireplace became the room's centerpiece.

We scraped the cottage cheese ceilings off and put down gorgeous black cherry hardwood floors. We painted some walls a muted light green. We put a thick white shag rug in the center of the room, directly in front of the fireplace.

The shag rug rested between a sofa I picked out; it had mid-century lines but was upholstered in a knotty fabric that looked lived in. Across from the sofa stood two distressed, parakeet green leather chairs with dark wood accents that Elio found at CB2 on one of our trips to the Grove.

We adopted a couple of kittens: a male orange tabby named Guapo and a grey and white female tuxedo cat named Petunia. We decorated all the rooms and made the back yard an oasis surrounding the pool.

Our home was a sanctuary, and I loved living there with all my heart. I was living a life I couldn't have dreamed I'd be living just three to five years prior.

Although the original plan was for Leo to rent one of the three bedrooms to help us pay the mortgage and other monthly expenses, he moved out not long after we got there to go live with his new boyfriend in Pasadena.

Then Elio got laid off when the economic crash finally hit the Los Angeles hospitality industry. He became despondent one day and told me he didn't think he could handle it. I asked, "Handle what?"

"The house! The mortgage! All of it!" he replied.

I told him we were fine and we could manage until he got back to work. I told him if he left me alone with the house, I wouldn't know what to do. Elio knew my history and understood that I had a deep-seated fear of abandonment.

Even though the hotel he worked at had practically shut down the banquets department due to business falling off a cliff, whenever they had a random event for one of the studios or some other business that managed to be doing well enough to afford to have an event there, they'd always call Elio in to be one of the skeleton crew who worked it.

Over time, things got to the point of feeling perfect, and I couldn't believe how well my life was going. I was advancing in my position at work, getting raises left and right at what seemed like a suspiciously accelerated rate, and that brought me into an income bracket I'd never even come close to touching, ever. I was working out religiously first thing in the morning. I'd be out the door by 4:15 and off to the gym, back home an hour or so later, quick shower, make my coffee, drive to work in my new car, the first and only vehicle I've ever bought new (I'm still driving it).

I was living the dream, as I understood the dream to be. I'd achieved my life goals and thought that now it was just a matter of maintaining the life I'd grown into until I retired. I didn't foresee anything that could possibly go wrong and fuck it all up. I was inexperienced that way.

◆◆◆

Second Law

When I try to identify the beginning of the end, or the moment when my relationship with Elio ceased to exist as it had prior to that point, I land on a Christmas that we spent with my mom in Ashland, Oregon. We drove up there at night, and as we hit Grants Pass a blizzard landed on us. At the top of the pass we were required to put chains on the tires. We managed that just fine and made it down the other side of the pass.

At the bottom of the mountains the snow had let up and the roads were clear. I pulled over to remove the chains. The chain on the front passenger side was caught up on the tire, and for the life of me, I couldn't get it to come loose. It was one o'clock in the morning, the highway was muddy and wet, it was cold as fuck, my fingers were numb, I couldn't figure out how to get this chain off the tire, and I had a meltdown.

I ranted and raved and kicked the tire and bitched and complained about the stupid fucking chain and the stupid fucking tire and the stupid fucking cold and the stupid fucking dark that I couldn't see in. After I was done, I reached into the wheel well and tried again. The chain came undone immediately and fell to the asphalt

It was as if the universe were saying (because, you know, the universe has extra time to focus on little old me) let's see how far we can push you until you snap. Oh. Only that far, huh? What a huge disappointment you've become. As you were.

The visit went well, as far as I could tell. We went to Mt. Ashland for a day and skied, and we had dinner with my mom in Downtown Ashland, which was all decked out in holiday lights and decorations.

We were going at it late one night in front of the bathroom mirror, and as I was fucking him from behind, Elio was shoving his ass back in time with each thrust. We both had our porn faces on and were doing the whole, "Fuck yeah!" gay sex thing.

I looked at our reflection in the mirror, and we looked so funny that I removed myself from the passionate intensity of the moment. And when I saw our reflection removed from the context of that passionate intensity, we looked ridiculous. I burst out laughing.

Elio asked me why I was laughing and I told him we looked so stupid and funny, and then I imitated him executing his backwards ass bump, pursing my lips adding some porn-flavored dramatics to it, and he took offense to that. I mean, I had no intention of hurting his feelings or anything like that. I was laughing at both of us. I just happened to imitate him to illustrate my point. But I certainly regret it if I hurt Elio's feelings to the extent he said I did.

At any rate, things were never the same after that.

We didn't have sex again for months. By that time, business at Ociel's workplace was back to almost normal, and Elio usually worked nights during the week and on weekends. We came to resemble two ships passing in the night. Every night. I was busy at work, so it was easy not to dwell on it. But I asked him several times why we weren't having sex anymore. Elio gave me stock, disinterested answers: he was tired, work was too busy, he was stressed out.

Finally, he told me he lost interest in me sexually the night I made fun of us in front of the bathroom mirror in Oregon. I couldn't understand how, of all the things that could murder our sex life, that was the thing that did it. I couldn't understand how he would think I was making fun of him to be mean. We tried a couple of more times to get it on, but the vibe just wasn't there anymore. It was a huge disappointment.

The reason he gave me didn't make much sense, but I had a lot going on, so I just kept doing stuff. I threw myself into work, I continued to push myself harder at the gym, my orgasms grew more intense, by biblically epic proportions, even though they were all self-induced and experienced solo.

One thing I can say about myself is that I live my life in a way that allows me to sleep at night without pharmaceutical assistance. I live by a code that generally requires me to treat others no worse than I would ever want to be treated. That doesn't mean I don't stick up for myself. But I don't fuck people over. I don't lie about, manipulate or mischaracterize the intentions of others in order to destroy their careers so I can look good or advance my own. This makes me bad at capitalism, but I'd rather be able to sleep at night.

At work, I became the target of a smear campaign. I opened myself up to it, I can own that now, but it blindsided me, just as it was designed to.

A woman I'd paired myself up with so I could be mentored in the ways of court operations management, which I was moving into (or so I thought), fucked me over because I expressed independent thought, and my belief that loyalty between a court clerk and a federal judge had to be a two way street in order for it to work.

Not a controversial position to take, I would think. I mean, those judges have lifetime appointments. They never have to worry about finding work again. Why would I be selflessly loyal to a federal judge without being certain that they had my back as well? Yeah, that was a mistake.

A coworker of mine, whom the other Black female employees in our department referred to as The Great Black Shark, used a heated email exchange between us to accuse me of being racist. The federal judge to whom I was assigned, who was also Black and eager to fuck the Great Black Shark, adopted a position of outrage, insisting I'd committed a cruel, unforgivable racist attack upon her.

This incident coincided with my mentor's decision to inform said federal judge of my comment regarding loyalty being a two-way street.

Well, the shit hit the fan. I was removed from my position as that judge's assigned courtroom deputy, and the Great Black Shark moved in, set up shop, and began fucking the judge in short order. In his chambers. During regular work hours. Of course, I never witnessed this myself. I was just told about it by others, including people I knew and had recently worked with from the judge's chambers.

The day I learned I'd been fucked over and removed from my assigned position with that judge, I went up to his chambers and told him I'd been informed of his decision to terminate my assignment, that I'd enjoyed working with him and wished him the best. Then I asked him why he'd made this decision. He declined to give me a reason. He said he might let me know. One day. In the future.

And that, as they say, was that.

Court management treated me like a pariah from that point forward. I didn't get fired, but I was made an example of. I became a floating courtroom deputy. I wasn't assigned to a specific judge. Instead, I worked with all the judges, wherever I was needed, based on other courtroom deputies who'd called out or were on vacation or whatever.

They didn't fire me or lay me off. They did this thing where they gave me just about every courtroom assignment possible and praised my ability to adapt and perform in any given set of circumstances, with any judge. They gave me satisfactory reviews. But they behaved as if none of that was of any value to them. I was left to stagnate, with no apparent route to advancement or professional growth.

I liked the job a lot, but I eventually left because it had become a dead end. I was ambitious back then. I was full of piss and vinegar, as my grandfather used to say. At the same time, I didn't believe in being cutthroat to get ahead. I'm just not built that way, and I have no interest in it. I consider this aspect of myself a personal strength, even if it's considered a character flaw by the established standards of capitalism.

During this time, I attended graduate school for a master's degree in public administration because I still had ambitions to get into public sector management. Even though my instincts told me the court was a dead end, I held out hope that things would change if I just kept doing a good enough job and could get along with as many people as possible (save for the horny judge and the Great Black Shark, who were scandalizing the courthouse with their ongoing, barely concealed shenanigans).

◆◆◆

Miss Congeniality

While I eventually worked through my feelings about this sequence of events and can see that it spurred me on to better things, at the time I went through it I was devastated. I put so much energy into that job, and it was a lot of fun to have that many balls up in the air each day: scheduling hearing calendars, maintaining case management, leading jury selection for trial, being the primary point of contact for the judge. I loved it.

I worked so much overtime that my supervisor eventually reached out and told me I needed to slow down. That I was making myself a prime candidate for burn-out. He reminded me to take time off and aim to achieve a healthy work life balance. That the work would be here when I got back.

As the drama with the judge and the Great Black Shark unfolded, it became clear to me that my "mentor" had fucked me up the ass with a twelve-foot-tall Saguaro cactus. She'd run to the judge and told him I was not properly subservient, and must be punished for exercising independent thought that did not prioritize him before my own wellbeing.

I was enraged to the point that I fantasized about causing that mentor bitch serious bodily injury. I also couldn't get past how the Judge and the Great Black Shark had thrown me under the bus, and for what? Alone time in the judge's chambers, apparently. What floored me is that the judge went the dirty route instead of just telling me up front, "I'd like to make a change, good luck in your future endeavors, I'll give you a reference."

When I went to Elio with all this rage and turmoil, I told him there was no way I could stay in this job with these people.

They were fucking assholes, who had fucked me the fuck over! I was out!

Elio's response was that this was just work. And things like this happen at work all the time. And that I should just get over it. I should not worry about my former mentor or the judge or the Great Black Shark. I should just focus on my own work and ignore anyone who'd betrayed me.

I tried to explain to him the depth of the fuckery that had occurred (and was still occurring) but he didn't hear me. He didn't really care. He just told me I needed to man up, swallow my pride, and keep going to work.

My husband was more concerned about keeping the house and maintaining our lifestyle together as a married, home owning same-sex couple than he was about being in love and taking care of each other emotionally. Any ideas I had of ways to extricate myself from the court, which usually involved adjustments to our lives so that we could make it work financially, Elio had no interest in.

I harbored resentment for Elio at this point for unilaterally removing sex from the equation that was our same sex marriage. But I had to admit we got along well, that I enjoyed living in our house, and that aside from the small detail that we were no longer fucking, the marriage was, for all intents and purposes, a successful one.

I leaned into this boulder I was forced to push up the hill every day, and at the end of the day I'd let go of it so it would roll back down, waiting for me at the bottom of the hill to rejoin it the next morning and start all over again. I numbed the emotional turmoil with a steady stream of Xanax, which got me through the first few months of my new reality. After that, I took care of myself unmedicated.

I got into activities that empowered me. I hit the gym harder and more regularly than I ever had before. I started running in 5Ks and 10Ks. I watched T.V. shows that specialized in dark, often mean-spirited humor, such as the *Comedy Central* celebrity roasts (I especially enjoyed the dark, often nasty humor of comics like insult queen Lisa Lampanelli and problematic yet strangely hot and fuckable button pusher Anthony Jeselnik). I watched T.V. shows about morally ambiguous, often corrupt characters breaking the law and fucking each other over for career advancement or financial gain, shows such as *Damages*, *The Good Wife* and *Breaking Bad*.

I tried to power through my circumstances and process the storm of bitterness, resentment and rage I had brewing inside me.

For a while, I interviewed for every job in the district that came up, and at each interview the same H.R. manager would eventually ask me, "Why did Judge So and So terminate your assignment as his courtroom deputy?" And every time, I'd answer, "He declined to give me a reason."

The purpose behind this response was to demonstrate peak poise, with a facial expression of politeness but remove, indicating that I no longer gave much thought to those circumstances. Ancient history, and all that. Which apparently was not the answer she was looking for.

What I really wanted to say was, "So he could dick down the Great Black Shark, you fucking idiots!" Why didn't they ask *him* about why he terminated the assignment if they were so fucking curious? Of course, I assumed they knew. They just enjoyed rubbing it in and keeping me in the dark. Eventually I stopped applying for positions in the federal court system and looked elsewhere.

As my job search intensified, something became clear: the court was paying me so well that I couldn't find a job I was qualified for at a comparable salary. The ones I qualified for, based on my education and experience, especially jobs in the public sector, didn't pay nearly as much as the court did.

In a very real sense, I was trapped. The court had me locked into a career holding pattern that deprived me of any opportunity for growth or advancement and paid me very well to maintain that holding pattern.

I wrestled with the fidelity question for a while, because this time I was officially married. But when I weighed the pros and cons of maintaining the status quo in my head, I always came out dead last. I'd played by the rules and was getting the shaft. Not in a good way.

I was insanely frustrated by the fact that I wasn't getting laid. Like, ever. And I was jacked up at the time, I looked good. I was quite fuckable and I knew it. I wasn't about to beg for it from Elio, or pressure him into it. Why pressure someone who doesn't want to fuck you into sex? Where's the appeal in that?

I started trolling hook up sites for dick. I figured, I'm doing all this hard work, putting up with all this bullshit at the court to make the mortgage payments and get my car paid off. I was attending graduate school and incurring insane debt to advance my so-called career. I should be getting laid regularly too! That's the least of what I should be getting!

32. Enter the Monkey

○

—DIAMOND RINGS

TRASHY + FUNNY = PERFECTION

I found Monkey on a hook up site. His profile was unlike any I'd ever seen, and trust me, I'd seen a lot. He posted pics of himself showing off his assets and allure, which was standard hook up site fare. But he also employed other elements in his profile pics that intrigued me.

He held up a mask of a blockhead on a stick to hide his face in one of the pics. He photographed himself in strange environments with weird handmade masks and stuff always hiding his face. His profile was trashy and funny. I like a guy who doesn't take himself all that seriously when he puts it out there. It reveals an ability to relax and have fun that not many people possess in this day and age. I messaged him, he replied, we arranged a meeting at his place.

Monkey was of Italian descent and had grown up in the Gulf Coast Region of the Deep South. He was diminutive in stature, standing about five feet seven inches tall, give or take, and had a slender build. His white skin looked snow-lit, somewhat translucent and, as I would soon learn, threw his dark pit and bush hair into sharp relief. The hair on his head was dark blond, as was his mustache, and his green eyes were reflective prisms. He was seven years younger than me.

Monkey was an artist. His home was filled with pieces of his own work and of works by others he'd collected. He also had a vast, overwhelming collection of tchotchkes. Every surface in his room, and almost every inch of wall space, was covered with something.

Monkey's artistic style leaned into hyper commercialism parody and appropriation art. My favorite piece that he'd done was a black on white drawing of a seated orangutang smoking a cigarette and reading *Valley of the Dolls* with a bored expression on its face.

Throughout our time together, Monkey generated most of his income through costume, stage and set design. He had recently worked with a flamboyant, up and coming television personality with national exposure, who had decided, mid-ascent to fame and fortune, that he didn't want to put in the work it took to become famous, and that Monkey was becoming a drag. Their parting of the ways was not amicable, and Monkey's wounds were still fresh when I met him.

Monkey was into astronomy, futurism and building complicated Japanese robot models. He drove a beat up, late 1980s Oldsmobile 98, which he painstakingly painted with gold paint (it was a dark brown car) to resemble a Louis Vuitton bag. You can google it, there are pics of it on the internet. It was fucking hilarious.

For him to drive that car around L.A., the birthplace of car culture, where cars and high-end fashion brands are worn as status symbols, was just a good-natured middle finger to all of it. The absurdity of brand obsession and consumerism, in the form of a beat-up Oldsmobile painted to look like a Louis Vuitton bag? Priceless.

I fucked him the first time we met, and I fell in love with him somewhere between the moment we got naked and the moment I nutted inside him. After I came, I looked down at him, my dick still throbbing in his hole, sweat running off my body, my head about to spin right off my neck, trying to catch my breath, and said, "I'm keeping you." I meant it.

The next day I went to a shop in Little Tokyo, which was within walking distance of the courthouse, and found a complicated beyond belief model of some fancy Japanese robot. It looked like a cross between a Power Ranger and Venom, but much more intricate and detailed. Monkey eventually christened it ManSpider.

I returned to his place on my way home from work a few days after we'd met, unannounced, because he hadn't returned any of my calls or messages. I wasn't about to let that stop me.

When I got there, he came to the door and was not in a good state. He looked like he'd just woken up, and he was hostile toward me. He kept asking me questions like, "What are you doing here?" and I was like, "I brought you something. It's really cool, I knew you'd like it. I thought of you as soon as I saw it."

I ignored the questions he was asking me and just kept telling him about the robot model. I figured, if I didn't argue with him about whether or not I should even be there, or about whether or not the way I'd unilaterally decided to reconnect with him without getting an okay from him first was appropriate or acceptable, then I didn't have to reach a point in our conversation where he said something stupid to me like:

"No," or

"I'm not interested."

"You're not my type."

"I'm not looking for anything serious."

"I like playing the field."

"I have a boyfriend."

"I'm not really gay."

"I don't think we're sexually compatible."

"I need space right now."

"My mother warned me about homosexuals like you."

And other reasons not to give real love a chance.

I didn't manage to win him over that day, but he finally accepted the model, acknowledged it was very cool, hung out with me for a while so we could talk, and agreed that we could continue seeing each other.

It didn't take long for my relationship with Monkey to become my driver. He gave me hope that my life could have some kind of meaning in it that wasn't tied to paying a mortgage, being a lackey for federal judges, or being gay married. There were elements of those three things, my home, my job and my marriage, that I loved, valued and felt a deep sense of gratitude for.

But where Elio had grown indifferent toward me, Monkey focused his attention on me. He was into me. In Monkey's eyes, I was a stud, and he treated me like one. I worked out even harder so I'd look good naked for him.

I also assumed the role of protector toward him. Whenever we were out together, I was the big guy. He was the imp who could jump around and cause mischief. I was the one who kept an eye on him and made sure he stayed out of trouble.

Unparallel Lines

I found myself in an untenable set of circumstances, though. Married to a guy who had no interest in fucking me, responsible for a mortgage that ate up a majority of my income, trapped in a well-paying federal job that was slowly destroying my sense of self-worth. I had everything I'd ever dreamed of having, technically, but it didn't look and feel the way I needed it to.

I conducted this affair with Monkey for a couple of years. My relationships with Elio and Monkey ran on parallel tracks inside the framework that was my life. I pulled it off for a good amount of time and was quite proud of myself for doing so.

The friends I'd had for a long time were mostly supportive of my relationship with Monkey, save for one from high school who was a Log Cabin Republican and had been searching for a husband for a very long time. I'll just add right here that this guy makes bank, and he's also a Republican, so I can only feel so sorry for him at any given time.

One night Monkey and I met up with him at the Hard Rock Café at Hollywood and Highland to see a performance by none other than 80s legends Bananarama. The ladies were awesome, they both had affable personalities and made the most of basically just standing in the middle of the bar area with a couple of mics in front of them, singing to karaoke tracks of all their biggest hits.

Back to my Log Cabin Republican friend, who was pissed that I had a boyfriend and a husband. He said, "I can't even find one guy, and here you are with two!"

I could have said, "Well, it sucks to suck, bitch," or something equally cunty, but I didn't need to. I was just living my life. This was how it looked. If my husband and boyfriend didn't have a problem with it, why should he?

Elio didn't know about the affair at first, but then one New Year's Eve we had plans to go to Leo's for a party. Shortly before we left, Elio looked at my phone and came across my text message stream with Monkey. In it, we said we loved each other. Miraculously, Elio suddenly gave a fuck.

He was angry about something very specific: Monkey and I had said we love each other. That was crossing the line. Apparently, fucking Monkey wasn't a problem. But he was PISSED that we'd said we love each other, and he didn't hold back.

As for me, my relationship with Monkey was a no-brainer. It was a pathway back to my humanity, to a world where I was valued and appreciated, not because I was paying a mortgage, but because I was me. Monkey not only found me fun to be with, but he also found me to be funny, interesting, and hot. The feelings were mutual. All of them.

I considered Monkey, to quote something I once saw on the internet, "an enigma, wrapped in bacon." Monkey was mysterious, and bacon is my favorite food.

I couldn't help but think of Monkey as a chaos agent. He challenged me all the time. He was always bugging me to divorce Elio, sell the house and move in with him. And I wanted to be with him, but what Monkey didn't realize was that, for me to maximize my return on everything I'd invested in over the past several years, I had to plan my exit and execute it methodically, in a way that wouldn't sell me up short.

One day I got off work early and drove home, excited because I'd beat traffic for once. I pulled into the driveway and noticed the bedroom curtains were closed. That's weird, I thought, because opening the curtains to let the sunshine in was one of the first things Elio did every morning.

I got out of the car, walked to the front door, and let myself in. I went to the bedroom, and when I came to the doorway (the door was open), I was treated to the sight of Elio on our bed getting spit roasted by a couple of middle-aged white guys.

I turned around and walked back out the front door. I closed the door behind me, stepped off the porch, and stopped, not sure where I should go. Then I thought: wait a minute, this is my fucking house. Why am I the one who's leaving?

I turned around, went back through the door, and instead of turning left toward the master bedroom again, I turned right and headed to my media room. A few minutes later, Elio came in and apologized. "I'm so sorry. I didn't intend for you to see me that way." Obviously.

"Where are they?" I asked. Apparently, after I'd seen them, turned around and gone back out the front door, one of them had asked Elio, "Are you in trouble?" Elio had said, "Just a little," at which point those spit roasters grabbed their clothes, got dressed in record time, and hurried out the side door so they wouldn't chance running into me.

The thing is, I wasn't hurt that Elio had been fucking someone other than me. We hadn't fucked in a long time, and it didn't take a rocket scientist to figure out that he was probably getting laid elsewhere. But in our bed? That was low.

We talked it out a little, and I suggested we go to same sex marriage counseling to see if we could salvage what was left of our marriage. He agreed to give it a shot.

Elio told me that day I could have anything I wanted, to make up for what had happened. I didn't have to think very long before I responded: I wanted to spend the night at Monkey's place one night a week. Elio didn't like it, but he was a man of his word, and it became a part of our arrangement.

Look, I know we all have dreams and aspirations about our ideal life partner, but no single blueprint for marriage works for everyone. Each marriage is unique, and as long as no one is being exploited, abused, or held against their will, the only people who ever have a right to say anything about a marriage arrangement are the two people who are married.

We went to several counseling sessions together, but Elio never really gave it a chance. He said, "I don't need to hear some white guy tell me it's okay to let my husband cheat on me." I figured, okay, fair enough. But also, he should talk. What did he want me to do instead? The passion we shared from the time we met until after we moved into the house was completely absent from our marriage. We didn't even try to have sex anymore. After a certain amount of time not fucking, you lose interest in the idea of it altogether.

Elio and I had love and affection for one another. We hardly ever argued and coexisted quite peacefully. But I needed to have love and passion in my life. If I couldn't get it from Elio, but was lucky enough to find it someplace else, then I was going to run with that and enjoy myself. Why shouldn't I?

Why should I deprive myself of love, passion and excitement, which all made me feel really good, just because my husband decided that I said the wrong thing once and was therefore cut off from that part of our relationship forever? Did I owe it to Elio to suck it up, keep paying the mortgage, keep working at a job where the environment was toxic and debilitating, and deprive myself of the one relationship in my life that lit a firecracker under my ass? I refused to give that up.

I didn't know what else to do, but I wasn't going to remain stuck in a sexless marriage, no matter how well we got along as roommates. By the time we'd reached this crossroads, it was too late for us to negotiate new ground rules. We should have addressed these issues as they occurred; when Elio lost interest in me sexually, and when I became frustrated as a result. The time to have those conversations had passed, though, and the damage was done.

I didn't marry Elio to be roommates. I didn't pay a mortgage on the house just so I could be miserable in it. And I wasn't going to stay at a job where I was treated badly, devalued and gaslit by leadership until I was convinced that I was incompetent, unnecessary and disposable.

◆◆◆

EXTRICATION (THIS WON'T HURT A BIT)

A couple of things happened that cemented my decision to do what was right for me, and not what was required to uphold these fake markers of success that I'd become entangled in.

The first thing was that Monkey moved back to the East Coast. He missed New York City, where he'd lived for a time, and there were ample job opportunities there tied to the theater and drag scenes that he could explore. Also, he was tired of waiting for me to leave Elio.

Monkey's departure had what I'm pretty sure was its desired effect on me. I started making an exit plan. I visited Monkey twice in Jersey City, which is right across the Hudson River from Lower Manhattan. I flew into Newark and would spend a week at a time with him.

The first thing I had to do was extricate myself from the court. For years, I managed to withstand the bad energy, the hostile work environment, the deliberate attempts to destabilize my equilibrium by constantly reassigning me to different units whenever they felt like it. To drive their point home, they wound up relocating me to the cubicle I was assigned to when I started working there. On top of Monkey now being gone, this was the last dig from the court that I was going to take.

I learned from several court employees that the court made a practice of paying all unemployment claims applied for by former employees of the department I worked in. The federal, judges we were there to support had been given lifetime appointments. Like most people in positions of authority with no systems in place to enforce accountability, judges could abuse their power, break rules, engage in conduct that was, if not prohibited by law, then at the very least, frowned upon in the context of a professional work environment.

At the same time, judges are basically attorneys on steroids, and like most attorneys, they like to do whatever they want without much regard for how it impacts others. There was no one at the court whose job it was to advocate for the courtroom deputies. Which meant, judges could theoretically do whatever they wanted, without giving any thought to how it may impact the livelihoods of whatever courtroom deputy they may be fucking over at any given moment.

The court also didn't want to be drawn into any messy lawsuits, where sordid details about the upstanding, lifetime appointed federal judges' unseemly behaviors might come to light. So, word on the street was, the court paid all unemployment claims filed by former staff no matter what.

Having been stuck back in the desk where it all began, I knew that it was time for me to get the fuck away from those people. I requested a desk job and a set of duties that would not require that I be reassigned every few months. I disclosed my HIV status and stated that the upheaval and constant reassignments were very stressful and affecting my health.

It's important to mention the turn of events that brought me all this turmoil and grief. When I'd responded to the Great Black Shark's email with a cunty tone that I did not bother trying to soften for her, I was already irritated with her because I knew she was working against me. I just didn't know how.

In my email response, I corrected her grammar in a sentence she'd used that was, in effect, African American vernacular. But it was also grammatically incorrect, which in that moment, I chose to point out and correct her on. Very cuntily. So, that is what fucked up my life for a few years. Keep that in mind each and every time you're tempted to email someone with even a whiff of cuntiness in your prose. It can and very often does come back to bite you in your ass, and the people who write things to bait you into telling them off know this.

I applied for unemployment, and they approved it, no questions asked. I cashed out my 401K and lived off it for a year while I purged myself of the toxins the court had polluted my psyche with. I worked out like a maniac, I enjoyed myself, I worked an online editing job, I enjoyed my last summer at the house. I soaked it all in.

I also informed Elio that I wanted to sell the house and list it in September so we could hopefully be out by the end of the year. He pushed back. He didn't want to sell, but I told him I would only pay the mortgage through the end of the year. When he finally accepted it, he allowed me to handle most of the arrangements.

The house sold almost immediately. It was a seller's market, and its value was higher than it had been when we bought it. Escrow was excruciating because a new California law had just gone into effect that extended the escrow period to what seemed like an interminable length of time.

Over the course of the past few years, I'd not only been under pressure to make the mortgage payments so we could keep living in the house, but my mother was also circling me, hoping that I would be able to get her into a property where she could relax and not worry about trying to live off social security without becoming homeless.

Before Elio and I started looking for a home in L.A., we'd planned on purchasing a property in Oregon that my mom could live in and maintain until we secured employment there and could make the move up. We planned it this way because we didn't think we could afford a house in Los Angeles. But the housing crash in 2008 suddenly made home ownership in Los Angeles possible.

This of course changed our Oregon plans, much to my mom's disappointment. We'd been toying with the idea of a remodel of the detached garage to convert a portion of it into a living space with a bathroom and kitchenette. My mom was hoping this would pan out. When news of the rocky state of our marriage got to my mom, she of course sided with Elio and did her best to convince me that I was making a mistake by leaving the marriage and the house.

Having assumed the mantle of He Who Makes Living In Our Fabulous House Possible, the idea that I would be letting down my husband and my mom created a lot of anxiety for me. I knew they didn't want to sell the house. I knew they'd push back and do their best to keep things as they were. I needed to figure out a way to lessen the pressure they would try to exert over me. I already had a lot of doubt and insecurity about the path I was taking and the changes I was making to my life. I didn't need both of them to further complicate the process.

During that final year in the house, specifically the last half of the year or so, I engaged in what I came to identify as my Year of Living Dangerously. I embarked on an odyssey of meth consumption and sexual adventures with a fairly large number of L.A. tweakers. I hadn't used meth since at least a couple of years prior to moving in with Elio, so it had been over a decade.

I knew that if I became engaged in this behavior, to a level that was unprecedented for me and was noticeably alarming to the casual observer, I would succeed in pushing Elio and my mom away from me, because I knew they would not be equipped or inclined to do the work it would take to disentangle someone from the level of meth use I was about to embark on.

Elio had shared with me before we got married that he'd had his own period of meth use when he was younger, but he'd quit cold turkey and hadn't used since. He had a very low, close to nonexistent tolerance policy for it in his life.

I knew my mom's existence was precarious due to her financial circumstances. I knew she wasn't equipped, and didn't have the resources, to "save me from meth" when the time came. I knew her keen instinct for self-preservation would trump coming to my rescue. And I didn't begrudge her for it. I just knew it to be true.

Besides, I didn't need her to come to my rescue. I'd quit meth before. I could do it again. To her credit, she did express concern for me when what was going on became apparent to her, but that's as far as it went.

It was hard to see my mom and Elio look at me in a way that showed they considered me a lost cause. A casualty. A ghost of my former self who was already gone forever.

At the same time, I was giving them an out. If they didn't want to chase me down the tina rabbit hole, who could blame them? There was only so much you could do. At the end of the day, we each must take responsibility for our actions.

This was an effective way to extricate myself from their lives by making them think it was their idea. And I could go on without the ongoing pressure to change my mind about selling the house and return to what I hadn't even yet freed myself from.

I've always been a strategic thinker. I always plan ahead and I've always got a back door that I'm prepared to slip through should circumstances suddenly dictate it. These are the planning tools of a survivor. I've relied on this toolbox on more than one occasion in my life and, while I'm pretty sure I'll always have an exit strategy in place, no matter how happy I may be, I do hope that I'm never required to utilize one again. I'd prefer to leave through the front door from here on out.

Go!

The day before he was scheduled to fly out from the East Coast, I called Monkey and came clean about what I'd been up to. I told him I'd been using meth for the past several months. I told him I was out of money, that I wouldn't have any until escrow closed, and that if he wanted to change his mind and not come, that was okay, I'd understand.

Monkey was a pothead, but that's as far as he went. He didn't even drink. He'd had a bad ecstasy experience at a Hollywood party when he first got to L.A., and I guess it was embarrassing enough that he decided he was out. Monkey didn't falter or hang up on me. I was so grateful when he said of course he's still coming. It made me feel like there was a chance I was going to get through this.

My appearance had gone through a dramatic change during late summer and early fall that year. My tina brain kept telling me I was hot because I was able to fit into clothes sizes that I hadn't fit into since high school. But I had gone from a solid 195, in the body of a guy who works out like a maniac, to 145 within the space of about four months. I was emaciated, but strangely enough, I photographed well. For a while. Then I continued to lose weight. My plug Jason kept saying to me,

"You gotta eat." I didn't know what the hell he was talking about.

I picked Monkey up at Burbank airport the next night. When he saw me, he was taken aback. He didn't say anything to me right away, but he got on Metafilter that night and asked for advice on how to fatten up his once beefy boyfriend and how to get me through withdrawals.

As difficult as withdrawing from tina can be, it's just a matter of managing your cravings. Don't get me wrong: they're BIG cravings. Fucking huge. But it's not the kind of withdrawals that make you violently ill, like heroin or other opioid withdrawals.

The cravings are severe though. You feel like shit. Half the time, I felt like I wanted to jump out of my skin. And it fucked with my brain by giving me bouts of brain fog, and general confusion. My brain didn't process information as easily as it used to. Luckily, I got my brain back. But it took time.

For me, what it came down to was pushing through the impulses to use. Your brain LOVES tina. It mimics dopamine, then triggers your brain to produce more dopamine, then traps the released dopamine inside the synapses so that the dopamine rush doesn't subside for a very long time. Which feels euphoric.

Then, when you deprive your brain of the chemical that triggers the euphoria, your brain does everything it can to talk you into doing it again. Your brain will tell you *anything* to convince you that doing more tina will make everything better. And that may seem true if you're going through withdrawals. If you break down and use, everything will feel better. For a while. Until it doesn't.

Then you'll be back on the tina merry go round, using while you're planning to stop using, but being back at the pre-dawn of no longer using. You'll be back at square one. You'll have to stop using all over again. And that's a long, often painful and challenging process. Just because it's difficult, though, is no reason to not stop using and doing your best to stay off it.

When I stopped doing tina, I just stopped. I made sure my home environment was very organized. I made sure I filled my days with a lot of shit to do, to keep me busy. I worked out a lot, which helped empower me and helped me work through the frustrated energy created by the cravings. I had to be ready to argue with myself and be relentless in talking myself out of choosing to get high again. Your brain will not give up. It will keep pushing you to use. Eventually, your cravings and impulses to use begin to subside, the arguments your brain makes become weaker, your strategies to redirect yourself when triggered become habits that give you the strength to say no.

This process isn't something that happens to you. It's something you design for yourself, in a way that maximizes the likelihood that you will succeed. It's the work you put into redefining yourself into a person who doesn't use. It's extremely difficult, but it can be done.

The house became a ghost of its former self. Elio had moved out and all his stuff was gone. Monkey and I stayed there together, packing shit up and waiting for escrow to close. The sofa was still there, and I had a video projector, so we hooked the Playstation up to it and played Fallout on the living room wall to pass the time.

With all traces of Elio gone, and the rooms only sparsely furnished, the wait became intolerable. I'd lie on the sofa and just stare at the lines of the living room, the eaves, the fireplace, the hardwood floors. I'd go out back and run my fingers through the leaves of the pomegranate tree I'd planted a few years prior, and that already produced full sized pomegranates. I'd walk through the empty rooms in the house and soak up as much energy as I could.

The house still represented a dream of mine, and it wasn't going to be easy letting that dream go. If it wasn't tied to my former toxic workplace and my soon-to-be ex-husband who'd decided to check out, I wouldn't be leaving. I appreciated the good times I'd had there, though.

Besides, this was my plan, and my plan was unfolding just the way I wanted it to when I designed it. Now that I was about to leave the house behind, the gravity of the plan hit me with full force. My mind scrambled for ways to fix this, to do it differently so that it worked. But it was too late to keep hanging on to this life. I had to let go.

The hardest part about leaving the house occurred when I was blindsided by memories of Elio and I, what our relationship had been like during the time we'd met, got to know each other, lived together, got married and purchased the house. I'd shut down my emotions about our marriage for so long, in an effort to protect myself and get through the day-to-day business of living, that I thought those feelings were long gone. They weren't.

They came flooding back to me: all the high hopes, the good intentions, the love we felt. I realized those feelings were still alive in me. Elio and I started out just like most other people who get married. But then other things started drawing our focus away from making it work, and as time passed, it became more difficult. At one point, each one of us, in our own timeframe, decided to check out.

Where our relationship had once been the source of all the rest of it, what eventually happened was that the source, the driver, the why for our lives together, became the house. Our relationship, our connection with one another, became secondary. We allowed that to happen. But I don't think either one of us realized it had happened until after the fact, and by the time we did, it was too late.

Even so, I had so much fun in that house. It was a fantastic home. We made it great. It had style. We had some epic pool parties. We turned that house into a home, and that home was the shit. So were we for making it that. Yes, I was going to miss the house, and all the plans, ideas, and dreams I had with Elio that didn't pan out. I just had to keep reminding myself that some of those plans, ideas and dreams did pan out. And they were worth it. Things just changed.

Now it was all about me and Monkey. I had both sets of feelings at the same time: I could appreciate the awesome and happy times we'd had in that house. But it was also time for me to get the fuck out of L.A.

I knew I'd probably bitten off more than I could chew, but I've always been a Go Big or Go Home kind of guy. That might be confidence, foolishness, recklessness, or something else. And the funny thing is, I didn't have a home to go to if I didn't go big. Going big was my only option. That's the choice I made, and that's the choice I'd live with. I had some fear, but not enough to stop me or make me change my mind. Throughout my adult life, things have always had a way of working out. I didn't expect this time to be any different. All that was left for me to do was to go. I took a deep breath and I went.

33. Plugs 3: Jason

○

Boss

Because I didn't know how to dive off the deep end into tina, I needed to find someone who did. I found a guy on a hook up site who referred to himself as Twisted Fuck Boss. His pictures were slightly above standard hook up site fare. There was an element of self-awareness detectable in the way he posed, the way he gazed into the camera, and the way several of the shots were framed.

Seeing how playing it safe had landed me in the dead-end life from which I was currently trying to extricate myself, I figured I needed to reach far outside my comfort zone for the wildest person I could find. This guy might be twisted, but he looked fun as well, and I've always been of the opinion that fun and danger go hand in hand. I messaged the guy and heard back from him quickly. He invited me over. I accepted.

Jason lived in a subsidized housing complex in Altadena. It was newer as far as buildings in Altadena went, with an intercom and tenant directory out front, and a person who manned the front desk at all times of the day and night.

Jason lived on the third floor, and when he greeted me, he was affable, friendly and hotter than his profile pics had indicated. Our first meet up was pretty much so I could introduce myself and he could evaluate me to see if he thought I was someone he'd want as a client.

That first night, I was sitting in a chair facing him as he stood before me. He told me he fucked his clients as a way of forming a bond with them. To make them loyal. I reached up and cupped his bulge in my hand. He smiled down at me without protesting, and that was the only green light I needed.

Jason was a true professional. He was thick and meaty, and his balls were a mouthful that I never got tired of. My fascination and enjoyment of Jason never diminished the entire time we hung out together.

Jason was an alpha, and I assumed our sexual activity would consist of me bottoming for him. I was fine with that if that's how it had to be, but Jason never allowed that dynamic to establish itself between us. He allowed me to assume the dom role, and since I was willing and able to take the reins and run with it, that's where we went.

I got off on knowing he was showing me something not many people got to see. I was privy to this deeply hidden side of Jason, and I was honored that he trusted me enough to show me what that looked like.

I'm pretty sure part of the turn on for him was that I presented as such a square, Wonder bread suburban type, clueless and polite most of the time. When I got dominant, I was playing against type. My position in our relationship as dom was limited to when we engaged in sexual activities and had decided beforehand that's what we were doing. Jason remained an alpha dog at all other times.

Jason was never boring. The way he effectively took me in and allowed me to share space with him was very generous. I needed it at the time.

One of the walls in Jason's apartment was covered with weapons: swords, daggers, a machete, hunting knives, and those stars that secret agents kill people with by throwing them into the necks of their enemies.

Jason had grown up in Chicago Heights, living on the streets from a young age with a posse of other street kids he led. They would frequently travel to Chicago to make money. He told me they'd hook up with gay johns, who would get a motel room they could stay in for a day or two, which they'd use to turn tricks after the first john left.

Jason and his posse looked out for each other and backed each other up when necessary. He assured me that they didn't make a habit of targeting gay men to commit crimes against them, but they did rough up the men who tried to steal from them, assault them, change the terms of their arrangements after they'd been agreed upon, and so forth. I've no doubt they did, in fact, fuck up a few gay men who had it coming.

Jason and I became emotionally entangled with one another very quickly. The men I find most attractive are the ones who are authentically themselves, without explanation or apology. What you see is what you get. That's what works best for me.

Jason put it all out there, and while there were layers of artifice in how he presented himself to the outside world, the layers were authentically him, if that makes sense. They were just him at different volumes, tailored to the situation at hand.

I hung out with Jason all the time, usually at his place. We'd get high and hang out all day or all night. We didn't spend all our time watching porn like I usually did when I was high. Not that we didn't watch porn, we just didn't do it all the time. We had long conversations and got to know each other pretty well.

He dealt out of his apartment, and since I was spending so much time with him, I was there when his clients came over. It was interesting. His clients came from all walks of life: laborers, doctors, athletes, soccer moms, you name it. And Jason had a story for every last one of them. I still wonder what story Jason tells about me, if he tells one at all. I also wonder what his clients thought of me. Most of them probably paid me no mind.

Jason had a big personality. His presence dominated any space he was in. Underneath his tough exterior, he was a sensitive man who could be very loving. I don't mean he was feminine or weak, because he wasn't. But he had access to his emotions. He was at home in them. There aren't many men I've met who I can say that about.

There was a marked difference between the way Jason behaved when we were alone, and how he behaved when we weren't. Around others, he kept me at a distance but went out of his way to include me in the conversation or the group dynamic. He never ignored me or tuned me out.

Jason had a wicked sense of humor and could make the darkest scenarios sound hilarious, making me wish I'd been there to partake in them. He'd been to prison, and he suffered some psychological issues because of the trauma he'd endured as a kid. His street kid persona had matured into a streetwise adult, but I could still see the kid every time I looked at him. He also had an inner spark that shone through his eyes and illuminated any room he was in.

Jason's laugh was quick, sharp, loud and infectious. He was a man who'd been subjected to some of the harshest conditions a kid can face, but he'd come into adulthood with his killer sense of humor intact, along with a deep appreciation for intensity and pleasure.

Jason's humor was a tactic he'd developed as a kid to put those around him at ease so he could observe them, take note of any tells they let slip, and learn as much about them as possible. He told me he didn't have to ask questions. People love to talk about themselves. He'd interject conversations with a joke or an observation to prompt the person to reveal more information or to guide the conversation to where he wanted it to go.

◆◆◆

OPEN

Even though we got close, Jason started to do things that raised red flags. Incidents occurred from out of left field that forced me to reconsider our relationship. One afternoon I arrived at his place, and a cute young guy was lying on the bed. He was friendly and chatty, so we hung out together while Jason took a shower.

The guy was an ex who, about a year prior, had gone on a leave of absence from his management position at a government agency so he could go to rehab, detox, and get his shit together. He'd gone on a meth binge and disappeared from work with no explanation, and the only way he managed to salvage his position was by doing a stint in rehab and filing for federal disability protection, which was predicated on his being in rehab and not being an active user of illegal drugs.

After rehab, he remained clean for about a year without any problems. He also ghosted Jason, who was a trigger for relapse and a threat to his sobriety. He said he'd just come over to hang out for a while. I didn't stay for very long that day because I could tell that Jason was really into the guy and I didn't want to be a third wheel.

I came back the next night, and the guy was still there. The vibe in the apartment had changed. The guy went from being charming and cute to being fearful and strung out. Jason had slammed him, which meant he'd administered meth to him intravenously. Jason was well known for being a good admin, and people would sometimes come by just so he could find a vein and inject them, then they'd leave. I'd never slammed, and Jason never asked me if I wanted to.

At one point, Jason went to the restroom, and I asked the guy if he was okay. He said, "I can't let him keep me here." I just played it cool because he seemed on the verge of panic, so I reassured him that he was fine, and he could leave any time he wanted.

Jason came back out and we sat around for a few minutes and talked some more. After a lull in the conversation, I said, "Well, I'm gonna take off."

The guy, who'd been lying prone on the bed, sat up and asked, "Can I come with you?"

"Sure," I said. "Where do you need to go?'

"I don't know yet," he said.

He jumped off the bed and darted around the room, collecting his things.

Jason slipped into a mode I'd never seen. His affability disappeared, his face became dark and threatening. He raised and deepened his voice to tell the guy that he better not leave, that he was making a mistake, that he'd better stay. The guy paid Jason no mind.

"Jason. Relax," I said, "He just needs to get out of here. Nothing's gonna happen."

"You two better not leave together!" he shouted.

"Jason, nothing's gonna happen. He just needs to get home."

Jason got up and started storming around the apartment, shouting about how fucked up this was and how we were fucking him over.

The guy signaled to me that he was ready. I waited for a pause in Jason's ranting and said, "Jason, we're not gonna do anything. I'm taking him to my place so he can figure out where he's gonna go. That's all. I promise you, nothing's gonna happen."

But Jason was off on a tirade and it wasn't going to end any time soon. I went to the door, opened it and waited for the guy to exit the apartment. The whole time, Jason was like, "You better not leave! Don't fucking do it!" until the guy walked out the door, and then Jason said, "Fuck! God dammit!"

"I'll call you," I managed to say when Jason came up for air, then closed the door behind me. I drove the guy to my house and told him he could crash in my bed for however long he needed. I went into my office and got online, looking at hook up sites to see if there were any interesting prospects worth pursuing.

A couple hours later I went to the kitchen to get something to drink, and when I passed the bedroom on my way back to the office, I saw him sitting up in bed, looking at his phone. "How ya feeling?" I asked.

"Much better," he said. "Thanks for getting me out of there. This happened last time. He kept shooting me up and wouldn't let me leave."

"It's okay," I said. I was still playing it cool and not asking too many questions, but I was wondering to myself, What the fuck went down between these two when they were together? Was he saying Jason held him captive in his apartment and kept him high so he couldn't leave? That bordered on horror movie material, and I couldn't imagine Jason doing that to anyone.

I asked him where he wanted to go, and he told me he was ordering a Lyft. I went back to my office and got back to the hook up sites. When his Lyft arrived, he thanked me again and left.

Jason was still pissed off at me the next day. He was convinced we'd fucked, but I told him he was wrong. I said, "Jason, he got too high and panicked. He hadn't slammed since the last time he was here. And I heard that didn't go too well."

Jason shot me a look and narrowed his eyes at me. "Why do you say that?"

I shrugged. "He said you kept shooting him up and wouldn't let him leave."

"That's bullshit!" he said and broke into a laugh. "Jesus!"

I shrugged again. "It's what he told me."

The thing about Jason was that, even though he was volatile and could fly into a rage at the drop of a hat, he would also snap out of it on a dime and forget about the whole thing. His rages came and went but never lingered for too long. And the way he'd stop being mad was that he would sort of announce it with a joke and laugh his funny laugh, which usually got everyone else in the room to at least smile, if not laugh along with him.

One night a few people were over at Jason's to hang out for a while. One of them was an attractive young woman whose beauty was on the fade due to her heroin habit. She and Jason were talking about people I didn't know, so I was on my phone and pretty much tuning them out, but at one point she said, "Oh, I *love* taking K. That feeling you get when you fall into a K-hole?"

I took note of her comment because I'd never heard anyone describe falling into a K-hole as a positive experience. Pretty soon after that, she and her friends left.

"You want a line?" Jason asked me.

"Yeah, sure," I said. I hadn't snorted tina in a while. We always smoked it, so doing a line seemed fun. Old school. A throwback to the 90s. I was game.

Jason cut out a fat ass line and handed me the book it was on. We were both sitting on the bed, Jason at the head of it, leaning up against the headboard, and me at the foot, facing him, my right foot on the floor, my left leg up on the bed and folded in front of me. "Try to do it all in one pass," he said.

I was up to the challenge. There was a bill on the book next to the line, so I set the book down, tightened up the bill, put it to my nostril and inhaled. I got the whole line in one pass.

There was a mirror in the headboard, and I could see myself in the reflection. Jason's weapons collection hung on the wall behind me. I was waiting for the rush to hit me, but instead I became paralyzed.

I saw a figure in the mirror's reflection standing behind me. I could see the figure up to the top of his chest, but not his face. The figure pulled up his left arm just enough to reveal that he was holding Jason's machete. I realized the figure in the reflection was Jason (Voorhees, not the plug) and I knew what he was about to do.

If I'd been able to move, I'd have tried to get away. Jason (Voorhees, not the plug) spoke to me telepathically. He said, *Relax your body. Let it happen.* I relaxed my body just as I was told to do. The figure in the mirror behind me drew back the machete, then thrust it into my rib cage. As the machete entered me, tearing through flesh and severing bones as if they were toothpicks, I accommodated the blade the way I accommodate cock. Jason (Voorhees, not the plug) drove the machete through my torso, and as it burst out through my lower chest, I arched my back and my arms jerked out reflexively.

It didn't hurt. I felt I'd done a good job at getting stabbed.

Jason (Voorhees again, not the plug) pulled the machete out of me, and the figure behind me evaporated. I looked over at Jason (the plug, not Voorhees) and the frame of my field of vision shrank down into the bottom left corner, so that it was a small square within my usual field of vision. It was similar to seeing a screen in screen video display, with only the "in screen" screen containing any visuals. The rest was pitch black.

The image of Jason (the plug, not Voorhees), sitting on the bed in front of me, displayed within the "in-screen" screen, in the bottom left corner against the pitch-black background, observing me with no expression on his face, began to multiply and fan itself back into the distance. It seemed to go off into infinity.

I couldn't speak and I couldn't move. Jason kept saying my name, but I didn't answer him. I shifted my gaze back to my reflection in the mirror and stared at myself for a while. I couldn't speak but I kept trying. Eventually, I asked myself out loud: "Am I dead?" It seemed possible. I'd never been in this state before.

Jason said, "No. You just snorted a line of K."

"Okay," I said. It helped to have a reason for what the fuck was happening.

Then I slowly fell over onto my left side and stayed there. I was in another realm that I had no context for. I couldn't make sense of it because it wasn't a physical realm. It was void of matter and shapes. There were just fields of energy and lots of negative space. That's as good as I could do in comprehending it.

Jason started asking me questions like who was I, why was I there, who did I work for, that kind of shit. As if I were an undercover agent with the CIA or FBI or maybe even the DEA.

The joke was on him if he thought any of those agencies would touch me with a ten-foot pole.

All I could say was that I liked hanging out with Jason, that I cared about him a lot, and that I didn't have an agenda, I just wanted to have a good time together.

Later, Jason dismissed what he'd done as just fucking with me and seeing what I'd do when I fell into a K-hole. I didn't get mad at him, to tell you the truth. That I'd experienced being murdered by an apparition of Jason Voorhees wielding Jason the Plug's machete, and that I'd opened myself up to be penetrated in such a sexualized way, made for some good conversations with Jason after it happened.

ROUGH

Things between Jason and me came to a head, though, a day after he'd had hernia surgery. I'd driven him to Cedars Sinai, helped him get checked in, hung out with him in his room, then waited while the surgeon did his thing. The surgery and recovery time took several hours. By the time he was discharged, it'd been a long day, but it was still just a day.

Jason had asked me if I'd spend the night at his place in case he needed help getting around. I was up most of the night online, but I finally crashed around four. When I woke up around ten, Jason was up puttering around. I greeted him and he didn't say much. I splashed water on my face, brushed my teeth and came out of the bathroom to get dressed.

Jason started talking to me, but he spoke to me differently. He was cold. I immediately got the feeling he was ending it. And as soon as I got that feeling, all the panic and fear of abandonment I'd ever experienced came flooding back into my system, all at once. I suddenly felt I'd been cut off, that all love and goodwill for me was gone, and there was nothing I could do to get it back.

Even though my brain knew I was experiencing this situation with Jason, a guy I'd only known for a short time, my emotions hit me as if I were experiencing this situation with my father. The intensity of the feelings were up at the father/son level, not the level where Jason sat on my spectrum of emotional connections.

My fear of abandonment and my panic at being left behind were on a scale I wasn't equipped to handle that morning. Jason was being dismissive and sounded bored when he spoke to me, which exacerbated the already out of proportion feelings that were hitting me.

The last few mornings, Jason had noticed and mentioned a street kid who looked to be about twenty who was sleeping against the wall of a mini mall across the street. Again, Jason pointed the kid out to me. He was on the ground, lying on his stomach, resting his head on a backpack. It looked like the backpack was all he had.

Jason made some comments about how lucky I was to have everything I had, and how I'd partied all night when my reason for being there was to ensure he didn't need any help while he recovered from surgery. I told him I'd been up all night, keeping an eye on him. Jason didn't respond.

Instead, he said he'd put together some food for the kid and he wanted me to take it over to him. I thought to myself, what the fuck? I put my shoes on, telling him he could deliver the food to the kid himself. I became paranoid, feeling chills and getting the shakes.

My car was parked across the street in the mini mall lot. I had stuff at Jason's because I'd been staying with him off and on for a few months, but I gathered what I could and put it in my gym bag. I told him I was taking off.

He kept insisting that I take food across the street to that poor kid down there, who obviously needed some help. Was I just going to let him starve? Where was my humanity?

When I opened the front door, Jason's homies were walking down the hall, slowly, their movements and conversation looking very practiced and deliberate to me. They were all talking at once.

My paranoia intensified and I got the feeling that if I left the apartment and tried to make it to my car, something was going to happen to me. His homies were going to jump me in the hallway or the elevator. Or someone was going to run me over as I crossed the street. If I took Jason's care package over to the kid across the street, he'd pull a gun out of his backpack and murder me right there in the mini mall parking lot.

Then Jason would invite him up and have a new bud to hang out with. I'd be ancient history and forgotten by all the people in my life, which really stung. They already had a hard time remembering me as it was, and I wasn't even dead yet.

The logic behind these scenarios I kept imagining wasn't really backed up by facts, but the fear I felt was palpable. It felt like I was a five-year-old kid whose parents were abandoning him and throwing him to the wolves. I was afraid that if I went outside, even though it was daytime, that devil monster in the tree was going to swoop down and get me.

I was overwhelmed and on the verge of panic. I shut the front door, dug my cell phone out of my pocket and called Elio. I thanked God when he picked up. "Hey what's up?" I asked.

"Nothing."

"You home?"

"Yeah."

"I need you to come get me."

"Of course. Where are you?"

"I'm at Jason's place in Altadena. I just need some help getting my stuff out of here."

"Okay."

I gave him Jason's address, hung up and waited for him.

I assumed Jason had heard my side of the phone call, but when his phone rang thirty minutes later and the front desk told him he had a visitor, he shot me a look. "Who is it?" he asked the lobby guy. "Elio?" he said, furrowing his brow.

I nodded. Jason said, "Yeah, he's good. Let him in," and hung up the phone. "What's he doing here?"

"He's helping me with my stuff," I said.

"What?! You called your husband to come get you? What the fuck!" Jason started ranting and raving about how I was overreacting and shouldn't have called for help.

"You're being weird," I said in an effort to explain. "I don't wanna leave on my own."

There was a knock on the door and when I opened it, I was relieved to see Elio. He was here to provide me with safe passage back to my real life, away from this tweaker hell hole I suddenly found myself stuck in and unable to manage.

Elio waltzed into Jason's apartment like he owned the fuckin' place and asked me what I needed help with. I handed him my gym bag and laptop, then picked up my dumbbells. Jason was tense but making it a point not to lose his temper.

Elio walked back into the hallway. As I followed him, I turned my head back and said, "Get the door, Jason. My hands are full. I'll call you."

As Elio and I approached the elevator, Jason's homies walked past us, observing us both with mild curiosity. Jason slammed the door to his apartment and resumed his ranting and raving behind it.

The elevator door opened, and I stepped in with Elio. After the doors closed, Elio gave me a long sideways glance and said,

"I had no idea the people you're hanging out with are so *rough*."

I sighed, looking down at my feet. "Thanks, Elio. For getting here so fast."

"Who *are* these people?" Elio asked me. But it was a rhetorical question, asked not so I would answer him, but so I'd reflect on the life choices I'd recently been making. When the elevator door opened, Elio stepped into the lobby and moved toward the front door without waiting for me.

◆ ◆ ◆

REFLECT

I liked Jason when we first met. He was a charmer, a rogue, a performer and a stud. When he let his guard down for me, I fell in love with the guy beneath the armor, the one who came out from behind the façade because he'd decided I was worth getting to know and spending time with.

But my time was up, and the guy I fell in love with had disappeared back behind the public-facing persona. Except now, he didn't have a need to charm or win me over.

Jason may have no longer wanted anything from me, or he may have realized what he wanted from me was something I wasn't going to give. Either way, he decided the best way to disengage was by lashing out, to remind me how tough he really was underneath the charming, funny, rogue façade.

Something Jason told me during one of our more intimate, confessional conversations, was that people who liked him or fell in love with him never stuck around for very long because of who he was. He said he's always been too much for people.

Jason was never too much for me. Somehow, I felt safe when I spent time with him, despite his sporadic volatility. I was accustomed to functioning in that type of environment.

Familiarity with periodic chaos helped me stay regulated in this lead up to some of the biggest changes in life I'd ever made. It kept me preoccupied and helped the time pass.

From the first time we met, I was up front with Jason about my situation. I told him I was getting out of a marriage and selling my house so I could move to the East coast to be with Monkey. At the beginning, he said he was fine with that.

But at a certain point we realized we'd fallen in too deep. Jason and I jumped into an instantly deep emotional relationship with each other because, I assume, we were both in the mood for it, and we both knew we had an out. Once we got to know each other better and learned each other's histories, we bonded over our trauma.

While our life experiences differed, we understood the effects trauma had on us. We gave each other a certain amount of grace to allow for erratic or confusing behavior. We understood that we'd both experienced things that could break people and often did. We'd managed to survive and forge paths for ourselves, even though the journeys were often messy, just like we were.

Jason and I didn't have anything to lose by connecting emotionally and sexually, because we knew it couldn't go anywhere. We didn't risk losing anything because the part of a relationship most tied to risk, determining whether it will work out in the long run, didn't factor into the relationship we agreed to have.

We took the ride for the sake of taking the ride. Our personalities fit and we got off on each other. Being together was fun, and we let it be, without any expectations about a future together to fuck it up. And for as long as it was fun, it was fun. I saw and loved Jason for who he was. He gave me the same in return.

He also gave me something I was in dire need of. I was shedding every trapping I'd been conditioned to believe would grant me entry to happiness, fulfillment and prosperity. I'd quit my job, I'd ended my marriage, and I was about to sell my house. I needed the love of a fucked up, flawed, funny, twisted survivor like Jason to distract me from the feelings of panic and impending doom I was living in the shadow of.

I knew from the outset that when Jason turned on me, it would be brutal. But I stuck around anyway. The payoff was worth it. I was that much closer to unearthing the sometimes uncontainable chaos, insanity and rage I still harbored, so I would someday no longer have to carry it with me, and struggle to contain it, wherever I went.

Jason showed me how to stop pretending that those aspects of myself aren't there. He helped me see that I'm still worthy of love, I'm still worth being seen and heard, not just in spite of the uncontainable chaos, insanity and rage that live inside me, but also because of it.

Those elements are worthy of attention. They've earned the space they inhabit. They must be acknowledged and respected. You can try to erase them all you want, or pretend they don't exist, but they will always find a way to resurface and remind you (and those around you) that they are, in fact, there. Better to work with them, don't you think?

A few weeks later I found myself still pining for Jason, feeling like a jilted lover who'd been thrown over for someone else. I went back on the hook up site we'd met on, looked at his profile pictures and realized: for fuck's sake, he looks just like my fucking dad. A younger, hotter version of my dad, no doubt, but the dude looks just like my dad. The eyes, the gaze, the shape of his head. The resemblance was uncanny, and my failure to notice it until after the fact puzzled me. How could I not have seen it when I was interacting with him, face to face, for days, weeks, months on end?

I realized it was high time I got off the I-wish-my-daddy-loved-me merry go round, once and for all. I needed to own, embrace and embody my innate human value, which I knew already existed at its fully maximized potential. Independent of my father, or anything he ever felt about me, did to me, or tried to do to me. Despite anything he ever said to me or didn't say to me.

I understood that I was on the doorstep of my twilight years, and I needed to come to terms with these things before I could move forward on my life path.

Once again, I'd jumped into a relationship with a plug I built up in my mind as an idealized and romanticized version of my dad. A version of my dad who chose me. I reveled in his attention, sexual and otherwise, for one hot, messy summer, as the life I'd been hell bent for years on creating for myself was dying a slow, ugly death.

Once again, I'd bonded with a man I thought could help me recreate something I longed for. Something that never existed. Not in the way I was recreating it, anyway.

Then I watched him change his mind about me.

I was fed up with playing this role. It was time to let go of it. I knew there were so many other things I was, that were not this same, tired old character. This character who didn't learn anything. Who thought if he just did it over, one more time, but differently, he'd get it right. He'd finally be good enough, and his dad would love him.

I found myself standing in front of the medicine cabinet mirror that day, watching my reflection speak to me.

He fastened his gaze to mine and said: "My dad doesn't love me. He hasn't for a long time. He tried to pin the sexual abuse crimes he committed against my sisters on me. He sexualized me. He roughed me up. He tore me down. He hated me. I wasn't good enough for him."

I heard my reflection state the truth I'd been afraid to accept for fear that those things, if true, would annihilate me. But I heard the truth. I accepted it. And I remained. The truth didn't erase me.

But there was more I needed to accept.

There's a younger version of myself who may still emerge periodically. He can't accept the rejection. He refuses the erasure. He can't yet bear the weight of the truth.

He's volatile. He's impulsive. He's relentless in his pursuit of what he thinks is paternal love and acceptance. He's addicted to that love and acceptance, or the illusion of it, because he thinks he's defective and incomplete without it. Without it, he doubts his right to be alive.

I haven't always been able to control him. I don't know that he'll accept me as a solution to his problem. I don't know if I'll be able to stop him. I don't know.

But he knows all this. He knows I'm here. He knows what I'm offering. Maybe him knowing these things will make a difference. Maybe what I can now offer him is finally enough.

It's hard to say. Let's see what happens.

34. Boxes

*

I struggle with the scissors as I cut it open. My mom spared no expense on packing tape. She's sealed it with such precision and authority that I'm reminded of simple, inexpensive products (dental floss, razor cartridges, phone chargers) that are over-packaged to the extent that opening them often requires a razor sharp cutting instrument, a minimum of one power tool, and a pair of safety goggles to round things out, just in case things get out of hand.

I rip some tape off the box. It lifts portions of her confident, oversized lettering, made with a black Sharpie. "Precious Pix," P-I-X, followed by an exclamation point and underlined with a succinct happy face quite out of line with the person I once knew her to be.

Not a real happy face, but a happy face that looks like one she imagines someone similar to her, at a similar age, might be drawn like. I can only guess how much time and effort went into scrawling what is meant to appear, to the casual observer, or to me, to be a carefree, impulsive afterthought. Hours. Days.

It's at times like this I wish I just had a box cutter instead of this pair of scissors, which came with a set of hair clippers I bought, and which I've used for clipping everything from coupons to nose hairs, and gutting boxes, or at least breaking their skin apart at the seams, just to get in.

I peel open the flaps at the top of the box to find a green Hefty bag lining the box like an inner membrane. It's knotted at the top but left loose so it can be easily undone once you're in. I pull the knot apart and spread the edges of the green plastic bag apart, and now I've arrived at the meat of this expedition. I can finally see inside.

They're all like this. Taped to death on the outside, written on, smiled on, and once inside, a large green garbage bag to protect the contents from whatever elements might harm them: water, air, perhaps me.

Filled to bursting with photographs and documents that span the last century. My history and lineage, or the evidence of it. Proof that I'm a part of something that exists (or existed) beyond the walls of my immediate family unit. Proof that my history does not begin and end with me just being a product of my parents. There's more to me than just them.

Turns out I'm a part of a history that's been sealed away in boxes in my mom's storage units, moving from state to state, taking up anonymous rented space as I've tried to realize an identity for myself. A history that has been hidden from me until now.

Now she's Zen, she's trying on Buddhism. People need to try on different philosophies and world views, until they find the size that fits. This one's all about letting go of worldly possessions, and the past, and the monthly storage fees that get harder to afford each year.

I stepped in and offered to store the stuff for her in my garage because it isn't as if we park our vehicles out here. We just use it as storage space anyway. She was thrilled to take me up on it. And how could I blame her? I really don't mind.

Look what I have. Photos. Birth, marriage and death certificates. Scrapbooks. Keepsakes. Locks of hair. China. Knick knacks and tchotchkes.

And diaries, or at least one very interesting diary. I am sitting out here in the garage, reading the diary my mother kept when she was fifteen years old. It's the most fascinating window I've ever had the opportunity to look through, especially given who I've known her to be over the course of the past forty some odd years that make up my life. This is only the beginning of an archive I'll construct.

But before I construct it, I'll keep digging.

35. Quarantine

Fatigue has become something extraordinary.

I don't know about you, but I've been slogging through this pandemic as if through a vat of sludge. Now that the end of the year is near, time drags at an unbearably slow pace. Funny how time speeds up and slows down depending on how you're feeling about it. Thank God there is less than a month before 2020 is finally dead. Dead to me, I say! You can be sure of that.

At the beginning of lock down I went on a weird, manic shopping spree. I created a collection of enamel pins that I enjoy immensely. The pins are fun to look at and didn't cost much. I have a Joe the Tiger King pin, a Jason Voorhees on a skateboard pin, a flying saucer pin, as well as pins with witty sayings on them like the CLOSED sign modified to say "Sorry, we're closed off emotionally" or "The Price is Wrong Bitch." A bowl of guacamole with the words "I know I'm extra" stenciled on the side. I keep them in a distressed Goodyear Tire bin on the shelf next to books about introverted leaders and the art of programming.

I bought clothes that I can now barely fit into because of the COVID weight I've put on over the past several months.

Whether it's my middle age or my ice cream habit, those 33s aren't always an option, and I've only got a few 34s.

Right after lockdown started, I got a subscription to a clothing company that mailed boxes of clothes to me at agreed upon intervals, then I would choose which items I wanted to keep and send back the rest. I had a personal shopper that curated my boxes just for me. It was fun. It felt like I was receiving a gift every month, because I'm special. Gifts that I paid for. Patterned long sleeve button downs and dressy casual pants in the color of Phantom.

But then my waist expanded, and I had other bills I needed to focus on paying, and the fun of new clothes wore off, just like the initial fun of the shutdown started to wear off. I had new clothes and I looked fabulous but all I did was put them on and parade around the living room, shaking it to dance anthems on Spotify (Charli XCX, Todrick Hall, Dua Lipa), getting my gay on and looking out the window and thinking to myself, this is all well and fun, but when am I actually going to put these clothes on and go out again? How long is this quarantine thing going to take?

The longer this year stretches out, the more people who get infected, the higher the staggering number of deaths from COVID climbs, the longer that twat in the White House keeps trying to wreak havoc and create chaos before he leaves...you would think I'd just shut down and give up.

Surprisingly, that isn't the case. Anticipation and optimism abound. I can feel it, in myself and in others. It's the exhilaration of avoiding a car accident or dodging a bullet. Pure adrenaline pushes me forward in a state of excitement. We carry on. More aware, more frightened, yes, but more determined than ever to face this down and make it work. To honor the dead by making sure it never happens again.

I envision a massive party one day next year. We're all invited. The pandemic is over, the vaccine has done what it needs to do, people are not dying anymore, and we're all going to get together and smile and hug and dance, and there's going to be an explosion of joy and happiness the likes of which we've never seen in our lifetimes. And I'll be right there in the middle of it, laughing uncontrollably and crying tears of joy as I dance and hug it out with everyone else.

36. Gameplay Instructions

Read all instructions carefully.
Check that all parts are present before assembly.
Press play.
Please begin.
Start with what you've got.
Identify your daily mission.
Game on.
Follow the prompts.
Here we go! (5x)
Break the ice.
Consider perception.
Recognize patterns.
If it's not a good fit, don't wear it.
I'll know what I need to know when I need to know it.
Get out of your own way.
Be mindful.
Don't overthink it.
State your question clearly.
Use your own resources.
This is how we do it.
Take what you want and share the rest.
Be the interface.
Run with it.
Feel the fear and do it anyway.
Everything can change.
It's a puzzle. Solve it.
Identify triggers.

Have an answer for every question, even if you don't know the
answer.
Always provide an out.
Help others help themselves.
When dazed and confused, take the path of least resistance.
Save it for later.
Innovate.
Take five (minutes: set a timer).
Learn how to thrive in chaos.
It's all right.
Please try again.
Please try again.
Please try again.
Restart.
Have fun with it.
Get game.
That's why I'm here.
Stay focused.
Identify your spirit animals.
Make it manageable.
Edit.
We are all playing the same game.
One task at a time.
Patience is a virtue.
I'm working on it.
I'll get it.
No worries.
It pays to be kind.
Music calms the savage beast.
Shake it off.
Let it go.
Keep moving forward.
Actions speak louder than words.
Remember who you are.
Choose your personal data collection/tracking device wisely.
Do what you need to do.
This is a stress test.
Good to know.
It's a joke. Get it?
What do you do.

Fix it.
Waste not want not.
Keep it simple.
Know thyself.
Pay attention to outcomes.
No hate.
Observe and learn.
Categorize.
A place for everything and everything in its place.
Consider the source.
Think fast.
Chew with your mouth closed.
That's it.
The rest is up to you.
All in good time.
Fuck is no longer a four-letter word.
I can do better.
Ask yourself: is it reality or is it a glamour?
It's a fair question.
Everybody has a heart, except some people.
Look it up.
Enjoy the ride.
Time is of the essence.
You gotta dance.
Present it effectively.
Adapt.
Do the right thing.
Raise your frequency.
Stay the course.
Think before you speak.
Offer assistance.
Ask for help.
Floss daily.
It's all good.
Use what you've got.
Leave a light on.
Look for clues.
Use your voice.
Think for yourself.
Roll with it.

Conserve.
Remember to take the trash out.
We and I are the same thing.
All in a day's work.
Does it have legs.
Swallow the biggest frog first.
When you're overheating, wet your head.
Make it better.
Timing is key.
Put the right fuel in your tank.
You have talents and abilities no one else has.
You're beautiful.
Take inventory.
Stand your ground.
This is how we learn.
Don't believe everything people say about you.
Write your own narrative.
Spend time strengthening mind, body and spirit.
Don't assume authority wants what's best for you.
Finish what you can.
Learn how to juggle.
This is it.
We design this.
Please make a note of it.
We'll see each other when we get there.
That's my story and I'm sticking to it.

Verse:
ca.2024. Age 58.
Not initially constructed as verse. I've curated a collection of maxims, instructions, & statements over the years. In 2024, I assembled them into a single form.
When not thinking clearly, I rely on them. If I'm in a panic spiral, they calm me.
They've pulled me through frightening times.
They're anchors. Action steps. Reminders. They've never failed me.

37. Mad About You

■

*How Getting to the Root of Your Anger Can Be a
Catalyst for Positive, Transformational Change*

Have you ever had one of those days?

When one thing after another seems to exist only as an obstacle between you and what you need to get done?

Or perhaps you've had a day that's been going swimmingly, and you're feeling unstoppable. You're on top of the world!

But then...it happens.

A bossy boss. A surly barista. Karen. Perhaps it's your big sis, your little bro, your mother-in-law. Your frenemy, your fwb or your work spouse. Maybe it's even your (gasp!) REAL spouse. Words are exchanged. At least one temper flares. Feelings are hurt and the emotional aftermath is often enough to ruin the rest of your day.

Bao, et al. contend that "conflict can be a positive creative force, when it increases communication, releases stored feelings, leads to the solution of problems, results in the growth of the relationship between parties in conflict, or improves performance."

And that's all well and good...in the same way that starving yourself will help you fit into that size 2 dress you've got your eye on. The outcome may be desirable, but the process of getting there sucks.

Let's just assume it's you who's butt-hurt after a nasty exchange. Your pulse is racing, maybe you're a little dewy on the brow and in your pits, and you're berating yourself for overreacting, for letting that person even get to you in the first place.

But why are you angry, really? What's your anger's bottom line?

First things first: who pissed you off? Was it a coworker you barely know, a family member you know too well, or a complete stranger you don't know at all? The first step in putting the spat into proper perspective is determining who your beef was with and how much space they actually take up in your life.

Next, what exactly did they say or do? Did they critique your output unfavorably, laugh at your appearance, or insult you for seemingly no reason? Was it a work thing, a family thing or a rando thing that happened at the supermarket? Be sure to categorize this spat accurately so you can determine how much emotional and mental space (if any) you need to allow for it in your life.

Now let's take a look at how you reacted to this person who got a rise out of you. Did you suck it up and choose to be the bigger person, even though you were pissed? Did you respond in kind, meet them where they were at, so that the vibe intensified and the interaction escalated, fueling and drawing out more of your anger? Or did you laugh it off and play dumb, but then carry it with you into the rest of your day, ruminating on the injustice of what that person said or did to you?

And how does your reaction make you feel? When we snap back, challenge their diss or up the ante with counter shade, we often wind up chastising ourselves afterward for taking the bait. As if the fact that we pushed back is proof positive that our antagonist is right about us.

Even if we take the high road or play dumb, the feelings of being slighted and the resulting anger often remain. We feel bad about letting that person get to us, and internalize that anger, telling ourselves we should have spoken up, we should have corrected them, we should have stood our ground. We shouldn't even be upset! We stifle our response, but the anger still festers where it lands, which in these instances is within us.

In the U.S. we're taught that if someone is able to get a rise out of us, then that person has won. But operating from that viewpoint gives all the power to the bullies, bitches and bad actors out there. They only need to poke you at the right time, and in the right spot, and produce a negative reaction from you...and they've won?! You lost because you let them get to you?! Hmm...interesting.

Meanwhile, no one holds them accountable for their bad behavior. As a matter of fact, we're taught to protect bad actors from experiencing the consequences of their bad behavior. What a very pro-capitalist lesson.

A person who pushes back against bad treatment is usually categorized as the troublemaker, the bad apple (think unions, whistleblowers, etc.). The focus shifts from what your antagonist did to antagonize you in the first place, and lands on how you reacted, and whether your reaction is appropriate.

We tend to beat ourselves up for getting angry because we are socialized to avoid conflict. Conflict, we're told, invites us to expose ourselves by letting our emotions take over. If we do that (we're told), we're at risk of "losing control," and who knows what might happen then!

This way of thinking takes for granted that we move through our lives "holding it together" and maintaining our composure no matter what is occurring around us, or happening to us. Anyone who reaches the point of being fed up, who pushes back or says out loud what they really think, is eyed with suspicion. They're seen as a weak link in the human chain of keeping things as they are.

If too many of us begin to react appropriately to what is happening to us, then the entire network of social constructs that is holding up the patriarchy and current powers that be with spit, rubber bands and chewing gum might begin to collapse under the weight of its own repugnance. Heaven forbid!

Anger usually arises when we feel that we're being disrespected, condescended to, gaslit, demeaned, abused or some awful combination thereof. We all know there's a correct way to interact with others. We all know how to be polite. Unfortunately, there's a class of people out there who often forget (or choose not) to be polite. Instead, they steamroll over others with their ill will, arrogance and bile. And this puts the rest of us in the position of needing to react to their nonsense in a productive way. And how we define "productive" is determined by the outcome we desire.

If you think about it, your anger arises because you know, at the core level of your being, that what your antagonist is communicating to you - that you're stupid, ineffective, lazy, too much of this, not enough of that - that you're worthless, basically, is incorrect. Your antagonist is trying to convince you, by treating you a certain way or by saying certain things to you, that your lack of human value means you are deserving of the poor treatment they are subjecting you to. And that part of you who knows that this is bullshit is what rises up and fights back.

Your anger is coming from a place of strength, not weakness. You know your true human value, and the way this asshole is speaking to you, the derision they are aiming at you, is in direct conflict with what you know your true human value to be. Your antagonist is wrong, and it is up to you to educate them on how they are wrong, because no one else is going to do this for you.

But how?

Of course, context is everything. If you're pumping iron in the prison courtyard and suddenly find yourself surrounded by a hostile group of fellow inmates who proceed to insult and antagonize you, it might not be the right moment to point out that you know your true human value and that this is about them, not you.

If it's a work situation where your horrible boss is chewing you out because her coffee was cold, or some other lame, privileged non-reason, just remember that if you choose that moment to tell her where she can stick her unacceptably cold cup of coffee, you might just get fired.

And lest we forget, we are living in these here United States, which means that any time you choose to stand up for yourself might result in you being shot.

But that's a chance we all have to take if we choose to live authentically, and if we insist on being treated by others in a way that is in alignment with our true human value. Just remember that this is not a you problem, it's a them problem.

Sometimes you decide to just chuck it in the fuck it bucket and let it slide. Other times you decide that obnoxious fool needs to get schooled. Just use your better judgment and keep your priorities straight. The rest will take care of itself!

From the micro-level, individual lives of single human beings and their daily interactions with one another, to the macro-level systems that are crumbling under the weight of their own inequity and corruption, desperately looking to us to continue to uphold them (as if that's gonna happen), the world truly is changing one corrective fuck you at a time.

Just remember to use your discernment. And be grateful that you're here to experience and witness this change as it happens.

38. Feature, Not Bug

I don't relate to the things they say,
And I don't wanna be like them today.

-THE CARS

I don't mind what you do,
If I can do the same to you.

-NONA HENDRYX

◆◆◆

If there are any kids reading this collection, even though you've been told you're too young to be reading it, I have one thing to say to you: Good for you, you sneaky little bad-ass! You already have the presence of mind to seek out information the adults in your life (or some of them, anyway) have decided you shouldn't have access to.

You may be young, but you're already thinking outside the box and being creatively resourceful in how you obtain information. These are good qualities to have, and I've no doubt you have many more. Continue developing these qualities. They'll serve you well in life.

The efforts made by capitalist christians to shame queer people and erase us from public life have consistently, and historically, failed. Spectacularly. The fact is, we've been here longer than they have. We didn't just spring up in the Middle Ages, or in the Renaissance, or in the 1950s. We've been here the entire time.

I acknowledge that their influence on the communities they've infiltrated and inhabit does enjoy a certain level of reach and effect on the many people, including queer adults and children who, through no fault of their own, were born into them.

I know there are children and adults out there who are indoctrinated to believe, and often adopt, toxic fundamentalist ideologies that shape their views on queer people. And when they themselves are queer, they often internalize messages and beliefs that demonize queer people. They believe what their fundamentalist communities say about them.

Even so, queer people continue to exist and thrive, despite the malicious efforts of capitalist christians and other fundamentalists, to make them feel shame, force them into hiding, and erase them from the face of Mother Earth.

Many queer people who were raised in fundamentalist communities or households escape to live lives that defy what they'd been taught to believe about themselves. Many queer people escape and go on to embrace and live in their authentic queer identities, free from the toxic, patriarchal, backwards-thinking fundamentalist values they were groomed to adopt from a very young age.

Others are unable to accept their queer nature and try to make lives for themselves within those communities, hiding behind facades they construct to pass as heteronormative. For some people, it's just too scary to move beyond what they think they know.

Look, I'm not gonna lie: being your authentic queer self can be scary, especially at first. All the people who have so much invested in you pretending to be something you're not will come for you, and for very selfish reasons. Try to remember, those reasons are their reasons, not yours.

If there are any queer people reading this collection who do feel shame for being queer, or are surrounded by people who would despise and reject you if they found out that you're queer, please hear me: you are a beautiful, perfect creation of the Source of all things. You are made exactly the way you're supposed to be. I'm sorry it's been drilled into you that you should be ashamed of who you are. I know it hurts to hear that from people you love, trust or think highly of, and it hurts even more to believe it.

Please know this (and if you don't know it, keep saying it to yourself until you do): you have the strength and the power to embrace, accept and love your authentic queer self unconditionally. You were born with the strength to withstand the lies, the abuse and the bullshit those people have been subjecting you to.

Best of all, THEY'RE WRONG! Look at them. See them for who they are. Most of them are miserable and frightened. Many of them relish the power they wield over you by repeating the same old lies about queer people, as if those lies are the truth.

Look at them. See them for who they are. Let them show you who they are. Observe how they live their lives. Observe how they treat and talk about other people. Observe how they treat and talk to you.

If they can't appreciate what you bring to the table when you are being your true, authentic queer self, then the shortcoming exists on their end, not on yours. If they can't love you as you are, as you were created, and as you're meant to be, they don't deserve your attention.

You are made exactly the way you're designed to be. Our source doesn't make mistakes. Our source doesn't create beings who are abominations. Our source doesn't create beings that it hates.

There is no defect or flaw in your design. The defect is in the belief system that tries to convince you that you are *not* divine. That you're an abomination. That belief system is, at best, misinformed and at worst, dishonest and corrupt.

I invite you to reconsider those assumptions about your queer self. Consider the source of that messaging. Even if you believe the source is the Bible, remember that the Bible was written by men, at the direction of wealthier and more powerful men, who had political, economic and other self-serving agendas.

If you're conflicted because your leaders (religious or otherwise) are delivering the message that queer people are bad, and this upsets you, then congratulations! You've won half the battle. You know your value. If you didn't, you wouldn't be confused or upset when others don't.

You already know, innately, that you are divine and good. I repeat: you are divine and good. What they're telling you about queer people is wrong. You already know, in your heart, at the deepest core level of your being, that you are divine and good. Embrace that knowledge. Practice knowing it's true. Get comfortable with it. Then, run with it and put it to good use.

I know how it feels to ache for the acceptance of people you care about, and to be denied that acceptance because of who you are. But please understand that your acceptance of yourself need not be contingent upon the acceptance of others.

Take your innate knowledge of your value and build upon it. Draw strength from it. The more strength you draw from it, and the more strength you exercise in your life, the stronger you become. If you don't feel strong, fake it. Fake being strong, and eventually, you will be. Keep exercising your strength. It increases the more you pay attention to it and practice using it.

Try not to despair. You will periodically experience feelings of sadness, rage and fear. Don't avoid or deny those feelings. Embrace them. Feel them. But don't live in them. Instead, release them. Clear your mind of them. Stay focused. Stay centered. Persist. You are stronger than they are. That's why they put so much effort into trying to control you.

Find and feel your joy. Whatever brings you joy, DO THAT! Whether it's creating art, playing sports, working out, activism, community service, spending time with family, friends, or pets, or being out in nature...whatever does it for you, make time to do that. Get used to engaging in activities that bring you joy. That make you feel alive. Living in your joy, and bringing that joy to others, is the most effective form of resistance against tyranny.

The people who believe the lies told by capitalist christians and other fundamentalists about queer people are of a weak character and don't deserve your mental or emotional energy. They only deserve your attention when you assert yourself, establish boundaries, claim your space, or fight back.

All you will ever get by waiting for them to accept you is wasted time. Accepting yourself now, no matter who's ready or not, will allow you to move past your fear of their rejection, and their inability or unwillingness to understand you.

Accepting yourself now, without their permission, allows you to live your life freely, right now, and to focus on the things that matter to you.

You don't need to ask if it's your turn. If you pay close attention, you'll know when it's your turn. And when it's your turn, you go. Don't wait for a green light from anyone other than yourself.

Yes, queer people are different. Each of us is here for a reason, and we're designed with the power, the talent and the skills to make that reason happen. The self-reliance we're forced to learn and develop as queer children makes us stronger than most other adults.

Queer people stand out because, while there aren't as many of us, we create a much larger impact by virtue of our talents, abilities and practices.

We don't require permission or approval to act. And we don't need to ask for permission to become who we're meant to be.

They do not control us, as hard as they try. They will fight to oppress us. We will evade them and avoid their control. They will fight to beat us into submission. We will stand firm and defeat them instead.

They will scream from the tops of their highest ivory towers, using all the resources their hoarded and stolen wealth can buy, that we are errors to be eliminated, abominations. And yet they'll fail, as they have for centuries, to erase us.

Own and embrace your queer nature. It is your superpower. You can out feel, outwit, and outmaneuver them. You can be who you were designed to be, and thrive, without their permission, love or approval.

The days of demonizing queer people, of erasing us from society, of criminalizing our nature, and of shaming us into submission are over.

Always live in service to love, justice, and the personal safety of you and your loved ones. Justice for those who would oppress, harm, or eliminate us. Guard the personal safety of yourselves and your loved ones in the most effective ways that you can. Don't be a sitting duck. There's no reason to be. We know too much about what they intend to do to us. Be ready to respond accordingly.

Feel and express love, for yourself, your chosen family and the brothers, sisters, siblings and allies that make up our queer community. Because, despite its flaws, it is a community. And it's only as strong, resilient, beautiful and formidable as each of us makes it. Bring only your best to our queer community. Expect nothing less from the rest of us.

Our presence in this country and around the world, our existence, our willingness and ability to engage in the daily life of the societies we live in, is nothing less than a triumph. We live, we engage, we thrive in this world, despite the patriarchy, despite the forces of organized religion and political oppression.

Our strength is so powerful, our queer take on the existing social hierarchies is such a threat, that they spend untold hours and millions of dollars to use lies, disinformation and propaganda to suppress our collective voices and erase our presence.

Despite their efforts, they fail. Queer strength, queer resilience, queer power and queer joy survive and flourish. They are no match for us: they know it, and so do we.

The time has come to face the battles being brought to our collective doorstep. Instead of focusing on the cowards who flee, turn against, or otherwise abandon us, I invite you to focus on those who are joining our forces.

Bring your A-Game.

Don't forget to serve.

And believe me when I say to you: they aren't going to know what hit them.

39. tl;dr/fu

2000 and 2 maybe,
I became a thing.
The Eminem Show
J to tha L-O!

Pop culture
Main function:
progress after 9/one-one.
Rosie came out, Halle won.
Let Go, low rise jeans,
hailed rebellious.
Refreshing.

Hit an old guy with no face.
Stupid old guy, waste of space.
Rear view mirror is for my face.
Listening to andrew tate.

He walked right in back of me.
Berated him and watched him bleed,
while sitting in the driver's seat
of my shitty Mitsubishi.

I'm complaining all about it
how the world is total shit.
Girls hate me, deal with it.
Don't know how to deal with it.

Hair too long, waist too thick,
dick too short, beard too thin,
hair too short, arms too thin,
dick too eager, skull too thick.

Eyed through an unfiltered lens:
united states as terrorist.
No pursuit of happiness.
Never owned a fuck to give.

congress high court president
Bought and paid for, all of it.
Doesn't matter, no one wins.
May as well embrace this shit.

If truth to power doesn't speak,
but truth has power to delete
Strength in numbers can delete
the nihilist elite.

Who destroy and hoard and kill for free.
Who choose to fuck humanity.
It falls upon humanity
to fuck the nihilist elite.

Verse:
ca.2024. Age 58.
Hadn't written verse in 30 years.
A young driver nearly hit me with his car in a Walmart parking lot.
As I walked to the store entrance, he followed me in his car and berated
me for not staying out of his way.
As if I'd almost hit him. As if I'm the enemy.
I got the inspiration to write verse! Heeded the call.
Written while listening to DUTY NOW FOR THE FUTURE *on my headphones.*

See you when we get there.

Acknowledgments

HEARTFELT THANKS:

To the following people, who have enriched my life by making it more tasty, colorful and memorable than it would have been, were they not essential ingredients:

Dru Ullery, the guy I call my guy. He saw me standing on the edge of a great chasm, distracted me until I stepped back from the edge, paid me attention, showed me care, gave me love, and put up with me until I remembered my reasons for being here. Thank you, Dru, and congratulations: you're stuck with me.

Tammy and Tina, for showing me how to be and do love, courage, grit, strength and badassery. You make it look easy, even though I know it isn't. You're both in my heart 24/7.

To my mother, who gifted me with the opportunity to live this life. She made sure I knew I was loved, which was integral to my survival. She did what she could with the tools she had, and there were times those tools cut deep. But she also showed me love, which is the most important thing a parent can do.

Dan Nussbaum, who facilitated the APLA Writers' Group in L.A. back in the day. Dan was gifted at unlocking creativity and teaching us how to harness it. He had a knack for singling out the best thing you'd written that day (a turn of phrase, a metaphor) and bringing it to your attention, which then reconfigured your brain to include that vein of creativity and develop it for future use. That's a talent not many people have. Dan is one of the reasons I still write.

To Kenn B., Steve L., Gary S., Ken H., Ociel M., Jerry S., Steve S. and Ash. You were exactly how I've always liked my men to be: fun, beautiful, dangerous, and messy as fuck.

Finally, to any plugs out there who may have served as inspiration for characters or incidents described in this collection: we're good, right?

In Memoriam:

Don Watson: A Vietnam vet and former cop from Albuquerque who sauntered into the Roosterfish one night, challenged me to a game of pool, and charmed the pants right off me. He was the first adult in my life who got through to me. He opened my mind to the concept that there is no direct correlation between my value as a human being and the level (or the absence) of my father's love for me.

What my dad thought of me, did to me, said to me, or failed to think, say or do for me, has nothing to do with my human value. Just because my dad didn't love me didn't mean I was undeserving of love. "After all," Don said, on the night he got through to me, "your dad isn't a very good person."

Don was my chosen father figure. He was insanely intelligent, fearless, disciplined and focused. He scuba dived with shivers of sharks, flew planes, and when not piloting them, jumped out of them, trusting that his parachutes would open (they did). He was the manliest man I've ever known, and this made him hot, frustrating, inspiring, intimidating and a lot of other manly-man things. I miss him a lot, and whenever I think about him, I'm smiling, impressed, inspired and grateful that we crossed paths. I don't know where I'd be right now if we hadn't.

If you've read this collection, thank you! I hope it resonated with you. Writing is the communication method I'm best at. I've written stories since I was in elementary school, I wrote lyric poems from my adolescence well into adulthood, and all through college I loved the process of conceptualizing, researching, writing, refining, finishing and then sharing things I'd written.

Writing stories for others to read and live in is my primary reason for existing on this planet. Creating those spaces through effective writing is always the goal. I share and explore intimate, personal, awkward, painful, inspiring, funny and empowering thoughts and feelings through my writing. When I create that space for us to share and live in is when I'm most alive. It's when I'm happiest to be here, and when I know I'm doing what I came here to do.

I receive pushback on some things I write and share. I sometimes write outside the boundaries of acceptability, as defined both within and outside queer literary spaces. I write from a perspective that doesn't prioritize conforming to societal expectations. Some believe I deserve to be shamed or censored for sharing a perspective that makes them uncomfortable.

But the stories I tell, and the characters I tell them through, depict life experiences that are rooted in truth. No one's life experience is more legitimate, or more valuable, just because it occurs within the confines of the acceptable, or produces outcomes deemed legitimate by capitalism. Stories told about messy lives (especially those told by the messy people who've lived them) are valid, interesting, and worthy of attention.

I don't write to exploit people who've had painful life experiences. I want readers to be entertained, but I don't write trauma porn. I write to capture moments of existence and share them in ways that I hope transport readers into the worlds and moments they're reading about. If they've never experienced similar circumstances, I hope they gain insight into what living through such circumstances might be like. If they have experienced such circumstances, I hope they feel less alone.

I also write because it's fun and it makes me feel good. Sometimes, it just boils down to something that simple and self-serving.

When I decided it was time to put this collection together and share it, I knew it would consist of a few things: works I'd already written; works that existed as beginnings or fragments that I'd need to further develop; verse I'd written that captures the essence of who I've been at different stages in my life; and new works, started from scratch, that I wasn't even sure I'd be capable of writing until I wrote them.

What emerged as this collection took shape was a queer narrative arc, my queer narrative, told in spirals that circled back upon one another as it kept moving forward. My commitment to producing these chapters in their best, most engaging, fully realized and impactful form meant that I had to really dive into the memories and excavate the feelings required to write them in a way that did them justice.

What I experienced, without anticipating it, was an unexpected life review that ultimately provided me with clarity, healing, and closure. The Reflections chapters, in particular, required that I revisit events, as well as mental and emotional states, that I thought I'd left far behind me. Reinhabiting those memories, and returning to the worlds in which they occurred, was empowering, harrowing, humbling, and revelatory. I accessed things I didn't know I was still holding onto. I also released a lot of baggage that I've been carrying, in some cases, for 50+ years.

The Reflections chapters in this collection are rooted in fact and draw directly from my lived experience. Some brand names and locations have been altered or genericized; others appear as remembered. I did not invent any of the events, conflicts or meaningful moments described in those chapters. However, recalling events from my memory bank decades after they occurred isn't quite the same thing as providing a transcript of what happened in real time. In service to the narrative of each Reflections chapter, I sometimes took liberties with pacing, atmosphere and scenic framing. But those chapters are categorized as Reflections for a reason: not just because I'm reflecting on my life, but because they are reflections of events that occurred; images of those moments as seen, felt and recounted by me, many years later.

The older poems in this collection granted me access to a younger version of myself in a way that surprised me. Poetry is an artistic creation that often pulls things out of the writer that they don't necessarily have a conscious understanding of. My young adult self lives in a different time space, and he inhabits that space separately from me and the one I inhabit right now. I say "he" not because I think of him as another person, but because that iteration of myself is as close to being a different person as he can be.

The poems in this collection provide a direct connection to him and his emotional states at different moments. Reading them taps me into these states of being. Because he is me and I am him, it opens up those states of being for me. I connect with him through time in a way that memory can't accomplish. Memory is vague, an echo of what happened. These poems feel like transmissions from him that open a portal between us through time. Those experiences are stored in my brain, and when the poems recall the experiences, I'm living in both states of consciousness simultaneously.

This process has been a gift, and I've changed significantly as a result. I'm deeply grateful for this amazing experience. I get the sense now that the iterations of myself that have existed throughout the course of my life are existing simultaneously, and whether by chance or instinct, my adolescent and young adult self figured out a way to connect and communicate with me directly.

It's been a privilege and a blast taking you on this ride. I hope you'll join me again for the next one.

Until then, "J'adore ton trou de livre!"

Up Next:

SUPER SIZE
minis!

———————————

THE NOVELLA COLLECTION
Feel the mouthful!

Stay tuned at raymondgneal.com

One More Message:

You might have noticed that drugs and alcohol have played complicated, significant and shifting roles in my life over the years. There have been periods when my relationship to them has been central, and others when it's been peripheral.

If you or a person you care about are struggling with substance use challenges and would like to connect with someone to discuss them, the following resources provide support tailored to the queer experience and at varying levels of engagement, based on your needs:

The Pride Institute/Foundations Minnesota "provides LGBTQ+-centered addiction treatment and co-occurring mental health services for adults seeking inclusive, identity-informed care." Treatment is provided at a wide range of care levels, from partial hospitalization to virtual, and the organization has a 40+ year history of providing treatment to members of the queer community.
https://foundationsminnesota.com/addiction-treatment
/lgbtq-drug-alcohol-rehab-pride-program/?redirect=pride-institute.com

Gay & Sober is a non-profit organization that aims to "create a safe space for LGBTQ+ people to gather in-person and online for health & wellness, educational recovery programming, and fun social activities." The site provides a directory of daily online addiction support meetings that are available worldwide and free of charge, a calendar of events, and other resources.
https://www.gayandsober.org/

CREDIT WHERE IT'S DUE:

The jacket concept and design for this *Author's Cut* edition of *minis.* (based on the original *minis.* cover, conceived of by Raymond G. Neal and created by Dru Ullery) is by Raymond G. Neal, and created by Raymond G. Neal and Dru Ullery with the assistance of AI.

Excerpts and/or information culled from the following copyrighted works appear in this collection (listed in order of appearance):

Berger, John. *Ways of Seeing*. London: BBC and Penguin
    Books, 1972. ISBN-10: 0140135154; ISBN-13: 978-

0140135152. Repr. London: Penguin Books, 2008. ISBN-10: 0141035796; ISBN-13: 978-0141035796.

"Cloudbusting," recorded by Kate Bush. Bush, Kate (composer and lyricist). Published by Novercia Ltd., administered by EMI Music Publishing Ltd. Released in 1985 on *Hounds of Love* (EMI Records).

"Come Upstairs," recorded by Carly Simon. Simon, Carly, and Mike Manieri (composers). Published by C'est Music (ASCAP), Quackenbush Music Ltd. (ASCAP), and Redeye Music Publishing Co. (ASCAP). Released in 1980 on *Come Upstairs* (Warner Bros. Records).

"What Is Love?," recorded by Deee-Lite. Kirby, Kierin Magenta, Dmitry Brill, and Towa Tei (composers). Published by Delicious Vinyl Music (ASCAP). Released in 1990 on *World Clique* (Elektra Records).

Dewey, James W.; Reagor, B. G.; Dengler, L. A.; and Moley, Kathy. *Intensity Distribution and Isoseismal Maps for the Northridge, California, Earthquake of January 17, 1994.* Open-File Report 95–92. U.S. Geological Survey, 1995. https://doi.org/10.3133/ofr9592

National Institute of Standards and Technology (NIST), Engineering Laboratory. *Earthquake Northridge California 1994.* Created June 1, 2011; updated January 29, 2025. https://www.nist.gov/el/earthquake-northridge-california-1994

U.S. Department of Housing and Urban Development, Office of Policy Development and Research. *Preparing for the "Big One": Saving Lives Through Earthquake Mitigation in Los Angeles, California.* Washington, DC: U.S. Department of Housing and Urban Development, January 1995.

https://www.huduser.gov/portal/publications/destech/
bigone.html

Brighton, Connor. "The World's Costliest Earthquakes."
WorldAtlas. July 19, 2024.
https://www.worldatlas.com/natural-disasters/the-
world-s-costliest-earthquakes.html

U.S. Geological Survey. "Executive Summary." *The Northridge,
California, Earthquake of 17 January 1994.* Open-File
Report 96-263. Accessed November 2, 2025.
https://pubs.usgs.gov/of/1996/ofr-96-
0263/execsum.htm #impacts

Grant, Jan; and Crawley, Jim. *Transference and Projection:
Mirrors to the Self.* New York City: McGraw-Hill Education,
2002. p. 38. ISBN 978-0-335-20314-7.

"Bitter Sweet Symphony," recorded by The Verve. Ashcroft,
Richard Paul (composer and lyricist). Published by
ABKCO Music Inc. (BMI). Released in 1997 *on Urban
Hymns* (Virgin Records).

"Runaway Love," recorded by Diamond Rings. O'Regan, John
(composer and lyricist). Published by Secret City
Publishing, SOCAN. Released in 2012 on *Free Dimensional*
(Secret City Records/Astralwerks).

Bao, Y.; Zhu, F.; Hu, Y.; and Cui, N. (2016). "The Research of
Interpersonal Conflict and Solution Strategies."
Psychology, 7, 541–545.
https://doi.org/10.4236/psych.2016.7405

"Hits Me," recorded by The Cars. Ocasek, Ric (composer and lyricist). Published by Lido Music, Inc. Released in 2011 on *Move Like This* (Universal Music Publishing Group).

"Living On the Border," recorded by Nona Hendryx. Hendryx, Nona and Ronnie Drayton (composers and lyricists). Published by Legacy Recordings. Released in 1983 on *Nona* (RCA Records).

www.ingramcontent.com/pod-product-compliance
Lightning Source LLC
Chambersburg PA
CBHW032037050726
47590CB00001B/33